The Gol
Sedu
Rippl

There was before her a man with powerful arms and chest muscles. Vee wanted to paint his portrait like this. Lightly she smoothed the salve along his bruised ribs, touching him as little as possible, but drawing a gasp from him all the same. Her hands shook as she wound gauze about his chest and tied it off.

She thought about never knowing Max the way she wanted to and began to undo the buttons of his riding breeches.

"Veronica, what are you doing?" Max asked warily. His breath smelled not of wine but of strong whiskey, and it was intoxicating her.

"Undressing you and putting you to bed." She resumed her careful work.

"Do not start something you cannot finish." He grasped her hand and held it to his crotch so that she might feel the urgency of his arousal.

"I want to finish it. I want to see you, all of you."

"Are you speaking as an artist or as a woman?" Max asked.

"Both." She embraced him gently, and felt the warmth of his hands caressing her through the thinness of her nightdress. She watched the candle flames set Max's eyes to glittering as he gazed at her.

"Oh, Veronica, do you know anything at all about this?" He sat on the bed and pulled her toward him.

"Max, I have bred horses the better part of a decade. I know all about it."

The Critics Adore the Romances of Barbara Miller, Writing As

LAUREL AMES

"*Infamous* is a wonderfully engaging tale from beginning to end. [The heroine] is absolutely incredible. She is strong, highly intelligent yet vulnerable. . . . The dialogue is sharp and provocative, while the characters all have a sophisticated flair that makes for edgy, dramatic storytelling."

—*Rendezvous*

"[In *Infamous*] Laurel Ames spices the light flavor of her innovative Regency hybrid with scandal, stirring in prose that finely echoes the barbed undertones of nineteenth-century high-society discourse."

—*Romantic Times*

"*Nancy Whiskey* is a spirited, moving story written with style and wit. Richly textured with strong, heartwarming characters and a riveting plot that will keep readers on the edge of their seats. A spellbinding romance guaranteed to quicken hearts everywhere."

—*Rendezvous*

"*Tempted*, a well-written journey into the lives of an early 1800s wealthy English family, is mysterious, romantic, endearing, and entertaining. Add to this a multitude of suspicious characters and a shocking conclusion and you have one terrific romantic thriller that will surprise and delight you at every turn."

—*Rendezvous*

"Once again, Laurel Ames creates a delightful tale that is fun and romantic! This time around, she throws in a dash of mystery for good measure. Her writing evolves with each book. . . . Regency fans will be thrilled with *Tempted!* A rollicking romp filled with romance and mystery! . . . If you love Regencies, you will love Laurel Ames! Her writing is fast-paced and fresh!"

—*Literary Times*

"*Tempted* is an exciting, unusual, and delightfully quirky Regency romance that stars two unique individuals who immediately capture reader attention. Laurel Ames is an excitingly original author whose star is definitely on the rise. Readers will indubitably want more tales . . . from the luminous Laurel Ames."

—*Affaire de Coeur*

DEAREST MAX

BARBARA MILLER

SONNET BOOKS
New York London Toronto Sydney Singapore

This book is a work of fiction. Names, characters, places and incidents are products of the author's imagination or are used fictitiously. Any resemblance to actual events or locales or persons, living or dead, is entirely coincidental.

An *Original* Publication of POCKET BOOKS

A Sonnet Book published by
POCKET BOOKS, a division of Simon & Schuster Inc.
1230 Avenue of the Americas, New York, NY 10020

ISBN: 0-671-77452-2

First Sonnet Books printing February 2000

10 9 8 7 6 5 4 3 2 1

SONNET BOOKS and colophon are trademarks of Simon & Schuster Inc.

Front cover illustration by Gregg Gulbronson

Printed in the U.S.A.

For the
Western Pennsylvania
Romance Writers

DEAREST MAX

1

Surrey, England
April 1820

*L*ady Veronica Strake prodded the fitfully burning logs in the drawing room fireplace, hoping to encourage them to give up some of their heat to the distant sofa where her old companion Miss Flurry sat knitting. Laying the poker by the hearth, she walked past the rest of the grumbling members of the Strake clan to sink down beside Flurry, pulling her merino shawl about her shoulders and surveying the family. They were now gathered at Byerly House like vultures on a corpse. Her aunt, Lady Margery, was stabbing at her needlework as though she were trying to put it out of its misery. Her aunt's faded gold ringlets danced at her ears, distracting Margery's son George from his contemplation of his boots. George uncrossed his legs and touched the hairline that had just begun to recede with the coming of his thirty-second year.

Good for him, Veronica thought. After all the trouble he had caused, she had no sympathy for either him or his brother Freddy, who was now tugging at the waistcoat that kept creeping up his slight paunch. Two years younger than George, Freddy had always looked and acted like a bulldog, and his new weight only enhanced that impression.

Lady Margery had married the Strakes' legal advisor, Austin Comish, and her three children had been a charge on Veronica's father since Austin's death, the year Veronica was born. So they had seemed like disagreeable siblings to her rather than cousins. And the most bitter pill was that they were never grateful for anything that was done for them. Veronica's mind flitted over all the years of struggle, all the things she had given up because Freddy had run into debt, George needed a new hunter, or Mercia wanted a ball gown.

She had hoped that since her papa's death the Comishes now realized it was useless to descend on Byerly like a plague of locusts. But even with the spartan dinner that had been set before them, they had not been discouraged enough to leave. She sighed wearily and glanced at Mercia Comish, still unmarried in her twenty-eighth year. Good for her, too, after all the lies she had told. If not for Mercia trying to trap Max into marrying her, Veronica's favorite cousin would never have been banished from Byerly.

Lady Margery's fair-haired sons and daughter always made Veronica feel sallow, though Flurry assured her that her dark hair and eyes showed to great advantage against the weepy-looking Mercia. Veronica had the same jet black hair as her father, John Strake and his cousin, Robert, who had been Max's father.

The absent Max intruded on her mind and it shocked her to realize that she no longer had any idea what he really looked like. She had painted his portrait a dozen times over in as many years, trying to imagine how he had changed during the time of his absence. Surely he was not getting like George or Freddy. If that were the case, she never wanted to see him again. She would rather hold in her heart that image of her cousin as a wronged and desperate man, persecuted by all his family, including—unjustly—her own father.

Her papa had been gone more than three months now and she bit her full bottom lip to keep it from quivering with either grief or anger. Her emotions were swirled together inside her now, causing a dizzy queasiness that made her shiver. Flurry glanced at her with concern, but Veronica forced a wan smile to her lips and gave her head a slight shake to let Flurry know she was coping with all of it, even the Comishes. Thunder rumbled outside, shaking the old windowpanes in the promise of an early spring storm that would hit Byerly House on top of its hill with far more violence than the villages in the valley below.

Veronica's formidable aunt-by-marriage, Dora Strake, sat apart from the Comishes, ostracized as usual. Veronica did not mind Aunt Dora's shady past as an actress. But for the life of her, she could not see any beauty in the woman, nor any likeness to Max. Thank God he had not developed a resemblance to his mother by now. Dora was staring about, her gray head twitching from side to side as she took a speculative inventory of the vases, statues, and other artifacts in the large room. Veronica supposed the place looked more like a museum than a room for a family to gather in, but her papa always liked to have Max's treasures where he could admire them.

The managing Dora had insisted that Veronica hold the meal in expectation of Max's arrival. In spite of Dora's assurances, the better part of the dishes had been ruined, and Max had not come. After the anticipation of seeing Max, his failure to appear had left Veronica bereft as though he had died. She gave a shuddering sigh and Flurry sent her a sympathetic look.

"Just like Max to be late," her cousin George complained, tugging at his cravat and inching along the sofa, away from both his mother and the heat of the fireplace. "You have brought us all this way for nothing, Mother."

"Why did we bother to come? That dinner was atrocious," Freddy said loud enough for Veronica to hear as, she surmised, he had meant her to. The insult lost its effect when he had to tug his waistcoat down over his slight paunch again. Veronica nudged Flurry when Freddy finally found the heat too much for him and moved to a chair on the other side of his sister Mercia.

"We may finally get the estate settled now," Lady Margery replied. "Besides, we must wait on Max." She turned her head to stare menacingly at George. "It is his due as head of the family."

"Head of the family, indeed. The little bastard—" George caught Dora's hawklike glare and bit back the rest of his sentence.

"George is right," Freddy said. "If you think Max will part with any of his inheritance you do not really know him, Mother."

"Why would he not be reasonable?" Lady Margery asked. "After all, we must live."

This drove George and Freddy into silence, for Veronica knew they could never tell their mother how much they had tortured the youthful Max on their annual summer visits to their Uncle John's estate at Byerly. They had lied about Max and beaten him up at every opportunity. And because they backed each other up, Veronica was the only one who defended Max to her papa. He had even sometimes believed her, except that last time.

She could still hear her papa's angry voice condemning Max for being found in Mercia's room naked. Vee had run to witness the appalling scene when Mercia's shrieks had brought the whole house to her door. Freddy had been leaning against the door and when Veronica's papa had thrown it open, a barely conscious Max had tumbled out of Mercia's bed and dragged a coverlet around himself. His legs had been muscular and his chest growing a man's hair by then. And Mercia had still been in her nightdress.

Veronica had seen that much, before Flurry had dragged her away. Max had fled by the open window, a perilous exit considering the twenty-foot drop. Veronica had carried clothes out to the stable for him, guessing correctly at his hiding place. He had told her what Freddy had done, knocking him out, stripping him, and dumping him in Mercia's room.

Their conference had been interrupted by George, who had attacked Max with a bullwhip. Veronica had shouted the truth at George, but he had not heeded her, systematically beating the still-dazed Max, until she had hit George over the head with a shovel. She could remember the blow very well and how it had hurt her arms. She had thought George dead.

She and Flurry had patched Max up and given him enough money to get him to his mother's house in London. And that was the last time they had seen him. Papa had adamantly refused to reconcile with Max and now it was no longer possible.

The thunder rumbled closer and a brisk wind flicked leaves and a smattering of raindrops against the north windows. She looked around the room at all the things Max had sent her and wondered why her papa had let her keep them if he really still believed Max an infidel, as he had called him. Had he come to realize the truth, finally, but was too stubborn to admit his injustice? It was criminal that Max and her papa had never reconciled.

Veronica shook her head to clear it of useless thoughts. Her papa was dead now and Max was too late. The wind began whistling around the cluster of chimney pots on the roof as she turned to her old governess. "Do you want another candle, Flurry?"

"One does not have to see to knit. I vow I could do it blindfolded now."

Veronica gazed at the intricate web of knitting that moved in Miss Flurry's hands like an affectionate pet. She thought it was another shawl, but with Flurry you never knew. "I wish you had taken dinner with us," Veronica whispered.

"I did not wish to put myself forward." Flurry clamped her lips shut, tugged a length of yarn loose from the ball in her workbag, and plied her needles again.

"What a bouncer. You simply did not wish to break bread with this family."

"It is true; they do not aid my digestion." Miss Flurry glanced at George, then Freddy, before giving a slight shudder. She sat erect, her dignified gray head bent over her work.

"Rain," Mercia noted at the sound of more pronounced tapping on the drawing room windows. "I do not think Max is coming tonight."

"Max said he was coming today," Dora stated firmly. "He will be here."

Freddy consulted his watch on its long gold chain, then slipped it back into his waistcoat pocket before another habitual tug. "Did Max say he would arrive today or did *you* tell him to be here today?"

"It comes to the same thing," George said with a snicker.

"If only Max were as obedient as you two," Dora said, not realizing the insult beneath her compliment.

Veronica gave a little gasp of laughter but silenced it with a hand to her mouth. They were both adult men, yet their mother, Lady Margery, reduced them to the status of children. Was that because their father had died when they were so young? Veronica had lost her own mother when she was still in the cradle and she thought it had made her more self-reliant. Now that her papa was gone too, she would have to think of a way to get rid of the Comishes herself.

"Hiccups?" Flurry asked kindly. "Take a bite of sugar."

"I am all right now," Veronica said.

The rain beating against the windows and the rumbling of thunder nearly masked the thump of the knocker on the great front door. Veronica heard murmured greetings and the tramp of booted feet in the entranceway. If it was Max, she could not pick out his voice from those of the servants in the hall. They were all staring at the entrance. Just as the double doors to the drawing room were thrown open, a clap of thunder made everyone jump.

A tall man paused on the threshold, illuminated by a flash of lightning as well as the sconces of candles. As the women's gasps subsided, he raked the room with dangerous gray eyes under his dark eyebrows. He looked older than thirty, the years of sun and saltwater having browned him and caused permanent creases around his eyes. He was dressed all in black, from his boots to his greatcoat, which he flung from his shoulders into the arms of an Indian-looking retainer as though it were a king's coronation robe. An emerald ring glittered on the middle finger of his right hand, while his left rested on the hilt of a walking stick he carried as though it were a trusted weapon. Odd that he could look so military without wearing a uniform.

Veronica thought it strange that the entire room was so silent and discovered that Freddy was gaping and that George was nervously touching his hairline as he regarded Max's full head of black hair with the raindrops glistening on it like jewels.

The real difference in Max, Veronica thought, was in how he carried himself. He was no longer awkward but paused now in the doorway with the supple grace of a cobra taken aback by the sudden discovery of a nest of mice. Veronica found herself wondering which of them he would have first.

Veronica realized she had been holding her breath as she examined Max, searching for some element of the youth she had known, some sign that the boy still lived inside the man. For this figure seemed nothing like her Max and, magnificent as he was, she found herself frightened of his very size.

She searched his face with her artist's eye as though she were going to paint his portrait. Perfect faces were not at all interesting and Max's was fascinating. She found that scar under his lower lip that George had given him the night he had left. And that right eyebrow raised like a question mark. Max's face was far from perfect and it was unique.

Veronica resented the intervening years that had kept them apart and rose from her chair as though his gaze were drawing her to her feet. Forcing herself to breathe and feeling she must add some element of normalcy to the event, she said, "Dearest Max!" as she bravely went to him with outstretched hands.

"Vee?" he asked in a hard voice, staring at her as though she were a stranger.

"Yes, I am Veronica. Who did you think I was?"

"You look different," he said, taking her hands and holding her at arm's length to scrutinize her hair, which she now wore swept up in a knot of curls rather than trailing down her back in an untidy braid. His hands were cold and strong, yet the sight of those long supple fingers lit the wick of some candle of memory; Max playing the pianoforte in this very room, putting his arms around her to show her the scales. She grasped his hands tighter, trying to convey to him some of her warmth, trying to bring him back to her.

Their gazes locked and there it was in his eyes, that intensity that was Max and no one else. Perhaps he had not changed so much after all. "Why, thank you, Max, but it has been twelve years since we last saw each other," she said breathlessly. "Come and sit by Flurry and me."

"Thank you? I did not say I liked you better for having changed," he replied with a challenge as he walked to the settee by the worktable, laying his walking stick on the scarred surface, as though to say he was home and their lives could resume now.

"Oh, it does not matter if I have improved or gone downhill," Veronica said shakily. "It only matters that I have changed."

"Flurry, lovely as ever," Max said as he bowed and kissed Flurry's veined hand, seating himself adroitly as he carefully ignored his mother.

"My compliments, Max," Flurry countered primly. "You have been working on your manners."

"Thank you, Flurry," he said, the ghost of a smile gracing his firm lips.

"Max, stop being rude," Dora contradicted. "Say hello to your cousins and aunt."

"You here, too, Mother?" he asked without looking at her. "Great-Uncle John does not like you. Does he know you are here?" Max acknowledged the presence of the others with no more than a nod and went back to his scrutiny of Flurry's knitting.

"That is not funny, Max," Dora said flatly.

"But it is the truth. Why are you here? I would have got round to seeing you in town, Mother. You make me wish I had not written you that I was coming."

"There are things to be settled," Dora stated. "It is about time you put in an appearance. I think you might have given me a ride from town in your carriage."

"What is there to be settled?" Max asked with a raised eyebrow. "I have come to visit Flurry. That is all."

"I told you, Mother," George said with finality. "I told you there was no point in coming."

Veronica watched Max stare at his cousin as though he did not recognize him. George pulled nervously at his cravat and was about to touch his slightly receding hairline when he, like Veronica, saw Max purse his lips in that way he had of keeping something funny to himself.

Veronica grinned at George's discomfiture until Max turned his penetrating gaze upon her in such a way that she blushed and toyed with the ribbons at the bodice of her dress.

"Very pretty, my dear," Max said as he stared at them. "But much as black becomes you, they are a bit somber."

"We are still in mourning, of course," Flurry said, looking up at Max, and hesitating. "Or did you not know?"

The words hung in the air between Max and Flurry, giving Veronica a chill as Max glanced around the room with a frown, taking census. He looked at Lady Margery's bronze silk gown, Mercia's frivolous frock, and Freddy's jade green waistcoat before turning his regard to Flurry's gray dress and Veronica's black one. Many things passed over his face; shock, disbelief, then grief. But this was gone as quickly as all the other emotions to be replaced by resignation and acceptance, all in the amount of time it took Veronica to draw three or four breaths. How unfair, she thought, when it had taken her more than three months to reach such a state. She was staring at him in fascination, her lips parted in wonder at the rapid transformation.

"No, I did not know," he said grimly, his eyes hardening to glittering gray diamonds.

"Max, surely you got my letter saying Papa had died," Veronica said. "I mailed it the next day. Or surely Aunt Dora told you."

"She must have neglected to mention it," Max replied sadly as he stared again at the intricate web of knitting Flurry was holding.

"Max is shamming it," Freddy said. "He knew Uncle John was dead or why did he come back?"

"Shut up, Freddy," Dora said, drawing a glare from her sister-in-law, Lady Margery. "When do I even get to talk to you, Max? If you ever come back to London you never come to see me. When you wrote you were going to Byerly, I assumed you knew. Otherwise, why else would you come? You do not even like it here."

"Why, to see Miss Flurry, of course," Max said childishly.

"So you did not even know Byerly Hill is yours," George said resentfully.

Max did not move, except to dart an angry glance at George before he looked toward Veronica, as though assessing how she was feeling. He did still care about her, Veronica thought, no matter how much he might feign indifference.

"I suppose I am saddled with it now," Max said with resignation. "I just thought it would not happen for a while. I am sorry, Vee." This last was whispered to her with such a rushing return to his youthful familiarity that Veronica looked up in surprise and smiled at the intense look in his gray eyes.

"Vee is a child's name," she said to distract him. "I am Lady Veronica now."

"What a pity," Max said sadly.

"You are come very late, Max," Veronica observed, hoping this comment, too, would not be a conversational blind alley.

"Yes, I know," he said softly.

Veronica knew he meant too late to see her father alive. "Well . . . was there trouble on the road?" she asked valiantly.

Max glanced around the room, then replied, "No, my journey went as planned."

Mercia looked toward him accusingly. "But you have missed dinner, after making it very late."

"I dined on the road," Max said abruptly.

"Where?" asked George.

"At Horsely," Max replied.

Freddy stared. "But that can be no more than three miles from here."

Max glanced at Freddy as though he were an obnoxious child. "Yes, I know," he enunciated.

Veronica clapped her hands and laughed. "Max, you are as provoking as ever. You meant to be late for dinner."

"Have you the same cook as ever?" he asked with a lift of his right eyebrow.

"Yes, of course," Veronica said.

"Then my judgment was not amiss," he replied lightly.

"Really, Max, this is too bad of you," Lady Margery scolded.

"A wise woman," Max warned loudly, "might be content to have me blame the cook." This wrung a shocked gasp from his aunt.

"Max, I am ashamed of you," Dora said. "You do not even attempt to get along."

"You must excuse my surprise at walking into a family reunion. I had thought that the clan would have dispersed after the holidays. If it comes to that, why are all of you here?" He glanced around at the assembled family, "in what appears to be my house."

"Max, how dare you?" Lady Margery demanded.

"Perhaps we should retire early," Mercia suggested. "We must all be tired from our journeys. I know I am. Shall I walk you to your room, Aunt Dora?"

"Not now, Mercia," Dora said dismissively. "I must speak to Max."

"It was not my idea to come here," Freddy warned.

"As you do not have many ideas," Max said, "I did not think this was one of them."

Freddy looked confused for a moment before he turned resentful and stormed out. George stood up, resisted the urge to brush his hair back and took his mother's arm. They heard him in the hall ordering the servants to light candles for them. Dora rose and Veronica got up to attend her.

"Stay, Vee," Max commanded. "I want to talk to you."

Veronica sat down before she realized how much she should resent such an order. This was very unlike the old Max. She was about to correct him on her name again when Dora loomed over them. "Not talking to me will not get you off the hook, Max. Are you going to keep your part of the bargain or not? You know the consequences if you do not."

"I shall discharge my obligations as I perceive them, but not because of you," Max replied with so much ill will one could hardly credit he was speaking to his own mother.

Dora held her head up and left. Mercia shot Veronica a confused look as she was going out the door, but Veronica could do nothing but shrug. Whatever was brewing between Max and Dora would explode eventually. She personally had no desire to inquire into it prematurely.

"Alone, at last," Max said with satisfaction as he got himself a brandy.

"Are you forgetting about me?" Flurry asked with a click of her knitting needles.

"Why, it is you whom I want to be alone with, dearest Flurry, but we need Vee for propriety's sake."

This caused both women to laugh. "I cannot stay angry at you, Max," Veronica said.

"No matter how much he deserves to have his face slapped?" Flurry questioned.

"Oh, I do not care if Max is rude to everyone," Veronica returned. "He only says the things I think of and suppress."

"I should hope you are never rude to people even if they do deserve it. How would it reflect on me?" Flurry now laid her knitting aside.

"It is only that consideration which prevents me from disgracing myself, dearest Flurry." Veronica hugged her.

"This is like old times," Max said, pushing a small glass of brandy on Flurry as well.

"Except you are much changed, Max," Veronica said, looking him up and down.

"What is so different?" Flurry took a sip of the amber liquid and pursed her lips. "He still taunts Freddy and George. Perhaps now they realize it more."

"But Max looks positively dangerous now," Veronica said. "I really think they are afraid of you, Max."

"Do you think so?" Max got up to preen in the looking glass over the mantel. He ran one hand through his long, straight black hair, stroking back the dark lock that had fallen over his brow, but it immediately dropped back down to brush his forehead. Veronica stared in fascination. She could remember brushing back his hair many a time when they had been in some scrape and were trying to make each other presentable for Flurry. But this new Max . . . would he resent such a familiarity? He looked expectantly at her, and she suddenly realized he had asked her a question.

"Yes . . . yes, most assuredly you could beat them now, even if they both attacked you together. For Freddy has gone very soft in your absence and you know George has no heart for a fight on his own."

"Especially if you are there," Max said, "to climb on one of their backs or get in a good kick now and then."

"Or a blow with a shovel," Flurry added.

Veronica thought Flurry's reminder of the night he had been banished might offend Max, but he smiled, propped his right boot up on the fireplace andiron and laid his arm along the mantel. It was a pose he had often taken, but now the legs encased in tight pantaloons were well muscled, and the coat was well cut and in no need of padding. Max had grown up, as she had, and he was giving her a funny feeling in her stomach. She was proud of him, of course, and joyful that he had put all their annoying relatives to rout, but there was some other emotion at work in her.

He was not Max, the wretched boy in the torn shirt whom she had befriended during her childhood. He was a man, and an extremely attractive one. But she had always known he would be. In point of fact, if he had come back to them the same bedraggled youth who had left, she would have been just as glad to see him, for only Max relieved the tedium of life at Byerly. She had missed him more than she had realized. She could feel the color rise to her cheeks. They were only second cousins, after all, she told herself, though they had been raised closer than most cousins. Under normal circumstances it was not outside the realm of possibility that they might make a match of it. Veronica tore her gaze away from him.

"Vee? What is the matter? Are you ill?" Max inquired, his dark brows drawing together.

"What? Oh, but I am still a featherweight. They would only throw me in the dirt as they used to."

"That never embarrassed you before." He walked back across the room to look more closely at her.

"But I am a lady now," she said, smoothing the front of her skirt as an excuse not to face him. "And I must not be brawling anymore, not even to help you, Max. So have a care you do not pick a fight you cannot win."

"Sage advice, Max," Flurry agreed. "I would take it if I were you. I am going to bed now," Flurry announced.

Max took her hand to help her to her feet.

"Do not stay up talking forever, you two," Flurry said as she walked to the door.

"Will you not breakfast with us tomorrow, Flurry?" Veronica asked.

"If Max is to be there, I expect it will be worthwhile. Yes, I will. Good night, then."

Max closed the door behind Flurry, then came to sit beside Veronica and take her hand, laying her thin fingers between his large palms. "So when did this transformation take place? When did you become *Lady Veronica?*"

"I always have been. I just find I get more respect if I do not get into such stupid scrapes as I got into with you." She met his eyes proudly and with a welcome return of her composure. "I swear I have not done anything embarrassing or deserving of censure since you left." She detected a smile tugging at the corners of his mouth and thought perhaps there was more of the old Max left in him than she had reason to hope.

"Has it been sadly flat for you?" he asked abruptly.

"Unbearable," Veronica crowed, then gave her rich, bubbling laugh. "I cannot get over how different you are. Not just taller, I think, but bigger somehow."

"At least I was a grown man when I left. You were just a child, eleven or twelve, as I recall. Absurd as it seems, I expected to find you the same. Certainly your letters never led me to believe you had grown up." His voice slowed and dropped. "Except perhaps for the last one."

"Well, I tried not to, Max, but life has a way of forcing itself on you no matter what you would rather."

"I know, and I am sorry I did not heed you."

Max stroked her hand, sending some sort of shock wave through her. Why would she be afraid of him, now that she had discovered he was still the same old Max underneath all the bravado? He raised one of his hands and gently turned her face up to study her. She felt strange, exposed in some way, though truly there was nothing she had ever sought to hide from Max.

"Was it very hard on you, your papa's dying?" he asked gently.

Veronica turned her face away from him and fingered the black ribbon at her throat. "It came on quite suddenly, but fortunately the family were all here for the Christmas holidays. We took turns sitting with him, all but Freddy."

Veronica stared into space, remembering that last somewhat happy Christmas. "Papa had been very much involved in some research on Nonsuch Palace, Henry the Eighth's last residence. You know the site is not so very far from here and Papa had become convinced that some treasure from that dismantled building was hidden at Byerly." Veronica shook her head to rid herself of the memory. "But that last part might have been an imagining caused by the high fevers. They left him weakened . . . and his seizures became more frequent . . . and he simply died in his sleep," she whispered, trying to lessen the impact of her account.

"What did the doctor say it was?" Max stared at her so intently she could scarcely face him.

"Dr. Morris had no explanation for the illness." She could hear the tears in her voice but swallowed them so as not to cry in front of Max.

"You should have sent to London for another doctor." Max clenched his hands together, studying the floor.

"There was no time," Veronica insisted, hurt that Max would blame her. But the face he turned to her was not accusing. He was in pain himself, saddled suddenly with a grief as deep as her own, but with no outlet. He would never have let the Comishes or his mother see how much he cared about her papa.

"Max, is it true? Have you been back to London before and never thought to come here?"

"When I had to—when I had a particularly valuable

cargo to ship, I came with it." Max averted his eyes. "There are always matters better settled in person than by letter, the mail to the East being what it is."

He said this so coldly, Veronica knew it for a lie, but passed over it as she had always ignored Max's faults and went on to something that did him credit.

"You came because you got my letter that Papa was ill, not because you knew he was dead."

"Of course." Max leaned toward her with his hands on his knees. "I am not one of those vultures. Why are they here again?"

"They did leave after the funeral. There was nothing more to be done until you returned," Veronica said tiredly. "Last week your mother wrote that she was coming. I tried to discourage her, but I cannot do it in person, let alone on paper. The rest of the family simply arrived without asking, as they usually do. I do not know why Papa put up with Margery's brood. It seemed to me sometimes, just from little things she let drop, that she had some kind of hold over him."

"Hmm, I cannot imagine what." Max raised his right eyebrow again, a new trick for him. "Mother must have written to them. I wonder why. She would not want them here unless it was to get back at them." He stood up to wander about the drawing room, regarding the artifacts he had sent home over the years.

"I suppose Dora expects them to formally acknowledge you as head of the family. You would have thought Freddy and George would have had more sense than to come, after the way they treated you while you were growing up."

"Oh, no. I just had a horrifying thought." Max turned from his scrutiny of a marble Venus.

"What?" Veronica was becoming annoyed at having to shout across the room at him.

"Are we to have your two sisters and their broods inflicted on us? They must have seven between them by now."

"Eight, if all goes well. Janey is imminently expecting and Lucy has gone to attend her. She wanted me to hare off to Cornwall to look after her children while she is with Janey."

"I hope you do not make a practice of doing things like that." Max strolled back over and sat down again. "I should hate to think of you becoming a mere aunt."

"That is the most grating thing, to be called *Aunt Veronica* as though I were a spinster."

"I cannot take it in. How old are you now?"

"You are as clumsy as ever, Max," Veronica said, wriggling under his scrutiny. "I am twenty-three. Do you often go about asking women that question?"

"But you are different," he argued, gesturing with his sun-bronzed hands. "We used to play together. We were . . . friends."

"We are still friends, Max," Veronica said shyly, scarcely able to believe this was the same person as the boy whose wounds she had doctored under Flurry's guidance. They had been best friends and now there was some barrier between them. She wanted Max back, impetuous and foolish, rather than this arrogant, competent man. She felt her want of him as a hungry longing tugging at her heart. "Do you mean to stay now?"

"No. I was planning to go back to Spain in three weeks."

"Well, I suppose you will lease the house then." Veronica listened sadly to the storm that had resolved itself into a determined rain.

"Lease Byerly to strangers?" he asked. "Are you mad? This is your home, and Flurry's. What would you do?" Max jumped up and resumed his restless pacing.

"I have plans," Veronica said staunchly, raising her chin to stare up at him. "We have only been awaiting your arrival to turn the keys over to you. Then Byerly is your responsibility, Max."

Max paused, one hand locked around his brandy glass. "Plans? Are you . . . are you going to be married then?"

His voice dropped as though this would be a fate worse than death for her, and Veronica thought she detected a note of panic in his tone, but perhaps that was wishful thinking.

"No, but I am an artist of some note."

"Still painting your miniatures?" He came closer to half sit on the worktable and stare at her.

"Yes, and it is a respectable occupation for a lady, one of the few open to us. I have exhausted all sources of commissions around Byerly. I mean to broaden my horizons."

"Make your own living? But that is absurd," Max said. "You should not have to work, either you or Flurry."

"But I can do it," Veronica asserted, a flush of anger this time kissing her cheeks.

Max sighed tiredly. "I know you well enough to know you can do anything you set your mind to, but you belong at Byerly. I cannot picture you anywhere else," he argued. "For you to leave would be like a jewel abandoning its setting."

"Max, I love the place dearly, but how can you ask it of me? I am not one of your china bowls or statuettes to be locked away and only got out every decade or so

when you have a notion to admire me. I am determined
to see something of the world before I dwindle into
Aunt Veronica."

She stood up and walked to the door with determination, but turned to look back at him. She did not
want to argue with him tonight, though she usually
enjoyed disagreeing with Max. The face he turned to
her was a man's face, but those gray eyes looked just as
lost and confused as they had the night he had left
Byerly twelve years before. He was her dearest Max still.
Satisfied, she went out and closed the door before he
could think of any more arguments.

Max glared at the fire, drained his glass, and threw it
against the brick at the back of the fireplace, watching it
shatter with a surge of satisfaction. Vee had not changed
so much after all. She was always wanting to go her own
way. He would find a means to dissuade her. He pulled
a well-folded letter from his inside coat pocket and read
it over again.

5 January 1820

Dearest Max,

I know I have written to you before of Papa's illness, but it has grown very serious. Perhaps it was
brought on by the stress of having the entire family visited upon us for the holidays. If you expect
to see him alive and in his right mind, you must
come to Byerly as soon as you can manage. Dr.
Morris has no explanation for these fevers and
seizures. I know you think I exaggerate, but not
this time. Papa is failing very fast now, Max. You
will hardly know him. He does still speak of you
and wants to see you.

I know that you are busy and that it may be weeks before this reaches you, but it is most important that you come if you are not already on your way.

I would normally entertain you with a lot of prattle about Papa's latest research, but I am not in the mood to be entertaining. And do not write back telling me I am being melodramatic. You have been gone twelve years. In this case I do know what I am talking about and you do not. Papa is very ill and he wants to see you. Remember, you are his favorite nephew.

Please come.
Lady Veronica (Vee) Strake

He had meant to come for the holidays, but there had been that revolution in Spain to claim his attention. After all Wellington's hard work to make peace in the peninsula, it was a slap in the face to have the restored King Ferdinand VII set aside the Constitution of 1812. Perhaps the troops at Cádiz would have mutinied without him, but it was Max's direction that set the troops to march on Madrid, and it was he who had gathered the strands of the northern revolutionary movements into one concerted effort. Finally Ferdinand had yielded and agreed to a restoration of the liberal Constitution of 1812. It was also Max who had kept Ferdinand from being summarily executed, thus plunging the country into even worse disruptions. He shook his head. There was much work yet to be done to assure peace in Spain.

And he had actually been in London by the beginning of February, but if not for him the Cato Street conspiracy would have been an utter disaster, with the entire cabinet of ministers assassinated at the Earl of Harrowby's house. It was the intelligence gathered by his contacts that had led to the discovery of the plot and the arrest of the conspirators. Did he have to do everything himself? Here it was, April already . . .

He was just making excuses and he knew it. He had gotten a letter from his mother warning of Great-Uncle John's illness and ordering him to come to Byerly before the end of last year, but it was Vee's letter that had brought him. Had it really been twelve years since he had last seen her? He remembered it well enough. He had been hiding in the stable after being exiled by Uncle John for an attempted rape against Mercia—as though he would ever desire that woman. Vee had brought him clothes. George had discovered them there and had systematically beaten him with Vee watching.

That had been the hardest part, that Vee had seen it all. Thank God the girl was not above wielding a shovel. She had knocked George out cold. He could always count on Vee. She had sneaked him into the house then, and she and Flurry had patched him up and lent him enough money to make it back to his mother's house in London.

They had no idea how far it had carried him eventually—to India, China, and a host of exotic islands. Once he had pried loose from his mother the inheritance his father had left him, he had bought a plantation in Madagascar, but his real fortune he had made trading in ancient Chinese porcelain. And every voyage brought him more wealth and more assurance that he would never be dependent on anyone again. Why was it not enough?

Perhaps because he now realized his most cherished memories were of Byerly and those times he, Vee,

Flurry, and Great-Uncle John had been together here. How could so much time have flown by? He must stay long enough to lay to rest Veronica's notion of leaving Byerly. He wanted her to stay here where she was safe, and he wanted to take care of her. It was his duty. More than that, it was his fondest wish that she should be happy. Perhaps the government would simply have to do without him for a while.

He stared into the fire, thinking of all the evenings he had spent in this room playing chess with his great-uncle as Flurry knitted and Vee painted her botanical studies. He knew she was an excellent painter, was more talented by far than he would ever be, but the world so seldom recognized such qualities, even less so in a woman. He did not want her to find that out, that she would be as unappreciated by others as she had been by her own family.

Why had he not come back to her? He had reconciled with John two years ago, had indeed met him in London. But Vee did not know that. Her father had decided Max's return was to be a surprise. Then he had been called away on matters of state. Still, if he had known Vee was being plagued by their relatives he would have managed to come back and rescue her.

Perhaps that was it. She had always been the one defending him, if not actually saving him from George and Freddy's persecutions. His uncle had told him that it was Vee who had interceded for him and eventually convinced her father that Max had been innocent of wrongdoing to Mercia. Vee had rescued him again and he had been embarrassed that he still needed her help.

This time he would be the resourceful one. He would put the Comishes to rout and set Vee up so well at Byerly that she would never want to leave. Then . . . what?

Would she marry if she could? His stomach recoiled at the thought of a man, any man, taking Vee to bed. They were, none of them, good enough for her. Yet he did want her to be happy.

He could not picture Vee's future any better than he could imagine his own. Perhaps there were some women, like Flurry, who were complete without a man. Perhaps Vee was one of those women. Max realized that in spite of her letters he did not know Vee at all anymore, not this woman she had become, this Lady Veronica. Beyond this passion for travel he had no idea what she wanted from life, and he must make it his business to find out.

3

$\mathcal{V}$eronica glanced at her gray morning frock in the cheval mirror. What a lowering reflection to have gray actually become one. Did it mean she was fated to be in mourning all her life? She could spend another ten minutes pinning her hair up or she could let it loose and see Max ten minutes earlier. She chose the latter, pulled on her half boots, grabbed a shawl and ran down the stairs.

She paused midway to listen to the creaks and groans of the ancient house, much like the endearing moans of an old person getting up for the day. The Strake family, like the house, was an old one. Neither was without flaws; in the case of the family, many flaws. But they shared a dogged persistence that Veronica admired. Byerly would go on without her, would survive anything the Strakes could do to it, with no more than a whimper. Veronica felt a sense of comfort in that. Byerly was the only home she had ever known, yet she felt a most persistent need to get away from it. The memory of her papa's last days was too vivid in her mind. She would come back someday when she could

enjoy the crooked doorsills and creaky stairs again, but
for now she must escape.

Especially now that Max had raised the specter of her
neglect. Without meaning to he had made her wonder
if there had been something she could have done to
save her papa. Veronica pushed the thought away as she
ran the rest of the way down the stairs. Everything Max
said mattered so much to her. Why did she let him torture her like this?

She plunged into the empty breakfast parlor and
glanced apprehensively over the array on the sideboard.
It was a skimpy breakfast by anyone's standards: toasted
bread, eggs, and ham—no fish, but large pots of tea,
coffee, and chocolate. Her only hope was that everyone
would rise so late they would think the others had eaten
everything.

When they had all been here over the holidays there
had been plenty to eat. But that was before her father's
death, before the tradesmen had begun demanding
payment of long-overdue accounts. By rights their man
of business, Henry Steeple, Lady Margery's second husband, should have paid all such bills out of the estate.
He had delayed any such settlements until the will
could be read. And Veronica had managed on her own.
Now the relatives had all gathered again at Byerly and
she refused to go into debt to feed them.

She took only tea and toast. It was good tea, some of
what Max had sent them. The aroma held for her all the
spice and magic of India and other far lands. She hoped
she could get Max to tell her what she would need to
know if she meant to journey to such places. She had
seated herself and closed her eyes in pleasant contemplation of the Ganges, which he had described in a letter, when the door burst open and Freddy entered.

He heaped his plate with four eggs and fully half the ham on the platter. This alone would have made Veronica look daggers at him, if he had not said, "Veronica, the stables are nearly empty. What happened to all the hunters?"

"I had a sale, Freddy," Veronica said defensively. "I needed the money to keep the house up. Besides, what would be the point of having them idle for an entire year?"

"But what am I supposed to ride?"

"You are perfectly welcome to send for one of your hunters," Veronica offered.

"I . . . I don't keep a stable of my own."

"What about George?"

Freddy sat at the table and shook out his napkin. "He keeps only a couple of town hacks. You had half a dozen prime hunters as late as Christmastime."

Veronica wondered what had happened to the last expensive hunter her papa had bought George. "If you must know I had to sell them all to pay the tradesmen."

"Damned encroaching devils. You should have—" Freddy gave a start at something he saw out the window and Veronica turned to find Max sitting on the sill.

"What do you mean by climbing in the window like that?" Freddy demanded.

"Tea!" Max said, swinging his booted legs and his walking stick over the sill and stepping in. "I am not even human in the morning until I have had some tea."

Veronica poured him a cup and Max grasped it, his cold fingers brushing hers in his haste. The touch reinforced her awareness of him as a man now, a powerful man whose hands could do anything he wanted them to. Veronica gave her head a mental shake to clear it of this thought. Why would she be having such fears of Max. He would never hurt her.

She noted with satisfaction that Max drank tea plain as she did. His taking a sip and giving a nod of approval doubled her enjoyment of the brew. She had trained Cook in how to steep it, and had got it right. How strange that a mere nod from Max could give her so much satisfaction.

"I told Mother there was no point in coming," Freddy pouted with his mouth full.

Max sat beside Veronica and stared across at his cousin as Freddy hunched over the breakfast table, wolfing his food.

Veronica knew that calculating look. Max was going to bait Freddy and start an argument. How childish.

Freddy finally sensed Max's stare. "What are you looking at?"

"Why did you come then?" Max asked coldly.

"Mother wanted to come, not me, and certainly not George. If it were up to him, he would have given Byerly a wide berth. Uncle John never took to him, you know."

"Indeed?" Max set his teacup down with a clatter. "I was not aware that Great-Uncle had *taken* to you, either."

"He only had two real nephews," Freddy said, looking piggishly at Max. "Stands to reason he should have left us something since we are more closely connected than you."

"Does it?" Max asked sharply.

Freddy glanced warily at him. "You were the one who was cast out. Trying to rape my sister."

Max jumped to his feet so quickly Freddy had no time to react and overturned his chair in an attempt to get out of Max's reach. "I would not take your sister if she were the last—Ouch, Vee, you kicked me," Max complained, reaching for his ankle and slowly seating himself again.

Mercia came through the open doorway, looking inquiringly at Max, who was still rubbing his ankle, and shaking her head at Freddy, who was righting his chair and tucking into his meal with one eye warily on Max. Mercia took a plate from the sideboard and began to load it with biscuits and jam.

"Did I?" Veronica asked. "Well I expect you had it coming, and stop calling me Vee."

"You are a savage little brute, but then, you always were." Max smiled at her, causing Veronica's heart to flutter a little. "Ah, here is Flurry now. This tea is well made. You must have some while it is hot, Flurry."

"Veronica instructed them in how to make it," Flurry assured him, letting him pull her chair out for her.

"I might have guessed. Our ever-competent Vee. What else shall I get for you?" Max offered.

"Just the tea," Flurry said as Veronica poured her a steaming cup.

"That is all I have in the morning," Max said. "I dislike eating anything heavy until noon. Otherwise, it is so easy to let oneself go."

Freddy paused in his mastication and glanced uncertainly at Max. Mercia looked down at her figure. But since George was just entering the room he assumed the discussion had been about him. He stared so hard at Max that Veronica thought surely Max could feel the scorching through his coat. George took perhaps half of what he would normally have eaten, Veronica thought, which did leave some food for Dora when she came in a moment later, but very little for Lady Margery, who was the last to arrive.

"The chocolate is cold and someone has eaten all the eggs," she complained.

Mercia stared at her mother guiltily, but Dora merely recommended Margery ring for whatever she wanted.

"May I?" Margery asked Max, who was not attending. Veronica nudged his arm.

"Oh, certainly," Max said with an arrogant tilt to his right eyebrow. "I am sure you may ring for anything you want." He actually let her rise and pull the bell rope before he added, "Whether they will be able to supply it is another matter. I have sent my man Mustafah to the kitchens, and he finds the larder in a woeful state." Max turned to Veronica so suddenly she almost overset her cup. "Why is it that you have not been given adequate housekeeping money?"

"I have not been given *any* housekeeping money," Veronica was startled into replying.

"You well know that my husband Henry is executor of the estate," Lady Margery said coldly. "I am sure he sends her what is proper. Veronica has just forgotten."

"Believe me, if Henry Steeple had ever sent me any money I would remember it," Veronica said, more angry at Max than Aunt Margery, for Max had drawn her into this argument.

"I doubt any amount would be adequate if the whole family descends on her like a plague of locusts several times a year."

"How dare you?" Lady Margery's nose twitched with anger. "You have not even been here for twelve years. What do you know about it?"

"But if your husband is going to be such a nip-far-thing, I do not see how you expect to come here and eat in style," Max said ruthlessly.

"Henry is not—I see no need to sit here and be

insulted." Lady Margery folded her hands in her lap but made no move to leave. "George, are you going to let him talk to me like that?"

"What do you want me to do about it?" George complained, as he pushed his plate away. "It was not my idea to come here."

"Now, Mother, you cannot deny that Henry Steeple is a bit on the cheese-paring side," Freddy agreed. "Here, Veronica has had to sell all her horses to keep the house up."

"Shut up, Freddy," Lady Margery said tiredly, as though she said it often and to little effect.

Mercia stared at Veronica in astonishment. "Surely you did not use your own money for the household?"

"The servants had to be paid," Veronica said, trying to calm herself.

"Henry recommended you turn some of them off," Lady Margery countered, staring pointedly at Flurry.

Veronica gritted her teeth and would have ripped up at Lady Margery had not Max laid a calming hand upon her fingers, arresting her crumpling of her napkin. She took a deep breath. "But they are mostly older." Veronica's liquid voice rose on a note of injustice. "Where would they have gone?"

"As I see it," Max said, "there is scarcely enough help now if we are to be plagued by unexpected company. Did you write Vee and ask if you could come?"

"We are *not* company. We are family," Lady Margery stated. "Besides, she must have known we had to be here for the reading of the will."

"Which makes you all the more unwanted," Max countered dismissively.

"I am not going until I know what you mean to do," Lady Margery demanded.

"Me? About what?" Max asked vacantly, his teacup halfway to his mouth, his right eyebrow arched in surprise.

"About George and Freddy." Lady Margery nodded toward her two grown sons. George stared resentfully back at her while Freddy tried to sink into his chair.

Max stared at her, then at his two cousins, who shifted uncomfortably in their seats under his appraising glare. "My dear madam, if you and Henry Steeple have not been able to do anything about them in all these years, I cannot see what I am expected to do."

Veronica choked on her tea and was glad she had not just taken a bite of toast. Flurry patted her on the back.

"You are expected to provide them with incomes as my brother would have done if he had been sane," Lady Margery said with finality.

"There was nothing wrong with Papa's mind," Veronica said, jumping up. "If he only chose to leave them a pittance each, that is because . . . because . . ."

"Well?" demanded George, calmly pressing his napkin to his lips.

"Because he did not like you," Veronica finished. "You never came to visit him unless your mother sent you."

"Bravo," Max cheered at Veronica's retort.

"And I suppose you saw to it that he did like Max, who has not been next or nigh the place in years." George looked appraisingly at Veronica.

"Max wrote to me regularly, and we all shared common interests, art and history," Veronica said proudly, though she felt the weakness of her defense and really thought Max should help her out since he had provoked the argument.

George stood. "I spent four years studying art at

Cambridge and Uncle John would not give me the time of day."

Veronica sat down, trying to think of a reply. "Perhaps if you had been kinder to Max over the years, not been always harrying him."

Freddy shifted in his chair, causing it to creak alarmingly. "What would Uncle John have known of our harmless pranks if you had not tattled on us, Veronica?"

"Knocking Max off his hunter could hardly be considered harmless," Veronica retorted. "Tossing him into the bull's pen was scarcely a prank. And you are blaming me for telling Papa you were trying to kill Max? Now you do sound like a child." She had risen again as she delivered this tirade, then Max pulled her back into her chair with a grin. This felt like old times, a pitched battle with the Comishes. Why had she imagined things would turn out any differently now that they were grown?

"Childlike!" Lady Margery pounced on the word, completely ignoring Veronica's accusations toward her sons. "That is what John was like toward the end. When my first husband, Austin, died, John promised me that my children would be taken care of, but he never made any permanent arrangements. We should have had a competency hearing like I said."

"Papa was ill, but there was nothing wrong with his reason," Veronica stated angrily. "He made that promise when they were little children and he did take care of them. He educated them, insofar as it was possible," she said with a glance at Freddy, "and he paid for Mercia's come-out." Of the three only Mercia had the grace to blush.

"Then why did he leave his art collection to you and

make no other provision for you?" George asked quite reasonably.

"Because I have an interest in art," Veronica said, feeling she should not have to defend her papa's decision. "I am a painter."

"A miniaturist," George corrected.

"A portraitist," Veronica argued.

"An unattached female without a roof over her head," Lady Margery said cuttingly.

Max directed a menacing glare at their sharp-faced aunt, a look that exuded contempt and repugnance, and Vee had the satisfaction of seeing Lady Margery quail before Max's gaze.

"I imagine the reason Great-Uncle John did not leave an income for Veronica is that there was nothing to leave, thanks to you and Henry Steeple." Max smiled unpleasantly. "It has been rather convenient for you, marrying the family's man of business, the one who sold off Uncle's investments and took such severe losses for him after Waterloo, the man who has been able to help himself to whatever he pleased all these years and blame hard times, the man who is executor of the estate or whatever is left of it."

"Max," Veronica said in some shock. "Do you have proof that Henry Steeple had been stealing from Papa?"

"I told you we should not have come, Mother," George reiterated for the umpteenth time, leaning on the back of his chair.

"I should have thought family pride would induce you to keep your cousins out of debtors' prison," Lady Margery persisted, becoming tearful enough to conveniently ignore Max's accusations.

"Mother!" Freddy shouted.

"I should like you to tell me why I should help

George and Freddy," Max said, his eyes glittering like ice. "I certainly have no feelings for them. However, if things are that desperate, I will offer them both positions where they can do no harm."

"Positions?" George asked suspiciously. "You mean *work?*"

"That is how the better part of the world's population earns its daily bread," Max said casually. "I do not see any reason why you should be different."

"But to engage in trade," Lady Margery said with distaste.

"I engage in trade, madam, and I must say I enjoy it." Max leaned back in his chair. "There is nothing so exciting as driving a hard bargain. What do you say, boys, to a few years in Madagascar or the East?" Max asked.

"Well . . ." Freddy bit his lip and glanced at George, who looked thoughtful.

"Shut up, Freddy," Lady Margery commanded. "Max is only trying to insult us."

"Let Freddy speak," Max encouraged.

"Freddy, if you agree to such a thing, I will never speak to you again," Lady Margery warned.

Freddy's eyes lit up. "Do you mean it, Mother?"

"Yes, I mean it," Lady Margery enunciated.

Veronica saw her aunt catch Freddy's meaning and would have laughed if she had not been so angry with Max for provoking the whole situation.

"Nor will Henry help you out of your current predicament," Lady Margery warned, "if you decide to go into trade."

"Oh, well, that being the case," Freddy said, "I guess I will not go to Madagascar."

George chuckled. "I would not worry, Mother. Max is

just taunting us. But we really should leave Byerly and return to London."

"We are not going anywhere," Lady Margery said belligerently. "It is unfortunate that Henry has been detained in town these last few days. We shall discuss all this after he arrives."

"Oh, no! Not Henry Steeple, as well," Max said with so much feigned despair it made Flurry choke.

Veronica could not help but notice that Dora had been strangely silent during the argument, almost as though she had expected some such dustup to occur. Veronica wondered what sort of satisfaction Aunt Dora got from watching Max vanquish the Comishes. He rarely treated her any better than them.

Once Lady Margery and her children had finished breakfast and gone their separate ways, Veronica turned to Max. "You will not get them to leave that easily."

He seemed not at all surprised by the remark. "I shall merely have to try harder then." The corners of his mouth hinted at a smile.

"And you certainly will not get rid of me with such tactics," Dora added.

"My ambition scarcely soared that high," Max acknowledged without looking at her.

Dora snorted and tramped out of the breakfast parlor. Flurry followed her out, chuckling to herself, a graceful foil to Dora's clumsy exit.

"Alone, at last," Max said with satisfaction, as though that had been his only purpose. "I must say, even though you are short of help, someone should have answered that bellpull after all this time."

Veronica grinned. "That one has not worked for years."

"You imp." Max smiled with satisfaction. "Aunt Margery was fated never to get any breakfast."

"That will teach her to get up earlier. What shall we do today, Max? Would you like me to show you over the house?" Veronica was beginning to feel easier in Max's presence, but she was not sure how to entertain him.

"No, too dull." Max glanced out the window. "Let us take a walk. I want to hear what you have been doing all this time."

"I would rather hear what you have been up to, Max. It has all been very dull here." Veronica grabbed her shawl, the one Flurry had knitted for her out of dark brown merino wool. She led the way down the hall, picking up a flower basket at the back door before throwing it open and stepping out into the warm spring sunshine. She remembered how much her papa had liked to walk on such days. Rather than continue to mourn his loss, she should be grateful she had him as many years as she did.

She should be grateful for Flurry and strive to take care of her. And she should be happy that Max had finally returned. She had always been so much younger than the boys that she would never have been included on any ride or hike if not for Max. No matter how long it took her to push her pony through the hedge or how tired she got on their rambles, Max always waited for her, whereas George and Freddy abandoned them.

Veronica unconsciously started toward the stables, then remembered too late that there was nothing of interest there, so she turned her steps in the direction of the gardens.

She wanted to gather some mint for tea anyway. Two stone walkways crossed in the middle of the garden with a sundial and bench at the center. The quadrants held the kitchen garden, the rose garden, the culinary herbs, and the medicinal herbs.

The daffodils stood out bravely yellow in the flower borders that framed the bare vegetable garden. Veronica trod past the dead stalks of last winter's bean plants, drying on the trellises, to the herb gardens.

"There is not much here this time of year," Max said as he stooped to gather some sprigs of spearmint for her. He crushed one in his hand and inhaled it with a sigh of pleasure.

"Only mint and parsley," Veronica observed, "although it looks like a lucky rabbit has made a meal of the parsley."

"Rhubarb!" Max said with delight as he broke off a small early stalk and munched hungrily on the tart red stem.

Veronica shuddered. "How can you eat that raw with no sugar?"

"An unjaded palate. What are these dried stalks?" Max indicated a crumpled mass. "They are huge."

"Those were ricinus plants from the scarab beetle seeds you sent Papa."

"Oh, I remember. *Ricinus communis.* I found them in a market in South Africa. I had no idea they would propagate in England."

"The gardener generally keeps the medicinal herbs separate from the culinary ones, hence the two beds, but when I told him the scarab beetle plants were reported to drive away moles, Marsh cultivated them throughout the garden."

"I did not realize they were good for anything." Max picked up a stray pod and broke it open. "I just thought the seeds were unusual."

"They make a pretty bush and the seeds could be

used for necklaces, if I had the time." She poked at the
half-dozen seeds, mottled beige and chocolate brown,
that lay in his hand like a group of beetles, no two alike.
"See how prettily they are spotted, and they do not
wrinkle when they are dried but retain their shiny
appearance."

"Yes, very pretty, Vee," Max said as though she were a
child, before putting them in his pocket and taking her
hand to draw it through the crook of his arm. She had
the most odd feeling that something momentous was
about to happen as she strolled about the garden, but
she could not imagine what. Of course being with Max
had its own importance.

"Well, there is a lot I would have time for if I did not
have to run this place."

"Has life been so hard, Vee? You never told me, and
certainly your father gave me no notion of it."

Veronica watched the way he carried his walking
stick in his left hand and had the most obsessive illusion that it contained a sword. "Not enough for me to
notice ... except when we have company. I do not
mind doing without, but the family makes me feel our
deficiencies as though they were my fault."

Veronica broke contact with Max to pick a few jon-
quils for Flurry's room and would have carried her
bouquet back to the kitchen had Max not taken her
arm again and dragged her ruthlessly to the stable and
down the empty row of box stalls. Aside from Max's
team there was only the cart pony and an aged mare left
in the end stalls. Veronica could not rid herself of the
feeling that she was on trial again. She expected condemnation from Lady Margery and her brood, but not
from her dearest friend Max.

When Ned Beatty, the only remaining groom, saw

that they meant to stay and talk, he left off cleaning the stalls and went toward the sheep barn where he spent the better part of his day.

"Why did you not keep one of your young horses?" Max asked, walking toward the mare.

"You remember Bonnie," Veronica said, stroking the velvety brown nose with one hand. "She is the mare who gave me many of my young horses. I sold them to good riders. But no one would have wanted her. She is too old even for a brood mare."

"This is not fair," Max whispered fiercely as he scratched the horse between the ears. "If only I had known you were in dire straits. I begin to suspect Henry Steeple has been feathering his own nest."

"And knowing that, Aunt Margery married him to try to hang onto something?" Veronica asked.

"I do not give her that much credit. It is a step up for Henry Steeple to marry a Strake, even secondhand. After your father began to trust me again, he was still very close about financial matters, and I did not push him. I simply assumed everything was fine."

"So Papa did start to write to you again. I am so glad," Veronica said with a sigh of relief. "You are here now and everything will be fine." Veronica gave Bonnie a reassuring pat, trying to think of an excuse to touch Max again. She liked the warmth of him against her—perhaps too much.

"But I am too late," he said in despair.

"Never mind, Max." She squeezed his arm as she walked past him, looking about the spacious building with its wrought-iron mangers and stone lion-headed bosses between each stall where the bridles were hung. Most of the box stalls were empty now, but she still had her memories. "I had almost thought never to see you again, that I would be trapped here forever with the house coming down about my ears."

"I was going to remark that the house has not changed at all," he said gently.

"Of course not," Veronica snapped. "I have had no money to make repairs." She forced composure on herself before she turned to him. "Sorry, but I get very impatient at being so powerless."

"It was not your job to take care of Byerly." He came to stand behind her. She could feel his breath on her neck, could almost feel the heat of his body, and it confused her. She did not know how to take Max now, and it made her edgy.

"No, it was Papa's job, but after a time he did not see peeling paint or broken copestones. He thought only of his research and finding the Nonsuch treasure. It became an obsession with him." Veronica turned to face Max. "Papa and I had always done everything together, all his research on plants, the folio of botanical studies. But he shut me out toward the end, and I cannot make out why. He made trips to London and did not include me, when I would have given anything to have gone with him. He made other trips without telling where he was going. After being so close to him, it hurt me to think we were growing apart."

Max smiled sadly and hugged her. Her shawl slipped from her shoulders and she could feel the warmth of him, the all-embracing comfort of him, and wondered how she had done without him for so long. His size was no longer frightening, but oddly exciting.

"Perhaps your father had the same problem that I do."

"And what is that?" Veronica asked, her cheek still pressed to his coat.

"A touch too much pride."

She looked up at him. "Pride? This is me you are talking to."

"Yes," Max said, not releasing her. "I am well aware you have seen me at my very worst on more occasions that I care to count."

"What of it?" Veronica asked. "We are friends, Max." She studied his lips intently, fully aware of his warm arms around her, his strong thighs pressed against her, and wondered what was happening.

"This was the last great thing your father would work on. He wanted the success, if he did find the treasure, to be his."

"Was he counting on it to restore our fortunes?" Veronica asked.

"I doubt that any artifact from Nonsuch could do so. The country is crawling with that sort of rubble. They are forever discovering bits of one ancient church or another used as foundation stone for some later building."

"Yes, Papa's notes say that Nonsuch itself was partially built from the stone of Merton Priory when Henry had it pulled down."

"I think he was trying to prove something to himself," Max said as he reached for the fallen shawl and pulled it close around Veronica in the chill of the stable.

She looked searchingly at Max. "Were we too close, Papa and me? Was I smothering him?"

Max's mouth wore that hint of a smile. "You do have a way of marshaling your resources that would stand you in good stead on a field of war."

"Thank you, Max. Let us hope I do not run out of strategies in the coming battle with Lady Margery and her brood. They will try to take everything, you know."

She stepped away from him, oddly disappointed that his arms were gone.

"I know," Max agreed. "I used to hate fighting with them, but they always managed to find the needle that pricked."

"Such as calling you a bastard?" she asked. She saw him flinch and regretted the remark.

"I do not know why I should have minded that so much." Max picked up the basket and handed it to her. "It is not as though the title, Viscount Byerly, carries anything with it."

Veronica's fingers brushed his hand and caused that momentary hitch in her breathing. "It may mean nothing to you, but George was always jealous of you because of it."

"But his father was not a Strake. Proving me a bastard does not make him a viscount."

"Depriving you of the title would take you down a peg."

"It is nothing anyone could prove," Max said, "unless Mother reveals some deep dark secret."

"No need to worry about that now. I have a surprise for you in the attic," Veronica said mysteriously. She picked up the bouquet of mint and sniffed the crushed petals, trying to calm her regrets over her papa.

Max scanned the deserted stable again. "Still, I wish you had told me things were come to such a pass."

"It did not get this way overnight, Max. If you recall I did write you to that effect when you were in Spain. If you chose to ignore my letters. . . ."

"I never got any letter that did not make light of your situation. I thought you were being frivolous, complaining languidly the way other ladies do. . . ."

"How dare you, Max," she said, thrusting the basket

so forcefully at him that he staggered. "I am not like other ladies. You were being insensitive and ignoring me because it was not convenient to come home." Veronica's sharp tone caused the mare to move nervously to the back of her stall.

"Except that last letter," Max said as Veronica turned and strode out of the stable toward the neglected rose garden, flinging off her shawl and trailing it behind her over the wet grass.

He followed her, looking with disfavor on the encroaching tendrils and the tufts of grass coming up between the stones. When she paused to break off some dead stems from the previous year, he picked up the tail of her shawl and restored it to her again. Vee always did have a way of seeing through him.

"And what is this surprise you have for me?" Max teased. "A leak in the roof?"

"I suppose I can forget about taking you over the house until your bruised ego has healed." She turned to regard him critically.

"You have never bruised my ego or any other part of me," he said softly.

"More is the pity," she tossed at him. "A stiff knocking about would do you a world of good at the moment."

He captured her gaze with those so compelling eyes. "You have always given me the plain truth about myself, even when it was the last thing I wanted to hear."

"I have a penchant for the truth, and I am surrounded by people who are self-delusional," Veronica said in that slow way of hers that drew his eyes to her lips. The flush of anger was receding from her cheeks but her eyes still snapped with dark fire.

Max shook his head and restored the basket to her.

"Shall I let Freddy have a go at me or, better yet, invite them both—"

"Max, I am sorry. I had forgotten why you left." Veronica resumed walking, bending her steps back toward the house.

Max kept pace with her, swinging his stick. "Slunk away in the dead of night with a split lip and a very bruised ego. They had finally managed to do it, to turn your father against me."

"It was not fair. And for the first time he would not listen to me. He just said I knew nothing about it. I shall never forgive Margery's brood for how they lied about you. It serves them right that you are left with everything—well, perhaps not. There is not much left except the house and it is in sad shape." Veronica gazed up at the crumbling four-story building, with its cracked roof tiles and blackened chimney pots. "I fear I have not done a very good job. . . ." She choked on a confusion of emotions.

"Crying, *Lady Veronica?*" Max asked as he turned her chin up to gaze at her. "This is not like you, Vee. You should have kept a few of your horses to cheer you up."

"And have Freddy laming them?" Veronica asked, wiping her eyes tiredly with the backs of her hands like a little girl. "No, Max, I am so weary of it all." She tucked a stray tendril of hair behind her ear with a resolute sniff.

"Tell me where your favorites are and I will get them back for you," he offered, playfully catching up a handful of her raven hair and letting it run through his fingers.

Her gaze followed the path of his fingers. "And what would I do with them now? Max, you do not seem to understand. I will not be here to ride them."

"You keep saying that, but you cannot mean it," he insisted.

"Dearest Max, as dense as ever in some respects. It was sweet of you to offer, anyway."

She stood on tiptoe and kissed his cheek so naturally he responded in kind; he wondered how such a simple act could touch him so much.

"At least now I do not have to worry about Byerly," she said. "You can take care of it."

Max was staring at her as though she were undergoing a transformation before his very eyes. In spite of her loose hair, her easy comradery, and her familiarity, she was a woman, not a child. He would have to remember not to treat her as though she were a hoydenish girl. "What did you say?" he heard himself utter numbly. She smiled and his heart leaped, making it difficult for him to focus on her reply.

"I said you can take care of Byerly now." Veronica tilted her head. "It is your turn. Why should that surprise you?"

He gave his head a shake. "I cannot get over how you have changed. As for Byerly, I can think of better ways to spend my money."

"What better ways?" she challenged.

"I could buy you anything your heart desires," he offered gallantly, the words spilling out as though he wanted to please her above all else in the world.

"My heart's desire is to be shut of this place. If you are going to talk nonsense, I will go do my book work." Veronica left him and strode back to the house, trying to look stern, but succeeding only in looking like a pouting young beauty, spurning her beau.

Max watched her go. Only when Vee talked did he recognize the dear friend of his youth. She had always been so much younger that he had always considered her merely a precocious child. Of course, it was because he had not seen her in so many years that he was having trouble knowing how to treat her. In a few days the awkwardness would go out of their relationship and everything would be as before. But he had some gnawing feeling that however much he got used to this new Vee, things had changed irrevocably, and she would be even harder to handle than the playmate of his youth.

*L*uncheon was an uncomfortable affair with the arguments of breakfast still fresh in everyone's mind. Consequently, no one said anything, except to remark on the food. Since this consisted merely of a thin soup, some cutlets, and a stuffed fowl of indeterminate age, the meal was not a safe topic either. As soon as she had finished eating, Veronica rose and practically ordered Max to accompany her on a tour of the interior.

A few minutes later Max snagged his coat sleeve on a nail and pulled his arm free with a ripping sound, looking down to scrutinize the damage as he ducked a low beam. "Veronica, I do not see why you must drag me over the entire ruin today. I did live here and know full well—What was that?" Max whispered as he froze in a crouch, attentively listening to a rustling and then a gnawing from a basket of rags in a corner of the attic.

"Just a mouse," Veronica answered, holding her skirts up as she made her way past piles of rubble to a stack of paintings leaning against one wall.

"I wonder that you have not trapped them," Max complained.

"They have to live too, Max," she said absently as she flipped through the paintings, holding the foremost one up with her knee and letting the heavy frames thump against each other, raising clouds of dust in the sunlight that streamed in through the round attic window.

"I see I was right about the leak. I can identify three holes in the roof from here." Max tripped over one of the pails that had been strategically placed under a hole and stooped to position it back where it would be needed next time it came on to rain.

"I have done the best I could with what I have. There is no way you will make me feel guilty about Byerly. Besides, it is yours now, mice and all. Have your way with them," she replied, still flipping through the paintings.

"You should have demanded that Henry Steeple make repairs," Max said.

"When he would not even pay the bills? Besides, I am not your helpless female always to be depending on someone."

"More is the pity," Max said under his breath.

"What was that? Ah, here he is. I found him when I ran out of canvases and was looking for something I could paint over. I put him up here so he would be safe. Look at the name plate. The fourteenth Viscount of Byerly, Jeremiah Strake. This was probably done around 1700. What do you think?"

"Passably ugly and the workmanship is crude," Max said, gazing at the portrait. "I do not see what impresses you about it."

"Max, without the wig and in modern clothes, it is you. You know how George and Freddy were forever riding you about not really being a Strake? This portrait proves that you are the heir."

"It does, indeed," Max said, his dark brows drawn in thought.

"Why was that, Max? Were you a seven-month child or something?" Veronica asked.

"I have no idea," Max said, "but I do not think George and Freddy thought of it themselves."

"Aunt Margery must have suggested the idea to them. Now, where shall we hang him?" Veronica asked. "I was thinking at the head of the main stairs."

Max braced his foot on an old trunk and rested the painting on his knee in the sole beam of sunlight invading the attic. He did finally perceive the resemblance Veronica spoke of. His ancestor's features had sprung out in him. He wondered if his brow would become quite so forbidding in middle age, his mouth so grim. As a peek into the future it would have made a stauncher man than Max shudder, but that was not what bothered him. The painting was not full proof, but it was insurance of a sort. "If only I had known about this before I left."

"Papa was so angry with you I do not think definite proof that you are a Strake would have mattered."

"But my mother got her way in one important matter in my life because she threatened to reveal my bastardy. And in those days I was fool enough to think that she would do so." Max hoped Vee would not inquire into what that matter was.

"But she never would have done it, Max. It would have cut her off from the Strake family as well," Veronica pointed out. "And however much she dislikes them personally, Dora enjoys the consequence of being a Strake and lording it over the people on the estate and in the village."

"Her threat seemed serious enough to me at the

time; at eighteen, I had not enough experience of women to know if she was lying or not."

"Ah, I see," Veronica said, straight-faced. "Now, with your vast experience of women . . ."

Max chuckled. "No, I still cannot tell if Mother is bluffing, but I do know what you are thinking."

"What?" Veronica asked.

"That I am the most pompous, conceited—"

"No, Max, never that." She brushed the dust off his sleeve in a familiar way that, all the same, gave him an odd feeling. "You may act the part for the family, but you are still Max underneath it all, as boyish and uncertain as you were when you left."

He stared at her a moment. "I do not want anyone else to see it."

"Your uncertainty?" Veronica asked. "But they cannot, for you disguise it so well."

"No, you wigeon, the painting," he said with a slow smile.

"Max, the painting is not that bad. I can clean it myself. I assure you I know how."

"Who have you told about this?" Max asked intently.

"No one," Veronica said. "I wanted it to be a surprise. It is so hard to think of surprises for you."

"Do not tell anyone." Max took out his handkerchief and dusted the frame.

"But why not? I was so looking forward to seeing the faces Freddy and George will pull when they realize they were wrong."

"I am not," Max replied. "Do you wish to destroy my enjoyment of their contempt?"

Veronica tilted her head as though that would help her to comprehend him. "You cannot mean that you like being wronged, having them resent you?"

"But I do. If they saw this, do you imagine they would come to accept me or even—the thought nearly gags me—come to like me?"

Veronica's rich peal of laughter echoed off the rafters. "I see your point. You would no longer have an excuse to be rude to them. You would have to become sociable and invite them for the holidays."

"It would be torture for me," Max said with a malicious grin.

"I do not know what came over me. By the time a man is your age he may turn from affable to recluse when he chooses, but he may never reverse his image."

"Oh, I should not do that." Max watched her appreciatively as her shoulders shook with laughter. "To be sure they would find some other reason to dislike me."

Veronica folded her arms and regarded him. "You do give them their pick of things to dislike about you. Why is that? I have always found it is much nicer to be liked than disliked."

"Ah, but you have no fortune. If I let a man like me, or even a woman, they begin to ask things of me, expect things of me." He looked away from her, thinking of the world in which he now lived.

"Because of your money, not yourself." Veronica gave up any pretense of keeping her dress clean and sat on the trunk. "But you should be able to say no without feeling guilty. A true friend would stand by you."

Max leaned the painting against the trunk and sat down. "A true friend would not ask. A friend like you."

She looked surprised, then smiled.

"Still," Max said, "I cannot quite forgive you for the mice."

"They may serve a purpose yet," Veronica said. "We will leave the portrait out here where they can get at it. Perhaps they will dispose of the fourteenth viscount for us."

"What? Out here where anyone might find him?" Max asked. "No, I think I shall take him into custody, if you do not mind."

"Help yourself. You may have all the paintings."

"Even your landscapes and still-life studies?" He looked around at the stacks of paintings.

"What would I do with them? Will you never let me paint your likeness?" Veronica studied his face and he inexplicably found himself blushing.

"Bad luck. Everyone of these fellows is dead now."

"But they—" Veronica stopped on a ripple of laughter. "I see, so long as no one paints you, you will live forever. Do not speak to any of my clients, sir. It would be fatal for business."

As they came down to the second story, Veronica shook her skirts hopelessly and followed Max as he carried the portrait into his bedroom and gave Mustafah, who was dusting there, a string of orders that sent him off, presumably to find wrapping material.

Veronica mused on how unobtrusively Max's retinue had fitted into the house.

"How many servants do you have with you? I was guessing you have half a dozen Indian men in your pay. So far as I can tell, only your coachman is English."

"There are only Mustafah, Karim, and Rajeev. I rescued them from a French naval vessel. It was sinking," Max said simply.

"I see." Veronica pushed aside her speculation on whether Max had anything to do with it sinking. She knew from his letters that his merchant ships were as well armed as many a British frigate and she half suspected he enjoyed the battle when one of his ships was under attack. But she let him retain his inscrutability. "And the dialect you use? I have a smattering of French, Italian, and Spanish, but this language is like none of those."

"It is Hindi. I find it convenient to be able to converse in native tongues. I have plantations in the Malay Islands, Madagascar, and the Indies."

"My, but you are far-flung." She glanced out his bedroom window and saw one of his men searching about the deserted gardens and wondered what he hoped to find at this season.

She was jolted back to awareness by Max closing the door. Why this made her feel odd she did not know. "Just think, this may be the last time we will all be at Byerly together," she said, turning and staring toward the door.

"What are you talking about?" He leaned against the footboard of the bedstead. "You must continue to live here, though I have no intention of inviting the rest of the pack again."

"We have already discussed this, Max. I am leaving."

"But that would spoil everything. You and Flurry are the only ones I want here."

"What would be spoiled?" Veronica asked. "Your victory over the family?"

"No, they have only come to sneer at the outcast. They thought they had gotten rid of me."

"You have gotten rather good at sneering back," Veronica observed. "If I did not know you so well, there are moments when I would be tempted to be offended myself."

"I would never give you offense. You are one of my few friends, Vee."

"You did offend me once." She folded her arms in front of her and looked up at him.

"How so? You never said anything. What was it over?" he prodded.

"I shall not tell you, for I have forgiven you." She stared at his neck, where she thought she had seen a glimmer of gold under his loosely tied cravat.

"Tell me or I will tickle you until you do." He stood up and grabbed her about the waist.

"Do not be a child, Max. As I recall, I was counseling you, wisely I might add, to make your peace with George and Freddy before—"

"How old were you then?" He let his arms slide around her waist and enfold her.

"Ten, I should think." She brought her hands up to rest them on his lapels just as any other woman might.

"And so very wise?" he asked, his mouth suddenly dry with the excitement of her nearness. He studied her face, trying to make out what it was that made her Vee; the midnight ringlets, those full, determined lips, or the brown wells of her eyes.

"Perhaps that is why you did not take me seriously." She reached for the thin gold chain about his neck and began tugging it outside his collar. He let her.

"And how did I give offense?" he asked as she pulled the locket outside his shirt.

"You kept them," she said. "The first miniatures I ever painted."

"You and Flurry. Of course I kept them." He took the object from her childlike fingers and worked the catch.

She and Max stared at the two small images, hers so young and Flurry's without the gray in her hair. Veronica smiled slowly and it warmed his heart to know she could still be touched by the past. He would be forever grateful that Great-Uncle John had brought him to Byerly after his father's death rather than leave him to grow up in his mother's house in London. Perhaps they had been afraid Dora Strake would go back on the stage and drag the family name in the dirt.

He remembered how much he and Vee had enjoyed arguing, just for the sake of conversation. Whatever he said, Veronica would play devil's advocate, just to keep the talk flowing.

"I suppose I made some comment about your hair," Max guessed. "If I did, I take it back." He picked up a curly black lock and twined it around his finger.

"You said I was like all the others," Veronica accused.

"That was bad of me, for you are nothing like the rest of our relatives. They are so sadly predictable." His gaze rippled over her. "And you are . . . unexpected."

"Odd, how we expect people not to age, how we carry an image in our mind that keeps someone looking as young and uncertain, as hurt as the last time we saw him." Veronica snapped the locket shut and tucked it under his collar. The gentle brush of her fingers brought back memories of her caring. But she had been just a child then, and he had never taken advantage of his strength or years to prey on her innocence in any way . . . in spite of what her father had thought.

The scene came back to him as vividly as an oft-repeated nightmare: groggily awakening amid Mercia's shrieks, then pulling a blanket about himself as Freddy laughed through the open door. Standing there with the rest of the family, Vee had protested as Flurry had dragged her away. Had she heard her father's condemnation of his depraved appetites? Had she heard John ask him if he had designs on Veronica as well? That was when he had jumped out the window.

He let his arms drop. He had not had such thoughts then and would not have them now. The Comishes had cost him a decade of companionship, of Uncle John, Flurry, and Vee. At least he had reconciled with his uncle before he had died. He would not now violate his promise to care for Flurry and Vee by doing anything to tarnish this relationship.

"Max, did you hear me?"

"I have grown a thicker skin," Max said with a brittle smile. "I am incapable of being hurt."

"Brave words. I suspect you are merely better at hiding it."

Her acuity had always been like a knife to the heart. She was right, of course. But no one else need ever know that. "It comes to the same thing."

"No, it does not," Veronica said softly. She turned to go, looking longingly back at him.

"Who has hurt you?" Max demanded, pulling himself together as he stared, entranced, into the depths of her eyes.

"It does not signify." She looked away.

"Not me," he croaked, feeling as though she were peeling away the years like the layers of an onion. How could he face a broadside from a French frigate to defend his cargo without flinching and still quake under the lash of Vee's tongue? Did she think it was easy to run Napoleon's blockade? But Vee did not care about his world of war and politics. She cared about him and somehow he must have erred grievously.

"I have forgiven you. Or I should rather say I have made allowances for your quirks no matter how outrageous."

"But I have not even been here in twelve years," he complained.

"You did not come," she said with her hand on the doorknob. "When all is said and done, you did not come. And you were in London, not thirty miles from here."

Max looked away as though seeking his answer out the window in the distant woods. "I did meet Uncle John in London."

"When?" Veronica whispered.

"Two years ago. He was visiting one of the libraries there."

"Surely he asked you to come to Byerly."

"Of course." Max's clipped answer sounded brutal even to himself.

"I see." Veronica looked down and seemed to shrink in height as though she were emptied of life. "It was me you were avoiding." She tried to open the door, but he crossed the room in two strides and leaned against it, trapping her on his side. He hugged her to him and would not let her go. She did not struggle, but rested her head on his chest.

"I can explain," he groaned. "I could not come back here before I was ready." He whispered this against her hair.

Veronica sniffed. "What do you mean, ready? I know you, Max. You are no coward. And what had you to face? Most likely you would not have encountered George and Freddy."

"They do not matter, anymore. I could not face you." He took her face in his hands and raised it to look her in the eyes. "Not until I had outgrown the bloody-nosed whelp who left here."

"What are you talking about?" Veronica stared at him in puzzlement.

"You have only ever seen me at my worst, in defeat. I wanted . . ." His words stumbled over the half-formed thought.

"Oh, Max," she said, looking worshipfully up at him. "You wanted to make your fortune first and make just such an entrance as you did last night."

"Yes," he hissed as she finally understood him.

"Of all the idiotic starts." She grasped his sleeves in her excitement. "Flurry and I would not have cared."

"Which is precisely why it was important to me."

"I will never understand you, Max, never," she said reaching up and running her fingers over his lips like a sculptor examining a work of art.

Max stared at her, his heart hammering in his chest, until she smiled self-consciously and withdrew her touch.

"It is just as well," he said, when he was able to speak. "I do not understand myself. Do you truly forgive me?"

"Of course." She stood on tiptoe to give him a quick kiss on the lips. Then she looked thoughtfully at him. "I must go change," she whispered. Veronica extricated herself from his numb embrace with a laugh. When she opened the door, Max saw Flurry in the hall looking grim.

He sat on the edge of the bed and tried to induce that meditative state Mustafah had taught him. *A man who did not control himself could never trust himself.* He could feel the blood racing through his veins in defiance of this chant he had repeated whenever his convoy of trading vessels sighted French warships. If it worked to control his anger and sharpen his mind, why could he not control other, more confused emotions?

It did not help that his personal servant now interrupted him to inform him that he was ready to make the trip to London for provisions. The city was scarcely a three-hours' drive. There was no reason to go anywhere else for foodstuffs. Without rising, Max gave orders for some items he thought would especially delight Vee. It took all his effort to remain indolent when he could hear the activity in the stable yard, the carriage being brought out, the horses being hitched. He was used to being on the go, but his defection at this time might upset Vee.

He forced himself to remain still until quiet once again reigned in the stable yard. He forced himself to think of his uncle, a scholar, a man in the prime of his life. Why had he died? Max pulled Vee's letter out again and reread the symptoms. Had she glossed over the worst of the illness as she had shielded Max from the situation at Byerly? Uncle John had been his advisor and mentor until their sudden rift. In many ways that relationship had been killed by the Comishes twelve years ago. And now the man himself had died and Max was feeling his loss, for he sorely needed to talk to someone about Vee. He could see the injustice of her being cooped up here all these years.

Now that the war was over, he could offer to take Vee and Flurry on his next trading voyage. The two of them could not go blundering about the world with no male escort. It simply was not safe. Flurry was the key, a competent, sensible woman. Max must enlist her aid in persuading Vee to stay put until Max had settled some things. But Max could tell by the glare Flurry had cast him from the hall that she was angry with him. What had he been thinking, talking to Vee alone in his bedroom with the door closed? He was angry with himself for that, and now he must think of a way to appease Flurry. Having formed a course of action, he came up off the bed like an uncoiling snake. He tossed aside his torn jacket, grabbed another, and went in search of the old governess.

5

After checking Flurry's room and the immediate grounds, Max invaded the kitchen, but his quest was initially unsuccessful, none of the servants having any knowledge of Flurry's whereabouts. Max's search did have the effect of convincing him Vee's dependents were neither indolent nor wasteful. The dozen people he encountered in a lightning survey of the house and out-buildings were engaged in lambing, wood cutting, clothes washing, or preparing for the next meal. The kitchen was a beehive of activity, and Max backed him-self out of it when he realized he was interrupting an exchange of recipes between Cook and Karim via sign language. It was a mark of Vee's ability to inspire loyalty that her people hung on here with low pay and little promise of future advancement. He would see that their devotion was rewarded.

And of all of them Flurry was the most devoted, Max thought, as he tramped back up the stairs. She had been a companion to Vee's mother, who Max had always understood to be sickly. Flurry had volunteered to accompany his mother, Dora, to Edinburgh for her confinement, though why he was not allowed to be born either in London or at Byerly, Max had no notion. He had been only five when his father had died and John Strake had either requested or commanded that his great-nephew and heir be raised at Byerly. Dora had complied, and Flurry had come along as a teacher until Max was old enough to be shipped off to school.

When Vee was born, Flurry once more became a nurse and nanny. Max had still been at Byerly the night Vee's mother, Olivia, had died, and he remembered Flurry's wails of despair and John's almost trancelike state. Flurry was the only mother Vee had ever known.

Max hesitated outside the drawing room door. He knew the women were gathered inside. Since none of the servants knew where Flurry was, he would just have to fall back on his mother's uncanny ability to keep track of people. He threw the doors open and glanced disdainfully around the room. This drew a spark of resentment from George, who was examining a folio of architectural drawings at the window. Max instinctively drew himself up even taller and raised an eyebrow in challenge. But Max's glare was mostly wasted on Lady Margery, who sniffed and went back to her embroidery, and on Mercia, who was deep into a novel. His mother could match him glare for glare. It was from her that he had learned some of his most effective looks.

"Mother, I cannot seem to find Miss Flurry. Have you seen her?"

"She said she was going to do some repotting," Dora replied. "So she is no doubt in that small greenhouse your uncle had attached to the library wing."

Max turned to go but was arrested by his aunt's whining voice. "That is not a genteel occupation. Why do we still need Flurry here? Veronica is well past the age of requiring a governess."

"Miss Flurry is a member of the family," Max asserted. He could not help but notice his mother's look of shock and wondered why she would be surprised at his defense of Flurry. Surely, after all these years, she knew how he felt about Flurry. Dora's concern seemed to abate and Max thanked her formally and made his way out the back door to the small greenhouse on the exposed southwest corner of the library wing. He would have thought it too cold at this time of year to be doing much with plants, but Flurry was bravely potting up some seedlings from a flat that had been started on the sunny side of the house.

"There you are. I have been looking for you, Flurry."

"And what have you been up to, Max?" Flurry asked, wiping her hands on her rough work apron and confronting him.

"Giving orders to provision the place." He bent to pick up a barrel of dirt she was reaching for. "And giving some thought to what to do about Vee."

"Locking her in your bedroom is not the way to treat a young lady no matter how well you know her," Flurry said cuttingly.

Max hesitated at the sudden attack. Usually Flurry was more subtle. "That did occur to me, but not until after that glare you shot at me."

"You admit you were in the wrong?" Flurry stared at him as though this was unprecedented.

"And most humbly do I beg your forgiveness." He bowed in an exaggerated manner that provoked an angry snort from her. "Closing that door was even worse than you leaving the two of us alone last night in the drawing room." Max smiled as he waited to see the effect of his counterattack.

Flurry pursed her lips and glared again in that way perfected by governesses. "After you had fogged my mind with brandy."

"That is why I rarely touch the stuff myself," he replied.

"Max, you are the most provoking boy." Flurry brushed back a lock of gray hair with the heel of one hand.

"But that is the point." Max propped one booted foot up on the aged potting bench. "I am not a boy anymore, no matter how you may think of me."

"No, you are not." She compressed her lips, then continued. "You are, in fact, a rather sinister character until you drop your guard."

"I have had a deal of practice being sinister," Max said proudly. "You might be surprised to learn that I am a powerful man in the world of commerce and diplomacy."

"Yes, I know. George told me."

"George? Why would he do that, even if he knew."

Flurry seated herself primly on the bench, deliberately keeping him in suspense. "I had the most uncomfortable feeling he was preparing me in case one of your *trading* expeditions ran afoul of a French patrol and you were shipped home to us in a vat of brandy."

Max laughed. "Brandy is reserved for admirals. And if I achieved more than trade on my voyages, where is the harm in that."

"What has that to do with anything?" Flurry demanded. "The point is you had Veronica in your room with the door closed." Flurry folded her hands in her lap as though awaiting his explanation.

"I already said it was ill-judged of me. But I have learned a thing or two in knocking about the world."

"You? Learn?" She cast him an incredulous look. "Well, I suppose it is possible."

Max looked away, admitting defeat. "I yield to your superior barbed wit. Is it possible that you would take my humble advice on a matter that touches both you and Vee?"

"What matter?" Flurry arched one eyebrow suspiciously.

Max seated himself beside her, ignoring the dirt on the bench. "Her plan to travel. I know she is thinking that since the war is over, the world is a safe place again, but nothing could be further from the truth."

"Traveling and painting new scenes has been one of Veronica's dreams. It is the only thing that has sustained her after her father's death. You certainly were not around to console her."

Max lowered his eyes. "I did not take her seriously, and not for the first time. I thought . . . I know it sounds absurd, but I was picturing a twelve-year-old writing those letters, and I was thinking she did not really know what she was talking about."

"Veronica has had the running of Byerly since the Comishes went to London for Mercia's come out. John provided them with the London house and told them to stay there, except for the occasional visit. He banished you, but I think he blamed them as well. Can I assume that she finally managed to convince him you had been victimized?"

"Yes, because she always believed in me." Max looked a challenge at her. "What about you?"

Flurry stared at him, then got a superior look in her eyes. "I knew you had better taste than to go after a little tattletale like Mercia."

"That is a backhanded compliment if ever I heard one."

"And better than you deserve, Max. Veronica used to ask me why I thought you had not come. And I got weary of making excuses for you."

"I was entrusted with important business for the government."

"I can see why that would sometimes be more important than your family. I cannot see why it was always so."

"The truth of the matter is that I was not sure of my welcome." Max took Flurry's hand. "Though my work is important, I hardly get public recognition for it. To most of the world I am no more than a merchant."

"You are a fool, and that will never change."

Max leaned toward her like a conspirator. "Are you with me or against me? I do not mean to keep Vee trapped here forever, but I want to escort you myself when I have the leisure."

"I will think about your proposal, but we *are* going, Max." She withdrew her hand and stood up, dismissing him.

"I had something else to ask you."

"What is it, Max?"

"Do you remember my father, Robert?"

Flurry's eyes took on a veiled look that startled Max. Flurry had always been frank with him, yet he had the distinct feeling that she was capable of lying to him if she wished.

"I did not know your father very well. He was . . . a charming man . . . by all accounts." Flurry moved toward the door that led into the room from the house.

"Do you remember why he took Mother to Scotland for my birth?"

Flurry turned her head but did not meet his eyes. "Dora was nervous about her pregnancy, after watching

John's wife go through a miscarriage. She wanted to consult with a particular physician there."

"And did she have any problems?" Max came to stand beside her.

Flurry flicked a pained glance in his direction. "No, all went as planned. When you were a month old we brought you to the house in London. Robert preferred London to Byerly."

"My father and John were not close, were they?"

"Robert was John's cousin and heir, but John had no hold on Robert, who had money of his own."

Flurry opened the door and made her way through a chamber outfitted as a bedroom, his great-uncle's bedroom. Max followed her, glancing at the bed and realizing that this was where his uncle had died, surrounded by his beloved plants and books. Some presence of the man still hung about the room in the untidiness of the piles of books and papers. Probably nothing had been touched since his death.

"John set this room up as his bedroom so he could avoid the family as much as possible," Flurry said. "They interfered with his studies." She moved on into the library and here stopped as though she had not quite decided where she wanted to go. "Do you remember the first time you came to Byerly?" Flurry turned to Max with something of her old energy in her eyes now. "You were five and had never seen it before, had never seen much of anything except London parks and streets."

"Yes, I asked you if it was a castle and you said yes, and we were going to live happily ever after."

"I did not lie to you, Max," she said, her eyes distant. "I truly thought we would be happy here."

"If I was unhappy it was none of your doing. Is there nothing else you can tell me about my father?"

"No, Max, nothing." Flurry leaned against the desk.

"But how did he die?" Max insisted.

"Max, you are being very tiresome," she growled. "I wish you would go away."

Max left her, chastising himself for tiring Flurry. He had to remember that she was not a young woman anymore and he could not tease her as he used to.

Veronica stood back from the painting as though she were waking up from a dream. It was finished, from the lightning strike in the midnight sky and the ruined castle in the background to the blasted trees in the foreground. And it was Max. She spun to glance around her bedroom at all the other portraits she had done of Max over the years, and this was her best. Those had been of Max the boy and Max as she had imagined him to have grown. She had guessed right that his eyes had not changed. They had remained clear gray and uncompromising. And his startling eyebrows set them off perfectly, but his jaw had hardened and his brow had become stern. His nostrils had a distinctive flare to them that was almost exotic. And those lips; the bottom one was full and promising. As she stared at the painting, it almost seemed to move. She reached out toward the canvas but stopped herself in time before she smeared the paint. She thought about the real Max, how he had looked when she left him in his bedroom, and a jolt of longing went through her.

She turned to focus on the small clock on the mantel and realized it wanted only an hour to dinner. She must be hungry and that was why she was feeling so giddy. Hastily she used linseed oil to remove the worst of the paint from her hands. Then she stripped off her painting smock and the gray morning dress and washed her face and hands. She felt odd, satisfied, and yet hungry at the same time. Instead of putting on her black evening dress again she pulled out a frivolous yellow frock she had made out of some of the muslin Max had sent her. Perhaps Papa would not mind so much.

But before she pulled the dress over her shift, she gathered up all of Max's portraits and put them back in the trunk. Even the wet one was carefully slid into the drying rack in the trunk lid and the whole safely locked. Why she needed to keep these secret she did not know, except that Max would be displeased if he found out about them.

Veronica was standing by the sundial at the intersection of the walks that divided the garden area into quadrants when next Max saw her. He was striding back from the direction of the home farm, hatless and with the wind whipping his long hair across his brow. It was a warm wind for early April, and Vee looked beautiful, like one of those wistful maidens in a painting of country life. Yet he felt his mouth turned down into a frown.

Max cursed himself, for a jolt of desire, as unexpected as it was unwelcome, raced through him. He almost turned on his heel and went back the way he had come, but he bit his lip and repeated the mantra he had invented for such occasions: *A man who cannot control his appetites is not a man but an animal.*

When she noticed him she pirouetted on the stone walk until he nodded his approval. "Is it very bad of me, to cast off my mourning color just for today?"

She looked on the point of tears. How could he answer her? "Your father would not want you to be so unhappy. Besides, the daffodils need some company. Where have you been?"

"I have been painting, Max," she said as she ran up to him. "I have not felt like doing anything these three months since Papa died. You have inspired me."

He shook his head as he smiled, wondering how making her angry could count as inspiring her. "What have you painted?" He cautiously pulled her hand through the crook of his arm and began to walk with her between the rose garden and the herb beds.

She hesitated. "The garden in winter, right down to the rabbit stealing the parsley. When I am painting it is like being in another world. I had forgotten how pleasant it is to escape this one."

Her answer surprised him. Why would she be painting a winter scene now with all the spring flowers bursting forth? "You should not feel as though you need to escape."

"Sometimes what I need to escape is me." She glanced at him with that impish smile that begged him to understand her, and he was not sure that he ever had. "Do you not agree that spending every waking hour in my company would be tiring?" Veronica asked.

Max gazed at her and felt something inside him begin to melt. Perhaps it was his resolve. "No, oh never. I would delight in spending all my waking hours with you." He brought her hand up and kissed the back of it, thrilling in the chuckle that escaped her.

"Max! I gave you a perfect opening for an insult. You had only to agree with me, but you did not."

"Disappointed?" He let go of her hand and gnawed on his lip, trying to regain control of himself.

"Surprised, at any rate. But I should not taunt you the way you bait George and Freddy."

"They offer you poor sport, I take it." Max glanced toward the house, wondering if Flurry were sending them disapproving looks from one of the windows. If so, he would be in for another tongue-lashing.

Veronica toyed with the ribbons that encircled her bodice and Max looked away. "George can be rather witty in an acerbic sort of way. Most everything I say goes over Freddy's head, which would not be so bad except that it makes him angry when he cannot understand what George and I are laughing about."

"You . . . you like George?" Max studied Veronica's profile. By her frown of concentration he knew she was choosing her words carefully. At least the subject of George was a distraction.

"George is not such a bad fellow when he is not being irritated by his mother . . . or you. He knows a great deal about art, and I think he did eventually realize that Freddy set you up."

"But I should probably not hold my breath waiting for an apology." Max smiled as he felt some easing in the tension of talking to her.

"It was twelve years ago. The sad fact is that George is merely the best of the lot. Mercia is shallow but not deliberately unkind. Freddy *is* deliberately unkind. He gets that from Aunt Margery, but he is not nearly so subtle about his remarks. Your mother is . . . well, you know what she is like. I must talk to someone." She tilted her head to look up at him and nearly caused his heart to melt again. "Think how dull it would be if we liked all our relatives." Veronica's steps were leading them beyond the gardens toward the wilder part of the woods and the steepest descent from the fertile plateau known as Byerly Hill.

"Hmm. When George said he did not come here willingly . . . ," Max said in an attempt to keep their conversation on safe ground.

"I think he meant that. Odd, he had many of the

same interests as Papa, but even after you left, he would never make a push to engage him. Perhaps George was too embarrassed by past behavior."

"Perhaps he did not want to appear predatory, as though he were hoping to curry Uncle's favor," Max pondered.

"But Papa's illness came upon him quite suddenly. It would not have looked as though George were just after money or something. I think rather that Papa's distaste for Lady Margery caused him to keep all the children at arm's length."

"Odd how one always seems to end up choosing sides without really knowing who is right or wrong." Max was thinking of how Vee had always sided with him, even though he had more than once been wrong.

"People are seldom all wrong or all right, Max. Certainly I own to my share of mistakes, but I try to do the right thing."

"Where are we going?" Max asked finally, in something of a panic. "The woods?"

"No, this is something entirely new that I created for you. So if you dislike it, please lie to me." Veronica grabbed his sleeve and pulled him along behind her as through she were still ten years old.

"Through these hedges?" Max ducked under the arch pruned between two tall box hedges that formed a windbreak on the southwest corner of the hill, and followed Vee down a winding path.

"Yes, this is the entrance to *your* statuary garden," Veronica said.

"Why *my* statuary garden?" Max looked around, recognizing some of the plantings as exotic.

"Because I created it for you, using many of the objects you sent me while you were on your travels."

Max took her arm again to keep her from tripping on the rough ground and steeled himself to the warmth of her touch. He vowed to praise highly whatever efforts she had made to create an artistic retreat.

"I did not think it mattered so much to have these out-of-doors," Veronica said, walking with him down a series of natural stone steps and gravel paths. "They are not all that valuable, are they?"

"No, and they were meant to be outside." Max smiled as he stared around him in wonder. "I admire how you have set the stone Buddha on that rocky promontory, and the wandering holy man next to that steep loop of path. If you came on him unaware you might take him to be real."

Veronica followed Max down the winding path, taking delight in his joy of the grottos she had created.

"Ah, the medieval gargoyle next to the spring." Max knelt to look at the statue, remembering the day he had rescued it from a pile of rubble in France. "What an inspiration."

Veronica patted the gargoyle on the head. "Just after winter, when the little waterfall is running very full, it comes out of his mouth as it should if he were still atop a cathedral somewhere."

"You have used the natural terrain as a set for the pieces. I never imagined they could look so well."

"Thank you, Max. Since you are presently pleased with me, there is something I have to tell you that I hope will not make you angry."

"At you, Vee? Never." He guided her to a bench under an ancient willow that was just beginning to bud out, being careful to touch only her sleeve.

"Right after Waterloo Papa had some bad reverses. Henry Steeple sold off his investments, either with or without his knowledge, and for far less than they were worth. Anyway, Papa had to sell some of the pieces you sent us. It broke his heart because he knew you would be expecting to see them here, the jade Kwan-yin, the ivory pagoda ..."

"Were you so desperate?" Max asked, listening to the trickle of the spring as he waited for her answer.

"Well, yes. There are many pieces left, of course. Papa kept saying if only we can find the Nonsuch treasure, as though that would solve all our problems."

"But what sort of treasure was he looking for?" Max asked. "Perhaps he was thinking that discovering a relic himself would make up for selling some of your pieces."

Max could see Vee's love for her father gleam softly in her eyes as she turned to him.

"I had not thought of that. I helped him with some of his research, and I still have no idea what he sought. I remember much of the relief plaster work had gold leaf on it, but that is not all that valuable."

Max cast his mind back to his university days. "I recall reading about Nonsuch Palace, and it did indeed have some gold statues, but I would have thought those had all been removed since the place changed hands several times over before being pulled down for building materials."

"Papa was so excited about it. Is it possible that a work of art from Henry the Eighth's palace would be worth something?"

Max hesitated to dampen her excitement, though he secretly thought not. "I suppose if it were intact and impressive enough, but all I have ever heard of being found are some painted panels and some of the building stone."

"If only we knew what we were looking for." Vee

smacked her palm with one small fist in a manner so characteristic of her father that Max smiled sadly.

"But you do not have to worry about it anymore, Vee. I have plenty of money."

She sighed. "But when I think of Papa's last work I feel closer to him."

Vee looked him in the eyes and Max felt his great-uncle's loss all over again through her.

"I thought—I thought he would live forever, Vee."

Veronica glanced down at her hands, now tightly clasped in her lap. "I had no such illusions, but I did not think he would go downhill so quickly. At times it almost seemed to me as though he were shaking off the illness. Then he would have a renewed onslaught."

"The doctor did everything he could, surely," Max said.

"Dr. Morris was mystified too and asked me all sorts of questions. I think he suspected food poisoning, but Cook is very careful how she stores food."

Max twisted on the bench to stare at her. "You said the family were all here when he was taken ill?"

"Yes, they had all come for Christmas, and it was on the eve of the New Year that he got sick. They all took turns sitting with him when Flurry and I were too tired."

"You let them near him?" Max blurted out incredulously.

Veronica sucked in her breath as a chill shot through her. "Max, no! I know they are awful, but they are family. Surely they would never harm him deliberately."

"Have you any reason to trust them, any of them, Vee?"

Veronica thought frantically of Lady Margery's campaign to get rid of Flurry, of Mercia's lies about Max, of

Freddy's sadistic trap, and the final hellish beating George had given Max. The Comishes were capable of violence and deceit, but to what purpose? And Max was talking about murder. Her hands shook as she pulled a crumpled handkerchief from her pocket and blew her nose. "I cannot credit it. Besides, what had they to gain? They knew the terms of the will. Henry Steeple is one of the executors."

"I must talk to Dr. Morris. Does he still live in the same house in the village?"

"Yes. But Max, if he could not establish anything then, what could he tell you now?"

"Something he would never tell you, his suspicions."

"If I knew there was something I could have done to have prevented all that anguish Papa suffered, if there had been a way to save him . . ." Veronica pounded her thigh as she trembled with anger.

Max realized he had done a savage thing to Vee, letting loose his half-formed suspicions on her without realizing how much it would hurt her. He put his arms around her as he would have in the old days. "Perhaps it amounts to nothing. When tragedy strikes we are wont to try to second-guess ourselves, to try to go back and undo the wrong, even though it is not possible. Even when it is no one's fault. Forget I said anything."

"I have spent the last three months regretting every moment I spent away from Papa. Now that you have planted in my mind the notion that someone may have done away with him, I will not rest until I know the truth of it."

"Then there is something you must do, Vee."

"What?" She turned her soft brown eyes up to look at him.

"This notion of yours about leaving Byerly—you must not just yet."

She stiffened in his arms, then pulled back to look at him. He released her when he saw the mistrust in her eyes. "I know you are sometimes unscrupulous, Max, but you would never cast the thought of murder into my mind just to trap me here."

"No, Vee, that was not my intent. This is your home, and you should not be forced out of it because of your father's will."

"Max, I need to get away for a while. Papa is still too much with me here. I need to let his spirit rest for a time so that I can think clearly about what happened. You must understand that."

Max stared at her intently and nodded. "Were your sisters no help to you during Uncle's illness?"

"I wrote to them, of course, but with so many children and half of them sick, neither Janey nor Lucy managed to get here before he died. In fact, they both missed the funeral, and when they did come they blamed me for not urging them to come sooner."

"They are as stupid as me in some respects."

"They were only saying that to save face." Veronica gave a tired sigh. "They have been gone from Byerly for a long time and were not as close to Papa as I was."

"They should have come for your sake," Max argued.

Veronica looked down at her hands. "We get along now that we are adults, but they never really liked me, would not even play with me when I was little."

"What? You are their sister. I know there was an age difference, and they spent most of their time with Mercia, but . . ."

"They blamed me for Mama dying." Veronica chewed her lip. "And she did die soon after I was born."

"That is absurd. No one would blame an infant. Surely you are imagining that."

"No, I head them talking. That is why I clung to Flurry and Papa, and you when you were around."

Max put his arm around her again, wanting to ease this added pain that he had not even known about. "Well, I never thought much of them, but really, to put that on you. I suppose they are upset now that nothing has been left to them?"

"More upset that their children are to receive such small individual bequests. After Aunt Margery divulged the terms of the will, they have been writing frantically to me and to each other."

"To what purpose?"

"Just whining. You know what they are like. They both report to me what the other thinks, so I have to hear it twice. They never liked you even when we were young and all thrown together here. And Mercia was just as bad as they were."

"I think that was because I never succumbed to the lures any of them threw out to me. Perhaps you have noticed that Mercia has been trying to catch my attention," Max observed with a frown.

"You are much changed. It seems only reasonable that Mercia might have noticed that, since I have."

Max glanced at Vee to discover she was blushing. "She is still Margery's daughter. I will never forgive the Comishes for making you wish to flee Byerly."

"Flurry and I have other reasons for leaving," Veronica said proudly.

"What other reasons?" Max rested his hands on his knees, staring intently at her.

"You will not talk us out of our plans," Veronica warned.

"I do not wish to stop you, only to delay you until I have time to make arrangements," he said firmly.

"Delay me? But why? What is it?" she asked of the sudden serious expression on his face. "What are you thinking, Max?"

"That you have changed much, as well." He put his hands up to frame her face and smiled slightly as he gazed upon her. She could not help but respond. Max smiled so seldom that she returned his smile to encourage him not to be so serious. But his expression changed to one of surprise as he leaned toward her and she wondered if he observed something amiss with her face or hair. She could feel his breath on her cheek and wondered what he meant to whisper to her when his lips brushed hers so fleetingly that she did not know what to make of it. One of his hands stole down her neck and the other to her side. His lips touched hers again and she could taste him. How odd that she had never thought of Max as having a taste before. He was exotic and heady, like a fine forbidden wine.

She did not know exactly what was happening, but she thought it safe to consider this a serious advance and leaned toward him, parting her lips and getting a hold on his lapels. Max deepened the kiss and nudged her mouth open with his tongue, invading her in a most teasing manner. She gasped and opened her eyes to stare at him. But he was too close to see properly and his eyes were still closed, his black lashes fanning his cheeks. She swayed a little on the bench.

Her emotions had taken such a beating that she did not know whether to slap him or to laugh in his face. So she leaned against his chest to try to get a grip on how she really felt about this man. His arms about her felt warm and comforting, but his mouth was hungry and demanding. She knew Max could be dangerous, but that was perhaps what she wanted from him right now. He kissed her again, longingly, as though he had waited all those long years to do so. And Veronica responded, devouring his mouth and making wretched work of his lapels as she grasped him to her. Her heart fluttered in her chest like a captive bird.

"Max!" Flurry's voice barked out of nowhere.

"Flurry, what are you doing here?" Veronica asked, surprised and somewhat abashed at being discovered in Max's arms.

"Meditating," the older woman growled.

"On the weakness of man or the folly of woman?" Max asked breathlessly while his mouth still hovered over Veronica's lips. The kiss had popped into his mind as a ploy to get her to stay at Byerly, but it had awakened that indecent longing he had for Vee and now his whole body throbbed with unsatisfied hunger. What tricks the mind played to give us what we wanted no matter how wrong it might be to take that thing.

"It comes to the same thing," Flurry said as she strode up the path.

"I do not see why Max may not kiss me," Veronica said, standing and shaking the wrinkles out of her dress. We are cousins twice removed."

"That was not a cousinly kiss," Flurry asserted, tramping determinedly toward them, brandishing her umbrella. "It was a lovers' kiss."

"Was it?" Veronica asked in surprise. "Was it that good?"

Max laughed wickedly. It took all his considerable stage presence to play the rake, but he needed to delay until he was able to stand without falling.

"And you, Max, if you mean to play fast and loose

with decorum you will ruin Veronica's reputation. I do not think the two of you can be trusted alone together."

"Jealous, Flurry?" Max asked with his false brilliant smile. He got up stiffly and came toward her to kiss her as well, but she hit him in the arm with her parasol.

"Ow! You are devilishly wicked with that thing."

"I am not joking, Max. Back to the house with you. I will walk between you."

Veronica laughed nervously as Max rubbed his arm. Flurry grabbed them each by the sleeve and made them walk in this regimented fashion up the hill, with Flurry nagging at them with all the breath she could spare.

6

Before dinner Veronica came to Flurry's room clutching her small hands tightly together in front of her yellow muslin dress. "Do you dine with us tonight, Flurry?" Veronica paced to the window, twisting her hands together.

"I think I had better if Max has so little self-control as to try to seduce you in the garden."

"I am not sure that he meant to kiss me, Flurry. He seemed for a time to be afraid to touch me, as though I would break, but when we talked of Papa's death he became softer, almost his old self again."

"So the kiss was a surprise to you?"

"At first, yes. Max seemed so clumsy about it. Then something happened. I realized that I wanted more, that I want Max." Veronica turned her head to look at Flurry. "Not just as a friend."

A long silence fell between them. Flurry looked into the distance as though she were trying to decide what to tell Veronica. This was uncomfortable, for Veronica had come to rely on Flurry's judgment and had never found it at fault.

"Listen, Veronica, there is something you should know about men. Sit down on the bed." She patted the coverlet beside her with one veined hand.

Veronica complied, willing to give this discussion all her attention, for she was not at all sure what was happening to her feelings for Max.

"A man can be a good man, and still not be morally strong."

"Are we talking about Max?"

"I suppose so. Max knows it is not at all the thing for him to be taking advantage of you in this way, and he will, no doubt, regret whatever dire consequences might befall . . . I mean, it may fall to you to stop him if . . ."

"Yes, Flurry?" Veronica was being as patient as possible, but Flurry seemed to be beating about the bush in a rather silly manner. And then it occurred to Veronica that such a discussion between an older maiden lady and a young virgin was not likely to be productive of any very useful information.

"If his urges should get the better of him. If he should force himself on you again . . ."

"But he was not forcing himself on me." Veronica thought back over the conversation leading up to that abrupt kiss. "Now that I think about it, I am sure his kiss was merely to distract me, to convince me to stay at Byerly. I am the one with the urges."

Flurry gaped at her for a moment. "Veronica, you have been raised in a very sheltered manner. You have never been around young men, except for George and Freddy, who hardly count, so you would not know what they are thinking, if they do think at such times." Flurry began wringing her hands.

"I imagine they are thinking only as much as a stallion is thinking when he covers a mare."

"What?" Flurry asked in shocked tones.

"I am not a total idiot, Flurry. I know what might come next."

"Then you know more than I did at your age, and I see now it was a mistake to let you haunt the stables. Who let you see such a thing?"

"Do not be silly, Flurry. I always led the stallion to the mare because he would listen to me, and it was dangerous for one of the grooms to try to handle him. Of course, afterward he was too exhausted to—Flurry, you look rather pale."

"Enough," Flurry whispered as she stared at Veronica in fascinated horror. "You have already told me more than I want to imagine. So you think you would be able to stop Max if he had such an . . . urge again?"

"You mean if he tried to kiss me again?"

"Yes, or anything else." Flurry waved her hand vacantly in the air.

"I am quite sure that I could stop him, but I am not sure that I would want to."

"God help us, then. The two of you must never be alone together."

Veronica toyed with the ribbons that adorned her dress. "Have you ever been in love, Flurry?"

"Once . . ." The older woman's voice vibrated with remembered emotion.

"Were you deliriously happy? For I am not, so I do not think I can be in love."

Flurry stared at her a moment. "I was miserable, uncertain of my own mind in a way I had never known." Flurry put her arm around her protégée. "What is worse, I was uncertain of his mind. He never said what I expected. It was a most uncomfortable time. I do not recommend it."

"Then I simply will not be in love with Max if it is that bothersome." Veronica sniffed decisively.

"You always were strong, my child. But you are up against an emotion that does not obey rational thought. Do you think you can handle it?"

"I have faced much worse things, Flurry, Papa's death, now Max's suspicions that it may have been an unnatural death."

Flurry released her and looked searchingly into her eyes. "What are you saying?"

"Max thinks one of the Comishes might be responsible for Papa's death. When he saw how much that disturbed me he tried to take it back, make light of it, but now I begin to wonder myself."

"That is absurd. John died of some sort of influenza."

"Which no one else in the house caught. And it was not like influenza. Dr. Morris said so. Flurry, why do you look so ashen? I did not mean to frighten you."

"I suppose all houses have seen their share of deaths, yet when your father died, I could not help thinking how like Austin's death it was."

"Aunt Margery's first husband?" Veronica leaned toward her. "Were the symptoms the same?"

"I think so, but probably it only struck me that way because it happened over the Christmas holidays." Flurry stared into space in remembrance. "That was the year before you were born, and the year after Robert died in London. Dora, Max, and I had moved to Byerly, and Austin was complaining of that to John. He said it was not fair for Max, a great-nephew, to be brought up here when George and Freddy only got to visit. It was not a peaceful time. Margery took up the argument and harped on it for days. Once Austin took ill, of course, Dora felt badly, and helped nurse him.

His death actually drew the family together for a little while."

"So when my mother died the next winter, that made three deaths in three years," Veronica said with a puzzled frown.

Flurry wiped a tear away with the tips of her fingers. "I suppose it is not uncommon for a woman to die after giving birth."

"What about Max's father, Robert?" Veronica asked, trying to make a connection between the deaths but finding none. "What did he die of?"

"Oh, he died in London," Flurry said vacantly. "I was taking care of Max so I did not go near Robert in case he should be infectious. What makes Max think there is anything suspicious about your father's death?"

"Probably only because it was inconvenient to him. Let us think no more about it." Veronica took Flurry's hand. "Come, it is time for dinner."

It was nearly dark and Max could see his breath in the air, but he did not feel cold. He carried his heavy walking stick and was making a circuit of the property. He had started out through the sheep fields and walked the trail that led along the west side of Byerly Hill, admiring the meager sunset. Walking the perimeter of the hill had been a favorite occupation when they were children. How often he had dragged Vee around the two-hundred-acre plot till her little legs were too tired to carry her. Yet she managed to keep up with him. All too soon he came to the rock outcropping that marked the almost clifflike descent down the north face to the village of Oakham. There was a footpath, and Max had taken his pony down it once on a dare from Freddy. He was lucky not to have broken its legs.

The smoke from the cooking fires curled languidly through the still warm air of the valley and leveled to a flat haze when it met the cooler air washing down the hill. There was a time when a trip to Oakham was a big event in his life. Byerly Hill had seemed like an empire to him, and he had always been told it would be his one day, first by his mother, then by his great-uncle. School had made it seem smaller to him when he came for the holidays or the summer, but he had learned what he needed to know about estate management at John's elbow.

Byerly had already begun to shrink in his mind by the time of his exile. What had hurt Max the most was not the loss of a piece of land but the loss of his uncle's esteem and his own place in the world. He had then set himself the task of making another place for himself, and he had done that.

When a member of the government had approached him about certain services he could perform while on his trading ventures, he had accepted the assignment, not from a sense of nationalism, but because he thought it would make his family proud of him. But his uncle had died with only the slightest inkling of all Max had done during the war. Vee and Flurry did not care about such things. As for the rest of the family, it did not matter to him what they thought of him so long as they continued to dislike him. He was so used to being the outcast he could not very well think of himself in any other way.

Max turned and walked along the brow of the hill in the gathering darkness, knowing that one misstep could plunge him a hundred feet to the scree at the base of the outcropping. Had he indeed dragged Vee along this trail without thinking about the danger to her? He had been sadly lax in his care of her then, and even more neglectful these past twelve years. If this world had shrunk for him, surely Vee would feel trapped here as well.

He padded back along the trail that came past the hay fields. A large owl hooted from close by, then with a gusty flutter of wings made a low pass over his head. Max had half drawn the sword from his walking stick by instinct before he flattened himself to the ground. The bird had mistaken his dark head for game, then diverted its attack at the last moment. Max dusted himself off and replaced the blade in the cane.

He had created a world for himself, but there was no comfort in it. He knew now that a world without Vee and Flurry was an empty place. But how to control these urges. *A man who cannot control his appetites is not a man but an animal.* That admonition lasted as long as he was away from Vee. As soon as he saw her his heart melted and his head felt dizzy and empty.

Would they miss him at dinner? Only Vee and Flurry. Mustafah might speculate but would give no sign of it. He wondered idly if his retainers had any awareness of his present struggle with himself. It did not matter, since their inscrutable observation of his privacy bordered on apathy. Yet they did care about him, and Mustafah had more than once put himself in the line of fire for him.

But Max had a feeling no amount of meditation could reestablish the serenity he had attained over the years. He had been prepared for the anger that welled up at his mother and the Comishes and had masked it with arrogant disdain. He could handle anger as coldly as a pistol or saber. But he could not handle Vee and he could not avoid her, not if he meant to guide her travels.

But before he could even think about the future he had one commitment in London that had to be discharged. He had let the obligation run on far too long as it was. So he must get Vee's promise to remain here for the present and get himself to London as quickly as he could.

Max was satisfied now that he had a plan and strode with alacrity along the trail. A plan always made him feel in control of the situation no matter how awry the plan might later go. Once Vee had some experience of the world, then perhaps . . . but he had best not think that far ahead. He could see a faint glimmer of light through the wooded hillside that must be Horsely to the southwest. Then the lights from the house came into view. How late was it? he wondered. The moon had not yet risen, but he must have been gone several hours. Would they all still be in the drawing room? Should he make an entrance and give them the suspicion that he had dined out? He chuckled to himself.

But the fun had gone out of the game of baiting the Comishes. There was a light in Vee's window and it reminded him of all the nights he had climbed the oak with the large lateral limb growing within an easy leap of her windowsill. They had plotted innumerable ways of getting even with George and Freddy in Vee's room in the middle of the night. He leaned his walking stick against the base of the tree and made the climb, remembering the old handholds as though they were imprinted on his hands and fingers. This was a damned bad sign, this disconnection from his brain that he was feeling. Why was he doing this? Had he not just vowed to stay away from Vee for the present?

Her window was still open and she was sitting at her dressing table in her thin nightdress, taking up her hairbrush. Surely she heard his boots scrambling against the bark, walking along the limb. Surely she heard his feet as he landed on the sill, dropped into the room, with its sweet scent of melting candle and the faint aroma of Vee's paints. Surely she knew he was behind her.

Silently he took the three steps toward her, removed the brush from her hand, and resumed the stroking of her long black tresses. She was not startled in the least. "I wanted to apologize," he said softly, surprised that his voice broke with regret.

"Apologize for what?" Vee asked.

He could see her swaying as he stroked her hair. Max let those long strands run through his fingers like some living force. Something was flowing into him. How had Vee become, overnight, such an obsession with him, when other women scarcely affected his composure at all? He closed his eyes as he brushed her hair, trying to imagine another woman—any other woman—to distract him from Vee.

Veronica wondered why Max brushing her hair felt so different than when Flurry did it. How like Max to climb into her bedroom and take up such a task as though he did it all the time. Had he meant to shock her? Even if she had not heard him scrabbling up the tree, she would have sensed Max there in the room with her. Even had she not seen his excited face reflected in her mirror, those black brows intent over his glittering eyes, she would have detected that hint of sandalwood soap. If she thought he had looked dangerous by daylight, Max by candlelight was a heart stopper. And what was she going to do about it?

"I should not have kissed you, not like that, anyway," he whispered.

With his fingers running through her hair, touching her nape, Veronica felt naked before him, and she did not care. Something was happening to her and even though she did not know what, she did not want it to end. "I should not have kissed you back," she said, staring at his reflection. "But I am not sorry that I did. At least we both know—" She caught his movement in the mirror and turned her face to meet his lips. They were warm and caressing, arousing her lips, then straying to kiss her neck, her exposed collarbone, and her ear before returning to massage her mouth, sending ripples of pleasure along her spine. The hairbrush fell to the floor, and when he reached to encompass her, one of his arms grazed her breasts, causing her to gasp and give his tongue entrance to her mouth. She felt wonderfully exposed to him and was surprised that this did not upset her.

His tongue slid back and forth alongside hers and held the tang of a mint leaf he must have picked on his walk. One arm gripped her so tightly to him that she did not need the power of her legs to stand. He literally picked her up from the seat, knocking the small chair over as he ran a hand down her back to cup one buttock. Her excited gasp caused him to break the kiss and regard her with wicked amusement.

"I am terrible," he said, lowering his mouth to nibble at the erect bud of one breast through her thin nightdress.

"I am worse," Veronica gasped, arching against him as she gripped his shoulders.

"What are we going to do?" he asked. "You are like a ripe peach."

"I do not know, but do it soon." Veronica presented her other breast for the same attention from his mouth, locking her hands behind his neck.

The sudden pounding on the door took several heartbeats to penetrate to Veronica. "Veronica, I am coming in," Flurry's rough voice warned.

Max ducked out of the circle of Veronica's arms and leaned on the dressing table, panting. Veronica was still feeling bereft when Flurry made good her threat, whisking through the door in her nightdress and wrapper and closing it behind her.

"Are you two insane?" Flurry demanded. "Bad enough you are here at all, Max, without announcing your presence in an unmarried girl's room to the whole house by knocking over the furniture."

Max's head came up and he got that devilish look in his eyes. "I will merely say I was trying for your window and missed."

"Max Strake!" Flurry tied her robe belt like a fighter tightening his sash and charged at Max. He resisted when Flurry pushed him toward the door. Flurry grabbed up the discarded hairbrush and whacked him on the shoulder. Veronica, still giddy from Max's caresses, giggled while Max put a chair between him and the outraged woman.

"This is no laughing matter, Veronica," Flurry said. "And Max, you must stop climbing in here or you will ruin this child. Now, out with you, Max. I am as displeased with you as it is possible to be. You are just as irresponsible as ever."

Max laughed recklessly at her as she grabbed the fireplace poker and ran at him. He danced around the room and over the bed, evading her lunges until he could gain the windowsill. He made the leap onto the limb of the oak tree from old habit, blew them a kiss and was gone.

§ 7 §

*V*eronica awoke, warm and lethargic, wondering if she was running a fever. She tried to retrace in her mind the path of the dream she had been following. It was of her and Max, somewhere else, on a ship, she thought. They were being thrown together by the waves, surging against each other. She had tried to finish the dream, but could not do as well with it awake as asleep. Then she spent an hour trying to get back to sleep but to no avail. Why should she waste time dreaming about Max when she could actually see him. If only Flurry had not intervened—God, if Flurry had not intervened, they would have made love last night.

She sat on the edge of her bed, reason returning like a hangover after an imprudent amount of wine. What had she been thinking last night when she let Max in here? That was the whole problem. She had not been thinking at all, just operating on instinct, and it had nearly ruined her. But that seemed to be what she wanted at the time. Veronica pressed her hands to her forehead and slowly pushed back her tangled locks as though she could so easily eradicate Max from her thoughts. She was so uncertain and unhappy with herself, she knew she must consult with Flurry.

She washed her face and prudently tied her hair back with a ribbon. She dressed and went to Flurry's room; not finding her there, she then went downstairs to the breakfast parlor. Only Lady Margery was still there and after a cup of lukewarm tea and stilted conversation, Veronica went to put on her riding dress. She would feel better if she took Bonnie for a ride around the hill.

The mare was eager for a trot after several days in the stable. Veronica let her have her head as they skirted the sheep pastures. There were baby lambs out with their mothers and Veronica wondered how she could have missed that. She usually knew exactly what was happening all over Byerly. That was because she was usually out and about, not moping around the house. Really, she was making a complete fool of herself over Max. How could she be letting this happen to her? She and Flurry had plans. She simply would not let any man interfere with those, not even Max.

She let Bonnie break into a canter for a few minutes as they rode along the west rim of the plateau. Veronica was beginning to feel better now, as decisive as she had been a few days ago. They would get this formality of the will out of the way. It had caused much grief in the family for Margery to have gossiped about its contents. Of course, it had been unconscionable of Henry Steeple to have divulged the gist of it to his wife.

Veronica shook her head. She wanted nothing more than to pack her trunks and be on her way with Flurry. Spring was a good season to set out for Paris. There were many English in residence there, and she expected to get quite a few commissions. She and Flurry would live by their wits just as Max had done all these years.

Bonnie slowed to a walk and pulled on the reins, asking permission to graze and Veronica let her, admiring the periwinkle and pure white wood anemones. And there were some bluebells farther along. She would have liked to pick some, but then she would have had to find a log to mount Bonnie, so she contented herself with picking the flowers in her mind. Perhaps that was how she should enjoy Max, only in her dreams. That was the only safe way. She had no control where he was concerned, and since he clearly had none either, it was stupid in the extreme to be anywhere near him.

She was about to take the inner trail, skirting the dangerous cliff on the north shoulder of the hill when she saw a figure outlined against the sky there. Her gaze locked onto the image, for it was Max, standing dangerously close to the edge. What the devil was he thinking? She urged Bonnie in that direction, the little mare's hooves pounding on the packed dirt of the path. Max stood still, coatless and with the full sleeves of his shirt billowing in the updraft of current from the valley. His hands were braced on his slender hips and he looked like a captain sailing a fast ship. He swayed and Veronica could not stifle her scream. "Max!"

He spun, lost his footing on the smooth rock, and slid over the edge. Veronica urged Bonnie toward the rocks, closer than she had ever ridden a horse before. The mare shied when her unshod hooves hit the stone outcropping and Veronica made an inelegant running dismount. She raced to the edge and knelt, looked down, fearing to see Max's broken body on the rocks below. Instead she saw his face, grimy and streaked with sweat as he clung to some fissures a yard from the edge.

"Take my hand, Max."

"Do not be an idiot, Vee. I am too heavy. I would pull you over, as well."

"Max, what should I do?" Vee pleaded.

Max glanced over his shoulder, then looked back at her. "Leave me, Vee. You cannot save me."

"Leave you? What kind of stupid answer is that?"

"I'm no good for you anyway, Vee."

"I shall think of something. Hold still, do you hear me?"

"Hold still?" Max gasped. "What the hell else should I do? I cannot very well go anywhere."

Veronica crawled back from the edge and looked frantically about her, feeling panic rise like a sickening wave within her. If she gave into fear she could not help Max, and she must. There was no one else. If she was to save him, she must put aside the love that was causing her terror. She took a few steadying breaths, then spied Bonnie's trailing reins and got an idea. Quickly she led Bonnie as close to the outcropping as she dared. She removed her bridle and tied the end of one rein securely to the stirrup iron. Then she threw the other end to Max with the bridle stretched out in the middle of the two reins, praying that the leather would hold.

"Can you reach it, Max?"

"Yes, what is it tied to?"

"Bonnie. Now wrap the rein around your hand and tell me when to lead her away."

"Ready," Max shouted.

Bonnie stared around at the heavy weight tied to the stirrup and sent Veronica an accusing look, but finally responded as Veronica tugged on her halter and walked her slowly away from the edge. Max scrambled up over the rocks, startling Bonnie, who bolted and ran toward home. She pulled Max off his feet but the rein came loose from his hand before she could drag him very far.

Veronica ran to him and helped him to his feet, pulling out her handkerchief to wrap around his bleeding fingers. "Max, you idiot. What were you doing perching there on the edge like some giant bird?" She searched his face for some inner hurt that would have prompted him to contemplate destroying himself and was shocked when he grinned at her.

"Meditating."

"Meditating?" She gaped at him. "Are you insane. You could have been killed."

Max wrapped her lacy handkerchief around his knuckles and fastened the knot with his teeth. "I would never have slipped if you had not shrieked at me."

"Oh fine, blame me for your stupidity. It would have served you right if I had let you fall."

"I am only saying that I would never had fallen if you had not shouted my name."

"You frightened me to death and now you say it is all my fault. This is just like . . . just like . . ."

"Like old times," Max finished for her with a chuckle.

Veronica gritted her teeth and cuffed his shoulder.

Max grinned. "You never could see the humor in anything."

"Death is very seldom amusing," Veronica warned. "If you do anything so stupid again, I shall . . ."

"What?" Max wiped his grimy face on his shirt sleeve. "Push me off a cliff?"

"I shall tell Flurry."

"Vee, I am surprised at you. You were never a tattle in the old days."

"Be serious, Max. Where is your coat?"

"I shall get it. Perhaps you should capture Bonnie unless you mean to walk the whole way back."

Max collected his coat, then watched appreciatively as Vee, the tail of her riding skirt hiked up over one arm, stalked Bonnie. The mare paused temptingly just out of her reach to munch grass, but as soon as Vee got close Bonnie tossed up her head and trotted on. With a laugh he gave chase himself, but the mare cantered off with amazing speed for an aged horse.

At the moment, with her riding outfit in disarray and her face red with frustration, Max felt for Vee only their old comradery, not desire. Perhaps his urges could be controlled if only he could contrive to put Vee in a temper.

"Sorry, Vee. Now you will have to walk home."

"And if one of the grooms finds my horse wandering loose he will probably run to Flurry with the tale. She is apt to think me dead."

"Remember when Flurry used to call us and we would run home as fast as we could no matter what the distance, just so she would not know how far afield I had taken you."

"Yes," Veronica said, getting a good grip on her skirt and revealing the leather riding breeches Max had always suspected she wore underneath. "I'll race you, Max."

"You could never beat me. Your legs are too short."

Veronica sprinted away from him, looking over her shoulder. "But you are exhausted from hanging off that cliff."

He ran after her, reaching out to grab her, but she evaded him in the woods with a laugh. "You are fast," Max conceded. "But like a mare, you will tire easily."

"Oh, do you think so?" Veronica taunted with a tree

between them. She squeaked past him and unleashed a limb that caught him in the face, slowing his progress.

Her skirts were definitely going to hamper her, he thought, and he finally broke through the underbrush and ran her down like a doe during a hunt. She squeaked when he grabbed her arm and spun her around. He tripped and she came down on top of him, laughing. She stared him in the face for a surprised minute, the laughter still bubbling, and suddenly kissed him, bringing back all his aching desire.

He groaned as her knee brushed his groin.

"Max, have I hurt you?" she asked innocently.

"Not yet, be careful where you place yourself, Vee."

"I think I like kissing you," she said as she lay on top of him, inspecting his neckcloth and then brushing his hair out of his eyes with one hand. Her other hand came to rest on his already throbbing manhood; he gave a startled grunt in anticipation of her leaning on him to get up, but she did not do more than excite him out of all reason. He was panting as though he had run a mile. He gritted his teeth to try to suppress his erection, but with everything throbbing and Vee touching him in that disarming way, it would be some minutes before he could stand, let alone run.

When she leaped lightly up and ran off laughing, he realized what had just happened had not been an accident, and there was not a damn thing he could do about it before she had a substantial lead.

Twenty minutes later they jogged into the stable yard to see a gathering of farmworkers standing around Bonnie, mumbling in hushed tones as Mustafah conferred with Ned Beatty over the bridle the horse was dragging from her stirrup.

"Is Bonnie all right?" Veronica asked. "She got away from us."

Mustafah turned and stared silently at Max—his bandaged knuckles, scratched face, and dirty shirt—then turned his gaze on Veronica with a speculative mixture of wonder and admiration. But his mouth remained firmly shut.

"We had a little trouble at the cliff," Veronica said as though she were discussing a defective piece of tack.

Mustafah bowed. "The luncheon is ready, sir. Shall we delay until you have . . . rested?"

Max cleared his throat. "No, go ahead and serve. I will change and be down directly."

"Aye, sir." Another bow to Veronica and Mustafah was gone.

Ned Beatty led Bonnie away to unsaddle her and the rest of the men dispersed to their assigned tasks with subdued chuckles. Veronica turned to Max, but he was already striding toward the house. So she tidied her hair and went into the breakfast parlor herself.

"Where were you all morning?" Flurry asked. "Surely not riding."

"I took Bonnie for a ride, but she got away from me, so I had to walk back."

"Did you fall?"

"Of course not," Veronica replied.

"Did you, by any chance, encounter Max out there?" Flurry pursed her lips.

"Yes, I did, and let me tell you, Flurry, he is just as stupid and bullheaded as ever he was."

"That is welcome news," Flurry said.

"You would not believe what he did." Veronica hesitated. "And why would that be welcome news?"

"Not that he is stupid, but that you should think so."

George came in then, so Veronica had no chance to quiz Flurry further on her response. The meal, like so many others, passed in relative silence, even after Max made his entrance and glanced arrogantly around the table. Veronica stared at him, wondering what had come over her last night. How could she love Max so much one day and be ready to throttle him the next? If she had just experienced a brush with infatuation, she was glad it had passed over her so quickly. She pointedly ignored Max, and after the meal went to change into an afternoon dress. This one was brown, and she had worn it even before her papa's death just because it became her so well. She went down the stairs, thinking to take her flower basket and cut some blooms when she heard the sound of carriage wheels on the drive that circled the house. Veronica went to the front window.

"Henry Steeple," she said to herself. "This looks like business. A gracious hostess would go out to greet him."

Instead Veronica picked up her basket and slipped out the back door, walking so rapidly down the stone pathway toward the sundial that not even the most suspicious person could accuse her of neglecting her duties.

§ 8 §

An hour later Henry Steeple sat behind the large library desk, making Veronica feel very small and insignificant.

"I have settled the pensions for the staff, including Miss Flurry's," Steeple said, looking tall and angular even in his seated position. He glanced at Veronica over his pince-nez as though, Veronica thought, he blamed her personally for this expenditure.

"And I have paid out the rest of the bequests, including those to the grandchildren." He frowned again and Veronica wondered if he begrudged those small amounts as well.

"Fifty pounds each," Freddy said. "What an insult."

Steeple glanced at George for his reaction and the older son simply shrugged at his stepfather.

"Byerly belongs to Max," Steeple continued, "but I am sure you all understood that. The art collection is left to Veronica."

Lady Margery glared at Max, then turned her contemptuous gaze on Veronica. "I think John may have been influenced when his mind was weak."

"How dare you!" Veronica snapped as she came to her feet. "That will was made two years ago, and Papa most certainly was sane."

"Easy, Veronica," Max said, laying a calming hand on her arm and persuading her to sit again.

"Enough," Steeple said. "I take it, Veronica, that you have some idea what this art collection consists of?"

"Of course," Veronica replied.

"I shall require a detailed inventory of both the art collection and the household goods," Steeple said.

"But that will take days." Veronica nearly groaned with the thought of how boring such a task would prove.

"Which particular item is the one John referred to as his *treasure?*" Steeple asked, holding his pince-nez as he focused on another document.

"How did you know about that?" Veronica asked.

"He wrote me a letter expressing his wish that you were to have it. If it is a piece of art, it is yours under the will, of course, but if it is in the nature of money then the estate may have a claim on it."

"Just a moment," Max intervened, speaking slowly. "If John wrote a letter leaving something to Veronica it is in the nature of a codicil. The estate can have no claim on it."

"There are unresolved debts," Steeple insisted.

"There cannot be," Veronica said. "I always paid cash. I have been most careful not to run up any tradesmen's bills both before Papa's death and after."

"There are debts in London," Steeple pronounced sagely, his sharp nose quivering in his effort to remain calm.

"If there are debts in London," Max snarled, "they were not incurred by Vee or John Strake."

Steeple coughed. "John was in the habit of settling some of the boys' more pressing debts."

"Oh, gaming debts," Veronica said. "It was not a habit. He only did it to get them to leave us in peace. But surely all that ended with his death."

"The debts were incurred before that," Steeple said.

"They were not settled before that," Max insisted. "The estate has no obligation whatsoever."

"The honor of the family is at stake," Steeple insisted. "Veronica must turn over this treasure so that we can settle the estate."

"You are out of luck there," she said, "for I have no idea what it is either."

"I do not believe you," Freddy accused.

Veronica sat up straight in her chair, a blush of anger kissing her cheeks. It pained Max to watch her on the defensive.

"Well, it is the truth," Veronica said. "Papa talked about his *treasure*. He called it the *Nonsuch treasure* since he suspected it came from Henry the Eighth's palace, but I always got the feeling that it was out of reach, that he had no idea where it was himself. If he had, he would have produced it rather than have me sell his artifacts. I do not see why you should care, Steeple. If Papa called it a treasure, you can be sure he was talking about an object of art or some reused building stone. And its fate should be a matter of agreement between Max and me."

"Well, it is a matter of concern," Steeple insisted, "since the residue of the estate is to derive to Mercia."

"But there is no residue," Veronica insisted.

"I am sure you were very careful that there should be none," Mercia chimed in.

"What?" Veronica seemed almost speechless for a

moment. "You make me regret every bill I paid with my own money."

"Silence!" Steeple demanded. "You had no money but what your father gave you."

"That is not true." Veronica shook with anger. "I make a respectable living painting miniatures and portraits."

"Respectable?" Lady Margery questioned, her mouth twisted in contempt.

"You may make an odd guinea or two with your paint box, but it is not what I would call an income," Steeple replied. "And it is hardly respectable."

"Very well," Veronica said, rising with dignity. "I am done with keeping the household accounts. From now on I consider myself a guest at Byerly, and not one who will overstay her welcome."

Lady Margery glared at her. "What is that remark supposed to mean?"

Veronica rounded on her aunt. "That I have always regarded it as highly suspicious that Papa took sick while you were all in residence and moreover died while several of you were nursing him."

Lady Margery gaped at her and Max thought his aunt looked fearful. The stunning effect of Veronica's accusation was somewhat reduced by Dora's commanding, "That is enough, Veronica. You are getting hysterical."

"Henry, do something!" Lady Margery said from behind her handkerchief.

Max stood and laid a reassuring hand on Veronica's shoulder. "Vee is not the only one who finds it strange that a perfectly healthy man should waste away and die within a fortnight. I plan to consult Dr. Morris about this, for I hear that he also expressed some reservations about the death."

Henry shuffled his papers together nervously. "You do realize that if you open an inquiry into John Strake's death you could delay the settlement of the estate."

"I am fully aware of that," Max replied.

"If I may point out," George said quietly, "only Max and Veronica seem to have benefited substantially from Uncle's death, and we all knew the terms of the will, except for this treasure you speak of. If suspicion were to fall on anyone . . ."

"Murder my own father?" Veronica staggered a little, but Max steadied her. "You must be mad."

"No more so than a distraught girl accusing her aunt of murder when she has no motive," George said calmly.

Veronica spun on her heel, wrenching herself away from Max, and left the room, letting the heavy door fall shut with a resounding boom. Max turned toward George. "The residue of the estate to Mercia could have been a substantial motive. I suspect it was substantial at the time of John's death. But with Steeple executor of the estate for three months that may have been severely depleted."

"I have heard enough!" Steeple enunciated as he sprang to his feet. "You are questioning my professional integrity. Let me remind you that there are two other trustees."

"Yes, the partner in your law firm, a firm that has not been doing all that well, and your banker, who would be delighted if the accounts were back in tune," Max pointed out.

"You cannot prove a thing."

"I daresay I cannot where the paperwork is concerned, but getting control of the estate could have been a powerful motive." Max reared his head back like

a snake about to strike. It was one of his favorite poses.
"And you were here, Steeple, for the holidays with your
wife, Lady Margery. If I find just cause I wager I can get
Uncle John exhumed and tested for poisons. So if anyone would like to confess and save us the bother . . ."

"Max!" Dora hissed. "This time you have gone
beyond the pale."

"I am used to being an outcast, Mother. And I do not
give a tinker's damn about the house or the estate. But
if I have enough cause to suspect that Vee's father was
poisoned, I will be relentless in my prosecution of the
murderer."

Max exited and left the room buzzing under his
threat. They had not taken Veronica at all seriously, but
he rather thought he had them worried. It was long
past time that he consult Flurry on the matter. She
could give him a less jaundiced view of his uncle's
death. He sprang up the stairs two at a time and
knocked on her door.

"Come in, Max."

Max opened the door, a puzzled crease marring his
brow. "How did you know it was me?"

"Veronica always scratches like a mouse and calls my
name. And who but you two would bother to come see
me?" she replied with satisfaction.

Max gazed at his old friend reclining on the daybed
with a book open in her lap. In the candlelight her hair
might have been brown again rather than gray. Her
face was now glowing with satisfaction like a young
girl's. Because she had been right or because he had
come to her? Just for a moment he saw what she must
have looked like in her youth, a beauty, and she had
never spoken of her early years to him and Vee. Strange
how he had never thought to wonder about Flurry's

history until now, after knowing her for twenty-five years. She had been like a mother to both of them, but he had just discovered a great gap in his understanding of her.

"Are you going to stand in the doorway and stare or come in and sit down?"

Max chuckled as he shut the door and sat in the sole wing chair, crossing his legs. "You always could reduce me to rubble with a sentence."

"How did it go?" she inquired. "I heard shouting, but that is only to be expected in this house."

"I think I may have botched it. When I was talking to Vee in the garden, my questions on the manner of Uncle John's death led Vee to believe I thought he was poisoned."

"Do you?" Flurry asked huskily, the age telling in her voice.

"Yes, but I did not expect her to blurt it out to everyone. She actually accused Aunt Margery of the murder when they had pushed Vee too far."

Max waited for Flurry's anger or at least her cold condemnation. To his surprise and regret she stared toward the darkened window. "I have . . . always wondered."

"So it is not an absurd suspicion."

"The suddenness of it, and with all of them in the house." Flurry's right hand gestured hopelessly. "Of course I never thought of it at the time. We were too busy nursing him. Frankly, Veronica and I were glad for any help. Now I wonder if I did not sign his death warrant by letting them sit with him."

Max leaned forward, his elbows on his knees. "You suspect Aunt Margery, too?"

"But would she not be killing the golden goose?"

Max rubbed his forehead. "Mercia had the most to gain, of course, but not the nerve, I think, to do it."

"Mercia would have been better off if John had lived, provided Freddy stayed out of the gaming houses." Flurry turned to punch her pillow, then settled back again. "The income from investments was almost gone after the war but the estate has a respectable income and John put away much of it. But Lady Margery would land on us in tears with the promise that Freddy would be thrown into prison."

"I would have let him go where he could no longer be a bother," Max said savagely.

"Easy for you to say, Max. You do not know how she can pick at you until anything is better than having her here. John always gave in, and we had to live off the land for a time until the rents were paid or the lambs went to market."

"So Mercia would have been better off murdering Freddy than Uncle John," Max concluded.

"Exactly, though I am not sure she is intelligent enough to know that."

Max clasped his hands together. "I suppose it could not have been Henry Steeple, having got himself into trouble and not wanting John to find out."

"He never went near John," Flurry said with a faraway look in her eyes. "Henry was afraid John might be infectious. George sat with John at night sometimes . . . though any of them could have let Henry in." Flurry raised her hand to cover her mouth and closed her eyes.

"Forgive me," Max said, coming to sit next to her and throwing a shawl about her shoulders. "I have unthinkingly upset you just as much as Vee. Perhaps it really was an illness. Some virulent fever to which he had no resistance."

"But Max, no one else in the house took it."

"An internal disorder then," Max said, chafing her hands and holding them between his own. "If horses can get twisted gut, I am sure—"

"But Dr. Morris asked *such* questions, Max. He almost made me feel that he suspected me."

"That is laughable," Max said. "What motive could you have?"

"An overly generous bequest that will now permit me my independence. He did not just leave me fifty pounds, like the other servants; he left me an income. I may travel if I like or set up my own household."

"Who said such a thing to you?" Max demanded. "You are quoting Steeple, are you not?"

"Yes," Flurry admitted with a watery laugh. "But at least he did not accuse me of murder, just of being too high in John's affections. Oh Max, if I unwittingly let this thing happen . . ."

"If it was murder, there is nothing you could have done to prevent it. What were the symptoms?" Max asked.

"A bloody flux. He could not take solid food, for it sent him into agony. He lived on meat broth, tea, and sugared coffee for that last week. I believe he had a fever the whole time."

"You had reason to think it was a contagious illness at the time?" Max asked carefully.

"That was my first assumption."

"But you must see," Max said as he put his hands on Flurry's shoulders, "under normal conditions would Margery have exposed Mercia to some unknown disease?"

"Oh, Max, you mean she stayed to help because she knew she would be perfectly safe?"

"It is a possibility." Max rose and paced to the door and back.

"But what are we to do now?" Flurry asked. "After all this time?"

"I shall think of something. I hate to ask it of you, but do you think you could speak to Vee yet tonight? They accused her of stealing the Nonsuch treasure Uncle was searching for, and she left the room in a rage. I think that is why she blurted out her suspicions about her father's death."

"I need a few moments to pull myself together, Max. Then I shall go to see her."

"And Flurry?" Max said as he turned to go.

"What now, Max?"

"I think there had better be one of us present any time Vee takes a meal in this house. If I read things right, whatever she inherits would go to Mercia if anything were to happen to Vee before this thing is settled."

Flurry turned a horrified face to Max, but merely nodded. "Max?"

"Yes?" His hand was on the doorknob and he hated the hesitation, trying to guess the question and knowing he would not like it.

"I know you are always playing jokes, but how do you really think of Veronica?" she almost whispered.

Max stared at Flurry, thinking of her giving little Vee spelling lessons while he sat in the library and worked his geometry problems, or of Flurry discussing philosophy with both of them. Vee was always very quick about such things. And the walks they had taken with Uncle John telling about all his plants. Vee had truly surpassed him when it came to nature studies. At the age of eight she had already been drawing botanical specimens. Yes, he still thought of her that way, but that was the past.

He thought of Vee also in an entirely different way now. "She is quite charming," he finally said. "You have done a wonderful job of raising her, Flurry."

"I mean, how do you relate to her?" Flurry tossed the book onto the floor, a gauge of her distress. "You were raised together. I would have thought you regarded her more as a sister or . . ."

Thoughts of Vee as a grown woman touched Max with an overwhelming longing for her. "Vee, a sister? Never. I do not think any sister and brother really like each other. There is too much rivalry. Vee was always my ally and my friend. I think of her now as a very attractive young woman who—"

"Who is particularly vulnerable to you because of your past closeness. And you had better remember that, Max." Flurry shook her finger at him.

"We are only cousins, Flurry, and not close cousins. I should think you would be happy to have us form an attachment. I begin to suspect Uncle John hoped so too. Why else would he leave me Byerly?"

"Because he knew you could fend off your encroaching relatives where Veronica never could," Flurry replied, the strength returning to her voice.

"Have you any objection in principle to my marrying Vee?" Max looked steadily at Flurry, trying to divine how she really felt, but she could be inscrutable when she wished. She was the one he had learned his impassive expression from.

"I have a very strong objection to you ruining her," Flurry accused, "and that is what will happen if you are ever alone with her."

Max's chin came up. "I think I have more control over myself than that. And I do care about her." He left the room and went outside for a walk. He was having difficulty reconciling the precocious child who used to dog his footsteps with the ripe young woman who had such an obvious interest in him. That the attraction was mutual he no longer doubted, but it was both confusing and embarrassing to want her like this. He bit his lower lip with the concentration of sorting Veronica back into her accustomed slot in his mind. He tried to think of some other woman he had loved, any other woman, but that just made it worse because he ended by comparing her to Vee and finding the other woman wanting. Perhaps he had better think of Vee as two people. He had loved the child, but he was in love with the woman, and in spite of what Flurry had said, Vee did not seem at all like a victim to him.

"Quite a dustup in the library," Flurry said, interrupting Veronica's packing without even knocking.

The light, airy room had been decorated with the bolts of gauze and muslin Max had sent, that Flurry had declared too thin to be anything but bed curtains or window hangings. So Veronica's room, where there were potted plant specimens under study, had the aspect of some tropical retreat, with the creamy muslin curtains fluttering in the chill late-afternoon breeze from the open window and the lemon yellow bed hangings and sheets forming a backdrop for the colorful array of Veronica's clothes as she sorted them.

"Flurry. I am so glad you have come. For I sorely need your advice." Veronica brushed her dark hair back from her flushed face.

"I know it was very bad, Veronica, but you should be used to them by now."

"This time I mean to leave. I have abdicated," she replied, trying unsuccessfully to stuff a green velvet riding habit into an already bulging trunk. "Max will have to deal with them now. Shall I take the black merino or the brown? The rest of my clothes will have to be sent."

"Had you not better first consider where we are going?" Flurry asked kindly.

"Will you come with me? I have not wanted to ask you, seeing that I am leaving so precipitously." Veronica's eyes were intense, the pupils dark and troubled. Flurry reached to stroke her hair.

"I can hardly stay here if you go."

"I was not thinking very clearly when I made that grand exit. I suppose you will have to leave too." Veronica slumped on the bed. "Do you dislike it very much?"

"Not in the least." Flurry sat beside her, undid her disordered hair, took up a comb from the bed and began to braid her long tresses for bed. "But it would be best if you wrote a few letters first to see where we will be welcome."

"I was thinking to go to London for a while, just a little while," Veronica said hopefully.

"Rent a house, you mean?"

"Oh, I do not think I can afford that. We could stay in lodgings. That would not cost so very much." When Flurry had finished the braid Veronica turned and took Flurry's veined hands in her desperate young clasp.

"I think if we are to live by our wits we had better start now," Flurry said decisively. "You cannot just leave your art collection for Steeple to dispose of."

Veronica looked startled. "No, I had not thought of that. He will sell it and keep the money."

"Exactly. Leaving now would play right into Steeple's hands."

Veronica turned a hopeful face to Flurry. "I could

give it to Max. He bought most of the pieces anyway. Perhaps they will be some comfort to him."

"But you have not found the Nonsuch treasure," Flurry pointed out.

"The very idea that Steeple has demanded I turn it over to him when I do not even know where it is . . ."

Flurry could see her efforts to calm Veronica were not working. "It is not like you to leave a job unfinished. And your father would be so proud of you if you solved the puzzle."

"Suddenly I do not even care about the treasure." Despair warred with anger in Veronica's face. "Not if someone really did murder Papa to get it. You are right about one thing. I cannot leave until I have satisfied myself that we have either found the murderer or that it was just an illness."

"And then there is Max to consider," Flurry speculated, wondering if Veronica's vow not to fall in love with him had worked.

"Yes," Veronica replied calmly. "He will never be able to manage. If we leave, to be sure, he will flee the place, never to return." She got up from the bed and dropped the riding dress in folds at her feet.

"There is a vast difference between a rout and an ordered retreat," Flurry reminded her.

"Yes, you are right. We must finish our investigation, however distasteful. And it would mean much to Papa if we could find the Nonsuch artifact." Veronica gathered up an armload of dresses. "If you must know, I am sadly disappointed in myself. I would have thought I would be the last to be haggling over Papa's estate."

"You were sorely provoked," Flurry commiserated.

Veronica carried the garments into the dressing

room and began to hang them. Flurry followed with the riding habit.

"Aunt Margery implied I took advantage of an incompetent old man, Steeple accused me of stealing, and George suggested I murdered my own father." Veronica went back to pick up a winter pelisse.

"Well, you can be sure none of them will ever have hot tea in this house again," Flurry said as she took the garment from Veronica and folded it for the trunk.

Veronica chuckled, then walked resolutely to the window to close it. "An ordered retreat, then."

9

*D*inner was a seething disaster, with the family all either staring frostily at each other or mumbling under their breaths. No wonder Flurry ate with the servants most of the time. Veronica maintained her new-found serenity with a determination that impressed even her. She addressed no remarks to anyone and thought only of the new foods set before her: the curries and spiced lamb, the fresh pineapple, obviously from one of Max's ships. She did send an occasional encouraging nod to Max. She must set a good example for him since he would have to deal with these people for the rest of his life. She had only to solve her two mysteries before she would be shut of them forever. That one of them might be her papa's murderer could not even depress her, for she felt finally to be doing something about it. And there was always the possibility that he had died of natural causes. That would certainly be worth knowing.

Later that night she turned restlessly on her bed, trying to puzzle out some clue to one or the other of her problems, but her thoughts and dreams kept returning to Max. She must have dozed eventually for they were back at the cliff and Max was reaching for her. Then, just as her fingers touched his, he let go. She awoke with a strangled cry and shuddered a little, grasping desperately in her mind for the truth. Max had not fallen. She had saved him, but it could so easily have been otherwise. How tenuous life was. She looked up at some flapping motion, like a giant bird, and realized her curtains were billowing in the chill night breeze. A footstep hesitated on the other side of the room.

"Flurry?" Veronica sat up and asked of the shadow that crept toward her bed.

"No, it is me," a husky voice replied.

"Max! You must not be here," Veronica whispered.

"But I was walking in the garden and I heard you crying."

"I was not crying." She sat cross-legged in the bed with the covers bunched around her.

"Vee, you cannot lie to me," he said, kneeling on the bed, and running his thumb across her cheek to dry her tears.

"It is only that they are all against me," Veronica said, knowing it to be a lame excuse.

"Except me." Max cradled her face in his hands. "I will always be on your side."

"I know that." Veronica stared at him, unable in the darkness to read his expression.

"Is that really why you were crying? You have suffered with our relatives' absurdities before and only laughed at them."

"Perhaps I was tired, or perhaps they do not amuse me as they did when I was a child." Veronica looked away, anywhere except into his eyes. But Max turned her chin up and gazed at her. She had the suspicion that he could read her much better than she could see into his thoughts.

"Or perhaps you are falling in love with me," Max drawled as he bent toward her.

"Oh, Max, I cannot love you," Veronica said, wringing her hands. "It costs me too much."

"Do you imagine either of us has a choice in the matter?" He leaned forward and crushed her into a devouring kiss, sliding his hands down her back and feeling her rounded buttocks through her nightdress. She shivered and groaned, pressing herself against him. He tugged up on the thin fabric of her nightdress until he could feel bare flesh beneath his hands. His hand on her creamy hip elicited a gasp of shock from her and she surged toward him. He disposed his other hand likewise and squeezed her buttocks apart, knowing what this must be doing to her. If he was teasing her, she had no idea what her merest touch did to him. It seemed that all the blood in his body had collected in his groin to pulse there and slam away at his resolve.

What resolve? Something to do with being a man. *A man who cannot control* . . . what . . . he could not spare the effort to think it through. Surely there was no controlling Vee. She broke the kiss to grasp the two fronts of his shirt and pulled in opposite directions, sending most of the buttons flying. Her arms snaked about his naked chest then, pulling a needy groan from him. This was absurd. He was the man and she had nothing on but a fabric so thin he could feel her hardened nipples through it, yet it was he who was likely to be disrobed first.

He laid her gently down on the bed to caress her breasts through the thin gauze fabric with his tongue as he shed his coat. Her shuddering sighs encouraged him to dispense with the shirt as well, all the while his mouth was busy suckling one breast or the other. She ran her hands along his back, rousing every nerve in his body. How much longer could he endure this? And what was delaying him?

He pressed his mouth to hers again, his tongue gaining easy entrance. From their last encounter like this, he assumed Vee understood the symbolism of it. She might be young but she was the most supremely intelligent woman he had known. She pressed her tongue alongside his and when he broke the kiss to chuckle at her it was her hands that reached up to pull his head down again. She coiled her legs around his bare waist like a python about to have him for a meal, and he liked the feeling that she desired him just as hotly as he wanted her.

Veronica felt Max slide one hand along her thigh, then slip it between them, and when she realized what he meant to do, she relaxed the grip with her legs and lay back on the bed, her breath coming in short gasps as she watched him and waited for that long-deliberated invasion. She felt pulled two ways about this, as though she wanted to thrust him away at the same time she wanted him inside her. Wanting his skin next to hers won out each time, but she felt herself writhing as his finger invaded her opening a little at a time. She was wet with desire as she thought of her mares and how they reacted when teased with a stallion. She also knew you should not push a stallion too far. She wanted to touch Max as he was touching her but confined herself to running her hands along his well-muscled shoulders, eliciting groans from him anyway.

As he penetrated deeper he said with a puzzled moan. "You have no hymen. Has someone . . . ?"

"No, silly. It happened after a fall from one of the colts I was training." Veronica gasped but continued. "For me to bleed at that time of month I thought there was something tragically wrong until I read what it might be. It hurt horribly for a few days, but there were no ill effects," she said in a desperate rush. "Truly Max, I have never lain with anyone before." She stroked his cheek, then tried to pull his face down again to kiss him.

"I believe you, Vee." Max did kiss her longingly again, but his hand left its position and she was hoping this meant they were moving on to the next stage.

"Max, I want to touch you now," she whispered reverently as her fingers worked their way toward the buttons of his breeches.

Max groaned as her fingers brushed his engorged member still in the confines of his breeches. "You should not have had to face that trial alone. You should have told Flurry."

"Flurry is very motherly, but once I understood what had happened there seemed no point in worrying her with it."

"How like you to spare her sensibilities," Max said, grunting as she undid the first button.

"But I have confessed my desires to her," Veronica said.

"You have?" Max asked in surprise.

"She is worried about us, but I find her not the best resource when discussing love."

"Flurry would not be, but she did warn me," Max said groggily, capturing Vee's adventuresome hand in an iron grip and trying to remember something very important. He felt as though he were half drunk and on the point of making a very grave mistake.

"Warned you about what?" Veronica asked, trying to get at his buttons with the other hand. But he imprisoned this one as well and managed to kneel over her.

"That I could not be trusted with you," he said through clenched teeth.

"But Max, I want you. What we are doing is my choice, not yours alone. I would never say you had seduced me."

Then some part of his brain that had been fast asleep realized with a shock what he had meant to do and he stopped himself. He was not used to playing the villain, not on purpose, at any rate. Vee had made it easy for him to ruin her and carry her off with him. The sense of power and the strength of her love both elated and frightened him. But there was something in the way, if he could just remember what it was.

"Max, why are we stopping? Have I pushed you too far? I was being careful."

Max sucked in a breath and moaned again. "There is something I must do first."

"What could be more important than this?" Veronica whispered desperately.

"We must marry, for one thing, and that will require a special license unless you wish to wait for weeks." Max released her hands and lay beside her on the bed, pulling the covers up over her.

"Weeks? But I cannot."

"You shall not have to. But it is Flurry's wish that we be married before we make love, not after."

"Max, what are we to do?" she asked when she began to recover her senses.

"I will go to London to get the license. While I am there I will take care of the other matter that stands in our way."

"What other matter?" Veronica asked unhappily as she snuggled against his chest.

"Nothing you need bother your head about. Trust me. And you are not to cry anymore."

He lay beside her, holding her until she fell asleep and until his arousal had abated. Then he disengaged his arm as tenderly as though he were laying down a sleeping child and covered her.

He left as he had come, unfulfilled and unhappy but with a better understanding of the consequences of his actions. He had been too much used to not counting the cost. Veronica had always warned him that it would get him killed someday, but he had been lucky. What did it matter if it was only his life on the line. He could not ruin hers as well.

One good thing had come of his visit. He was sure of Vee's love. The only difficulty would be tearing himself away for a few days to track down a bishop and eradicate the other impediment that had finally gnawed through his brain to his conscious mind. He could see the other woman's face now, plain and unhappy compared to Vee, but was it a face that could be bought? He would soon find out.

He slipped down from the oak to lean against it, musing on the narrow escape his and Vee's honor had just suffered. *A man who cannot control his appetites is not a man but an animal.* How could he have forgotten that? Even though he had not remembered, he had stopped himself in time. Perhaps Vee would never have regretted their mating this night, but Flurry, if she ever found out, would have been sorely disappointed in him. And he had to admit he would have considered it a defeat himself. So when he took up his walking stick, he was not feeling depressed, but secretly elated as though he had passed some difficult test.

The sound of a spade clinking against rock finally penetrated to his fogged brain and when he stared he could see a figure digging in the garden. It looked like Freddy. Max turned over in his mind various explanations for this uncanny behavior but found nothing that matched his cousin's temperament, unless he had struck someone in a fit of rage and was now disposing of the body. He watched Freddy for some minutes, then obeyed his curiosity and walked up behind him. "Digging fishing worms?"

"Max!" Freddy sprang around, holding the spade like a weapon at the ready. "You should know better than to go sneaking up on someone," Freddy whispered savagely.

"Well, what are you doing?" Max finally demanded, exhaustion making him irritable.

"Digging for the treasure," Freddy said as he tossed another spadeful of dirt out onto Max's booted feet.

"Here?" Max gestured with open arms to include the empty garden. "But what on earth makes you think there is anything buried here?"

"If you must know, I found a map. But do not think you can lay claim to whatever I find," Freddy warned.

"You must be joking." Max was getting angry now at the man's stupidity.

"It was stuffed in one of Uncle's old books. Now go away and let me be."

"Very well, but if you uproot something important old Marsh will have your hide."

"Who the devil is Marsh?" Freddy asked, tossing out some roots and another spadeful of dirt. "I do not plan on sharing what I find."

"Marsh is the gardener, you numbskull, the one who used to chase you with a rake when you swung on the apple trees and broke the limbs."

"Is he still alive?" Freddy asked incredulously.

"Yes, I saw him today and he looks just as able as he was twelve years ago. What the devil happened to you? You used to be a strapping lad. Now you have gone to fat. And George is thin and acerbic."

"None of your business, Max." Freddy tossed the shovel aside and grabbed the pick, causing Max to wonder if he should step back a pace from the hole.

"Odd how some people hardly change at all and others . . ." Max stared at the ever-widening hole and wondered how to break off the encounter without losing face. He would never again let Freddy see him afraid.

"If you must know, London happened to me," Freddy spit at him. "Balls and routs and eight-course dinners with enough wine to swim in. It is ruinous."

"It need not be for a man with some restraint," Max said with a superior lilt.

"For a man with some hope. That was dashed when we learned the terms of Uncle John's new will. At least when you were out of favor we got something."

"That was your own fault. You would have been far better off if you had not spent your summers at Byerly."

"We were sent here for the same reason Dora sent you, to ingratiate ourselves with Uncle John." Freddy plunged the pick into the soft earth as though he were killing something.

Max forced himself to remain motionless. "Then you should have done so, instead of spending all your time fighting with me."

"He favored you from the first," Freddy accused as he paused, the pick held in both hands.

"No, he gave us all an equal chance to involve ourselves in studies."

"But you were the only one who did. You deliberately stole his favor. And now we are left with fifty pounds. That will not last a day in London."

"Surely you could see this coming," Max reasoned. "And your stepfather somehow managed to become executor of the estate. Steeple knew how things were going."

"If he knew he never let on. Feathering his own nest, I imagine."

"Well, there is always my offer," Max said, beginning to tire of trying to reform Freddy.

"Stuck on your snake-ridden plantation? I would rather die in a gutter in London than in your jungle hellhole."

"Suit yourself." Max deliberately turned his back on Freddy and began to walk away. There was a time when it would have taken only this to provoke an attack, and Freddy did have that pick. But the ring of the tool fell on some rock, not Max's skull, as Freddy resumed his digging. Max felt no compassion for Freddy, but George was another matter. Considering that Freddy and George had started with the same mother and been saddled with the same stepfather, Max thought George could have turned out a good deal worse. George's attack the night of Max's escape twelve years before had been prompted by thinking his sister had been raped. Max thought that most of his scraps with George had been provoked by Freddy. And there was that point George had made at the reading of the will. In the same sentence he had managed to defend his mother and excuse Vee's behavior with so much justice that Max would have applauded the subtlety of it had he not been on the defensive for Vee.

If Freddy thought Uncle John had been easily won over, he was wrong. Uncle John had actually been rather severe with him, even before Max's disgrace. It was true that a warm regard had sprung up between them, one that was interrupted by Max's absence, but not killed. And it was not because of the artifacts he had sent home to Vee. It was their common interest in art and history. Why had the same rapport not existed between George and Uncle John even though George had studied art? Perhaps because Uncle had expected George to be as grasping as his mother.

The gleam of a cigar caught Max's attention and warned him that he was not the only one disturbed by Freddy's nocturnal antics.

In the ordinary way of things, Max would have slipped into the shrubbery bordering the house and made his way by a circuitous route behind the smoker. And as he wandered toward the pinpoint of light under the trees of the side yard, Max did think seriously about what a good target he made in the moonlight. But he felt no chill of fear as he always did when Freddy's ire was aroused.

"George?" he asked, turning his head to try to detect some movement under the trees.

"Over here," George said quietly, the pinpoint of light glowed again as he took a puff and exhaled. Max could tell from the scent that it was one of his uncle's cigars.

"Enjoying a last smoke?" Max asked.

"And the sight of my brother making a fool of himself," George said.

"Where's the novelty in that?" Max asked.

"Indeed, my turn came earlier." George pushed his shoulders away from the tree and crushed the cigar against the sole of his boot, signaling the end of the conversation. "You know it does not pay to try to play the role of peacemaker in this house."

"I surmised that was what you were trying to do in the library today," Max acknowledged.

"Yes, my efforts must have seemed clumsy to you, with your vast experience at starting wars and ending them," George said bitterly.

Max stiffened. "What do you know of that?"

"I am not totally without connections in London. I receive offhanded praise all the time for your activities, both diplomatic and covert. You have no idea how difficult it is to respond to such sallies with good humor."

"How do you respond?" Max asked suspiciously.

"As though I know all about it," George said. "I gain no credit by sniping at you to your friends."

"You seem to have gained a measure of restraint over the years."

George shook his head. "I must really look like a fool to you in the context of the family setting. But when I come back here I feel like I am a boy again and I do not like it."

It suddenly occurred to Max that George had opened himself to him, a thing he had thought never to see. If he were negotiating with an enemy he would not jump at the weakness but work around it to see if he could find out more.

"Why do we come back?" Max asked as George began to walk around the house toward the front entrance.

"Family," George said with disgust. "One holds out the eternal hope of actually winning against them, or changing them, or something."

Max caught up with him at the front of the house where he was surprised when George pulled out a key and unlocked the door. "But nothing ever does change, except we die, one by one," Max said sadly.

"And last one alive wins, I suppose," George said, holding the door open for him. "Do you think it will be you, Max?"

"Scarcely," Max said as he watched George close and lock the heavy oak door, "I think it will be Vee."

"Why?" George asked, taking up the one glowing candle on the hall table and lighting two off it.

"Because she deserves to win," Max said, trying to fathom what game George was playing.

"Veronica has already lost," George said somberly. "Uncle is dead."

Max began to feel unsettled by the matter-of-fact way George discussed this. "I have lost his companionship, as well," Max said bitterly.

"I never had it," George replied. "And there was a good possibility, with your dangerous occupation, you would never return alive."

"If not for Steeple's interference, you might have gotten control of the family finances," Max parried.

George turned to him, a devilish look in his eyes. "I am not a plotter like you, Max. Do you remember what you said when you left? You vowed to make us all sorry for the way we treated you. And you have."

"I am unaware of it," Max replied, having totally forgotten his empty threat. "You must have done it to yourselves."

George stared at him a moment. "Perhaps you are right." He turned and started up the stairs. "Well, I wonder what new horrors dawn will bring. I think I had better get some sleep."

Max started up after him. "Yes, for Freddy will be as cross as crabs when he does not find anything after staying up half the night."

"You are sure he will find nothing?" George asked over his shoulder.

"For the same reason you are." Max decided to play a card. "You know Uncle would not have regarded anything but a work of art as worth the search he mounted for the Nonsuch treasure."

George hesitated. "Yes, I know it."

"If we manage to find this treasure, it would set at least some of the suspicions to rest," Max offered. He realized this was the longest conversation he had ever had with George. They were still miles apart, Max still did not trust him, but perhaps an understanding was possible.

George hesitated, but Max could not fathom what was going through his mind in the dark. "I shall think about it."

10

"Max came to see me again last night, Flurry," Veronica said as she poured them both tea in the breakfast parlor. She had not meant to tell Flurry, but the older woman looked so worried Veronica thought that it would be best to put her fears to rest.

"Yes, I know. I heard him." Flurry scated herself erectly at the breakfast table, trying to look disapproving.

"I suspected we had made a deal of noise." Veronica got Flurry a plate with two scones on it. "Why did you not come to poke at him again?"

"I shall not always be around to save you two from each other. You must take responsibility for your own actions." Flurry took a bite and chewed for a moment. "Did he . . . did he . . .?"

"No," Veronica said, staring into space for a moment, "but I think he wanted to."

"What stopped him?" Flurry took an incautious gulp of hot tea and coughed.

"I do not know, except that it was not me," Veronica said in a puzzled way.

"What do you mean?" Flurry stared at her with her most severe governess's expression.

"I knew it was wrong, what was about to happen, and I did not care, I wanted him so badly. It was quite frightening, for I am used to being in such good control of myself."

"This is an absurd conversation. A girl your age should know nothing of these matters. And it is about time Max grew up. It is unconscionable of him to be seducing you."

"He has grown up," Veronica said with a sigh. "He is much more massive than I remember."

"Veronica! I am not even going to ask what you mean by that," Flurry snapped.

"Flurry, do you think Max has a flaw?"

Flurry set her cup and saucer down with an impatient clatter. "A flaw? I think he has many."

"But compared to most men, how bad do you think he is?" Veronica asked wistfully.

"He is selfish, that you know. He puts his own happiness before everyone else's."

Veronica pressed her lips together. "That comes from being alone so long, and never having anyone care about him, not since he left us. I think if he were living in the same house with someone who did not annoy him, he could be quite considerate."

"He has a damned nasty tongue in his head," Flurry added, as though that settled the matter.

"But so have I," Veronica claimed. "It is a necessity in this family. Besides, a woman of intellect would be a match for him."

"Are we talking about you?"

"Of course we are talking about me. I love him so much, Flurry, that I would forgive him anything."

Flurry rubbed her hand over the top of Veronica's smaller one. "You have had much practice being generous."

"Perhaps that is why I do not see Max's flaws as insurmountable," Veronica said as she cradled her teacup dreamily.

"No. Compared to Steeple or Freddy or even George, Max is a paragon," Flurry agreed.

"So you believe he may still be reformed in some way?" Veronica asked hopefully.

"I doubt it." Flurry took a savage bite of her scone and chewed it thoroughly before replying. "Max's character is set. You must accept that, Veronica. No matter how much he may wish to change, he cannot."

"I disagree, Flurry. I think the right woman might turn him into an admirable man."

"But is that what you really want?" Max asked from the window as he spun on the sill and unsnaked his legs to land on the carpet beside them.

"Max. You were eavesdropping," Veronica accused.

"Morning, Flurry," Max said after he had given Veronica a smacking kiss on the cheek. "And I was not. If you do not want people to overhear, you should not discuss their characters in such a public place."

"Max, I will thank you to remember that houses have doors for a reason," Flurry admonished.

"I cannot see that stepping in a window decreases a man's consequence so long as it is not a bedroom window," he replied.

Veronica burst into laughter.

"Since when did that hold you back?" Flurry complained as she handed him a cup of tea.

"So you think I am still capable of being reformed?" Max asked. "I should like to see you try, Vee."

"I think I will enjoy taking up the challenge of it," Veronica said.

She tilted her head and looked up at him through half-closed eyes in a way that sent his heart thudding against his ribs. The hot tea sloshed onto his thigh, abruptly claiming his attention.

"But I shall never try to make you consequential or stuffy," Vee said. "I shall only hope that you will be kinder and not joke so much that you upset Flurry."

"Flurry likes to be teased," Max said with a dry mouth as he stared at Vee and blotted his leg with a napkin. "No one has ever done so before."

This resulted in such a scalding look from Miss Flurry that Max relented. "Very well, I shall try to be good, but I have not had much practice." Max grabbed up a piece of toast and spread jam on it in defiance of his aversion to eating breakfast.

"Why were you out so early, Max?" Veronica asked.

"I wanted to inspect Freddy's hole. He was out digging in the garden last night."

"Freddy?" Flurry asked. "That boy has never done a particle of work around here. Are you sure?"

"Yes, I can show you the hole," Max said, taking a long drink of tea.

"No, I mean, are you sure it was Freddy?" Flurry stared at him as though she thought he was imagining things.

"Yes, we had quite a long conversation." Max took a bite of toast and chewed thoughtfully, keeping them in suspense. He had learned the trick of that from Flurry. "He said he had found a treasure map in one of Uncle's books."

"Treasure map?" Veronica asked. "I cannot imagine

what he could mean. If Papa had anything valuable he would never bury it in the garden."

"And why would he be digging it up at night?" Flurry asked.

"To keep anything he might find from the rest of the family, I suppose," Max replied. "Uncle John intended that Mercia get the residue of the estate so that she could attract a husband. If there was a cache of gold coins lying about, she would be the one to benefit from it, not Freddy."

"That is not at all likely." Veronica crumbled a muffin thoughtfully on her plate. "But do you suppose Papa left a map to something else, some stones that were from Nonsuch?"

"Let us go to the library," Max said excitedly.

When Flurry saw they meant to carry their tea away with them, she clicked her tongue in disgust and refused to let curiosity prompt her to such a solecism.

Veronica preceded Max and started to laugh as soon as she saw the volume that was lying on the desk. She set her teacup down and flipped through the pages of *Common Garden Plants.* "This was where Papa kept his garden maps. To be sure, Freddy will find nothing more than the roots of some long-dead specimen."

"Shall I tell him? Look, he is at it again," Max said, regarding the coatless sweating man as he dug away near the asparagus bed.

"Rather early for Freddy to be exerting himself," Veronica said, coming to look out the window.

Max noticed that she was wearing blue this morning. He wondered if there was a color that did not become her black hair and dark eyes. "Freddy looks desperate," Max said, trying to take his mind off Vee and not succeeding.

"He must want to finish before the rest of the family rises," Veronica guessed. "Let him go. Who knows how much of the garden he may turn over and save old Marsh the bother."

When Veronica bent to regard Freddy, her bare arm brushed Max's hand. He was prepared by now for his reaction to her, but not for the intensity of it, and closed his eyes for several heartbeats to suppress his need. "Is the library where Uncle kept his notes?" he asked hoarsely.

Veronica turned to stare at him. "No, all the books and things related to his researches are in his room, through here." Veronica led the way into the adjoining salon fitted up as a bedroom. "He mostly lived in this downstairs room and the library. We took meals together in the library—he, Flurry, and I. She would knit while we talked of history or I read to him." Veronica stared at the mussed bed with a worried expression.

"That was me," Max said. "I lay down in here last night so I could hear Freddy."

"Perhaps you should take Papa's room. Perhaps he really did leave something useful tucked away somewhere." She glanced around the untidy room, where stacks of books gathered dust on the floor and piles of papers marched across every available horizontal surface. "He always had notes stuck in books or odd corners of the desk."

Vee's pain communicated itself to Max and his desire gave ground to his instinct to shelter her. "I would give anything to have been here," he said. "Perhaps I could have prevented . . ."

"It is past time for regrets, Max," Veronica said huskily. "We cannot change the way things turned out. Here are his notebooks. You should really take this bedroom. It is close to the library and all the things he loved."

"Perhaps I shall move in here. So much easier to get out at night."

Veronica turned and walked back toward the library.

"Where are you going, Vee?"

"I consider it extremely dangerous to be alone with you, especially in a bedroom," Veronica said over her shoulder as she carried the notebooks into the library.

The teasing look she had just given him was worthy of a woman far more practiced at flirtation than Vee. Was it instinctive, Max wondered?

Max lunged after her, feeling like an awkward boy pursuing his first love. "We did not do anything wrong." He came up behind her as she stood at the desk, opening the first notebook. He put his hands on her shoulders, then slid them slowly forward to cup her breasts, and her response was instantaneous. She arched back against him as flagrantly as she had the night before in her bedroom. Her nipples hardened with desire and Max felt his groin tighten.

"But we came very close, Max," she whispered dreamily. "Even now we are a danger to each other. What if someone should come in?" She stepped resolutely out of his arms, pulled out the desk chair for him and patted the seat.

He groaned and came carefully around the desk to begin his task, trying to suppress the much more interesting prospect of seeing how far they could get in a library. Of course, they had a bedroom handy enough. He threw open the first of the folders in frustration, only to exclaim, "What the devil is this? A foreign language? That his letters were a scribble I knew, but this is unintelligible."

"Let me see." Veronica leaned over Max's shoulder, further torturing him with her nearness, but not slapping him when his arm stole around her waist. "I think it says 'Henry ordered granite from Perth.'"

"Are you sure?" Max asked, scrutinizing the note and even turning it upside down.

Veronica squinted at the scrawl. "Either that or 'Henry ordained goats from Perth,' but given the context . . ."

Max laughed unsteadily and Veronica wondered how he could appear so calm when her whole insides were aflutter. If he threw her down across the desk at this moment, she would never be able to stop him from having his way with her. Suddenly it occurred to her what a powerful man Max was, stronger by far than she. She should be afraid of him. She flirted with the idea of being afraid of Max, at least of his wilder impulses.

"I can see it will be no mean task to decipher this, and that you will be essential to the process." He said it with satisfaction. Veronica could feel the coils of entrapment tightening about her again as Max pulled her onto his lap.

"I did mean to transcribe them for him anyway," she said, wondering if the heat between her thighs was transmitting itself to Max, wondering if he desired her as desperately as she wanted him at this moment. She wet her lips and swallowed. "Who knows but that we may stumble onto a hint as to where some of the artwork is located."

"Read this one to me first," Max demanded, running one hand down her side to assess just how few undergarments she was wearing.

"That is odd," Veronica said as she flipped through

the written pages, laying the maps and drawings aside
for Max to scrutinize.

"What?" Max asked irritably. How dare she find
something historical more interesting than his atten-
tions.

"One of the builders who was hired to raze Nonsuch.
I have run across the name before, but I cannot remember where." Veronica stood up and wandered about the
room, looking at various books on the shelves. "I generally have a pretty good memory for names."

"If it is important it will turn up again," Max said
impatiently. "Does this drawing match up with anything else you have seen?"

"No, but that might have only been Papa's guess as to
what it looked like."

Max gazed at the lion rampant and the maiden's head
rising out of a rose, the symbol for Catherine Parr. Poor
choice for a woman married to such a famous beheader.
"Rather too much detail for that," Max judged, gazing
appreciatively at Vee's ankles as she climbed the ladder
to the upper shelves. "He must have copied it from a
drawing somewhere," Max said as he came purposefully
around the desk to the foot of the ladder.

"He did make a trip to London last year." Veronica
glanced down at Max and discovered that his eyes were
fixed upward, beyond the hiked up hem of her gown.
She smiled as that wonderful throbbing started again
between her thighs. "There was some book in particular
he could not get," she said breathlessly.

"What was it?" Max ruffled his hair with his hands
and blew out his frustration as he leaned against the
ladder.

"I cannot remember. He bought so many books. It
was in Montague House."

"Vee, they have a lot of books there," Max said, with his lips attempting to curve into a smile.

"I know that." Veronica started back down the ladder. "If only he had taken me with him."

As he stood ready to help her descend the ladder, Max contrived to get one hand under her skirt and run it up along her leg, causing Veronica to gasp. She paused for breath and the errant hand circled under her petticoat and slipped through the slit in her drawers to find its resting place on her silken mound. Veronica leaned her head back against his chest as one finger enticed her to her undoing. "He never told you anything about the treasure?" Max asked absently, cradling Vee in front of him.

"What treasure?" Veronica mumbled. "I mean, no, but he may have thought he had."

Max turned her slowly and kissed her hard on the mouth so long that she lost all track of time and every other aspect of reason.

"Max," Veronica gasped when he stopped for air. She studied his troubled gray eyes, trying to clear the kiss from her thoughts, the warmth of his lips from her memory, the touch of his fingers from her flesh, but she could not.

"Vee, do you feel faint?"

"No, I feel wonderfully awake."

"You look faint." Max lifted her down from the ladder and carried her into the bedroom, laying her like a treasure on the rumpled covers and continuing to kiss her. One hand cradled her head while the other massaged her breasts into peaks of awareness.

When he stopped for air, she said with some confusion, "But this is Papa's room."

"What does it matter?" Max asked as he freed her breasts and grazed first one and then the other with his wet tongue. "What does anything matter. If we are to be married anyway, what is one day more or less to us?" He ran his hand up along her bare thigh. But this time she did stop him with both hands.

"How could you think of making love here?"

He was kneeling on the edge of the bed, his racing pulse making him rock back and forth when she saw the realization come into his eyes.

"Oh, Vee, I hate myself." He quite deliberately took his hands and arms off her and strode from the room.

She got up and ran after him, pulling the front of her dress up demurely and catching him as he opened the doorway from the library into the hall. She thrust herself against it to slam it shut. She knew Max was still in a dangerous mood, knew that he could take her now if he wished and she would not be able to stop him, knew that she would not want to stop him. Yet she confronted him with her bosom heaving and no more than three layers of cloth between them. "How long did you say it would take to get the special license?"

Max stared at her and swallowed. "Two days, but I cannot leave you now. Not with the family here. I had hoped to be rid of them by now."

"Why not go to London and come back as quickly as you can?"

"Vee, I do not think it is safe, not if what we suspect is true," he said with anguish.

Her eyes stared at him, her lips trembling as she caught his meaning. "Forget the license, then. Come to me in my own bed tonight. We are wasting far too much time over silly conventions."

She opened the door and fled up the stairs then, leaving him reeling.

* * *

Max strode toward the gardens to work off his excess energy and to meditate on his dilemma. Yes, they could do without the license for now, but he still had to get to London to take care of his other entanglement, and that would surely be the more difficult task. He was beyond the gardens by now and through the hedge into the statuary garden, not paying any attention to where he was setting his feet.

He took an incautious step and skidded into a hole, falling flat on his back. Then he heard George's muffled laughter and felt the old anger rising. It was a familiar feeling, him on the ground, filthy, and George laughing, but in this case he was far too pleased and excited about Vee's capitulation to let anger take a hold on him. And he had over the years tried to cultivate a sense of humor that would prevent him from taking umbrage at others the way he always had at his family.

He looked around at the trap Freddy had unconsciously set for him and had to admit it was funny. He started to chuckle at his own clumsiness as George got up from the bench and walked across to him. George stared ruefully down at him before offering his hand, and Max hesitated only a moment before grasping it. George pulled him out of the trench and examined the elbow of Max's jacket.

"I should say that one is ruined."

Max tried to brush the worst of the mud off while contemplating what an advantage a sense of humor was now. In the old days he had never been able to laugh at himself. "Freddy is like an exuberant hound, always expecting each hole to have a bone in it," Max said, examining the damage to his boots. "Has he found anything yet?"

"No, but he is working off a lot of excess weight, so I

shall not try to discourage him. Look what I found."
George held out a small leather-bound book to Max.

"An account book?"

"The oldest Byerly account book. I found them all in
a row on a shelf in the estate office. Someone must have
saved this as a curiosity. These expenses were kept by
the fourteenth viscount in 1685. He bought a large
quantity of stone to build the library wing."

Max grasped the fragile book and focused on the
faded brown ink. "Does he say where it came from?"

"No, only what he paid. But the timing is right. Nonsuch was being dismantled by Lord Berkeley in 1682."

"And Lord Byerly may have acquired other things
than building stones," Max surmised as he carefully
turned the brittle pages.

"That is my expectation. This is exciting, is it not?"
George rubbed his hands together. "The thought that
we may discover some artifact hidden for more than a
century?"

"How well would a statue or the like hold up in this
moist earth?" Max asked, scraping the mud off the sole
of his boot.

"They molded a lot of the frieze work out of pow-
dered stone, which once moistened would take any
impression and become, through the natural drying
process, as hard as adamant. I am quoting the Earl of
Arundel's cleric. But what does a cleric know of such
things?"

"Much less than you, I take it." Max handed the book
back and looked speculatively at George.

"I have been reading up on it," George replied as he
tucked the small book in his pocket.

"You do know that if we find anything, it may not be
worth actual money?" Max asked.

"Of course, but I am so bored I would look into the matter for nothing."

"My offer of a position was originally made as a taunt, that is true, but now I have some thought of buying Vee's art collection from her rather than have her sell it to someone else. Then Byerly will need a curator as much as a steward, someone to take care of its treasures and keep the place from falling apart."

George stared at him, perhaps trying to see the trap in Max's offer. "Are you serious?"

"Quite serious," Max replied. "I will not be here most of the time. You have a knowledge of the collection, not to mention the estate."

"Why would you trust me after all the fights we have had?"

"Those were childish scraps, most of them anyway," Max shrugged, making light of their past years of quite serious discord.

"Not the night I almost killed you," George reminded him. He looked away for a moment, then stared Max straight in the eyes. "You never actually touched Mercia, did you?"

"No, but Freddy made a convincing case, I think." Max rubbed the scar on his lower lip with one finger, glancing ruefully at George.

"Not one of his more harmless jokes. I am sorry, Max." George said it in a puzzled way as though he could not believe his own ears.

"We are beyond that now, I hope. I am a businessman and I can recognize expertise when I see it. You are the expert I need for this job. If you wish to make the position more palatable to your mother I can set you up with an income from investments rather than a salary."

"I would do it for nothing if I could afford to," George said as he gazed at the gargoyle. A rare smile played about his lips.

"And that is why you will do the job well," Max concluded.

George nodded. "It is well past time I stopped listening to Mother and do what I want to do. I will take the job, Max, as a job." George held out his hand and Max took it with no hesitation at all.

"And you can start by getting someone to fill in that hole before Flurry breaks her leg." Max started walking back toward the house and George fell into step beside him.

George grinned, the corners of his blue eyes crinkling. "I shall take care of it, Max. What happens if Freddy does find something?"

"Keep him from damaging it and pay him a generous finder's fee. Above all, do not let it leave the property."

11

*V*eronica went to her room and got out her paints. It was the only solution when she was overwrought or excited. She pulled out the largest blank canvas she had and started another portrait of Max, a full-length portrait. His face she knew so well from memory that she had no difficulty sketching it in and laying in the planes of color. But there was something different about his features. He was not cool and distant, not inscrutable anymore, not detached, but with his attention fully engaged. Max was watching her and waiting for tonight.

When she painted in his eyes, it was almost like having him in the room. Veronica locked the door belatedly and cleaned her hands enough to strip off all of her clothes. Then she took up her paints again in a fever of anticipation. She had to pass the time before tonight somehow, and she wanted to be ready for Max, as taut with excitement as a bowstring. After spending the next few hours with his amorous gaze locked on her aroused breasts, she would be lucky if she did not waylay him on his way to the dining room.

Where on earth was she to keep this painting? For as she sketched in his shoulders, torso and slim waist she realized that the portrait was to be nude and that she had no intention of ever clothing it. Max would have to mind it for her. His servants would never snoop through his belongings, and if they did run across it, would never say anything.

Midway through the painting Veronica caught sight of herself in the cheval mirror and walked up to scrutinize her body with an artist's eye. She was perhaps too thin to be quite pleasing as a subject, but Max had not complained so far. Her hair was long enough to temptingly hide her breasts. She would have to remember that for tonight. She was too short, perhaps, but Max had not complained of that either. She stepped aside to view the reflection of the portrait and had the oddest illusion that it winked at her.

She must stop soon, for she frequently let her mind wander too far when she was intent on a work and got these strange illusions about it. But there had never been anything like this before. How would she ever be content to paint flowers or faces again?

She thought she had been at it no more than an hour or two, but Flurry's sharp rap sent her scrambling for a cloth to cover the picture, completely ignoring her own nudity.

"I am painting, Flurry," Veronica called. "How long until dinner?"

"Less than an hour, Veronica," Flurry called through the door. "What are you painting?"

"It . . . it is a surprise for Max. I shall clean up now and meet you in the drawing room."

"Very well. Do not be late or I shall eat in the servants' hall again."

Veronica breathed a sigh of relief and did, indeed, remove the worst of the paint from her fingers and one or two other places where she had inadvertently gotten it. She glanced at the portrait as she rubbed her hands in the linseed oil. It was nearly finished to the waist and she would have had to stop soon anyway for lack of specific information.

Once she had donned her most demure dress to tease Max, she emptied the large trunk at the foot of her bed and secured the portrait inside, tying the key around her neck by a ribbon, planning how she would entice him to open it. Then she made all tidy for the night. She supposed she should get some wine, but she seriously did not think they would need it. As an afterthought she threw open the window, for that was no doubt how Max would come to her.

Lady Margery and Mercia fawned so on Max during dinner that Henry and George stared at them. Even the dense Freddy gave them a suspicious glance. Flurry must have encountered some disquieting remarks while waiting for Veronica in the drawing room, for she had decided to absent herself after all. She received more news, she informed Veronica, about what went forward in the dining room from the staff than if she had been present at dinner herself; Veronica could hardly wait to hear the servants' version of the meal from Flurry.

Veronica had never taken the servants for granted, certainly had never pretended they were deaf as Lady Margery's family did. Therefore they trusted and confided in her. They would tell her anything, except something that would hurt her. She meant to see that Max took care of them and did not scatter them to the winds by replacing them with his own people. So far the two staffs had appeared to integrate themselves amicably: Cook's roast leg of lamb sat cheek by jowl on the table with the spiciest curry she had ever tasted; boiled turnips rubbed shoulders with carrots cooked with sesame seeds and honey; and the pork pie was chased down the table by a pretty platter of vegetables and bits of chicken fried up and spiced with what she thought was ginger.

They had not had such a wonderful meal in years that she could remember, and Veronica was just deciding which of the dishes she would sample a second time when she became aware of a dead silence and all eyes upon her. "I am sorry, I was not attending."

"That is obvious," Henry said. "I asked if you meant to sell John's art collection."

"Sell it?" Veronica asked, playing for time and glancing at Max for help. She asked for the sesame dish again and he passed this to her. She found herself glad Max was at the far end of the table, else he might feel the heat of desire emanating from her.

"What business is it of yours?" Max glared at Steeple.

"By what I can see from a quick walk about the house, Veronica would be in for a windfall if she sells the collection, either at auction or in its entirety. It seems only right, since the others have been left with nothing."

"Actually, most of those pieces I sent to Vee, not Uncle John. He must have felt it safer to mention them in his will to assure her possession of them. Veronica's windfall, as you call it, was Uncle John's way of providing her with an income that she must live off for the rest of her life," Max stated. "She is not going to waste it settling anyone else's debts."

Veronica wanted to speak up and say she meant to

live off her own painting, but she could do that in private. It would be foolish to weaken Max's position in front of the enemy, even if she did not agree with him personally. Besides, it was sweet of him to defend her.

"Something must be done for George and Freddy," Steeple said.

"I offered them both positions with me, but Freddy will have none of it."

"Positions? I heard nothing of this," Steeple said.

"He wants to put us to work in some godforsaken plantation growing coffee or some such thing," Freddy complained.

"Still . . ." Steeple said.

"You do not condone such an idea?" Margery asked, then must have remembered she was being nice to Max for Mercia's sake. "No offense Max, but we must think of the family position."

"You were the one who mentioned debtors' prison," Max said. "That is why I made the offer."

"Surely you could find something for them in England," Lady Margery insisted.

George cleared his throat. "I have accepted the position of steward of Byerly."

"But that is worse than being in trade," Lady Margery said shrilly. "Why George, you would be no more than a servant."

"Max is engaged in trade," Mercia said, looking for a way to impress Max. "It has not hurt him."

"But he has no position in society; neither has Dora. The only way he will be acceptable is if no one knows where his money comes from and he marries—"

"Someone who does have a position in society," Dora finished with a nasty sneer. Both Lady Margery and Mercia stared at her.

Max traded impatient looks with Veronica, who shook her head slightly to warn him that she was planning to stay out of the argument.

Rajeev brought in two platters of fruit and Veronica attacked them with pleasure. There was such sheer enjoyment in only thinking of yourself for a short while and how best to satisfy your appetite. It was wonderful to foist the burden of argument on Max for a change. She sent him a grateful look and smiled as though to signify she was finished eating. His eyes roamed hungrily over her as she rose from the table.

"It will not do," said Margery. "George, you are not to accept this position."

"You have nothing to say about it, Mother," George replied.

"So this is what it has come to. Max has turned one of my own children against me."

"Now, Margery," Steeple said. "Times change—"

"I deplore this English custom," Max said, "of talking business at the dinner table. Uncle John would never have permitted it. If you had nothing to say on philosophy, art, or politics you were expected to keep your silence."

George smiled at the discomfiture this caused his mother, brother, and stepfather.

"Well, ladies," Veronica said to get their attention. Mercia got up with relief, but other than she, only Dora responded.

"Who are you to be deciding when the ladies are to retire, you stupid girl?" Lady Margery demanded impatiently. "I have not finished talking yet and you should not by any means consider yourself mistress of this house."

"Until Max chooses a new mistress, I most certainly

am," Veronica stated flatly, enjoying Lady Margery's gasp. "The port and cigars follow the fruit, but if you wish to commit the solecism of sharing that course with the gentlemen, you should not perhaps flaunt your position in society."

Veronica got herself through the door into the salon before she turned to Mercia with an apology on her lips.

"But that was so well done of you," Mercia said with a wicked smile. "I demand to have lessons."

"If you take lessons from Veronica," Dora said, watching to make sure the footman closed the door, "you will be treated to many exciting meals."

"But it was not well done of me to snipe at a guest," Veronica admitted with a twinge of conscience.

"It was not well done of Lady Margery, begging your pardon, Mercia, to defy the customs of the house," Dora stated.

The door opened then, so no more was said. When the gentlemen entered the room, Max was not with them. Veronica guessed he had gone for a walk to cool himself down before tonight. She immediately began to feel overheated.

"I have a slight headache," she lied. "I think I will abandon you early tonight."

"No doubt it was all that rich food you stuffed yourself with," Lady Margery said viciously.

"Oh? I had thought it was the incessant chatter," Veronica replied, drawing chuckles from Dora and George. She would have to remember that line to tell Flurry.

Veronica did knock on Flurry's door and wished her a good night, yawning so blatantly that Flurry would never suspect she did not plan to sleep at all. Painting usually did wear Veronica out, but tonight she felt wonderfully alive and hungry in spite of the good meal she had eaten.

Veronica had no sooner locked her door and lighted a candle than she stripped off her clothes and let her thinnest of nightdresses fall down over her shoulders. Then she went to the window to look at the stars until Max came.

"Vee," he whispered from beside the oak tree. "Are you alone?"

"Of course I am alone. Did I not make an assignation with you?"

"I am coming up," he announced.

It was wonderfully romantic for Max to enter by the window, but a bit of an inconvenience. They would have to contrive some other meeting place for tomorrow. Odd, they had not yet accomplished this night's lovemaking and she was already anticipating meeting Max in secret again. How easily one fell from grace when the bait was as tempting as Max.

Max was so focused on Veronica he made a misstep on the stout lateral limb that reached to within a leap of her sill. He slid off and hit the limb hard with his side, only hanging on by one arm and that on his injured side.

"Max! Hold on. I am coming out." Veronica hiked up her nightdress and threw one leg over the sill.

"No. I shall just let go." He glanced below him to the yard.

"Do not be an idiot," she whispered frantically. "You will break both your legs."

"Wait," Max gasped. He got his other arm over the limb, and with a deal of squirming and an obviously painful effort he ended up straddling the limb.

"How badly are you hurt?" Veronica gasped.

"Just scraped." Gingerly he stood up and walked toward the window. He dropped inside with less than his usual grace, and when Veronica hugged him he groaned.

Veronica stood back and pulled Max's coat open to see blood on his shirt. "Flurry was right. You will kill yourself one day with your antics." Veronica made him sit on the bed while she eased his coat off and began unbuttoning his shirt. She thought Max was breathing rather hard and that surely his ribs were broken, but when she lit more candles and looked closely it was apparent that he had scraped his entire side but not caused any fractures. The golden light slid seductively over the ripples of his torso. He was so different now. The skinny ribs and thin arms of the boy were gone. There was before her a man with powerful arms and chest muscles. She had already painted his portrait thus far and wondered if it would be cruel of her to demand to see the rest of him in his injured state. Lightly she smoothed salve along the bruised area, touching him as little as possible, but drawing a gasp from him all the same. Her hands shook as she wound gauze about his ribs and tied it off. She thought of delaying their meeting for another night but did not think she could make it through another day without knowing Max the way she wanted to. She began to undo the buttons of his riding breeches.

"Vee, what are you doing?" Max asked warily. His breath smelled not of wine but of strong whiskey, and it was intoxicating to her.

"Undressing you and putting you to bed. You are not going by way of the tree again."

"I only do that to make an entrance," Max said slowly. "I can leave as easily by the door."

"But I do not want you to." She resumed her careful work.

"Perhaps this was a warning to you, a reprieve before I ruin you."

"Perhaps it was a warning not to waste any more time."

"Do not start something you cannot finish." He grasped her hand and held it to his crotch so that she might feel the urgency of his arousal.

"I want to finish it," Veronica said. "I want to see you, all of you."

"Are you sure this time, Vee? It must be your choice."

"Yes," she said desperately as she pulled off first one boot then the other. He stood and let her strip the rest of his clothes from him.

"Well?" he whispered.

"You are . . . magnificent." Her words caressed him, yet he tilted his head in suspicion.

"Are you speaking as an artist or as a woman?"

"Both." She embraced him gently, avoiding the ribs and felt the warmth of his hands moving up and down her back through the thinness of her nightdress. Then he began kissing her breasts again, that wonderful sensation that last time had preceded Flurry's violent entrance. But Flurry was fast asleep; no one would come between them this night. She reached for the hem of her gown and pulled it over her head, letting it fall to the floor.

She watched the candle flames set Max's eyes to glittering as he looked her over. His eyes alighted on the key.

"The key to your heart, lady?" he asked, running one finger from it down on a line between her breasts and finally to her mound, where he twisted it in the curls there.

Veronica gasped and drew closer, pressing her aroused breasts against his naked chest.

"Oh, Veronica, do you know anything at all about this?" He sat on the bed again and pulled her toward him.

"Max, I have bred horses the better part of a decade. I know all about it," she said as she straddled him.

He laughed and embraced her, cupping her buttocks in his hands appreciatively. Veronica thought over the dangers, few enough at this time of month for her. If she were breeding a mare, this would be the least likely time of the cycle to bring her to the stallion. How wonderful that humans still desired each other even when the woman was not in estrus. She kissed Max, bearing him backward onto the coverlet.

"Horses are somewhat different than men, Veronica."

"Fortunately." She wiggled on top of him, drawing a moan from him, but having no luck placing herself so that she could descend upon his shaft, and she was beginning to get desperate.

"Allow me," he said, gently rolling her onto her back and sliding a hand between her legs. She arched her back by instinct and gasped in amazement that his mere touch in that area could cause her such a jolt. She lay down, trying to calm her heart and fanned her hair out on the pillow so that it would not be caught under them. Max lay beside her, kissing her cool flesh with his hot lips and playing about inside her with his fingers until she became wet. She had the most overwhelmingly heavy feeling, as though there was something inside that she wanted out. No, there was something she wanted in. Max poised himself over her, his arm muscles alive and taut, his member engorged and hot where it touched her flesh. His progress was at first so slow and halting that she reared against him with impatience.

"So much for being gentle. I think you are too used to watching stallions at work." He began thrusting and she wrapped her legs about him in the fear that he might become dislodged. She could see the sweat glistening on his brow as he drove vigorously into her. This was incredible. She had no idea of the hunger she had been holding in check. Her internal muscles craved him, did not want to release him. The spasms of pleasure assaulted her again and again. Each time he rested until she had ceased trembling. She had no idea how long they had been at it, longer certainly than any stallion and mare she had ever seen. But perhaps time stretched out where so many parts of your body were engaged at once. Max gasped and swelled inside her to the point where she wondered if she had hurt him. But he chuckled then as he extricated himself and lay beside her to cradle her head on his arm and kiss her again.

"Have you hurt your ribs or . . . or anything?" she asked with some concern.

"No, I feel wonderfully well and sleepy."

When his regular breathing gave the proof to this, she pulled a coverlet over them and cuddled beside him. The only time in her life when she had felt such intensity was while she was painting. She had been substituting her art for this. That was the only way she could think of it now. Max had ruined painting for her in a very real way. It would be work from now on, not a passion. It would be second choice.

It was nearly dawn when Max awoke. He remembered instantly where he was and looked across at Vee. She was sleeping on her back with her long hair tumbled about her and her hands curled up by her face like a child. He had been wondering about the key and carefully untied the ribbon so as not to wake Vee. Then he pulled the covers up to her chin. Once he had the key in his possession there were a limited number of places to try it. It was clearly too large for her jewelry box, so he started with the largest trunk first and the latch clicked open. He was stunned. Did he indeed look like that? Either he was a handsome fellow or Vee loved him very much. But it was only half finished . . . of course, she needed to know what the rest of him looked like. He should be offended that her artistic needs almost rivaled her physical needs, but he was not. He could foresee many interesting paintings in their future married life if he let Vee find the time.

He carefully put the painting away and locked the trunk, placing the key in Vee's open palm so that she would know he had seen it. He slid off his sapphire ring and slipped it onto her finger. It was much too large, of course, but he wanted to claim her somehow as his wife now that they were finally one. Would she understand what this meant, a promise that they were to be together forever? It amazed him that they could have fallen in love so completely in just a few short days. He had a feeling Vee never did anything by halves and that, once his, she would never forsake him no matter what he did. He must live up to her estimation of him.

After he dressed, he kissed her lightly on the forehead and let himself out into the silent hall, creeping down the stairs to his new quarters so silently even Mustafah could not have heard him.

§ 12 §

Veronica slept so late that she thought she must have missed breakfast altogether. But there was a cup of chocolate and some scones on her bedside table. Flurry was such a dear. She was disappointed that Max had not awakened her, but she enjoyed the secret pleasure of what he must have thought of his painting. She threw on her oldest clothes and completed the work, getting so engrossed in her painting that Flurry was rapping on her door to warn her of luncheon by the time she was finished.

She was disappointed that Max was not eating and wondered where he could be. As soon as Flurry was safely disposed in the library with a book, Veronica took her flower basket and went in search of him. Now they would have to make plans for tonight. She began to wonder if actual marriage might take the excitement out of seduction, but no, not with Max. He was not in the stable, the breakfast parlor, or any of the gardens. She was almost in despair and thought of taking the riding trail around Byerly, but she had no idea which way he had gone and might miss him. So she waited on one of the benches at the back of the garden, her peach dress artfully draped. Normally she would have decried wasting so much time, but she was feeling quite lethargic and peaceful.

She saw him coming out of the woods before he caught sight of her and her longing came just as desperately as it had before he had made love to her. Was it possible for today's desire to exceed that of yesterday? His face was peaceful and speculative as he gazed about the garden, but when he saw her his eyes lit with excitement and he ran to her, his booted feet crunching through the gravel. He tossed his walking stick aside as she stood up and he caught her to him in a laughing embrace. She reveled in the feel of his strong hands as they pulled her against him, then slid down for a more intimate hug.

"What did you think of my surprise?" she asked shyly.

"Magnificent. I hope I was not a disappointment to you." He put her down, caught her face between his hands and kissed her briefly. "Come, Vee, we must somehow fill the long hours of the day. Have you eaten lunch yet?"

"Yes, but you have had nothing all day, and you have missed the meal."

"It does not matter," Max said with a sweeping gesture. "The servants will feed me now if I command it."

They had gone scarcely halfway to the house, hand in hand, when a carriage pulled up around the weedy drive and disappeared from their view as it made for the front entrance. It was a post chaise and pair, which economy led Veronica to believe that one of her sisters had arrived unexpectedly. Much as she would rather have slipped in by the back door, she led the way around the house to the front, intending to dutifully greet her.

"Who can that be?" Veronica asked, stopping to regard the two women, one old and one young, who were being helped out of the equipage.

"Oh, my God." Max groaned. "Vee, you must go inside. Let me take care of this."

Veronica could see the haunted look in his eyes and wondered how two women visitors could put him in such a sweat. "Who is it, Max?" Veronica asked, worried at the bereft look he cast at her.

Dora was striding out of the house to greet a woman as ponderous as Dora was angular and a prim young lady of about Mercia's age and coloring.

"Lady Eustace and Henrietta," Dora said, accepting a peck on the cheek from each of them. "How are you both keeping? Here is Max coming now."

Dora proceeded to introduce the guests to Veronica and Flurry, when she came outside. Veronica could not make out why Dora would invite extra company at a time like this. No wonder Max was scowling so badly. He barely tolerated their relatives.

"I thought we might look for a visit from you in London," Lady Eustace said to Max, "but Dora wrote us that you had come home. I must say, we did not expect to have to come the whole way to Byerly to see you."

"I did not expect it either," Max agreed grimly. "Etta, we have much to discuss," he hissed.

"I know, Max," Etta agreed wholeheartedly.

Veronica looked curiously at Max. She had so often stood as a buffer between him and the world in his younger days that she was tempted to intervene and keep him from saying anything cutting. But she was out of the habit of it, besides not knowing the source of his anger.

"It is a large house," Lady Eustace observed as she pointed with her cane. "How many servants?"

Though this question was directed at Max, Veronica stared at her and answered. "I do not see that it signifies how many we have." She was angry at the kind of remark she might have expected from one of the family, but not from a complete stranger.

"No matter. Now that we are here everything will be put to rights."

"Mother, I do not think they know," Henrietta suggested.

"What?" Lady Eustace asked in shock. "You mean you have neglected to announce it, Max?"

Dora stepped in. "Max has the most shocking memory. Ten to one he has not told anybody."

"Told us what?" Veronica almost shouted.

"Miss Eustace is betrothed to Max," Dora said proudly.

Veronica felt her pulse beating in her ears the way it did when she awoke from a nightmare, and her vision blurred for a second. When it cleared she was staring at the embarrassed face of Miss Eustace. Veronica whirled to face the patently outraged Max, commanding him with a tilt of her head to own up to it, if it were true.

"It is true," said Max with gritted teeth. He stared defensively at Veronica, expecting an outburst.

She was too proud to give him that satisfaction but was having trouble trusting her voice. "There is no wonder, really," Veronica said finally, turning her back on Max. "We have been so caught up in talking over the past, we have scarcely given a thought to the future. You must come inside and rest before dinner," Veronica chattered almost hysterically.

"Yes, that is best. Tomorrow will be time aplenty for

seeing the house," said Lady Eustace, taking Veronica's
arm and leaning on it possessively.

Henrietta followed them meekly, looking expectantly
back at Max, but Max did not take her arm. By now all
but one of his minions stood in a respectful line awaiting orders. Max gave these in a clipped barrage of Hindi
before glancing savagely at his mother and following
the others into the house.

Dora gave a chuckle as she turned to Flurry. "That
has spiked his guns, has it not?"

"If that was your intention, you have certainly
achieved it. But why do you wish to make Max angry?"

"I wish to make him live up to his responsibilities."

"I had no idea Max was saddled with that particular
responsibility," Flurry said sadly.

"Knowing Max, he would delay matters until Etta has
lost her looks."

"Is the engagement of long standing?" Flurry asked,
starting to walk toward the door.

"Ten years."

Flurry turned her head in surprise. "Why, Miss
Eustace could have been no more than a child and Max
not so very old himself."

"She was seventeen. Old enough to know her own
mind. It is a good match, an old family, well connected
in every part of the country."

"Is she an heiress then?" Flurry asked, knowing the
question would not offend Dora.

"Not to speak of, but that does not matter now that
Max has come into the title."

"It should be interesting to see what comes of this,"
Flurry said ominously. She suspected Dora was cham-
pioning Etta because Dora thought she could control
the girl and her mother. Dora had spent the better part

of her widowhood trying to control Max and had not once succeeded.

Suddenly Dora halted and asked in a fierce whisper, "You have never said anything to Max about his birth?"

Flurry drew in her breath, knowing she should be offended. "I promised that I never would. And I am a woman who knows how to keep her word."

"Good, let us see if Max knows how to keep his."

Flurry followed Dora into the house feeling her long association with the Strake family dragging at her heart. What a lot of secrets they all had, and like it or not, she was a party to many of them.

Half an hour later Veronica paced Flurry's bedroom, looking almost feverish, but maintaining a brave front.

"Was there ever anything to equal the shock?" Veronica asked with false bravado. "And Lady Margery does not know yet, only that we have unexpected company. You will not miss dinner tonight, will you, Flurry?" Veronica asked with too much excitement, too much brilliance in her eyes.

Flurry made her turn around so that she could make some adjustment to the ribbon Veronica had used to gather up a top knot of curls. "You are upset by this, as you should be."

"Does it show?" Veronica asked anxiously, turning to peer at herself in the mirror.

"I do not know what Max promised you, but he never should have led you on, knowing he was already betrothed. Thank God you were able to keep him at arms length until we found this out."

The climax of the lovemaking flooded back through Veronica's mind so powerfully that she swayed with the remembrance of it.

"Veronica, are you feeling faint?"

Veronica shook her head, trying to discard the image of her and Max together. "Arm's length is not nearly far enough to be from him now. I had no idea what to say to those women. Was I incoherent?"

"No, I found myself very proud of the perfect composure with which you greeted such unwanted company." Flurry arranged a stray lock of Veronica's long, black hair along her shoulder. "And such apparently unwanted news."

"That is all that matters then, that I did not show how angry I was." Veronica sniffed back a tear. "Really, it is Max I am angry with. What business had he kissing me . . . like that, if he was engaged?"

"What business had he kissing you at all?" Flurry consoled.

"Well, he acknowledged her, however grudgingly, so it must be true." Veronica looked at Flurry, hoping for a contradiction, knowing Flurry would have ferreted out this information.

"The alliance was contracted when he was not yet twenty."

"I suppose he might still have been stupid enough to do such a thing in those days." Veronica wandered to the window and leaned her head against the cool glass, wondering how she could have been so deliriously happy an hour ago when her whole world now lay in ruins at her feet. And the worst barb was that Max had lied to her, had promised marriage when it was not even a possibility.

As she ran over in her mind their many passionate encounters she came to that unfulfilled night when he had been brushing her hair. He had stopped himself from making love to her because . . . how had he put it?

There was a matter that stood in their way. What had he been planning, to post up to London and jilt the girl, then pick up a special license and come back to marry her? How could he do this to her?

"Did you always plan for him to come back and marry you?" Flurry asked casually as she arranged the gray curls that coiled at her neck.

Veronica jumped and turned to look at Flurry. "What? Oh, you mean years ago. I never planned that."

"Your father obviously did. Why else would he leave you so unprovided for?"

She considered this for a moment. "I suppose Papa might have had it in mind. Perhaps he thought only to make the opportunity for Max, if he wanted it. But I think Papa might have consulted me about it."

Flurry watched her compassionately. "It does seem odd that John trusted Max more than he trusted you."

"Why did Max not tell us, Flurry?" Veronica asked angrily, turning to gaze out the window into the gathering night. "If not when it happened, then anytime this decade would have saved me the embarrassment of today." Her voice broke on this last sentence.

"If you are going to cry, I suggest you get it over with before dinner," Flurry said lightly. "I do not take many meals in the dining room. And this one is likely to be trying enough without you turning into a watering pot in the middle of it."

Veronica had started to gasp with unshed tears and Flurry walked to her and hugged her as she had when Veronica was a little girl. She could not remember anything short of a broken bone that would reduce Veronica to tears, but Max had. And Flurry would not soon forgive him for that.

After ten minutes Flurry helped her wash her face in cold water and proclaimed her fit for company.

"I suppose I needed to do that," Veronica said with a sniff.

"I was sure you did. Do you think you will be able to face Max?"

"Without throwing something at him?" Veronica asked bitterly. "I am not sure. I shall try to pretend he just arrived as well, and I do not care a farthing what he does with his life." Veronica tidied her hair in the mirror and schooled her face into an expression of boredom. "I shall pretend I am merely a disinterested observer tonight. Just think how much more fun it will be to watch them all squirm."

"As Dora has been planning?" Flurry added.

"Yes, as though she had sprung a trap," Veronica agreed. "It is rather like a drama unfolding on the stage and we have no idea what will happen."

"No doubt this is what comes of having an actress marry into the family," Flurry jibed. "Are you going to let her stage-manage this dinner tonight?"

"No, I suppose I should have made more of a push to tell Aunt Margery, but she has not endeared herself to me either. Come, we must not be late." Veronica threw Flurry's shawl about her spare shoulders and picked up her knitting bag. Flurry smiled encouragingly, and they went down the stairs hand in hand.

As usual, Lady Margery and Mercia were the last to gather in the drawing room before dinner and Veronica rose to go into the dining room as soon as they had all entered and been introduced. Lady Margery was as puzzled as her children by the sudden arrival of company. Veronica sat at the foot of the table opposite Max, feeling bereft. He was replacing her as mistress here after he had taken everything she had to give. She was trying as hard as she could to hate him, but she could not. Not without loving him at the same time. The confused mixture of emotions was making her slightly dizzy. She sighed and carefully unfolded her napkin and placed it on her lap.

Lady Veronica Strake was still mistress of Byerly Hill and still in control of herself as well as the meal. Now that she thought about it, it might be more amusing for the revelation of the engagement to take place where there was wine to be spilled and food to be choked upon. Veronica looked on with satisfaction as the first course was laid. A tremendous pike was poised on its belly on a platter in front of Max. Dressed with the head on, it stared at him with a baleful eye as though its present condition was all his fault. Max, likewise, looked with disfavor on the dead fish as well as on the servant who had placed it there. Karim bowed himself away from the table to return with a dish of oysters for Max's right elbow and a platter of lamb chops for his left. A brace of chickens on a bed of rice and a tureen of soup occupied the center of the table, along with an aromatic pie, a sauceboat full of gravy and a sirloin of beef. A leg of mutton and a dish of curry were placed closest to Veronica and she smiled approvingly at Rajeev and Karim to make up for their master's frostiness.

The mix of dishes was so obviously a kitchen competition between Cook and Max's staff that Veronica could not help but grin at him. Really, nothing could be more delightful; a bountiful table, good wine, and the prospect of a once-in-a-lifetime performance. And Veronica was pleased with the way Max's eyes always drifted miserably to her, never to Henrietta. His inattention was giving Lady Eustace the fidgets.

"And what brings you to Byerly, Lady Eustace?" Aunt Margery asked.

"Why, to see Max, of course." The woman held her knife and fork suspended in the air as though she meant to carve him up.

"I only mean that this is a mourning period for the family," Lady Margery replied. "I wonder that strangers to us should be invited at such a time."

Lady Eustace glanced at Lady Margery's brilliant green silk and Mercia's frivolous pink frock as she chewed a mouthful of beef. "You are in mourning?"

Veronica snorted and nearly choked as Max rolled his eyes impatiently. Flurry glanced between the two of them, no doubt wondering if either or both of them would disgrace her.

"There are matters to be settled about my brother's estate, a lot of boring paperwork," Lady Margery stated. "Max will not be much of a host."

"That would not surprise me," Lady Eustace said, reaching for her wine glass. "He has not been much of a—"

"Then there is the inventory," Veronica burst out. It was not that she wanted to prolong Max's agony, but surely there was a better moment to let the news out. When Max looked at her it was with a gratitude that melted her heart. How could she be angry at him? Whatever he had done he must have had a reason. Veronica looked at the girl. She was ordinary looking, with her flaxen brown hair and blue eyes, and she was too quiet for Max, too cold a girl. "Perhaps you would like to help me with it, Henrietta?"

Henrietta opened her mouth to answer when her mother interrupted. "I am sure Etta would be delighted to help you in any way."

Lady Margery looked shocked. "Veronica, do you really think so? Someone not even in the family. Such a matter should be private. I am sure Mercia would be happy to assist you."

"I do not quite see why an inventory is needed," Lady Eustace said, "but if it is the thing to do, we had best start tomorrow."

"Really, Veronica, you should not have mentioned it," Lady Margery whispered urgently, knowing full well the others could hear her.

"But I have been putting it off and I do need help with it," Veronica continued. "You know very well Max will not be able to concentrate on separating household goods from works of art. He will just get impatient and tell me to take whatever I like."

"It should be obvious—" Max started to say.

"I do not understand," Lady Eustace said. "Art works?"

Dora intervened. "Veronica has been left John's art collection. I must say I had not thought there would be a problem distinguishing that from the household goods, but if you think so, Veronica, then I will help as well."

"Nothing has been decided yet," Lady Margery insisted, staring pointedly at Dora. "You are acting as though everything is to be packed up and sent away. Max may very well marry."

"Yes, I know," Veronica said emphatically, rolling her eyes. She happened to glance at Mercia and saw a flush rise to the girl's cheeks. Suddenly the situation was not so much fun anymore. Margery had intended for Max to marry Mercia. What a stupid idea, when it was Mercia's hysterical lies that had gotten Max banished all those years ago.

"What is the matter, Mercy?" George asked, interrupting his concentration on his dinner to stare at his sister. "You look like you are about to be sick."

"If anyone is about to be sick," Max said, "it is Freddy. How can you stomach all that greasy beef?"

"There is nothing wrong with it," Freddy replied, taking a breather and helping himself to another glass of wine.

"If I had my way, flesh would never be served on my table," Max said obstinately. "It is a disgusting custom."

"Not eat meat, you mean?" Freddy asked around a bite of beef.

"Yes, now that I think of it, the advantages are tremendous, a healthful diet and a lot less company," Max enunciated.

"Max, do not be ridiculous," Dora commanded. "You are making Etta uneasy. Recall, she has never been treated to a display of your temper. This is certainly not the time to do so."

Max glared at his mother and was about to resume his attack when Freddy said, "Got you there, Max."

Freddy immediately cringed as Max hefted a platter of ham with a glare that would have terrified one of the footmen. Veronica thought she would indeed get to see food flung across the table.

"May I have some ham, please?" she asked.

Reluctantly Max let go of it and Karim brought it to her with a bow.

"What precisely is in this art collection?" Lady Eustace asked. "Is it valuable?"

"Mother," Etta pleaded in a whisper.

"That is the problem," Veronica said. "The household goods are left to Max with the house, but I am to have Papa's art collection, whatever that means."

"We all know what the will says," Lady Margery recited coldly. "I hardly think this is the time to discuss family business."

"Why not?" Lady Eustace demanded. "We are as close to being family as matters."

"What?" Margery spit the word out disdainfully.

"Well, Etta is," Lady Eustace replied.

"Is she some sort of natural daughter to my brother John?" Margery asked with her nose as high in the air as possible.

Max broke into laughter, his eyes dancing wickedly at the absurdity of the situation. Veronica choked back a giggle and dared face no one but him. As their eyes met across the table it was as though they forgave each other and made some silent pact to survive this, as friends at least. Veronica still held her napkin over her mouth as she desperately sought Flurry's eyes for guidance.

"How dare you?" Lady Eustace demanded of Lady Margery. "Etta is engaged to Max."

Lady Margery gasped but did not choke. She did look as though she were going to explode for she kept taking in air without releasing any. Freddy was choking for her and George stared at Etta in stunned silence. Mercia looked as though she were going to faint.

"Max!" Lady Margery demanded, when she had at last found her voice. "Is this true?"

Every eye turned toward Max. Most of them were accusing. His mother looked on him with grim satisfaction and Flurry with resignation. Veronica knew she had every right to be angry, but sent him a look that told him it did not matter what he had done. She would help him anyway.

"It is true," he said, taking a large gulp of wine.

"I told you there was no point in coming," Freddy reiterated.

"Shut up, Freddy!" Lady Margery demanded. "Dora, how long have you known about this?"

"Dearest Margery," Dora said, putting on her most dignified expression. "I have known of the engagement any time these ten years. We were waiting to announce it when Max was back in England. Etta is like a daughter to me already."

"Of all the nerve!" Margery threw her napkin down with such violence she overturned her wine glass. "I would have thought . . . I would have thought you would have married within the family, Max."

As the wine stain spread across the white cloth like blood on a shirt, Veronica calmly laid her napkin over it, wondering if the family would go on wounding each other forever. It came as something of a shock to realize that she was not guiltless in this herself.

Max glanced at the blushing Mercia, whom Lady Margery had intended to be his bride, and then stared at his aunt, his lips curling into a mocking smile. "That sort of inbreeding is abhorrent to me," he said.

Veronica turned her head to stare at him, once again surprised. If he really felt that way, then why had he promised to marry her? She and Mercia were equally distantly related to him. Max had a great deal to answer for.

"Inbreeding!" Margery shouted. "I have had enough. Mercia! Come with me."

A silence fell after the exit of these two, and Veronica wondered, hopefully, if Freddy would follow them. But this was prevented, and the greatest part of the awkwardness covered, by the removal of the first course and the presentation of the delights of fricassee of rabbit, lobsters, glazed ducks, cheesecakes, dishes of oranges in a sauce, lemon custards, and wine sours.

"You do not suppose they are leaving entirely?" Veronica asked, as she helped herself to a crispy piece of duckling, her appetite not at all ruined by the recent scene. She was not used to feasting in this way, and she did not feel like ruining such a delightful meal by thinking very hard on any other matter.

"I doubt it," Max said. "My aunt has not vented her outrage to the full yet."

"Mother has every right to be offended," George said with a twinkle in his eye. "To keep such an alliance from the rest of the family smacks of, of . . ."

"Prudence?" Max asked.

Veronica laughed to have Max back in form. Whatever argument she had with him was between them and would not be aired in front of the rest of the family. She had not liked to see him surly and insolent, like the young boy who had left them. Perhaps he had been tricked into the engagement and had hoped Henrietta would grow tired of waiting for him. It would explain his lengthy absence from England. She glanced at Etta, who was looking rather woeful, but Veronica felt no compassion for the woman who unknowingly was going to make them both very unhappy. When it looked as though the ladies were all finished, Veronica rose and the remainder of the females followed her to the drawing room.

Veronica could not imagine what the men found to say to each other. She did listen with half her attention in case they came to blows, but she heard only Freddy's grumbling from the other room, with an occasional answer from George or Max.

Lady Eustace stationed herself and Henrietta on the

sofa by the fireplace. Henrietta took up some sewing from a bag that had been placed there. Flurry got out her knitting and Veronica settled down to a comfortable period of speculation as to what was going forward above stairs where she could from time to time hear her aunt's strident voice, probably ranting at Mercia. The girl could never tell her mother that her accusation of Max attacking her had been a lie. And probably Aunt Margery could not understand why Mercia did not make more of a push to attach Max. At least some of the sins of the Comishes were coming home to roost.

"Am I perhaps sitting in your place?" Henrietta asked when Veronica's eyes came to rest on her.

"What? Oh, no. I never get to sit there," Veronica answered. "I am so glad you made yourself at home."

Lady Eustace stared at Veronica. "This should have been her home years ago."

"If not for the elusive Max," Veronica said, choosing not to be offended by Lady Eustace. "We have not seen him in twelve years and he used to spend every summer at Byerly."

"Some feud with his uncle, I heard," Lady Eustace said with a nod.

"Yes," Veronica agreed. "Max simply does not get along with everyone."

"Face it, Veronica," Dora said, after a hearty sip of the cordial she had rung for. "Max does not get along with anyone, except perhaps Miss Flurry. Tell me, Flurry, what hold you have over my son." Dora folded her hands across her tall frame as though she were preparing for a long lecture and Veronica thought it unfair for her to put Flurry to the blush when her only real hold over Max was love and caring.

Flurry looked up from her knitting and stared at

Dora a moment before she answered. "It is very simple, really. He shows a marked attention to me, a servant, in order to discompose everyone else. That is why I am permitted to reprimand him without drawing his ire. Besides, I have known him since he was a boy, so he has no dignity to protect in front of me."

Veronica listened to this half-truth with great awe, for she knew the affection between Max and Flurry to be genuine, approaching that between a mother and son. And yet Flurry had touched on Max's use of her in a philosophical way that explained his behavior and gave offense to no one. All this Veronica noted with admiration and smiled at her companion.

Flurry returned a superior look as if to say, *See, that is how it is done.*

The men joined them finally, bringing into the room on their clothes the odor of port fumes and cigar smoke. They were none of them in a very civil mood. Max offended the Eustaces by sitting next to Flurry and Veronica.

George went to stand looking out the window and Freddy searched futilely for a pack of playing cards. Veronica knew precisely where they were, but did not rouse herself to tell him, since it would occupy him awhile to look for them.

"Ah, here they are," he said at long last. "Who is for a game of piquet?"

George did not even answer him, so Freddy looked hopefully toward Veronica.

"I will play you, but not for money," she replied reluctantly.

"Where is the sport in that?" he whined.

"I will play with you," Max offered.

Veronica smiled her gratitude at Max for taking on

the onerous task of keeping Freddy amused. It was like having to watch a child, a large petulant child.

"Pound points?" Freddy asked eagerly as he pulled chairs up to a small table.

"Agreed," Max said as he deliberately took the seat from which he could trade looks with Veronica. Perhaps this is all they would ever have from now on, an exchange of understanding glances. She rocked in her chair as a wave of desire washed over her. How could she still want him so strongly when he had just betrayed her so cruelly? Make what excuses she would, Max had played the villain in this. Yet, she knew full well that if he came through her window tonight she would take him into her bed and believe any lame excuse he gave her. She licked her dry lips and tried to disguise her distress from Max and Flurry.

There was little conversation to interrupt the slap of the cards and the grumbling of Freddy when he lost. George occasionally chuckled from the window seat. Veronica was beginning to feel sorry her father had sold the pianoforte. Suddenly Margery and Mercia came into the room, the one looking determined, the other abashed.

"I have decided to forgive you, Max," Lady Margery said formally.

"For what?" Max asked in a surprised tone that only Veronica knew was not genuine.

"It is a testament to your upbringing that you would not even know," Lady Margery said with a condemning look directed at Dora. Then she sat down within his field of vision. So, too, did Mercia, who was still looking embarrassed, especially after she was nudged by her mother.

"Max, why do you not tell us of your travels?" Mercia

suggested. Her voice still sounded nasal from her recent bout of weeping.

"What possible interest could you have in the East, your family being so down on trade?" Max replied caustically.

"We need not talk of business matters," Mercia persisted. "Surely you saw many sites that would be of interest to us all."

"I was not out there on a grand tour. It was hot, insect-ridden, and not infrequently dangerous," Max summarized as he dealt the cards and took up his hand.

"Max once visited the Great Wall," Flurry prompted.

"Yes, I remember that from your letter, Max," Veronica said. "You allowed it to be tolerably impressive, but a shocking waste of manpower."

"Did I say that? How presumptuous of me. But that was years ago. I made a lot of indiscreet pronouncements when I was green."

Henrietta raised her head from her sewing to stare at the back of Max's head, and Veronica thought it was ill-done of Max to poke at the girl in that backhanded fashion. Miss Eustace was not stupid, at any rate. She knew when she was being insulted.

"What about India?" Lady Margery asked. "You must have liked India."

"It has a certain fascination, if you like cobras," Max allowed.

"Max has a plantation in China," Dora said, before draining her glass and exposing a wrinkled expanse of throat.

"Madagascar," Max corrected.

"What is the difference?" his mother asked.

"They are thousands of miles apart, Mother."

"Damn!" Freddy said, throwing down his cards. "I used to be able to beat you at this game."

"You used to be able to beat me at a lot of things," Max said petulantly.

"Max can talk to elephants," Veronica said, jumping into the breach, just as Freddy was about to start arguing.

"Talk to elephants?" Freddy was startled into asking. "Whatever do you mean?"

"He knows their language, or rather they know some of—what is it, Max, Hindi?" Veronica asked. "So Max can drive an elephant himself."

"What has that to do with anything?" Freddy demanded.

"Nothing," Veronica said with a smile. "I just thought it was interesting."

"It would be to you. You talk to horses," Freddy said contemptuously.

Veronica cast her eyes down at this reminder of all she had lost, and when she glanced up again she saw that Freddy was biting his lip. She was surprised that he had enough conscience to be sorry for the remark.

"At least you used to," Freddy continued. "Max, are you ever going to refill the stable?"

"To what purpose? I shall be at sea the better part of the time."

"What?" Lady Eustace asked. "You do not mean to live here?"

"No," Max replied without looking at her, shuffling the cards again.

"But what about Etta and me?" she demanded.

"I suggest you live in town. Byerly is extremely isolated from everyone you know."

"Have you got a house in town?" Lady Eustace asked.

"No, I stay at a hotel when I am in London." Max dealt the cards with practiced flicks.

"Max!" Dora chided. "Stop being so provoking. Where are they to live?"

"With you, Mother, since you love them so well."

They finished the hand and Max rose and left before Freddy had toted up the points. Veronica went to stand looking over his shoulder.

Freddy spun in his chair. "I do not mean to cheat him, if that is what you are thinking."

"I was merely wishing to know how he did," Veronica replied.

"He is forty pounds the richer."

"He never used to be able to play cards when he was in a temper," Veronica observed. "In some respects Max has improved."

"That is a matter of opinion," Freddy said.

There seemed nothing more to be said or settled. Lady Eustace owned to being tired and Dora took the mother and daughter to their rooms. Veronica sought her own bed soon after that, bidding Flurry good night in the hallway.

Veronica sensed him in the room. Perhaps it was a whiff of brandy fumes or just the window curtain billowing on the night breeze. But without looking for him she set her single candle on the dressing table and quite deliberately undid the buttons of her dress. She let it drop to the floor and stepped out of her slippers. Placing one foot on the small upholstered stool she undid one garter and slipped her stocking off. Let him watch and regret what he had lost. She hiked her chemise the whole way up her thigh to remove her second stocking and ignored the gasp she heard. She reached under her shift to untie the string of her drawers, dropped them to the floor, and stepped out of them. She whisked a thin nightdress out of a drawer and was about to proceed with the torture when her eyes fell on the trunk. He had never seen the painting finished. This would kill him.

She pulled the key on its silken cord from between her breasts and stooped to unlock the trunk. His ring was on the same ribbon, a reminder that he had meant well? Throwing the heavy lid up she carried the painting to her easel and stood it in place to rest one elbow on her other palm and critically look at it. The pulse began beating in her nether regions and she had the sudden feeling that this might be a mistake. There he was, all of him, as she remembered. And in spite of what he had done she wanted him still. How was it possible that her body could be so at odds with her mind? And there was another part of her, her foolish heart she supposed, that loved Max unreservedly no matter what crime he had committed.

His arms reached around her to cross over her breasts and make her gasp as he grazed them, bringing her nipples to full arousal. Had he any idea at all of his effect on her? She hoped not, or her tightly reined in needs might once again be her undoing.

"I wanted to explain," he said softly, his voice broken with regret.

"You have much to explain, Max," she whispered.

"My mother forced me into the match when I was nineteen. It was the only way she would turn over to me the money my father had left me. I never expected it to actually come to marriage, that Etta would wait for me."

"I suppose you sold yourself for that plantation in Madagascar," Veronica said, trying to ignore the hand that slid down her thigh.

"I was not of age, you see, and would have had to wait more than a year. The opportunity would have passed me by. I saw Henrietta only three times in my life. The last time was . . ."

"The day you asked her to marry you," Veronica concluded as she stared at the mocking portrait. "You lied to her just as you lied to me."

"But I did not know it would matter to me someday. I knew I would have to marry someone. I thought one woman was much like another. But that was before . . ."

"Before what?" Veronica whispered, swaying in unconscious response to the seductive stroking of his hands.

"Before you grew up." Max undid the ribbon that held her hair and ran his fingers through the curls to arrange them on her shoulders. "Are you very angry with me?"

"For not telling me, yes, I am angry with you," she said sadly, wondering if he knew how much his playing with her hair affected her.

"And for seducing you?" he asked, pulling her hair back to kiss her ear. "There was no time to tell you. They drove up and Dora was introducing them before—"

"No, you fool." Veronica spun on him impatiently. "I mean why did you not tell me ten years ago? It would not have been such a shock. I might have gotten to know her." Veronica's voice broke. "I would never have let you love me."

"Would that have made it easier?" Max's voice rose. "Would that have meant we would not have fallen in love? If you believe that you are a bigger fool than Etta."

Veronica tore herself out of his embrace and folded her arms across her breasts. "I am most certainly a big-

ger fool than she. You have not played fair with either
of us."

Max leaned on the small table. "I told you I had
something to attend to in London. It was my intention
to buy her off. That is still what I plan."

"Buy her off?" Veronica stared at him. "You make
these plans, Max, as though people are servants who
have to do your bidding. I do not think it will be so easy
to get rid of Etta as you think."

"Trust me," Max pleaded.

She turned away from him, facing the door. "I do not
think I can anymore." When she heard the scrape of his
boot on the windowsill she knew he was gone and
regretted it. If she had not been so stubborn she could
have made love to him tonight. How foolish to deprive
herself just to hurt him. But Max, for all the hardships
he had suffered, was spoiled in one important way. He
had always had her unreserved, perhaps undeserved,
devotion. Now he would have to earn it.

*B*efore breakfast the next morning Veronica was gathering some violets for a bouquet, admiring the way the dew beaded iridescently on their lavender petals. Flurry would adore having these in her bedroom. Flurry still involved herself in the affairs of the house, overseeing the spinning of the wool into yarn, helping Cook and the kitchen maids with jam making, or assisting in the small greenhouse when there were seeds to start or plants to repot. But more and more Flurry spent her afternoons reading alone in her room.

Veronica heard a footstep and looked up to see Etta approaching her purposefully across the back lawn. She was hoping it to be Flurry and her disappointment must have shown in her face, for the girl hesitated, then commenced her trek toward Veronica. The girl had a deal of courage . . . or something. Etta showed to more advantage with the benefit of a night's rest and her own choice of costume. Where the vivid blue gown of the previous evening had left her washed out, today's blush pink muslin emphasized Etta's glowing complexion, perhaps her only outstanding feature. Veronica glanced down with regret at the brown walking dress she had chosen. But she was in mourning again, this time for Max's integrity.

"I have been wanting to speak to you," Etta said, falling into step with her.

"I did not know you were an early riser as well," Veronica said, wondering if all her mornings were to be plagued by unwanted company.

"It seems the thing to do in the country," Etta said lamely.

"You wanted to speak to me?" Veronica prompted.

"My mother and I were under a misapprehension. We thought everyone was aware of the engagement, and they thought us just idle visitors."

"That is my fault," said Veronica, stooping to pick a violet. "I should have warned Aunt Margery so she could have had her hysterics in her bedroom. But I was in shock myself. Max only just came back to us after a long absence. I thought, well, never mind what I thought. It never occurred to me he might be entangled . . . I mean . . ."

"Entangled?" Etta asked, her face becoming pinched. "Are you implying that I entrapped him?"

"No, of course not," Veronica said frankly. "You are not at all his type." She ignored Etta's gasp of outrage. "Dora trapped him. What I cannot make out is why. What advantage does this marriage hold for Dora? She still does not become mistress of Byerly Hill, which was always her ambition."

"I have no idea what you are talking about," Etta said, her cheeks flaming. "Dora has always been most kind to us."

"Then perhaps I should remind you that she was

once an actress," Veronica said unkindly. "I forget that myself sometimes, that she cannot really be trusted."

"How dare you? Am I to take it that you are a permanent resident here, that I shall be obliged to provide a home for you and your companion after I marry Max?"

"Certainly not," Veronica said, trying to stand tall enough to match Etta's height. "Miss Flurry and I plan to take a tour of the Continent."

"And after that?" Etta demanded, with her arms folded. "Dora spoke of you as though you were some sort of invalid, closeted here forever. Now I find that is not the case at all, that you are a perfectly healthy young woman who should be out seeking a husband of her own."

Veronica read into the comment *instead of stealing mine,* and bit her lip lest the encounter turn into a cat fight. "Before, I had to stay here to assist my papa in his studies."

"Did you not have a season?" Etta asked.

Veronica stared at the violet bunch with the whorl of green leaves she had so skillfully fashioned around it. "Papa was too busy with his work and the estate to bother with anything like that, and I did not feel I could leave him without both me and Flurry."

"What about your Aunt Margery?" Etta persisted. "Surely she could have introduced you into society."

"I think Papa suggested it to her. They had a terrible falling out seven or eight years ago. I thought that at least we would be rid of them as guests for a while, but as soon as Mercia was launched into society, their visits resumed."

"Is it possible that she felt the competition would be too stiff?"

"What do you mean?" Veronica asked.

"You are far prettier than Mercia," Etta said critically.

Veronica stared at her. "A compliment from you comes as a surprise."

"It was not a compliment, but I would be stupid not to acknowledge the fact." Etta began to stroll through the rose garden, where the greenery was awakening and one or two early varieties were attempting to bud. "Mercia's come out was not a success. Her portion was so very uncertain, you see. I had the feeling all the young men were waiting to see how much she would get when her uncle died. Lady Margery gave it out that he was in very ill health."

Veronica's head jerked and her heart set up a flutter of beats. The thought that anyone could want her dear sweet papa dead just for the sake of an inheritance . . . and for Etta to mention it so coldly as though it did not matter. "Papa was never sick until the very end. That is why Max and I think he was murdered," Veronica said, ruthlessly pruning an encroaching bramble from their path.

"Murdered?" Etta stared at her in disbelief, then broke into cruel laughter. "Max is a fool. He is only saying that to get your attention."

"Do not quote Dora to me," Veronica said angrily. "I know Max a great deal better than either one of you, and his judgment is to be trusted." Veronica thought Max would be shocked to hear her defending his veracity.

"Just how well do you know Max?" Etta asked suspiciously.

Veronica was tempted to tell the girl they were lovers, but she could see no particular advantage to playing that card just yet. She did know one thing. Etta was not the woman for Max. She was too scheming by far, and besides . . . she did not deserve him. "Did you have offers?" Veronica blurted out the most cruel thing she could think of. "How terrible of me to ask. I am as bad as the rest of the family."

"I do not mind. I had several, but I was engaged to Max by then. I did not need to accept anyone else."

Veronica nodded. "Did you have an offer you would have accepted if you had not been engaged?"

Etta thought for a moment. "Perhaps, if I had my own way," Etta said wistfully, "but that is all past history. I no longer regret waiting for Max, even though he looks at me so menacingly with those piercing eyes."

"You are afraid of him," Veronica said past the lump in her throat.

"In a way," Etta licked her lips in a manner that made Veronica uncomfortable. "He does not even like me, but I will marry him." She began to walk back toward the house.

"But if you dislike him you will both be miserable," Veronica pleaded.

Etta paused and looked back over her shoulder at her. "I do not dislike him. I shall be able to tolerate him. I do not even mind that he will be away much of the time."

"But you do not love him," Veronica said with conviction.

"Of course not," Etta replied.

Veronica had never felt more frustrated in her life. She was turning to walk off her ire with a tramp in the woods when she spotted Max coming across the yard. He saw the two girls and stopped, giving them both a piercing look before tucking his walking stick under his arm and striding toward the house. Max had looked worried, Veronica thought. Perhaps he deserved to worry, but Veronica felt as though she had betrayed him by consorting with the enemy. It did not matter to Veronica that this was not true; it only mattered that Max might think so.

"What would it take for you to leave?" Etta offered. "I have no money of my own . . ."

Veronica stared out over the garden toward the woods that rimmed Byerly Hill. Did she really want to leave now that Max was here? The answer was simple. She wanted to be with Max, wherever he was, even if in the most stinking jungle. But she answered truthfully. "I must finish the inventory and dispose of my art collection, but—"

"I will help you with that," Etta said impatiently.

"But I must also find out who murdered Papa, and for that I will need Max's help."

"And if you satisfy yourself that he died a natural death?" Etta asked expectantly.

Veronica felt herself backed into another corner. It had been unwise of her to talk to Etta at all without first finding out what Max planned to do. She was used to dealing with unscrupulous women, but she had been surprised to discover the trait in one so young. "We shall see," Veronica said and left Etta standing alone in the garden by the sundial. Veronica turned to look at the straight-backed young woman and sincerely wished she would turn to stone as hard as her heart.

Veronica thought Flurry's appreciation of the bouquet would be the high point of her day. Breakfast was a silent affair, with George and Freddy staring at her and Etta as though they expected the two of them to come to blows. Dora was smiling far too much. Lady Margery, Mercia, and Henry Steeple must still be abed.

She could hear voices arguing in the morning room, so she assumed Max had bearded Lady Eustace there before breakfast.

When she could no longer stand the punishing silence in the breakfast parlor, Veronica voiced the thought that they might as well begin the inventory in the library where most of the art collection and a good bit of the porcelain was stored. She found pen, ink, and a fresh ledger, then asked Henrietta to describe the items to her as she listed them in her fine handwriting. They could hear shouting in the morning room now, but since this was not such an odd occurrence at Byerly, Veronica merely asked Etta to repeat, whenever her description of some bowl or vase had been drowned out. They had done the enclosed glass cabinets that Veronica thought comprised the valuable part of the collection and moved to the objects on the mantel when Flurry came in, closed the door behind her, and rested against it as though she were prepared to keep out some evil force.

"So there you are, girls. I had pictured you both cowering in some quiet corner until the storm blows over."

Veronica shrugged. "Oh, I am so used to it I can very nearly ignore it and Etta may as well adjust. Are there only Max and Lady Eustace in there or did I hear Aunt Dora as well?"

"She is there, too, reminding him of his duty, of his word of honor, and of the ironclad agreement she had him sign." Flurry came to look over Veronica's shoulder at her penmanship.

"Poor Max," Veronica said, looking up at her. "You are feeling for him, are you not, Flurry?"

Flurry nodded sadly and said, "You must understand, Miss Eustace, that Max grew up here at Byerly. He and

Veronica and I are very close. I suspect it is the breaking up of that relationship, more than anything, that is causing him to have second thoughts about his marriage."

Veronica did not at all feel this was what was in Max's mind, but she silently thanked Flurry for the lie.

"I may have need of a companion for my mother," Etta said. "I should be glad if you wished to stay, Miss Flurry."

"A gracious invitation, my dear, but it will not do. I am attached to Veronica, and Max and Veronica must never live under the same roof again." Flurry pressed her hand on Veronica's shoulder to lessen the pain of this.

"That I can see for myself," Etta said as she fingered a Chinese vase. "What exactly is your relationship to Max, Veronica?"

A lie was the first thing that came to her mind, but a harmless truth was what she uttered. "Max still thinks of me as the companion of his childhood," Veronica said. "He would think nothing of crawling in my window in the middle of the night to report that he had killed a badger. He would expect me to be delighted to hear it."

"Hm, still, we cannot have that—"

Just then the argument moved down the hall. Dora and Lady Eustace burst into the library.

"Is it true what he says?" Lady Eustace demanded of a startled Veronica. "Does he love you?"

Veronica shot Etta a guilty look. "That is what he said," she admitted slowly, without rising from the desk.

Max appeared in the open doorway, looming over her, his black hair disarranged by him raking his hands through it. He said nothing, but just stared at her as though his heart was about to be torn out.

"You must be insane to be engaged to one woman and in love with another," Lady Eustace accused. "If you loved her why did you offer for Etta?"

"Because Vee was a little girl the last time I saw her. Besides, I was forced into proposing when I was under age." Max's jaw twitched with the effort he was exerting to keep his temper in front of Veronica. "I only fell in love with Vee when I returned to Byerly. I will never love you, Etta," Max said, shifting his gaze to the tall girl.

"I know that," Etta answered steadily from her position by the mantel.

Max stared at her, gaping. Veronica thought it must be beyond his comprehension that a woman would take him under those circumstances.

"This is absurd," he said, shaking his head and causing Veronica agonies of desire with his untidy hair. She wanted to fling down her pen and run to him.

"Why will you not let me buy back that marriage contract," Max asked, staring at Lady Eustace as though she were mad. "I have no intention of fulfilling it, and you cannot make me."

"But as long as the contract stands it would be illegal for you to marry anyone else," Dora said.

"Do you think that will stop me? What do I care if Etta sues me for breach of promise. The court of common pleas cannot make me marry her, just give her a settlement, which is what I am offering."

"But you will have to stay in London until the case comes up," Dora replied.

"I have contacts that can assure me a speedy trial," Max countered.

"And when it comes out that Veronica is the cause of the disquiet between you and Etta . . ." Dora left the threat unfinished.

"She would never be received in any English household, not even in Paris or Italy," Flurry said.

Max glared at Dora. "And I suppose you would see that it did come out."

"There is only one solution," Lady Eustace pronounced. "Veronica will have to go."

"No!" shouted Max. "Byerly is her home."

Lady Eustace went to stand beside Etta. "She must leave if there is to be any peace in this house."

"I know, Mother, and we have begun the inventory. I am doing everything I can to speed things up," Etta said.

"Damn and blast your inventory!" Lady Eustace shoved a vase off the mantel and watched it shatter on the hearth with satisfaction. Flurry gasped and Max stared at the broken pieces. Dora blew out an impatient breath.

Veronica let her aching heart throb for a moment, then courageously broke the fragile silence. "Was that Sèvres or Chinese?"

Jolted out of her trance, Etta bent down to examine the shards. "Sèvres, blue," she reported in a choked voice.

"Yours, I am afraid," Veronica said as she dipped her pen and scratched it off the list.

Etta stood, gritting her teeth and taking a deep breath. "If you ever do anything like that again, Mother, I shall make *you* leave," Etta promised, her cheeks flaming with a blush that spoke more of anger than embarrassment.

"What are you saying? Abandon me, who has fought for you all these years?" Lady Eustace's hands fluttered at her bosom, leaving Veronica hoping that she was not one of those women who went easily into hysterics.

"That does not excuse such behavior, Mother."

Flurry nodded her approval and Etta continued. "I will marry Max, and Veronica and Flurry will leave. But we have a deal of work to get through first and shall all be cooped up here together for some time. If that does not agree with your notions of propriety, then you may leave, Mother. I will not hear another word about it."

"I was overcome, child. Do not talk such foolishness." Lady Eustace's handkerchief appeared, followed by unconvincing sniffles.

Etta evaded her mother's attempts to draw close to her. "If you are going to dissolve in tears, I suggest you do it in private. Veronica and I have work to do here."

Veronica stared at Etta, and Lady Eustace retreated in disorder, giving vent to some gusty whoops of despair on her way out.

"I begin to think you will be a match for the relatives after all, Etta," Veronica said grimly.

Max stared at Veronica in disbelief. "Have I nothing to say in the matter?" he asked in shock.

"Apparently not," Dora said with approval. "Etta, child, I did not know you had it in you, and after only a few hours in Veronica's company."

"I had nothing to do with it," Veronica said resentfully.

"You sit here, dividing up the house," Max accused, "as though that is all that matters when our future is at stake."

Veronica thought that it were best to lull Dora into a false sense of victory until Max could reason with Etta, but Max was too angry at this point to think rationally about anything. She sent him a speaking look. "Somebody has to take a practical view, Max," Veronica returned. "We are trapped, all of us. I consider it undignified to struggle."

"Veronica, this is not like you," he pleaded, coming toward the desk. "You were always on my side."

"Max, there is nothing I can do about this." Veronica stared at his face, seeing the doubt, knowing that she was hurting him. Perhaps if he could not escape Etta's snare, it would be best in the long run if he thought she had fallen out of love with him.

"But you care, I know you do." He grabbed her hand.

"I must not care. Caring about you is far too costly," Veronica said, pulling her hand out of his grasp.

"I see." He dropped his hands to his sides. "I shall leave you then, as my company is so unwelcome." Max turned on his heel and strode out, pausing in the hall to look left, then right, as though he did not know which way to turn. Finally he went out the front door and Veronica breathed a sigh of relief.

"Do you think he believed me, Flurry?" Veronica whispered with a trembling lip.

"I almost believed you," her mentor said as she rested her hands on Veronica's shoulders and kissed her on the cheek.

"That is settled, then," Etta said.

Fighting the strong impulse to go after Max, Veronica cleared her throat. "Let us continue." One or two tears splashed down onto the ledger but she blotted them up and hardened herself to face the possibility of life without Max. It was as though Etta had been sent to bring everything to a head, so it was difficult not to blame the girl.

Max was at fault, to be sure, for not confessing the truth to Veronica, that he was already engaged to be married, but Veronica could not help but look upon

Aunt Dora as the real agent of her downfall. Why had she kept the engagement secret all these years and only revealed it now when it hurt the most? Why had she let Veronica have the chance to fall in love with Max only to wrench him from her?

But probably Dora was so caught up in her own scheme to finally be able to live at Byerly she was not even aware of the attachment Veronica had for Max. Veronica thought she had finally figured out why the marriage was so important to Dora. In London she was a nobody, but in Surrey she was one of the Strakes of Byerly Hill. The local gentry and country people treated her with a respect she did not even get within the family. And her charitable works, taking baskets of food to the poor or buying vestments for the church, though they had cost her little, made her a woman of consequence in the area.

It was pathetic that Dora had no higher ambition, but Veronica had always supposed her aspirations harmless enough. Of course, with Max married to Etta Eustace, a family well connected in every part of the country, Dora's consequence would be much inflated.

No, Dora had no idea of anything more between Veronica and Max than an old friendship. If that were true, Veronica decided she must do everything she could to hide her love for him. If her pride was all she had left, then she must guard it, at least.

14

Max stood once more on the cliff overlooking Oakham. The problem was not Vee and her foolish attempt to hide her love from him. Did she really think he could not see through her bravado? The problem was Etta. He did not know the girl well enough to know what would persuade her to release him. He had already offered Lady Eustace a reasonable amount in order to buy back his agreement. She might in time be pressed to settle. And he had assumed that Etta would obey her mother. Now it looked as though the girl was not an innocent pawn of her mother and his mother, but a woman of considerable determination.

Very likely a trip to London would have been a wasted effort on his part, rather than a simple matter of breaking an engagement. He did not know much about such matters, but he did know a contract when he saw one, and that was what he had signed a decade ago. Of course, if Etta were to break off the engagement, his mother would no longer have any reason to shred Vee's character. Or if Etta could be found guilty of some indiscretion. . . . He toyed in his mind for a moment with the idea of recruiting someone to seduce her, but desperate as he was to be rid of her, such a tactic smacked so much of the sort of trick Freddy would serve someone that Max discarded the idea.

He found no answers in the smoke drifting up from Oakham, no inspiration along the wooded trail as he walked back toward the house, kicking an occasional stone out of his path. He needed to determine first of all what his options were, what would happen if he simply carried Vee off and married her. There would be a scandal, of course, and that would hurt Vee. Was there a way he could stop Dora from executing her threat? He needed legal advice. Much as he shunned the company of lawyers, especially Henry Steeple, the man was at least handy.

The other thing he must do was lift Vee out of her dejected mood. She had been so gay yesterday morning when she had met him in the garden and now she was without hope. Max paused to look out over the sheep farm as he broke out of the woods. Byerly was like a Garden of Eden now that he had fallen in love with Vee. He had never thought much about women before. He had been thinking only of building his business and doing daring deeds. His ultimate goal, he supposed, had been to impress Uncle John. He had found himself at a loss when he learned of the man's death. But his intimacy with Vee had filled the void in his heart and gave him visions of a happy future he had never imagined before.

After contemplating marriage with Vee there was no way any other woman would do. Perhaps if he told Etta that she had better take the money or she would get nothing. Somehow he had a feeling she was not the sort of woman to take an ultimatum. Etta accepted his love for Veronica as though it was a weakness for strawberries. Perhaps that was because Vee, without meaning to be, was on Etta's side.

There was, of course, his mother's threat of a lawsuit, as though he cared about that. A breach of promise suit might be expensive, but the damaging thing was how long it would drag out. He had been bluffing about having the pull to get the suit pressed through the courts quickly. If he made any such attempts the judges might delight in delaying the process. Not only did he want Vee now, but he must leave England in a few weeks to attend to other affairs.

Sooner or later Etta must be brought to capitulate and accept a settlement. Money was all she wanted anyway. He would get his way. All he had to do was find the right price.

After lunch Etta and Veronica resumed their inventory under the watchful eyes of Lady Eustace, Dora, and Flurry. Veronica was glad they had finished with the main part of the collection since Lady Eustace seemed likely to challenge every claim, even to a miniature Veronica herself had done of her father. It was very wearying.

"It is worth nothing in terms of money," Veronica said, "But I do not see why you want it. You did not even know Papa."

"But it is not a work of art," Lady Eustace insisted to Veronica's chagrin.

Etta was looking impatiently from Veronica to her mother, obviously wanting to get on with the inventory and get rid of her unwanted rival.

"I think it would be best if I were to give it to Max," Veronica said finally. "He liked Papa and then it will stay in the house anyway."

"Have you ever painted a miniature of Max?" Etta asked.

"He has never sat still long enough," Veronica hedged, for she had painted his dear face a dozen times and now she had her full-length portrait of him hidden away in her chest. She could feel her face suffuse with color and her pulse start to pound in her nether regions at the thought of Max, both the painting and the man.

"Veronica, are you feeling unwell?" Flurry asked.

"What? Oh, I suppose I am a little tired. Perhaps we can continue this tomorrow."

"I should like to have Etta's portrait taken," Lady Eustace hinted. "Not a miniature, but a large portrait."

When Veronica did not fill the awkward silence, Dora chimed in with "Veronica can do it for you. You love to paint, is that not right, Veronica?"

"Yes, of course. I am just not sure I will have time . . ."

"Flurry and I can continue the lists," Dora said, ruthlessly volunteering Flurry's time.

Veronica sighed and turned to Lady Eustace. "Do you wish to help us pick out what Etta is to wear?"

"The celestial blue gown," Lady Eustace said without realizing how insipid it would make her daughter look.

"Very well. I shall get my paints and go to the library," Veronica agreed. "The light is best there in the afternoon."

Half an hour later as she set up her easel, Veronica looked a question at Etta as the girl entered wearing a blush pink gown. Veronica did not know whether she was relieved or disappointed. And she was not altogether sure she was up to this, studying her rival in minute detail. But sometimes one could do a painting that revealed the true character of the person—avarice, pride, intolerance—and the subject was completely satisfied, not realizing that the face they saw in the mirror each morning was not as pleasing to the rest of the world as it was to them.

It would be interesting to see if Etta was clever enough to see her own flaws or to know when Veronica was pointing them out to her. As an intellectual challenge it was not how Veronica would have chosen to spend her time, but it was not so deadening as cataloging every item in the house.

Dora should do well at that since she never missed a chance to run things. But she had waited so long to get Byerly. Since her husband Robert, Papa's heir, had been younger by a decade, it had not been unreasonable to assume that Dora would have had her turn to reign at Byerly. Her husband's early death had come after some whispers of divorce and had put an end to such a possibility. Veronica supposed Dora could not be blamed for making up for lost time by using Etta to get Byerly for herself.

Etta posed for an hour in the library in her petal pink dress and with the one plain wall as a backdrop. Veronica did her preliminary sketches as Etta discussed what her wedding dress would be like and how she would have her hair done that day. But they had to quit when Etta was commanded to her mother's room.

Veronica could already see a division there, and a tendency of Etta to prefer the stronger Dora for company rather than her sickly mother. That would lead to trouble, but it meant nothing to her. She really did not care about anything very much anymore.

After cleaning up her paints, Veronica felt she must go for a walk before dinner or perish for lack of fresh air. She had been used to riding morning and afternoon. A walk was something of a substitute. She had not thought this talk of the wedding would so depress her and could not keep from thinking that if not for Dora's scheming and the existence of Etta, it might now be her own wedding she was planning. She wanted to scream, *Max is going to marry me,* but the more the others planned Etta's wedding, the less likely Vee's own marriage seemed to her.

But then she had once some plans of her own, to travel when she had enough money and expand her commissions to include landscapes and famous buildings as well as portraits. She knew that she would overstep the line of respectability someday, with or without Dora's gossip, but since she could not have Max, she did not care to marry anyone else.

She walked as far as the sheep farm, which was looking as idyllic as any foreign scene, and felt the first suspicion that travel held not as much appeal for her as it once had. When she tried to analyze why, she realized she had been planning, or at least hoping, that she would meet Max on her voyages. Now that he was here, what was the point?

When she came back through the gardens she was not surprised to find Max similarly engaged in a walk, but to find him in close conversation with Henry Steeple was so unprecedented as to set her back on her heels. And they were not arguing. Henry was talking and Max was nodding with a furrow of concentration on his brow as though he agreed. This was very strange. Perhaps Max had finally convinced Henry that her papa had been murdered and he was agreeing to allow an investigation.

It occurred to her that she had bartered with Etta for

Max's help in solving that mystery, but it now came home to her as she held her hand over her fluttering heart that working closely with Max on anything might prove a temptation beyond her power to resist him.

And her secret self prompted her not to resist him, to take him into her bed, and to forget about the rest of the world. She wet her lips and ran over in her mind their most successful encounter. She had it memorized, every move, touch, and sensation. The very thought of it was enough to make her writhe and sigh. It was a potent memory and one she never trotted out unless she was alone and likely to be so until her pulse ceased pounding.

Veronica excused herself from dinner, something she had never done before, and Flurry whisked into her room when one of the housemaids brought her a tray of soup, bread, and fruit.

"Are you truly ill?" Flurry asked.

"No, of course not, but I am very weary of all of our houseguests. I think I shall read my travel books and begin to plan our journey. If you dine with them, save any really good tidbits of gossip for me."

"I shall give a good account of myself," Flurry promised. "This painting tires you out more than you admit."

"Perhaps it is the subject I find tiring. Etta is not so demure as I had originally assumed, and hearing every detail of her trousseau has given me a lively disgust of her."

"Poor child. It was not well done of Dora to land you that particular commission."

"But it is likely to be the only time I have Etta at my mercy," Veronica said with a wicked smile. "I can grow her nose by half an inch, add jowls if I wish, or make her squint like a bag of nails. Since I do not expect to be paid for my efforts, there can be no repercussions."

Flurry chuckled as she whisked out of the room, and Veronica did indeed get out her guide to Italy, but she could not stand the suspense of wondering if Max was going to come to her or not. When it was eight o'clock by her small mantel timepiece, she roused herself and, grabbing a shawl, crept down the back stairs to walk about the outside of the house.

She could hear voices in the drawing room—Freddy's whining, George's occasional rumble, and a high-pitched chatter that could be any of the women except Flurry. For the first time she felt like an outsider here at Byerly. She had always been on the inside trying to keep their relatives out. Once she left she would only return to this house as a guest, and not a very welcome one. But that was what she had wanted only a few days ago. Max had changed all that.

She was making her way around the small greenhouse, holding up her skirts from the damp grass, and wondering where Max was when a shadow passed across the light from the library window and she spun to stare in that direction. Now who would be in the library at this hour? The window was thrown up and Veronica jumped back.

"Vee?" Max called. "What are you doing out there with no cloak?"

"Walking," she said as though she had been caught in a guilty act.

"Shall I come out or do you want to come in?"

Since he reached down his hands to her the temptation was easy to overcome. "I shall come in if you can pull me up. It is colder than I thought."

He took her hands and pulled her up in a single lithe

movement to sit on the sill. Not content with that, he picked her up and held her, staring at her in a puzzled way.

She knew she should protest and make him put her down, but she wanted this closeness since it was all they were likely to have.

"You were looking for me, were you not?" he asked, his mouth so close to hers that she could almost taste the aroma of the port.

"Why would I be looking for you?" she asked, trying to keep from trembling, trying to ignore the urge to press her lips to his, to invite his hands anywhere they chose to go, to let him do anything with her.

"God, Vee, if I so much as kiss you it will be all over. I will never be able to stop myself." His intense gaze raked her and she felt that lethargic longing to take him to bed with her.

"You are right," she managed to say. "A kiss would never be enough now." She had one hand pressed against the center of his white shirt and she could feel his heart pounding urgently against his chest. Did he experience these uncomfortable surges just as she did? It suddenly occurred to her that if she were suffering, so was he, and probably more so since he was the agent of their unhappiness.

"You're arms are icy," he whispered. "Where is your shawl?"

"I must have dropped it on the lawn. I do not feel the cold much."

He stood her on her feet and stripped off his coat with one lithe movement, settling it around her shoulders like a queen's cloak. She did not need it, but she would never have said so. "Thank you, Max. What are you doing in here all alone?"

"Reading Uncle's papers—or trying to. It seems you have no time to help me. You are too caught up with that damned inventory. I thought that besides working on the Nonsuch puzzle, there is just a possibility that I may find something to give me a clue as to his murderer."

"I told Etta I could not leave here until I knew who had killed Papa."

"Good girl, Vee. That gives us time to plan, as well. Let us make a start, then."

"It is far better than spending the evening listening to the Comishes snipe at the Eustaces. And by the way, I wish you would not set them on each other."

"Why, I do not know what you mean," he said with a grin as he took her hair that had been caught under the coat and gently freed it, as though he were tidying a child.

Veronica swallowed hard and stared at those so competent hands. She remembered all they had done in the past for her; bridled her horse, restrained an anxious colt she had been trying to break, taught her the pianoforte, even baited a hook.

"Why are you staring at my hands?" he asked lightly.

"Because I remember them so well," she said. "Whatever you did for me, you always said, 'Watch me, Vee, and see how it is done, for I will not always be here to help you.' And you were right."

"Forgive me, Vee. I had not meant to leave you for so long." He pulled a chair close to the desk for her. "I had not meant to make such a muddle of our lives, either." Max seated himself behind the desk, clearly regarding this separation as necessary to getting any real work done.

"I feel such a failure," Veronica said. "I have scrimped

and finagled and managed to keep the house together for you, but *they* cheapen all I have done and make me feel like nothing. And now the thought that one of them may have poisoned Papa frustrates me beyond measure."

"Not to mention Etta showing up to displace you. Do not let them depress you. I promise you we will find the killer, we will find the treasure, and we will send the Eustaces packing along with our unwanted relatives."

"You suddenly seem very sure of yourself, Max. This is not just one of your moods, is it?"

Max cast her an accusing look. "No, I begin to see some ways out of our difficulties. I was thinking only in terms of our own resources, but we can buy advice, Vee, call in the experts. Tomorrow I go to see Dr. Morris and I have gotten some legal advice that makes the situation with Etta seem not quite so tangled."

"Is that what were you talking to Henry Steeple about?" Veronica's voice rose in disbelief.

"I was asking him about that contract I signed when I was underage. And stop looking at me as though I have taken leave of my senses. He is a solicitor, after all." Max got the brandy bottle out of the cabinet and poured himself a glass. "Here, take a sip of this to warm yourself up."

"I find myself not placing much confidence in Steeple's advice," Vee said as she took the brimming glass from him.

"It would have been better had I tried to break the contract long ago." Max set the decanter on the desk in front of her. "All these years of no action could look like acceptance on my part."

"But you were not even in the country most of that time," Veronica said. She took another small taste from

Max's glass and felt the pleasant burn flow all the way to her stomach.

"A point in my favor, according to Steeple. And the fact that I was frequently on government business . . ."

"But Steeple is one of *them*. Why would you ask him and why would he help?"

"Money, for one thing." Max took the glass from her and a much larger gulp, then set it within her reach again. "I would as soon pay him as Etta, and he thinks he can find me a legal way out of this tangle. And he is willing to threaten Mother with an action for slander if she so much as opens her mouth about it."

"Legal and honorable?" Veronica asked, feeling her lips heat from the brandy.

"Beggars cannot be choosers. I shall settle for legal. Steeple seeks a means of avoiding a scandal for the family, but he needs to run to London to consult his law books."

"Do you care about scandal?" Veronica asked, reaching for the glass again and that warm insensible glow it produced.

"Not the slightest bit."

"Good, for there is certain to be one when we find out who killed Papa." She felt Max's strength and certainty flowing into her like a strong drug.

"I begin to think it could not have been Steeple," Max said. "Uncle's death caught him short and I suspect he has had to do some scrambling to get the books in order."

"Then how much can you trust him to help us, Max?"

"He will have to do until I can find someone else. Now it seems to me that Uncle John's murder is somehow caught up in his quest for the treasure, if for no other reason than the killer needed money desperately."

"Perhaps they thought that in his delirium he might tell what he knew," Veronica said, trying unsuccessfully to focus on the pen Max was holding.

"I had not thought of that. Who did you say nursed him?"

"All of the women at one time or another. Of the men, only George, who sat with him when he was sleeping."

"That is neither here nor there." Max listed the few names. "George I do not suspect at all."

"I must agree with you there," Veronica said, feeling so relaxed that she thought perhaps the awkwardness of being alone with Max had gone from her. "How far have you read through these notes?"

"I have not made any progress," he said, pushing one composition book toward her. "You decipher and dictate. I will take it down."

Veronica managed to focus her eyes on the page. "This notebook starts with a description of the south facade of the courtyard. I do not know where he gleaned it from. He was rather careless about noting his sources, I am afraid. 'So many statues and lovely images'—no, that's lively images—'there are in every place, so many wonders of absolute workmanship and works seeming to contend with Roman antiquities, that most wordily'—no, worthily—'it may have and maintain still this name that it hath of Nonsuch.' "

"How on earth did you get all that from his scratching?" Max asked, taking another look at the page.

She smiled at his compliment. "Perhaps the brandy helps. Now that I think of it, that has the ring of Camden. I bet we shall find that someplace in his *Britannica*."

"You truly know about these things, Vee," Max said in honest admiration.

"Papa had to have someone to share his enthusiasm."

"I am sure you were a joy to him," Max said, making a note about Roman influences and looking appreciatively at her.

"Oh, do you think so, Max?"

Veronica's worshipful look touched him. She was the only one who could make him feel as though he were capable of anything, and he could feel confidence flowing into him like water into a well. "Yes, I am convinced of it." Her large brown eyes seemed far too misty and as an afterthought he tossed off the rest of the brandy so that she could not make herself tipsy.

"This bit is more descriptive," Veronica said. " 'In the middle gatehouse, which outdoes the first gatehouse by a tower, a clock, chimes, and six horses'—no, six horoscopes—'the projecting windows might be thought to have been hewn from the heart of the rock. Everywhere there are kings, caesars, sciences, and dogs.' " She held the book at arm's length and corrected herself, "He must have meant gods for that last word. He credits this to Watson. Oh, Max, would it not be wonderful if we could uncover some unknown bit of Nonsuch Palace? A statue or a fountain, even if it were worth nothing."

"I would build a shrine around it to Uncle," Max said with a smile. "I want to do everything as he would have had it. Nothing is to be changed in this house, except that the servants will have more help and a more generous pension than even Uncle could provide. And we will finish this research together and perhaps publish it. Would he have liked that?"

"Max, he would have adored it. I knew you could not abandon Byerly. I knew you had not changed so terribly much." Veronica dropped the notebook to get up and staggered toward Max. He leaped up and caught her as she fell. When he pulled her to her feet she threw her arms about his neck and kissed him.

The door creaked open. "I thought I heard voices in here," Flurry challenged.

"Join us, Flurry," Max invited without taking his arms from about Vee's unsteady waist. "We are doing research."

"I will not even acknowledge that with a reply," Flurry said stonily. "Veronica, you should be in bed."

"I quite agree," Max said, bending to return Vee's kiss, savoring the lush warmth of her lips, now that he knew it could go no farther than that.

"Her bed," Flurry corrected.

Veronica sighed and pulled away from him. "She is right, Max. It will be fun to work together, but I am far too tired to do any more tonight." Veronica let go of him and was making her unsteady way toward the door when Flurry pulled Max's jacket off her shoulders.

"Yours, I believe, Max." She tossed the garment onto the desk.

Max picked it up and watched them go. He buried his face in the coat to catch the last scent of Veronica, not her perfume so much as Veronica the woman. He must somehow fix it so that they could be together forever.

He looked around the library where he and Veronica had spent so many hours discoursing with Uncle John as Flurry sat knitting. It and the bedchamber comprised the end of one wing of Byerly with windows punctuating two of the book-lined walls. The wall that separated it from the bedroom was lined with glass cases of artifacts and racks of drawers underneath. The books and

the heavy velvet drapes made it a remarkably easy room
to heat. The leather-covered furniture made it snug. He
wondered that his uncle had never had shelves built
along the fireplace wall, but the plaster was badly
cracked. Perhaps it was too unsound or the heat would
have been bad for the paper. He would go over the
house from attic to cellar and send for workmen to pre-
serve everything. He would buy back Veronica's horses
and . . . and what?

And somehow marry her no matter what it cost. He
had lived a decade with the idea of Etta as his wife and
had not been much discomposed by it. Now that he
loved Vee he found the thought of any other woman
intolerable. He loved Vee with a mind-numbing hunger
and knew he would give up everything he owned just to
have her.

15

It was still early morning, but the fire in the grate had made the library uncomfortably warm for a gentleman in a starched shirt and wool coat. Max frowned at the back of Veronica's easel. Flurry raised an eyebrow at Max as though to say he had this coming, then she went back to her knitting. From the vantage point of the window Flurry could observe both him and Veronica. Much as he adored Flurry's company in conversation, Max was irritated by the chaperonage. Each time Veronica peeked around the edge of the canvas, she grinned at Max and went back to making sweeping strokes with the crayon she used to sketch in her drawing. She hummed a piece she had often played and Max suddenly wondered what had happened to the pianoforte that used to be in the withdrawing room. Probably sold to keep the house up. Why had he not realized what was going on? His damned pride had prevented it. He always had this vision of returning to Veronica a conquering hero. Now he realized he had come too late, and he was anything but a hero.

Veronica peeked at him again, wearing one of her

father's old shirts over her dress as a smock and looking faintly like the baby she used to be, playing games behind her papa's back while Max had been trying to attend to what Uncle John was saying. Max had always threatened to thrash her for making faces at him and breaking his concentration, but he never had. Instead he had taken her to fish the streams or set her up before him on his horse to ride the wilder parts of the hilltop that was Byerly.

Veronica's impish face popped around the easel again, her dark hair piled untidily on her head with stray tendrils kissing her delicious neck. "Just as a point of information, Max, are you going to scowl the whole time? For I am about to set those lines in now and if you refuse to smile you might at least achieve a dignified stare."

This brought a chuckle from Flurry.

"Whose idea was this damned portrait anyway?" Max demanded.

"Not mine," Veronica replied. "Lady Eustace thought that since I was doing one of Etta—and I was trapped into that—it might be well to have one of matching style of you."

"Must you hum and chatter the whole while, and pull faces at me?" Max massaged the stiffness out of his neck and tugged at his collar.

"That is how I paint. And you do not have to sit there like the Sphinx. You are allowed to move."

"If I move now I shall ruin what you have done," Max said, glaring at her.

"Not at all. I am used to subjects with a little more animation, such as bowls of fruit."

"I should rather think you would want your subject to sit absolutely still so as not to change the light."

"If you were a landscape or a vase of flowers I might expect you to sit still. But you will find I take a deal of liberty with the light where portraits are concerned. That is the key to making people spring to life. That and a little liveliness from the subject."

"Come now," Max said, jumping up and coming around to look at her work. "How can it be so different from any other type of painting?"

"If I painted you without talking to you, without knowing something of you, your face would be lifeless as a corpse. I must catch that look." She shook the crayon in his face.

"What look?" Max asked, bending over her shoulder and peering at the nebulous area that would be his face.

"That world-weary, patience-stretched-to-the-limit look."

He groaned, causing Flurry to laugh outright.

"Perfect, Max," Veronica said. "Now go and sit down."

"How long does this generally take?" Max demanded as he sat and crossed his legs.

"A day or two."

"Two days? Veronica, I have things I must see to."

"Not two days of your time, silly. Only two days of my time. Once I capture you I can finish it at my leisure."

"I do not know about this wall for a background." Max craned his neck around to gaze at the bare interior wall of the library over the fireplace. "It is cracked and stained."

"But it is Byerly and it has character, like you. A few cracks and a little discoloration makes the painting more tense."

"If you want tense . . ." Max leaned forward, trying for his most menacing look, but Veronica only giggled.

"Perfect, Max, and if you curl your lip like that once more I will have you."

"Enough!" Max jumped up. "You can finish it from memory. I have to ride into the village to see Dr. Morris."

The smile evaporated from Veronica's face. "Do you go to ask about Papa?"

"Yes, I want to hear what he has to say."

"Take me with you, Max. Please," Veronica pleaded.

Max took her hand and held it between his two for a moment. "I would, but I think he might be more frank with me if you are not present. Do you understand?"

"Of course, but you will tell me what he says."

"Everything." Max strode to the door with his heavy cane and was gone. It felt to Veronica as though all the life had gone out of the room.

Flurry rose from the window seat and came to observe the work. "Yes, I think it is going well."

"All my delight in seeing Max again is banished when I think of poor Papa. I have been far too glad to see Max and far too delighted at how he has turned out. I should have been more disapproving, but it is hard when he smiles in that particular way." Veronica ran the charcoal along the line of his lips as though she were actually touching his face.

"Yes, I know. I admire your determination to keep your distance from him."

"For now, but if it turns out that he can break the contract with Etta, then I will marry him, Flurry, or just sail away with him. I do not really care which."

"You do not think that this thing with Max is not simply a passing fancy, that you will not have gotten over it in a fortnight, like a bad cold?" Flurry asked.

"If loving Max is an illness, then I am infected for life."

* * *

Max's quest for Dr. Morris turned out to be a more difficult task than he would have imagined. He followed in the wake of Morris's rounds but took comfort in the sure knowledge, derived from the man's housekeeper, that every day the doctor fetched up at the Black Horse Inn for luncheon. When Morris finally recognized in the adult Max the boy he had occasionally treated for broken bones, he invited Max to join him.

"This may not be the best time to ask about my uncle's death," Max said as he watched Morris carve an entire chicken into manageable portions.

"Damned unusual," Morris said with his mouth full, his heavy jowls working. "I have never encountered anything like it that was not a poisoning."

"So you had your suspicions," Max said, staring with disfavor at the brace of lamb chops on the doctor's side dish as he requested bread, cheese, and fruit for himself.

"And that is all I had. By what Miss Flurry told me, there was no one there who would profit by his death except Lady Veronica, and who could suspect her?"

"So you confided in no one?" Max peeled an apple with his penknife and used the same instrument on the wedge of cheese.

"And who could I confide in? That child, already distraught at losing her father? Tell her I suspected one of her relatives of murder?"

"I see your point, Doctor. The logical person to tell would have been Henry Steeple, the executor."

"You know him. He would have scoffed at the idea and warned me off it. I had no evidence to carry to a magistrate, and I did look. I searched the bedchamber, the library, and the kitchen, including all the tea tins." Morris gestured with his knife toward the row of tins on the inn shelf. "Nowhere could I find anything that would have brought on such a violent illness."

"Would a murderer likely leave it about?" Max pondered.

"You would be surprised. Of course, I had no excuse to go through the other bedchambers."

"After all this time, what do you think it was?" Max stared as Morris chewed over his thoughts.

"It was nothing classic, such as belladonna or arsenic. I know those symptoms."

"What about foxglove? There was an extensive patch of it in the ornamental garden at one time."

"Not that either. It would have quickened his heart and might have caused convulsions, but it would have worked faster. What that man suffered."

Max swallowed hard. For a doctor to remark on the pain, it must have been extraordinary. "I want to find who did this. Can you help me?"

"There is one thing you could do. Make a list of all the herbs or plants growing at Byerly that might have been used. I can compare your list with my books."

"That should be easy enough. Uncle John was a collector of specimens and old Marsh, the gardener, is still there. To be sure he will remember what is planted there, if Vee does not."

"Perhaps not as easy as you think. That rhubarb sauce you are enjoying, for instance. The stems are edible, but the roots and leaves are highly toxic."

Max paused with a spoonful halfway to his mouth. "Indeed." As the doctor continued to stare at him Max ate the bite and polished off the dish of stewed rhubarb without a flinch.

"Even if you find a poison to fit the symptoms," Morris warned, "that does not answer who."

"Leave that to me," Max said slowly.

"And even if you know who, without a confession you cannot prove a thing."

"I must know. One does not like to think someone in the family, little though you see them in the usual way, could cut down a man like that without a thought for the pain they caused."

"But unless I miss my guess, someone did and got away with it. So they would have no qualms about trying again. And they might put the poison in anything."

"Yes, I appreciate that," Max said as he took a swallow of ale.

"If I may ask, sir, who is your heir?"

Veronica had nearly finished Max's face, since she knew it so well, and she had been able to work on Etta's portrait for a few hours, though laying in the green and blue skin undertones had make her queasy. The faster she completed these commissions the less content Lady Eustace would be with her continued presence, since the inventory was nearly finished. But Lady Eustace was so dyspeptic that she did not appear for luncheon, which restored Veronica's spirits. She must remember that Max had a plan to get them out of their difficulties. She heard his carriage return during the meal and escaped as soon as possible to hear his report.

She finally ran him to earth twenty minutes later in the library. "So here you are," Veronica said, finding Max on his knees in front of the seed drawers.

"Is this all the seed Uncle dried and saved?" Max folded five seeds from one compartment into a square of paper and labeled it.

"Yes, these metal-lined drawers are the only safe place to keep any of the seeds. Some dried leaves of the medicinal herbs are kept here too. The cooking herbs are in tins in the kitchen. If not for these cabinets, we would have the mice into the seeds and nothing to plant in the spring. What are you doing?" Veronica knelt by him to look into the satchel of packets he had already prepared.

"Taking samples. I mean to find an expert who knows more about poisons than Dr. Morris. These drawers have no locks on them. So anyone could get at these."

"Yes, of course. Who would have thought that could be a worry? Max, what did he say?"

Max rocked back on his heels. "If I tell you it will just upset you."

Veronica smacked him on the shoulder. "I will be a great deal more upset if you do not."

Max closed the drawer and got to his feet. "He is convinced your father was murdered. I am sure Morris is a competent enough fellow when it comes to medicine, but not an expert at poisons, so he could prove nothing."

"Then it is a certainty." Veronica stood slowly. "Papa was murdered."

Max put his hands on her shoulders. "I will not rest until I am sure. If we can come up with a list of possibilities, then we may find a match for the symptoms."

Veronica stared at his hands and Max removed them.

"I know, if we are to make any progress at all we must focus on the problem at hand and not get distracted by each other."

"That is very hard for me, Max."

"I know, Vee. Have you got a book here that lists effects?"

Veronica went to a shelf to fetch it. "But so many of

the medicinal herbs are poisonous in large doses and I rather think the symptoms are frequently the same."

"Still we must try. Are there any plant seeds that would not be in these drawers?" Max wandered around the large room.

"Only the grains and they are kept in large bins in the barn. Also, we would not bother to save seed from perennials or anything cultivated by root division. Let me get you Papa's lists." Veronica went to the bookcase nearest the desk and pulled out a notebook. She laid it open on the desk. "You can take this with you. I see Freddy has made off with the latest garden maps. You would think he would be smart enough to make the connection between the plant lists and all those little x's."

"Do not count on it. Is there anything else I should take with me?" Max scanned the room.

"No, only my hope that we are both wrong," Vee said, wringing her hands.

"Does anyone else in the family have any knowledge of herbs or plants?" Max leaned on the desk.

"Nothing that would not be common knowledge. Papa prattled about his plant specimens all the time and no one paid much attention. Anyone could have heard him mention one as a poison and taken note of it."

"How horrible, if he was the innocent agent of his own death. He never had any suspicion that he had been poisoned?"

"He was the most trusting of souls," Veronica said, slumping into the large desk chair. "No match for this family."

"Yes, I know what they are like." Max roused himself, strode to the satchel and closed it up. "I have work to do."

"You cannot leave yet. I have not been idle in this

matter. I had a long talk with Cook, half the morning, in fact, as she and Karim prepared luncheon, which you missed. She was rather insulted by Dr. Morris's interview with her when Papa died and she recited it in detail."

"What did you find out?" Max brought the satchel to the desk and rested his hands on it.

"Dr. Morris was more pointed in his questions to her than to me, suggesting poison rather than spoiled food. She flatly denied that anything could have been slipped into a dish while it was in the kitchen and she vouches for all the help."

"Yes, but after it had gone to the table or the sickroom," Max speculated. "That is another matter."

"I know," Veronica said. "Dr. Morris could not very well have gone to the magistrate with no evidence and no clear suspect."

"I suppose he did all he could. We are in the same case. Do you suppose Aunt Margery capable of it?"

Veronica rose and walked to the window. "Even the most timid of my mares would charge and fight a dog if it were threatening her foal."

"Not for herself then, but for Mercia. What did Cook make those last weeks for your father?"

Veronica turned. "She vowed Papa had nothing but broth of one kind or another, tea, and coffee."

"Who had the ordering of the food?"

"Flurry or Dora."

Max thrust his hands into his pockets and paced. "Who stayed with him at mealtime?"

"We took turns and ate our meals in his room when we were on duty."

"But do you not see? All sorts of food went into that room."

"But none of the rest of us got sick."

"Stop thinking like an innocent, Vee. The poisoner would add it on the spot to whatever she could get Uncle to take."

Veronica could not help notice his use of the female pronoun. "You are right, Max. I have been stupid. I must try to think like a murderer or I will never discover how it was done."

"You are not alone in this." He picked up the case. "Steeple must be ready to leave by now. I will take these lists and seed samples to an expert in London. But I dislike leaving you without protection."

"I should be safe so long as I eat with the others."

"I have told Flurry to stay with you every moment. I know. I will leave my sword stick with you."

"Do not be absurd, Max. I should look a proper fool carrying that great thing around."

"Here then," Max said as he strode to one of the display cases. "Strap this dagger to your waist under your dress." He held out to her the small ivory ceremonial knife with the jeweled handle.

"I had thought that was only for ornament," she said, taking the small blade from it's silk sheath.

"I may acquaint you with its bloody history someday. I assure you, it can be lethal. I am off."

"Not so fast. One kiss for luck." Veronica put everything into that kiss, all her hopes and prayers for Max's success and quick return. When she opened her eyes he was gazing at her under his heavy lids and he looked as though he had been drugged by her lips. He lowered his face and she could feel the scrape of his beard against her cheek as he begged entrance to her mouth. If they were not careful . . .

A sharp rap at the door and a "Max," from Steeple on

the other side caused Max to hesitate, hug her tightly, then pick up the satchel and depart.

"What does Max mean haring off in this irresponsible way?" Lady Margery demanded at dinner. "Does he think our time is worth nothing?"

The dead silence with which this question was met might have been blamed on the quality of the fare, which had resulted in quieter and more satisfying meals. George helped himself to a curry as Freddy passed it suspiciously, choosing the safer ground of ham and buttered turnips.

Flurry turned her wineglass over and said, "May I please have some lemonade, Rajeev?" This filled the embarrassing gap as innocently as possible.

Veronica stared at her aunt without seeing her, wondering if indeed this rather small irritating woman could be a murderess.

"Are you sure Max did not say what he was meaning to do?" Lady Eustace asked.

"Veronica, Max is coming back?" Dora prompted.

Veronica shrugged. She was too caught up in her inner turmoil to pay any attention to Dora or Lady Eustace or even Freddy. Time was that she would have kept a fearful eye on the sideboard lest they run out of food. Now they seemed to have plenty of everything. She had only her big problems to think about; the murderer, the treasure hunt, and the woman who was trying to steal Max.

When Veronica's gaze touched on Etta, the girl smiled in a self-satisfied way. Veronica sighed, wondering that it could hurt so much to have Max gone. It was silly of her. She should be used to missing Max, as she had so often in past years. If Max could not fix this mess, she might have to get used to missing him in future as well, for they would be apart the rest of their lives.

"It is rather dull without Max about," Etta agreed.

Veronica smiled wanly and took a sip of cold tea, trying to taste India or China in the brew, but it was only tea without Max in the room.

"You are sure you do not know where he went?" Freddy asked pointedly.

"You are the fourth person to ask and my answer is still the same. Mustafah says London. Why would Max tell me what he planned to do?" Veronica asked, not precisely telling a fib. "He does not tell anyone else."

"Stop this lying, Veronica," Lady Margery said impatiently. "Max is gone and he has dragged Henry off with him. If anyone knows Max's mind, it is you."

Veronica stared numbly at her aunt.

"Lady Margery," Flurry said, rising to her full height. "I am only a servant in this house, but to have a girl who has always been in my charge accused of lying goes beyond bad manners. It is unconscionable. Veronica does not lie."

Everyone stared at Flurry as though she were an aroused lioness.

"What do you know about it, old woman?" Freddy said in a lame attempt to defend his mother before he resumed cutting the ham on his plate. "It is as plain as day Veronica is in love with Max. She must be privy to what he is doing. And if I were you, I would remember my position lest I lose it."

Veronica was staring at Freddy, dumbfounded. If he had divined that she was in love with Max, then it must be more than obvious to the rest of them. Mercia was blushing and Etta was staring coldly at Freddy. "It is you, cousin, who has forgotten his position," Veronica said viciously as she jumped to her feet. "Flurry is my dearest friend and my companion. You are an unwelcome guest. Besides which, she knows just enough Hindi to get those men of Max's to throw you out on your ear if she wants to. Do not imagine they would not cut your throat if she gave that order, either."

Freddy gasped and rolled his eyes at the Indian who had just brought in a platter of turbot. Veronica looked at Mustafah apologetically and the man winked at her. She was stunned. So they did understand English! How clever of Max. Everyone assumed it was safe to talk around them. As soon as Mustafah had left, Freddy slunk from the room. Etta gasped, made a valiant effort to contain herself, then broke into whoops. George added his deep chuckle to the laughter. Even Flurry smiled primly, which was a large concession to her dignity. The rest of the women cast disapproving stares at Veronica.

"We have routed him, Flurry," Veronica said jubilantly.

"But you have embarrassed me, child. Here I was defending your veracity and you tell two bouncers in a row."

"Oh, about you knowing Hindi or about Mustafah being willing to do your bidding?"

"As it happens, I do have some slight grasp of the language," Flurry admitted.

"You do?" Veronica asked. "How is it I know nothing of this?"

"Not knowing where we might travel I thought it wise to get a smattering of new dialects."

"Then Veronica did not lie," George said, taking a satisfied drink of wine.

"I frankly cannot see Mustafah either throwing Freddy out of the house or cutting his throat," Flurry said with a note of regret in her voice.

"Well, perhaps not by himself," Veronica considered, "but if he had help."

"This is the outside of enough," Lady Margery complained.

"Wishful thinking on your part, Veronica," Dora jibed. "They would never attack an Englishman unless defending their employer."

"How can you know that, Aunt Dora?" Veronica asked. "We will ask Max when he gets back. Until then I have not lied." Veronica took up her glass, removed the sprig of mint and took a sip. It tasted suddenly of raisins and some exotic sweet fruit. It tasted like Max's clothes often smelled, of sandalwood and spice.

"A point for Veronica," Etta declared, causing her mother to frown at her defense of the enemy.

Veronica smiled vaguely at Etta's animation. Perhaps if Max did have to marry her, he would come to like her someday as well as he did—no, what a horrifying thought, that Max could fall out of love with her, when she would never love anyone else. Max leaving her for just a night and a day seemed almost a betrayal. Why could she not have faith in him?

Veronica stayed up late in the library that night, pushing forward the transcription of her father's notes. She knew that completing the portraits would be the easiest of the tasks she must accomplish before she might have to fulfill her promise of leaving. Making sense of her papa's research could take time, but it was necessary if she were to help Max solve the puzzle of the Nonsuch treasure and possibly her papa's death. She

had been making good progress with the transcription
and had a sheaf of notes describing Nonsuch artifacts.
As the hall clock chimed one o'clock she leaned back in
the big oak desk chair and rubbed her eyes, blurry from
so much reading by candlelight.

Considering that no one else could know as much
about the treasure, she really could not see how the
treasure and the murder could be connected unless
someone thought her papa was very close to finding it.
She hardly liked to think about the murder when she
was alone. There were many moments when she could
not credit that anyone who knew her papa could wish
him harm, but every display of avarice in the family
fanned the flame of her suspicion that this person
could be the torturer and killer. The thought that she
might be harboring a murderer in the house did not
frighten her so much as make her angry.

She sighed and went back to the portfolio of notes.
The next item was a list of building materials, the transcription of a bill really. What caught her attention was
the catalog of precise sizes of stones. If only it were light
she could measure some of the foundation stones here
at Byerly and see if it were possible that any had come
from Nonsuch. A thump caught her attention, not from
above stairs but from below her. But there was nothing
below her except storerooms. The kitchen was under
the other wing of the house.

She was on the point of taking up a candelabra and
going to investigate when the thought of the murder
caused her to lift her hem and slide the ivory dagger
from the sheaf she had strapped to her thigh. It looked,
on second thought, far too fragile to be an effective
weapon. She dropped her hem and slid open the bottom drawer of the desk. She hefted the antique Spanish

dueling pistol Max had sent her papa and checked the priming to make sure the powder was dry. Then she got the brace of candles and proceeded to the cellar door. This was standing slightly ajar so that she did not have to put anything down to pull it open. She crept down the wooden steps toward a faint light coming from the wine cellar. Some rattling and a thump assured her that someone was looking for something. Probably Freddy after more brandy.

She crept into the room where the debris had been cleared away from one wall and stared at the basement stones in the light of a lantern sitting on the stone floor. She got so caught up in mentally measuring the building blocks that she had almost forgotten why she had come.

"Veronica, what the devil—?" George blurted out, causing her to swing around with the pistol leveled at his midsection.

"George, what are you doing down here, besides almost getting shot for a thief?"

"With that old thing?" he scoffed. "I do not think it would actually fire."

"Of course it will. I tested it myself. Would I come down here with a gun that does not work?"

George eyed the piece with a shade more respect. "No, probably you would not. In that case, would you mind pointing it elsewhere?"

"Sorry." Veronica dropped the pistol to her side. "Did you find the measurements for the stones?"

"Yes, in one of the old account books. Also the number bought. These are the right size, some of them. But they may only have come from the same quarry."

"But most of the stone used to build Nonsuch was not newly quarried," Veronica pointed out. "See how some are broken and refaced?"

"Then I think it very likely these were reused from Nonsuch, which means . . ."

"They were originally part of Merton Priory," Vee concluded, "and if our ancestors bothered to carry away mere stones, they may have bought other items as well."

"Or stolen them," George prompted with a grin.

"Which would explain secreting something far more valuable," Veronica finished. "But what?"

"My guess is a statue," George said with excitement. "We may find one buried in the place, or even walled up somewhere."

"But it would be stupid to hide it where it may come to harm," Veronica argued, turning to look around the dimly lit room.

"Unless it *was* stolen." George held the lantern up to scrutinize the damp walls as the echoes of his voice died away.

"Very likely, with our ancestors." Veronica held the candelabra up to inspect the joints between the stones.

When she turned George was staring at her intently, a frown marring his still-handsome face. She had never been afraid of George, indeed she was not now. But she was not in the habit of having him regard her with anything more than contempt. What was he thinking?

"Were you serious when you accused Mother of poisoning Uncle John?"

Veronica thought for a moment before answering. He might be trustworthy, but Margery was his mother. How much to tell him was a problem, so she cloaked her suspicions with emotional uncertainties. "No, I was angry. Somehow I cannot imagine anyone doing that. Indeed, I hope we never find out it was murder."

"I have already accepted Max's offer, a new start away from my wretched family."

"So it is not just me?" Veronica asked. "You think they are impossible, as well."

"Yes, it is very depressing, is it not?" George picked up the lantern and led the way toward the stairs.

Veronica followed George up and watched while he secured the door.

"Poor Etta," George said. "What she must think of us." George blew the lantern out and trailed after Veronica into the library. "Max is convinced that Uncle John was murdered and, if I know Max, he will never let the matter rest."

"Who do you think did it?" Veronica asked, sitting at the big desk to tidy up the papers for the night and put the pistol away.

"Is there anyone outside the family? Anyone we are overlooking?" George asked, staring intently at Veronica over the candle glow.

"None of the servants would have any reason. Frankly we get no visitors except family."

George sat on the edge of the desk and asked quietly. "Who among us had the best motive?"

Veronica stared vacantly at the mantel, thinking there was something not quite right. "Financially, me or Max, but he was not even around."

"Precisely."

"The next most likely suspect would be Mercia," Veronica mused.

"If she were sure she would get anything."

"Perhaps she thought she had to dispose of Papa quickly before the estate was beggared by your stepfather."

George nodded. "And where did she acquire her vast knowledge of poisons when she does not know a pansy from a petunia?"

"Good point," Veronica said, shoving the portfolio of papers into the lower desk drawer. "For that matter, who among us knows anything about poisons? George, look, the elephant is gone."

He stared at her as though she had run mad. "What elephant?"

"The ivory elephant," Veronica said as she ran to the mantel.

"Are you sure? Perhaps it was moved during the inventory."

Veronica bustled back. "Of course I am sure, for we noted the location of each piece on the inventory." She flung open the middle desk drawer and swore softly.

"What is it?" George asked, peering over the desk.

"The inventory is missing as well."

"Perhaps you had it somewhere else in the house," George suggested.

"No, we always leave it right here in case anyone has time to work on it." She searched the other desk drawers but did not turn it up.

George rubbed his face tiredly. "Max may have taken it with him."

"I suppose he might have. I have not looked for it since he left. But why would he take the elephant?"

"I do not know. Ask him when he gets back. For now I am going to bed. I advise you to do the same."

Veronica nodded and preceded George up the stairs. He had said one thing that sent her to sleep with an unquiet mind. Mercia knew nothing of plants, let alone poisons. To her recollection Aunt Margery had never evinced the smallest interest in foliage of any kind. For that matter, the only one in the family who had possessed any expertise with herbs or plants had been her papa, herself, and Flurry. Perhaps he had died of natural causes and she only wanted to blame his death on someone.

As she undressed for bed she sorted through the last horrible days of her father's existence. One thing had not been her imagination. The close manner in which Dr. Morris had questioned her about what her papa had eaten and drunk. She had not thought much about it at the time, still numb with shock, but now she realized how suspiciously the physician had regarded the death. And Max had confirmed this. She must know the truth before she could get on with her life, whatever that was to be.

One good thing about the inventory disappearing, even if they had to do the whole thing over again, she would have more time here with Max. For the life of her she could not see what he would want with it, nor why anyone else would take it either. Of course they had been talking openly about the Nonsuch treasure, and someone as stupid as Freddy, for example, might think one of the items in plain view in the house could be that treasure, even though the provenance of all the pieces was well documented.

Actually there were a few items left that would far exceed in value anything that might have come from Nonsuch Palace. As she fell asleep her mind worried over the missing pages like a dog over an old glove. If there was one thing she did not need, it was another puzzle.

16

There was no denying it. Etta looked pretty, Veronica thought, not the quiet drab girl who had first come to Byerly, but a more confident miss. And her secret smile seemed to say that she could handle Max Strake and any threat to her plans to wed him. Veronica was extremely unhappy as she worked on Etta's portrait.

Etta was the perfect wife for Max, Veronica thought wretchedly, as she fleshed out the smiling face over the top of the dun-colored background with its simulated cracks and crazes. The textured background would make an interesting contrast to the smooth perfection of Etta's skin.

Etta had the connections and social adroitness to bring Max to a position in society where he belonged. No doubt his business would prosper even more with Etta as his hostess. Moreover Etta and Dora worked well together, and neither would suffer any nonsense from Lady Eustace.

Not only would Dora's position as matriarch at Byerly be secure, but the former actress would finally get the recognition in London circles that she had

always craved. How Dora must have searched to find
the proper wife for Max, how she must have schemed to
trap him into the contract, how she must have fumed
when he refused to stay in England long enough to
marry Etta. Now Dora must be furious to discover that
Max meant to give them the slip if he could. Furious
but not desperate. That meant that Dora had some
other card she had not played yet. Veronica decided she
would have to discuss this with Max.

When she compared herself to Etta, Veronica felt like
a nobody. She had never even been to London, and did
not care. She wanted to go somewhere else and she did
not particularly care where. She brushed in Etta's hair,
giving it for all time the red highlights that the kind
afternoon sun was lending it. At no time did Veronica
feel so powerful as when wielding her brush. She laid in
some blue, green, and pink in the underbase for her
upper arms to make the viewer believe there was blood
pulsing and a heart beating within the canvas. She felt
only the intensity or subtlety of the colors. It amazed
her that she could create on her palette a color that no
one had ever seen before.

When she was like this, she never heard what was
said to her but instead let things drift through her mind
like water. There was usually no connection to what she
was painting. She heard her papa's voice this time talking as though he were sitting in front of her with a cup
of tea. *Lovely but quite deadly, not only the seeds if the
extraction is taken in overdose, but the roots and leaves as
well.* Veronica held her breath. It was her papa's voice.
But he could not be talking about Etta, for they had
never met. Veronica closed her eyes for a moment to
retrieve the image of him, and she could see him holding one of the scarab beetle seeds. It was an inch by a

half inch and mottled brown, tan, and white like a crossbred pup. He held it up to the light and in a swirl of memory he was gone. She wondered if she should tell Max about this latent memory.

Etta sighed and Veronica moistened her dry lips and asked if she wanted to rest. No, Veronica was to continue. By the end of the sitting, when Etta came to look at the work, she gasped.

"Is something wrong?" Veronica asked.

"You made me pretty," Etta said in amazement.

"I had nothing to do with it," Veronica said numbly.

"But I do not really look like this. I mean I do not see myself this way."

"Trust me. This is what you look like. Flurry was right when she said I do not lie, not in the important things."

"But will Max ever see me this way?" Her impulsive hug touched Veronica.

"I do not know," Veronica said, feeling guilty about plotting against Etta, even though she had not made her ugly.

"It does not seem natural that we should get along," Etta said. "You should hate me and I should be jealous of you."

"Me, why?" Veronica draped the protective cloth over Etta's portrait and turned to Max's. She had thought of a way to capture that indentation under his lower lip that made it look so terribly firm.

"Why, Max's portrait is almost as complete as mine and he has not sat for you more than an hour by my count." Etta stood looking over her shoulder.

"It does not matter," Veronica said, running the small brush along his bottom lip as though she were caressing it with a finger. "I know his face so well I can paint it without even looking at him."

Etta was silent for a moment until Veronica had done with Max's mouth. "I never aspired to his love, you know. In fact, he scares me a little."

"You said some such thing once before." Veronica turned to look at the girl. "But he is not violent. It is all a sham. This resolve I paint into his face is for show." She gestured to the lines about his mouth and between his brows. "Max has always had to bluff his way through the world. Perhaps all men do. When the time comes . . ." Veronica felt a tug at her heart, contemplating Etta's wedding night. Why could she not believe Max would prevent such a thing?

Etta stared over her shoulder and Veronica thought that perhaps she revealed too much of her love through the tenderness with which she treated the image of Max.

"Oh, I am fully prepared to have his children. I know my duty in that regard."

"Children do not exactly spring from the head of Zeus," Veronica said with a forced laugh. "Are you sure you can make love to a man you do not care for?"

"I care about Max. I even feel sorry for him, but I do not love him. Perhaps I was not meant to love anyone. Let us hope so, at any rate."

Etta whispered this last so desperately that Veronica felt sorry for her. If Max was trapped, so was Etta. Veronica had only been thinking of her own sacrifice. Etta was giving up the future possibility of ever loving anyone. Suddenly Veronica knew that she was lucky to have the pain of loving Max. She could not imagine the emptiness of not loving him, even from a distance.

"What I am trying to say"—Etta continued to examine the portrait, almost as though she were waiting for its nod of approval—"is that he will only be my husband, he will never be my lover. If you and he should want to be together . . ."

Veronica was stunned, her mind reeling at what Etta was suggesting. She should be shocked, angry perhaps. "It would not . . . hurt you?" Veronica asked in an amazed whisper, not daring to take her eyes off the portrait and face Etta.

"I should be happy to think I had deprived neither of you of the love you feel, just because I can feel none."

Veronica shook the image of Max out of her head and draped the painting before it could influence her. "Feelings can change, Etta. You scarcely know Max. You may someday fall deeply in love with him and he with you. So I think you had best not give away your husband, especially as you have not really snared him yet." Veronica began carefully cleaning her brushes in the linseed oil, her emotions under tight control.

"Oh, I am not worried about that," Etta said confidently. "Dora can force him into marriage if he will not comply."

"She has some hold over him she has not used yet," Veronica returned with a puzzled look, "but I cannot imagine what it could be."

"Neither can I, but she assures me Max cannot evade marriage to me and she has been right about everything else," Etta said in a superior manner.

Veronica stared at her a moment, thinking about her dear Max trapped and Dora victorious. She wanted desperately to know what that hold was. "Everything else?"

Etta nodded. "She assured us he would come home when he heard about his uncle and also that he might try to jilt me."

"Of course he would come," Veronica said. "But what if he did jilt you? What if he simply left?"

"I asked that, too, but she said five minutes alone with him will bring him up to scratch. How much longer will the portraits take?"

"A few more sittings. For now I think we had better clean up for dinner. I have paint all over me and so do you now that you have hugged me."

Max's servants seemed to be able to lay on a delectable spread without his orders as easily as with them. Veronica tended to linger in the dining room, where the conversation, without Max's presence, now avoided any discussions of money or the art collection. Perhaps they all thought nothing could be settled without Max there.

Once they moved into the drawing room, since she did not want to play cards with George and Freddy, she could only choose between watching her Aunt Margery stab at her needlework or participating in whatever topic had been raised by Etta. Veronica thought her quite valiant to manage the other women so well, seeing as two of them hated her, and Veronica herself could never manage more than the pretense of liking her. But it was good practice for Etta, since she would have to deal with the family for the rest of her life if she married Max. Flurry no longer graced the drawing room with her presence since her run-in with Freddy. A pity, since she was the only interesting one to talk to. Flurry still ate with the family and Veronica knew why, that Flurry felt someone should be there to keep an eye on the food.

Veronica knew she was in a dangerous mood, a painting trance. It would only try her patience if she attempted to make conversation tonight, She rose mutely and simply left the room without excusing herself to anyone. She thought perhaps she did not always hear people when they talked to her because her mind was so busy thinking about the painting she was working on. She had to make conversation when she was doing portraits, of course, but when she worked on a landscape or some piece of architecture she neither spoke nor heard for hours. There was only an internal monologue that had to do with color and light and capturing her quarry, reproducing life on canvas. She had never thought much about it before, about the process of that transfer of image and spirit to canvas. You might start at one o'clock and be vaguely aware that time was passing, but it was always such a surprise to finish up and discover that someone—Flurry, presumably—had come and lit candles, that there was an untouched plate of food on the side table to be devoured cold because you were suddenly famished.

Time stood still like that when she thought of Max. She went to her room and got out her other portraits of him. They were all of a much younger Max, of course, but he was the one she had fallen in love with. She carried the best of these down to the library for comparison. There was not enough light and it was much too late, but she opened her paintbox anyway and pulled the sheet off the unfinished portrait. She lit all the candles she could find. There was a chill in the room but she did not regard it. She slipped a smock over her gown and stared at the spidering of the plaster cracks in the cream background representing the bare library wall. She had chosen a lighter part of the wall that had not been damp-stained to reproduce as the background for the paintings. It would make a stark contrast to Max's sunbronzed features. She should wait for him to pose but there was no need. She knew every line of his dear face by now, the slightest curve of those sensual lips.

It was while she painted him that she thought about Etta's offer. Here they were planning on betraying Etta, leaving her at the altar, so to speak, and the girl had generously offered Max to Veronica. She could not decide how she felt about it; outraged or embarrassed. If Dora did indeed have a way of compelling Max to marry Etta, perhaps it was a way out. Well, she did not think she could suggest it, that she become his mistress. It was surprising to her that the idea did not shock her more, that she did not reel away from it. No, she would not suggest it, but if the necessity arose and he were to make that offer, would she have the strength of will to turn it down?

There could be the problem of a pregnancy, of course, but she knew how to avoid that. That night she had made love with him was the least likely day of her month to conceive. As for the future, she had studied herbs enough to know which combination would prevent pregnancy without doing any permanent harm. Not pennyroyal or lavender, but a combination of chamomile, betony, savory, and motherwort. When a book touted an herb as one that could bring on women's courses, that was a euphemism for preventing conception. It was rather depressing to think that she would be keeping herself from having Max's children when there was nothing she wanted more.

Of course Flurry could not possibly be fooled. Veronica would not do so even if it were possible. Flurry would not like the relationship, but she would accept it. The other relatives she discounted except for their gossip. Even if she and Max were discreet, the Comishes would be bound to figure out that he was spending half his time in England with her and half with Etta. Unless Veronica were not in England. If she went to Madagascar or India, no one would even know she was with

Max. Suddenly the whole idea of foreign travel seemed more than just romantic; it was a desperate necessity.

She looked at the picture and realized with a start that it was finished. It was Max, proud and competent, a man so secure in his own masculinity that he need not smile to seduce a woman.

"Amazing," Max said.

She stared at the picture, willing it to speak again before she realized the voice had come from behind her.

She started trembling, afraid to turn and find him not there. Finally he stepped around beside her. "Max? I thought I was hearing things." She raised her hand to her forehead.

"It is past midnight."

"You came back?" she said, almost amazed that he had not deserted her.

"Surely you did not doubt that I would return."

"No. I knew you would come." She wiped her hands on the linseed oil rag, then discarded the smock and started to clean her brushes, sure now of the man she meant to have. How easy it was to accept once she had made the decision. But she was not at all sure if Max would make the offer.

"Leave that until morning. Come and look at what I have found." He spread a map out over the library table and leaned over it. "Here is where the palace was, the two octagonal towers with the onion domes here and here. The back came to around here. There was an artificial grotto that would now be part of this wasteland. I intend to go and see if that survived. Also, Losely House has some of the arabesque panels from Nonsuch. We must go and examine those to become familiar with the style, though of course many artists were employed throughout."

"Max! This is what you were doing?" Veronica asked in disappointment. "What about the poisons, investigating Papa's murder?"

He straightened up. "I found out something about that, but I do not know if I should tell you."

"How can you not tell me what it is?" Veronica searched his face and found hurt and resolve.

A shiver went through her that made her gasp and drew tears to her eyes. She cleared her throat bravely. "You are sure now he was murdered."

"I am afraid so. I took your father's catalog and specimens to Dr. Culper in London." Max pulled from his pocket the notebook where the late John Strake had recorded his plantings and opened it to an entry in the middle. "There are at least a dozen possibilities growing within walking distance of the house, but there is one that matches his symptoms most accurately."

"The scarab beetle plant," Veronica guessed in a strangled voice, feeling a chill steal through her veins as though she had just drunk strong poison herself.

"*Ricinus communis,* family Euphorbiaceae, the castor-oil plant." Max looked up at her. "But how did you guess?"

"Papa told me." Veronica stared at Max's finger, pointing to the entry in her papa's hand, commenting on how well the seeds had sprung up and how easy it was to propagate. There was a buzzing in her head as she pictured her papa, cupping a handful of what he called the scarab beetle seeds. She could see him standing in the garden so vividly she felt as though she were there and not here, and it made her dizzy.

"Whatever do you mean, Vee? How could Uncle have told you? He is dead."

When she found her voice it sounded distant even to her. "But . . . but that one is so pretty." The buzzing turned to a roar and she held her hands to her ears to block out the sound, but it was inside. A soft, woolly grayness enveloped her head and she could feel herself slowly falling.

Max saw her sway in time to catch her. "Vee, my darling!" He scooped her up and carried her upstairs to Flurry's room, bumping the door open with his knee.

"Max, what has happened?" Flurry asked as she fairly leaped from bed.

"She fainted, I think," Max said desperately, "though it was more as though she fell asleep." He put Veronica gently down on the bed and knelt there while Flurry counted her pulse.

"She finished that entire portrait of me and we were talking . . . of other matters, and she simply trailed off. Has she done this before?"

"Worked herself into a stupor?" Flurry asked, wetting a compress for Veronica's head. "Yes, she simply goes out like a candle that has burnt itself too low. Bring that blanket and pillow."

Max did as he was bid. "Shall I fetch the doctor?"

"No need. She simply must rest." Flurry stroked her hair lovingly. "Leave her here for the night. I will keep an eye on her."

Max looked up in concern at Flurry's old, worn, devoted face. "You do not have to guard her from me anymore. I have myself under control now that I am doing something."

"I know that, Max. As for guarding her from herself . . ." Flurry pursed her lips. "She has been distracted since you left. I knew she needed to paint. It is a physical need with her."

"Will she be all right?" Max could not seem to take his eyes off Vee's still face.

"She will be wonderfully refreshed tomorrow and her old self again."

"I never knew this about her. I knew she painted but . . ."

"She started her art in earnest after you left," Flurry said, pulling a chair closer to the bed. "If she heard you were in China, she would study Chinese painting. It was her way of being close to you, I think."

"What will happen to Vee if I cannot marry her?" Max asked sadly.

"She will, no doubt, become a very great artist," Flurry replied.

"She will drive herself to it, you mean?"

"She does not always think about what she does, Max. Sometimes she just paints until she has used herself up."

"She needs someone to take care of her, Flurry."

"I will always be with her."

Max looked at Flurry with mute regret, trying to frame his concern into words that would not wound as the older woman pulled a blanket over Veronica.

"I know, Max," Flurry said with a tired sigh as she covered Veronica and sat on the bed beside her. "I will not *always* be with her. At best I will have another twenty—"

"Flurry, do not say that." He leaned down and embraced her, held her as he had that night twelve years ago. He had been excited then. Now he was desperate. "Neither one of you will go anywhere alone. If you must travel you will have my best ship to do it in. I will not have you in danger. But about this painting, about this I can do nothing."

"There is no answer, Max."

"One of the other matters we talked of, the one I think that made her faint, touched on Uncle's death."

Flurry froze and released Max to hold him at arm's length. "You found something," she whispered desperately.

"The poison ricin is potent enough to have caused his death."

"*Ricinus communis.* But that is a medicinal herb. They use it to make castor oil."

"But the roots are highly toxic and the oil of the seeds too, if administered in sufficient quantity."

"Who would know that?"

"That is what we are going to have to find out. Say nothing of this to anyone else." Max glanced at the sleeping girl. "I should never have told Vee."

He turned toward the door, but stopped and looked back at Flurry. "When I think about not being able to marry Vee, it is like a hand squeezing my heart. I feel like I am going to die and I do not particularly care, except that it would give both her and you pain."

"And you do not care at all about Etta?"

"I will never marry her either, but I may never be free of her."

"There is no honorable way out, Max."

"I do not give a damn about my honor." He planted his fists futilely against the panel of the door. "Flurry, if we did something terrible, Vee and I, would you forsake us?"

"What terrible crime did you have in mind?" Flurry asked calmly.

"If I cannot legally marry Vee in England, I will take her to some country not under English rule. Would you still come with us?" he asked resting his forehead against the oak door.

"Why Max, what has come over you? You are acting almost responsibly."

"When I came to Byerly I became enchanted with Vee. She made me forget everything bad that had happened to me since the last time we met. But when I went to London I took up again the trappings of my business, the decisions, the risks, people depending on me. I remembered who I am, a man, not a stupid boy."

"The old Max would never have understood that. It is almost sad to see you grow up. For Veronica it happened slowly. But you have been gone. You expected everything to be as you left it. You did not expect to come back and be in charge."

"No, I did not. I was a fool to think time stood still. I have been thinking about my life, every decision I made was to better myself, to gain enough power and money to assure that no one could ever leave me bleeding in the dirt again. But I forgot what my goal was, to take care of the two of you." He turned to her. "Let me do that, Flurry. Say you will come with us."

Flurry walked to him. "There is nothing the two of you can do that will turn me against you." She hugged Max.

"So we will all go together. You see, the world is a dangerous place for a woman of beauty." Max smiled boyishly. "For two beautiful women it is even more dangerous."

"I see you have not lost all your youthful charm."

"You will trust me to make our travel arrangements, then?"

"And lend an air of respectability to our departure," she said, "no matter how clandestine."

*T*he splash of water woke her long before she was willing to open her eyes. A warm breeze was wicking in the window, carrying spring-flower scents and the damp, rich smell of plowed earth. Veronica opened one eye and saw Flurry spreading something in the bathwater.

"Is that for me or you?" she asked, pushing off the blanket to stare at her wrinkled gown.

"For you. I bathed and broke my fast hours ago."

"Is the day much advanced?" Veronica rubbed her eyes with her fists like a child.

"Midmorning."

"Did I tell you I finished Max's portrait? I had the oddest dream. It spoke to me." She got up and stretched. Flurry unhooked her gown and pulled the dress and her shift over her head.

"The painting did not speak. Max has returned."

"So that is how I got up here," Veronica said, stripping off her undergarments. "He carried me and I missed the whole thing."

"I give him a great deal of credit for bringing you to

my room instead of yours, or even his," Flurry said sternly.

Veronica said nothing and slipped into the bath, submerging her whole head so as to shut out any recriminations Flurry might add, if she guessed they had already made love. But when she emerged, Flurry had only soap to offer her. Of course, she did not know that Veronica and Max were lovers, nor what Veronica had decided to do, if Max only asked it of her. Something else had happened last night, but she could not quite remember what it was.

"You said you were in love once, Flurry?" Veronica soaped her hair as Flurry stood ready with a pitcher of rinse water.

"Once," she said, kneeling to pour the water over Veronica's long black locks. She handed Veronica a small towel to dry her eyes.

"Well, you never elaborated," Veronica said as she soaped an arm.

"Must I?" Flurry asked, sitting on the daybed.

"If you do not, I will set Max on to worry you about it."

"I nearly married once. He was a younger son set to dedicate his life to the church. I was a girl of no fortune. He married someone else and has a congregation in Herefordshire, seven children, and a fat wife."

"That is rather sketchy," Veronica said critically as she scrubbed at the paint stains on her hands. "Did you ever meet secretly?"

"He was not the one I fell in love with. That happened later."

"Ah, now we are getting somewhere," Veronica said with satisfaction. "Did you have secret assignations?"

"We made a lot of silly vows that we never kept."

"Would it not have been better to be together, to live in poverty even, than to take the comfortable way?" The splashing stopped as Veronica waited for Flurry's answer.

Flurry flapped open a bathing sheet to dry Veronica in. "Decidedly not. Then I would never have come to live at Byerly and encounter you."

"Me? I can scarcely be considered compensation for giving up the love of your life." Veronica perched a small foot on the edge of the tub and gave it a swipe.

"I am not sure he was the love of my life. We never stood the test of time, you see. But you—I have made no secret that you are my favorite. You are almost like a daughter to me."

"Oh, Flurry. You should have had a life of your own." Veronica stood and helped Flurry secure the sheet around her before she stepped from the tub.

"Raising six children on a clergyman's pay, even a clergyman with his own congregation?" Flurry toweled her hair vigorously.

"You said seven children," Veronica corrected from inside the towel.

"What is one child more or less. And to a man given to prosing in a pointless way. You see I did go back to sit under him as minister. But only the once."

Veronica emerged from the towel to stare at Flurry, who was not looking at all misty-eyed.

"Indeed, he caused me to cut short my visit to your sister Janey. I could not believe how old he looked and stout. Whereas I have not changed at all."

Veronica giggled. "No, you are as trim and pretty as the first day I saw you."

"Perhaps not, but I should say I have held up rather well."

There was a tap at the door and one of the maids brought in a tray.

"Ah, your breakfast. I had them make scones for you, but do not expect such treatment all the time."

Veronica knew the minister was a fiction, but there had been someone. She barely waited for the maid to leave before she dropped the sheet, threw on Flurry's wrapper and grabbed a hot pastry. "This is heaven, but I earned it. At least I hope I did. Surely I did not dream I finished Max's portrait."

"No, I went to the library and looked at it. It is the best one you have ever done. Do you think everyone will guess that you are in love with Max?" Flurry began brushing out the tangles in Veronica's wet hair.

"You always couch your most disapproving comments as questions. If Freddy guessed, then everyone will. But loving anyone at all is not wise. It is exceedingly painful, and I would not have missed it for the world."

Veronica put on her most childish gown and a work apron. She felt childish and meant to take the impulse at its flood. She absconded with the last of the cakes wrapped in a napkin and ate bits of the scones as she made her way about the estate. She spent a delightful few hours roaming her favorite haunts and ended her ramble at the sculpture garden. They were all there, her old friends and reminders of Max. She sat beside the gargoyle, which must once have adorned some cathedral to spout rainwater and ward off evil spirits. It looked like a pathetic baby dragon, its wings just unfurling. She always felt sorry for it not having a mother dragon and began to wonder if she liked it so much because she had lost her mother without ever knowing her.

She playfully put the last bite into its mouth and patted its head. She emerged from the garden and started across the back lawn, wondering that she had not as yet encountered Max. Then she saw him come around the house, mounted on a white horse that looked suspiciously like one of Bonnie's colts. He made it rear, then cantered it toward her. She stood waiting, trusting both Max and the horse to stop. But he kept coming. She reached her arms up just as he swooped to grab her about the waist. The white horse ducked his head and whinnied when Max swept down on Veronica, but he never broke stride. They cantered across the lawn with Veronica gripping Max tight around the waist. It was wonderful to have an excuse to hug him.

"You are very practiced at this, Max. One would think you carry off maidens all the time."

"How do you know I do not?" he asked with his wickedest smile.

"That is true. You never said what you have been doing these past twelve years other than making your fortune."

"I admit to carrying off a frigate or two, but maidens are hard to come by on the high seas."

"Where did you find Strider?"

"At Tattersall's in London." Max eased the horse to a trot. "Walk, Strider," he commanded.

They were almost to the woods now and Max guided the hunter as easily one-handed as with two. His left arm was locked securely around Veronica's waist to keep her from sliding off.

Only Max would buy a horse and bring it the whole way from London to make such an entrance. He was indeed the sort of man they wrote fairy tales about, the sort of man who could carry off any situation, or any maiden, for that matter. She pulled her right leg up and got it over the saddle, hiking her gown so far up her thighs as to be positively indecent. Max handed her the reins and ran his free hand up her thigh, encountering the dagger with a laugh. "You are a lethal-looking lady." His hand went up beyond the top of her drawers to press against her bare stomach. "Where can we be safe?" he whispered into her neck.

"I know a place," Veronica said, guiding Strider up a rocky streambed, under a fallen oak, and into a small glen that contained just enough grass to keep him happy for an hour.

Max slid off first, then pulled Vee off, letting her dress ride up to her waist. She gasped as his hands grasped her buttocks and massaged them through the soft material. Veronica's arms snaked inside his coat to run over the muscles she could feel through his shirt.

Max's mouth found hers and there was no more talk until they had drunk of each other and met there in a metaphor that teased their hunger more than it satiated it.

Max was breathless when he broke the kiss. "I told Flurry I had control of myself, easy enough to say with you safe in her room. It was a lie," he said in amazement, his gray eyes looking bewildered. "I have no control where you are concerned."

"I do not care," Veronica said. "Take your coat off."

Max let go of her with a laugh and stripped off his coat, hanging it on a branch of the fallen tree. Veronica removed her apron and added it to the fabric wall of their bower. Strider raised his head from grazing to look curiously at them.

Veronica began to unbutton Max's shirt and he said,

"Do you have any idea how hard it is to explain to a servant losing all one's shirt buttons?"

"I do not think Mustafah needs any explanations about us at all," Veronica said as she pulled his shirt tails out and removed the garment to lap it over a limb.

"You are so brown," she said as Max knelt and lifted her dress over her head, adding it to the collection of clothing. "My turn," Veronica said. She knelt to unbutton his riding breeches, causing him to groan more than once as she ruthlessly stripped them down. Max sat on a limb of the fallen tree to pull off his boots.

"There's not much left," he said, tracing the aroused nipple of one of her breasts through her thin shift. He knelt again and ducked under it, untying her drawers and letting them fall, then making his way up her body with slow seductive kisses.

"I cannot see what you are doing," Veronica complained, laying her hands on the rippling muscles of his back.

"Just reconnoitering." Max stood up, lifting the chemise above her head and looking down at her admiringly. He arranged her loose hair about her shoulders. "Leave the dagger on. I like dangerous women." He bent his head to suckle one breast, causing her to sway in his arms. "Not going to faint, are you?"

"Not from exhaustion," Veronica said. She moved a tentative hand to his arousal and was rewarded by feeling his manhood move against her hand. She untied his smallclothes and pushed them to his ankles, then stared in awe at him.

"Am I as you remember me?" he asked, lifting her up and hugging her against him. She was so aware of his engorged manhood that she felt perhaps she was not paying enough attention to Max. By candlelight he had been magnificent. In the light of day she began to feel not equal to the task of satisfying him.

"Gooseflesh?" he asked. "I suppose it is a bit chill." He pulled his shirt off the tree and spread it on the grass for her. "Your bed awaits, lady."

Veronica lay down and looked up at him, standing brown in the sun that filtered through the new leaves into the secluded glade. "I cannot get over how dark you are, Max."

He lay beside her and she stroked the hair on his chest that was as fine and black as that on his head. He teased one of her nipples into an erect bud, then followed up with his tongue. Veronica watched the long supple fingers of his hand and wondered what he would have become if he had not gone to sea. Hands so talented should be doing something. She arched and sighed, running her fingers through the sleek hair of his chest. She began to wonder if she should perhaps give sculpting a try.

Max turned his attention to her other breast with the single-minded purpose of driving her insane with desire. "Frightened, Vee?" Max asked. "You are trembling. If anyone should discover us, what would they do, but go away?"

"It is not that. You just seem so much larger by daylight." She rolled onto her side with her legs slightly parted and he purposefully slid his manhood up between them, delighting in the surprised look on her face.

"I assure you that if anyone is going to get hurt it will be me," he said. "Most women have no appreciation for how vulnerable this equipment really is."

"Really? I shall be very careful," Veronica said, closing her eyes as waves of hunger throbbed in her nether regions. She no longer felt cold in any respect and parted her lips on a gasp of delight as his left hand squeezed her buttock.

Max took advantage of her gasp to plunge his eager tongue into her mouth again, probing and withdrawing as though he were showing her what he meant to do. He rolled her onto her back. "Wrap your legs around me," he whispered. "You have teased me far too long. Any other stallion would be breaking his tether by now."

She did as he bid, and felt his male hotness against her now wet tissues. He carefully brought the tip of his manhood to bear on her opening and teased it in so slowly she wanted to protest his reticence, and when he withdrew it she grasped his bottom and pulled herself toward him.

Max laughed. "Too slow for you? Very well."

He adjusted his position and slid his length into her, drawing a surprised gasp from her.

"Max, something must have happened to you. I remember nothing like this." She wiggled under him and gasped again.

"I was injured that night, so not at my best during out first encounter." He withdrew slightly and plunged in with more vigor this time. Every muscle in her torso fluttered in response. His withdrawal and thrust became faster until she was so pulled and pushed, deprived, and satisfied that she did not know which to complain of. The thrusting became so rhythmic she thought that surely it would never end and that the tremors that shook her periodically meant that she was dying from ecstasy. She did not care about dying or any other earthly problem. Max was beginning to pant now and she could see a sheen of sweat on his brow.

"We can stop if you are tired," she whispered, though she desperately wanted him to continue.

Max gave a crack of laughter. "Do you want me to stop?"

"Never," Veronica gasped. A liquid explosion inside her set off more waves of euphoria. Then he withdrew, gasping for air and rolling onto his back, his chest heaving.

Veronica snuggled against his side and held him. "I had no idea it was such hard work or that it hurt you so much," she said penitently. "The stallions never complain, but then they would not unless a mare kicks them in the leg."

Max chuckled weakly.

"Oh, very well. I will stop comparing you to a horse. But it is all I have to go on."

"Believe me, Vee, making love does not hurt me and it is the very best kind of exhaustion for a man."

"So you are not permanently injured?" she asked, glancing down at him.

He followed the direction of her gaze and laughed. "No, I promise you I shall be completely restored to my former health and size as early as tonight. Shall I come to you then?" he challenged, sliding his arm around her waist.

"No, I do not want you climbing in that window again."

"But you smell so sweet, like fresh soap, and I have been away so long."

"I will come to you." Her small hand crept up his chest. She could feel the heat from his body and the chill of the morning air washing over her at the same time. It was pleasantly confusing to not know if she were warm or cold, to wait for each sensation as though it were a feast for the senses. She toyed with the idea of adding herself to the full-length painting. That would be an added surprise for Max.

"You will come to me? That is novel." He pressed against her to shield her from a chill. "I will await you."

"Max?" Veronica asked without removing her head from underneath his chin.

"Yes." He managed with one hand to grab the tail of his coat and pull it down to wrap around her.

"Did you exhaust yourself frequently when you were in other countries?"

"There was always a lot of work and fighting to be done, and—oh, you mean . . . are you asking if there were other women?"

She pulled her head back to look up at him. "Yes, it would seem to me that it would have been a necessity."

"There were women, but I do not remember them at all now."

"And Etta?"

"Was certainly not one of them," Max answered with finality.

"I mean, what did Steeple find out in London?"

Max paused as he tried to find a way to tell her. "We may not be able to break the contract. Will you run away with me even if I cannot marry you in England?"

"Of course," Veronica said, snuggling closer. "Did you ever doubt me?"

"Not for a moment." He kissed the top of her head and felt himself drifting toward sleep.

Veronica found dressing again not nearly so much fun as undressing with Max, and the prospect of returning to the house not appealing at all. When Max took her up before him she rode demurely with both legs on one side. She had already started to use the herb tea after their first time together, so that if they could not be married any time soon, there would be no repercussions to make her regret this day, this hour.

"Strider is the first colt I raised, Bonnie's first colt in fact," Veronica volunteered.

"Will they remember each other?" Max asked.

"Not as mother and son, perhaps, but horses have a keen memory for smells. They will remember each other."

"How do you know that?" Max carefully guided the horse along the trail.

"When Strider was only a few days old, Freddy hit him in the nose, which is as bad a place to hit a horse as you can find. Bonnie went for Freddy like an avenging angel. She still tries to bite him every time she sees him."

"Strider too?"

"He is a little more subtle. He lets Freddy mount, then he dumps him at the first fence. He has never thrown anyone else on purpose. George is able to ride him with no problem."

"Good boy, Strider." Max patted the horse's shoulder. "Did Freddy give you any trouble while I was gone?"

"A little. He spent most of the time digging holes all over the yard and grumbling. Speaking of Freddy, I suspect he may have made off with the inventory and the ivory elephant."

"Freddy? I know he has many flaws but I did not think he was a thief."

"Well, you did not take them, did you?" She turned her head to look at him.

"No, of course not. And I cannot see what he would want with them." Max guided Strider into the statuary garden from the downhill side. He dismounted near the stream. Veronica could easily have slid off but she waited for Max to hand her down. His hands lingered possessively about her waist as he looked up at her. Then his smile turned sad and faraway as though he were going to kiss her but had thought better of it. When he set her on the ground she went to the baby gargoyle and retrieved the bit of scone. Max stared at her as though she had produced the treat by magic, but Strider accepted it without considering whence it had come.

Max shook his head. "What else did Freddy do?" Max leaned against the willow.

"He was rude to Flurry, but we took care of him."

"Tell me," Max demanded as though they were children again, sharing a joke. He slid down to sit on the grass and when he saw Veronica meant to do the same he pulled her onto his lap. "A snake in his bed, treacle in his tea? What?"

"He insisted I knew where you had gone," Veronica said, snaking an arm around Max's neck. "I was not about to tell him and he accused me of lying."

"And who put him in his place?" Max prompted.

"I merely suggested that since Flurry is the only one who can command your servants when you are not about, he better not offend her."

"And what would Flurry have ordered them to do, extra curry in the rice?" Max speculated.

"I might have said something about them cutting his throat in the night."

Max gasped and rumbled with laughter, holding her tighter.

Veronica delighted in making him laugh. "Probably they would not really do it, but Freddy seemed impressed."

"Probably not just on Flurry's say so," Max confirmed.

"But yours?" Veronica asked hopefully.

"Yes, of course." Max cleared his throat to convince her of his sincerity.

"I knew you were dangerous, Max. And Freddy is a coward. He is afraid to be in the same room with Flurry and any of your men."

"Surely that is unjustified. A cut throat would not go unnoticed. No, I am afraid he is quite safe."

Veronica laughed with him then. "It is still fun pretending with you, Max, but it is only a fantasy. I hate to say it, but we should go back."

"I do not want to." Suddenly all of the gaiety went out of Max and he hugged her tightly.

"What do you want to do?" Veronica asked hopefully, pressing herself into his lap, aware of the heat of his loins through her clothing.

Max glanced at the great white hunter grazing placidly. "Take you up before me on Strider and set out for the ends of the earth."

Veronica jumped up and went to pet the horse. "Even Strider would grow tired, eventually. Life does not work the way it does in books. We cannot really go on a quest, like a knight and his lady. Much as we both hate to admit it, we have grown up." Veronica came back to take Max's hand to pull him up. She could not budge him, of course, but he sprang up gracefully as though she had.

"And I missed it. I am sorry, Vee. I have made such a mess of things."

"I forgive you, Max." She managed to keep any trace of regret out of her smile.

"I wish I could have prevented this disaster." Max came to pick up Strider's reins.

"You could not," Veronica said. "You were trapped, perhaps even victimized, many years ago. But that was not Etta's doing."

"No, it was Mother's," he said sadly.

"What hold does she have on you, Max, other than that contract?"

Max laughed. "Besides threatening to tell the world I am a bastard?"

"But that would mean the ruin of all her plans. She is bluffing."

"Yes, she makes the mistake of thinking I set as much store by the title as she does, when I do not care at all." Max kicked at a rock. "The lawsuit I can handle, no matter how long it takes. As for the scandal . . ."

"Whatever scandal there may be, is justified," Veronica decided. "Dora has miscalculated, then. She has no real hold on you. Of course, it will look very bad for Etta if you just ditch her."

"I know. I will speak to Etta again," he decided. "She may yet listen to reason."

"I feel sorry for her, Max. Because she waited for you, all her other chances to marry are gone." Veronica said this as she ran her fingers through the horse's forelock, then scratched between his ears.

"I know." Max stared at her hungrily. "Time does not stand still no matter how much I want it to."

She felt his hunger for her charge the air between them and knew that if she took a step toward him, their arrival at the house might be delayed for some time. Such power she had, yet someone must be responsible.

"Vee," Max whispered and nearly pulled her off her feet with his embrace. His kiss was familiar yet searching. He was asking her a question and she answered him with her hungry response. She drank his kiss warmly like a sweet familiar wine, tasting still of youth and sunshine, lingering for heartbeats locked to his mouth. She could never be sorry she had loved him no matter what came of it.

It was Veronica who came to her senses first and broke it off. She laid her face against his coat, then said. "We really must go now. We will be very late. The sun is going down. Perhaps they have even started dinner without us."

"When would you like to go in search of Nonsuch?" Max asked as he picked Veronica up and put her on Strider's back. He gathered the reins and, stepping into the stirrup, mounted with the strength of one leg, off balance though he was.

"Now," Veronica said vaguely.

"Now? Mounted in front of me? As you said, very romantic, Vee, but not very practical. Besides, Flurry is coming too, and I do not think she will like to ride pillion." Max guided Strider up the path toward the stable.

The image of Flurry bouncing along behind them was too much for Veronica and she started to laugh. "Flurry would never ride behind. She is a better horsewoman than I am."

"If it is all the same to you, I think we will take my coach."

Veronica reveled in the press of his body against hers, the strength of his arm around her. "Max, you are becoming much too staid."

"Yes, I shall have to watch myself."

Their euphoria might have lasted longer had their return route not taken them past the herb garden. "Stop!" Veronica said, almost not waiting for Strider to halt before she slipped out of Max's grasp and went to look at the dried ricinus stalks. Some seeds from the previous year must have dropped, for a new plant had sprung up in one of the corners of the patch. Veronica trampled it quite deliberately, and when she turned to see Max dismounting, she could see the regret in his eyes. "Oh, Max, I wish we really could ride away like that together."

"It could be like that." He led the horse up to her.

"No, we have work to do." She took a fortifying breath of air and hugged herself, for with the parting sun had gone the warmth from the day.

"I wish I had never told you about the ricin," he said, acutely aware that she was now trembling with the cold.

"When I woke up I thought I had dreamed you came back and that it was all a dream, you telling me it was the scarab beetle seeds that did it. But it is not a dream. Papa really was murdered. Part of my mind tried to forget, but Papa's words came back to me, almost as though I had the answer all along."

"So that is how you guessed. I am sorry, Vee," Max said, laying an arm on her shoulder. "*I am sorry.* I should get those words engraved on a medallion and hang it around my neck. It would save time." Max slid out of his coat and clapped it around Vee's shoulders.

"It really is not your fault, Max. I want to find out who did it for myself. If this is what was used and the murderer did not come prepared with a supply of seeds, then seeds from Papa's stores would have had to be used. The plants would all have been killed by the winter."

"Let me put Strider away and we will go measure your store of seeds." They led Strider back to the stable where Ned took the horse's reins with an accusing look.

Max followed Veronica into the library to watch her kneel and draw open one of the metal-lined draws under the bookcases.

"How many seeds did you take, Max?"

"Only five of each. How many ricinus seeds were there?"

"This partition was almost full in the fall, and now there are scarcely a dozen left."

"Who would have known about them?" Max reached for her hand and helped her to her feet.

"That they were here? I and Flurry, or anyone with the patience to listen to Papa ramble on about his plants. But how would they have given it to him? If I remember aright, the extract is supposed to taste very foul. He would have known." She pushed the drawer shut with the toe of her shoe.

Max groaned. "Frankly, Veronica, unless someone confesses . . ." Max leaned against the bookshelves, his brows drawn together in thought.

"There must be a way to catch the killer. We have only to think of it." She paced to the window to stare out at Freddy digging near the strawberry bed.

Max roused himself and came to see what she had been observing. "What about Freddy?" Max tilted his head toward their sweating cousin.

"I do not think he knows one plant from another. And he is so clumsy at things that if he were looking for a plant poison we would all have noticed him skulking around the garden and library."

Max compressed his lips and stared into space for a moment. "No motive. And I am sure it was not George."

"Did you arrive at that logically?" Veronica watched his expression, never getting her fill of his face.

"No, just a gut feeling," Max replied. "Was anyone else here besides the family?"

"Just your mother, but she knew Byerly would come to you someday. She was so happy before the holidays because she was convinced you were coming home. And Aunt Dora is very seldom really happy. But you never came." Veronica slumped against the window frame, wondering if her papa would have been saved if Max had come. He might have figured out what was going on.

"I must have written that I meant to come. Poor Mother. It was that business in Spain that delayed me." Max rested his hand on the window frame and leaned close to her.

"What business in Spain?"

"Just a revolution," he said, kissing her gently. "Nothing to concern you," he murmured, his face so close that she could feel his warm breath on her cheek.

"Perhaps if you had apologized for disappointing her she would not be so angry with you now." Veronica toyed with his untidy cravat, trying to fix it for him.

"Perhaps I shall," Max said regretfully. "Perhaps I shall reform and become a model viscount. Why do you smirk so skeptically?"

"Perhaps Strider will sprout wings like Pegasus and carry us across the ocean," Veronica said with a laugh.

"Mmm, well anything is possible," he said as his lips met hers again and his body pressed her against the window frame.

"We shall be shockingly late for dinner, Max." Veronica broke the kiss and pressed her fingers over those so tempting lips of his. "I shall not even have time to change."

"Yes, I know," he said, not releasing her from the comfortable prison of his arms. "But we have to plan. My ship is at the East India docks. It is called the *Escobar*. Flurry has agreed to accompany us, regardless of what our circumstances are." He looked intently into her eyes.

"You mean whether we are married or not," Veronica guessed.

"Yes, if Etta will not listen to reason, I will send you and Flurry to London. Then I will tell Etta what I mean to do and give her one last chance."

"Completely shielding us from all blame. That is handsome of you, Max."

"That is also not my first choice. If it plays out that way, neither you nor Flurry will ever be received again . . . in England, but you have been yearning for foreign travel. There are many countries where they will not care how or even if we are married or whether I am being sued in England. I will take you to all of them." He kissed her lower lip, tugging at it to get her to open her mouth.

She pulled back with an impish smile. "But will they buy my paintings?"

"They will adore your paintings." One hand stole up to fondle her breast.

"Much as I hate to play the coward I can see that your plan will never work unless we go on ahead of you. I agree, Max. You are all I want. I do not care about anyone's opinion of me."

"I knew you would say that." He lowered his mouth over hers again and did gain entrance this time as his hands moved hungrily over her. He was just speculating on the likelihood of them being missed and whether it would be possible to invent an excuse for their absence when Flurry's strident call penetrated his love-fogged brain. Vee froze, for she heard it too, and it sounded very much like when Flurry used to call them as children.

"Max, she has agreed to cast respectability to the wind to come with us. Let us not worry her now."

Max released Vee with a regretful sigh.

When they went into the hall Flurry was coming down the stairs. "Flurry, did you see Strider? Max found him." Veronica tried to shed her somber mood, tried to forget about poisons and murderers for the moment.

"And you felt the need to make a spectacle of yourself by riding away across his saddle. I saw you from my window." Flurry handed Veronica a circumspect shawl to cover the childish blue dress.

"Did we look romantic?" Veronica demanded.

"You looked wanton. I might have expected such behavior from Max, but I would have thought you would have more sense, Veronica."

"It was my fault," Max said, striding to catch up with Veronica. "Do not blame her, Flurry."

"I blame myself for not keeping more of a watch on her." Flurry quickly tidied Veronica's hair and brushed her dress, as though that would get the white horsehairs off it.

"We shall go in as we are," Veronica said, giving her curls a shake. "How do I look, Flurry?"

"As though you had been kissing Max in the stable."

"Nonsense, Flurry," Max said coolly, giving her a smacking kiss on her own cheek. "We were kissing in the library."

Veronica's delicious laugh sounded a bit forced, but it was still on her lips when Max threw open the door to the dining room and they confronted his mother, as angry as Vee had ever seen her. Lady Eustace was mumbling to herself and Etta looked at both Max and Veronica as though they had betrayed her. Max groaned inwardly. Good Lord. You would have thought Henry Steeple would have had the sense to keep his errand to himself. But if he had told his wife, that was as good as shouting it from the rooftop. The rest of the family stared at Max with patent interest.

Henry frowned at his wife and sent Max a speaking look. Max seated Veronica and Flurry, then shook out his napkin and sat down as though nothing had happened. Veronica avoided Etta's stare.

"I will see you later, Max," Dora threatened.

He arched one eyebrow as though the prospect bored him.

They had scarcely settled down to the soup when Henry said, "I think I have found a solution to our difficulties."

"*Our* difficulties?" Max asked. "I think you have said quite enough for one day."

"Not yours, Veronica's and ours."

"Veronica has no difficulties," Max said obtusely, smiling at his former playmate.

"She is part of this family," Henry insisted. "She should take some responsibility, as you should. But I know better than to expect anything of you." Henry tore nervously at a slice of bread.

Lady Margery glared at Henry as though she wished

he would stop talking. But the repressing stare that was so effective in silencing her sons was lost on her spouse.

"I took the inventory to London," Henry announced.

"You took it?" Veronica shouted. "I thought Freddy had made off with it."

"Why would I want it?" Freddy asked as he passed a platter of fish.

"You have absconded with all Papa's garden plans, and you did not ask if you could have those."

"I can get good prices for most of the collection," Henry said as though he were making idle conversation. "Is there any butter?"

Veronica gaped and Max directed a menacing stare at Steeple. "Vee has no need to sell her collection and certainly has no intention of doing so."

"Did you take the elephant with you?" Veronica asked.

Steeple looked at her as though she were a raving lunatic.

"The ivory elephant," George explained. "It was on the mantel in the library. You remember it, gold-banded tusks and ruby eyes. It has gone missing."

"Well, I did not take it," Steeple claimed. "Why would I want to carry such a monstrosity to London?" He was frowning at the cut of meat placed on his plate.

"Steeple," Max barked. "If you have any sense you will restrict your activities to the matter for which you were engaged and not meddle in one that is none of your concern."

Lady Eustace directed her accusing stare at Max. "And the matter for which you engaged him is to break my daughter's heart."

"I was not aware Etta had one," Max said. "If she did

I think she would release me since I was clearly coerced into the marriage agreement."

Etta's thin lips were compressed into an even more uncompromising line than usual.

"You will never get out of it, Max," Dora said, rising to tower over him. "No matter how many scriveners you hire."

"Now see here," Henry said as he jumped up.

"Please, sit down, everyone," Veronica said more loudly than she intended. "I see no reason that dinner should be spoiled by Henry's . . . indiscretion," Veronica announced as though he had taken a mistress. "If you want to argue later you are welcome to do so, but Papa would never permit talk of money or petty bickering at table."

"Well said, Vee," Max agreed. "Well, Steeple, shall we leave now or will you meet me in the garden later and settle this like men?"

"I am staying, and you need me whether you realize it or not." Steeple went back to cutting his meat.

"And what is this about having no brandy left out?" Freddy complained.

Veronica ignored him and helped herself to another portion of fish.

"Do not look at me," Max said. "I know nothing of it."

"Damnable household," Freddy grumbled. "When a man has to buy his own brandy . . ."

"If you do not stop this instant," Veronica warned calmly, "I will have Flurry tell Mustafah to dispose of you as we discussed."

The fact that Freddy subsided and silence fell over the table earned Veronica looks of approval from all but Freddy and Lady Margery, though Steeple was patently puzzled. Max rolled an appreciative look at Veronica, the corners of his mouth twitching as he passed Henry the spiciest dish on the table to assure a case of indigestion for him later.

Veronica lingered purposefully over the sweetmeats. The walnuts in honey were heavenly, and there was pineapple candied and sprinkled with sesame seeds. Also, a dish of orange slices in a milk-and-butter sauce required a second taste. Finally, when she became aware that she was the only one still eating she sat back with a luxurious sigh and noted that all eyes were on her. She had not realized she was so hungry, but she had missed luncheon. Having eaten this much, at least if she looked satiated, no one would think it was for another reason.

"I think the ladies will rise now," Veronica finally said.

Max pulled out her chair. When Mustafah opened the door for her and the ladies to file out, Max engaged the man in Hindi speech for some minutes, sending him off with a purposeful look. Vee surmised that Flurry had followed part of that conversation and was aching to ask her about it. But Flurry decided she had had enough of the family and went up the stairs, cautioning Vee in an under voice not to take tea before someone else had tried it.

Veronica seated herself on the sofa closest to the fire this time. Etta and her mother sat on the far sofa in a war council with Dora. Mercia and Lady Margery whispered together as they took the chairs next to the chess table.

To her surprise Max joined them immediately in the drawing room, but chose to sit on the chair by the fire, rather than the sofa where he might be distracted by her. "I thought you had a mind to fight with Henry Steeple," Veronica observed.

"Oh, later, perhaps. Let him sweat it out." Max lounged back, crossing his booted feet at the ankles. "He may be stupid but he knows what he did was unconscionable."

"If he is so unscrupulous, I do not see why you rule him out as our murderer," Vee said morosely.

"I have not," Max replied quietly, glancing at the two groups of women who seemed from the buzz of their conversation to be plotting something. "But poison is a woman's weapon."

"Oh, really? What makes you say that?"

"Women are too squeamish to use guns, Vee. You want it to be Steeple because you like him the least."

"There is not much to chose between them, except for George," Veronica admitted. "An unfortunate family by any measure."

Max's brow furrowed over his gray eyes, distracting her from the problem.

"Does it seem the Strakes have more than our share of ill luck in the survival department as well?" Max asked.

"I was talking to Flurry about that and she agreed that Austin's death was suspicious, since it happened over the holidays when all the family were here."

"Would Lady Margery have had a reason for disposing of her first husband?" Max whispered.

"That is the problem with all of this, Max. No one seems to have a clear motive. Of course, my mother's death was my fault."

"Do not say so, Vee," He leaned toward her with a sympathetic look. "No child should regret being born."

Veronica sighed and tried to remember what her

companion had said about the deaths. "Flurry owned that Austin's symptoms were similar to Papa's. But when I asked her about Robert, your father, she became evasive. Max, I believe she lied to me."

Max uncoiled from his relaxed pose and brought both feet flat on the floor. "What are you saying, Vee? Surely you do not suspect Flurry."

"Not of murder. But she said she did not know Robert well, yet she had resided in the same house with him for five years when she was your nurse. I think Robert was the man she was in love with. That is why she did not want to speak of him."

Max nodded. "I see. So she is a woman of passion after all. But that is neither here nor there. How did he die? No one ever told me."

"She did not know. Most likely there is no connection between the other two deaths and Papa's, but about him we are sure," Veronica said.

"Of course." Max sighed heavily, stretched out his legs and rested his elbows on the chair arms, as he stared out the window instead of at her. If Veronica knew Max, he was hatching a plan.

"Considering our lack of success at solving the murder so far, I would have to say the safest course would be to try to get rid of all of them."

"Get rid of them?" Veronica stared at him, wondering if he meant to do them all in. "What do you mean?"

"Get them out of the house, so you and Flurry will be safe."

"Or we could leave," Veronica suggested. "It might be easier than dislodging the rest of them."

Max nodded. "As a last resort to escape Etta, yes, we will flee the country. But I dislike the notion of foisting the rest of the brood on poor George to dispose of. I would say we might have to make a deal," Max concluded.

"Pay them off?" Veronica whispered.

"Not that kind of deal," Max corrected.

"What then?" She leaned toward him eagerly.

"What if we were to get them to agree to leave when Uncle John's treasure is found. If it happens to be gold and silver coin, I am sure Henry Steeple will be able to get Mercia's permission to administer it. Or perhaps the expenses of the estate will consume all of it, and Mercia will have no say in the matter."

"But the treasure is not gold," Veronica insisted. "You know it is not."

"Let me finish," Max said. "If it is a work of art, it is to remain in your possession."

"But would they agree to something so indefinite? And that assumes we can find Papa's treasure. No Max, I do not think that will serve."

"Well, how do you usually get rid of unwanted relatives?" Max asked.

"They get tired of being ill-fed and leave of their own accord. There is no hope of that with your staff helping in the kitchen."

Mustafah entered with a sheaf of papers and a long explanation to Max. Max replied briefly and sent the man on another errand just as the rest of the family entered. Veronica recognized the pages of the inventory, but Max shook his head at her. Henry Steeple took the wing chair by the glass cabinet, guarding his precious supply of brandy, she supposed, and George and Freddy pulled two chairs up to an occasional table in preparation for an evening of cards.

"Why that is . . . ?" Henry sputtered. "That is the inventory. How did you get your hands on it?" Henry had risen and meant to snatch up the pages Max had turned over on the chair arm, except that Max whisked them out of his grasp.

"You must have dropped it in the hall on your way in," Max said without looking at him.

"I did no such thing. I had it locked in my writing case."

"Oh, really?" Max glared at Henry with that one eyebrow raised speculatively. "Considering you made off with it, I would not inquire too closely into the manner by which it was restored to its rightful owner, Vee."

"I have every right to the inventory. As executor of the estate—"

"I think we both know your rights have been overreached in that respect. Do you see these tick marks?"

"I did not put those there."

"No. Mustafah did while we were eating. It would appear that the ivory elephant is not the only item missing."

"Nonsense," Steeple said.

"Evidently someone thought the Chinese dogs and the antique Spanish pistol of value, for they are gone. Not to mention a Chinese vase."

"That is absolute rot!" Henry spun on his heel and flicked his angry glare around the room. "If they are missing, then some of your people must have made off with them."

"I will not have my men accused when I have absolute faith in them," Max said calmly.

Steeple began his usual pacing. "As to that, it could be one of Veronica's people, seeing the household about to break up."

"After not touching anything for decades? It is painfully obvious nothing disappeared until your family arrived," Max said. "I could have your room searched, you know."

Veronica saw someone flinch out of the corner of her eye, but could not tell who.

"You would not dare." Lady Margery was on her feet and trembling with rage.

"I will wait until tomorrow morning for the missing items to be restored," Max promised.

"That is a bit high-handed," Freddy complained. "Can he do that, Mother?"

"I have never been so insulted in my life," Steeple said.

"Actually you have been," Freddy said. "Remember that time, George—"

George laughed. "Best not tell that one, Freddy. If you are going to argue all evening, I am going off to read." George rose and walked to the door. "You can search my room if you wish, Max. Unfortunately, I cannot speak for the rest of the family."

Freddy strode to the door as well. "I have had enough fun for one night. Bad enough to be stuck in this godforsaken place with nothing to drink without being called a thief."

The door closed on the last of his complaint. Veronica entertained some slight hope that Freddy's anger might carry him as far as the village, where he could catch the mail or an accommodation coach for London, but since he had not threatened to leave, she felt his anger would play out before he got as far as packing. Perhaps he had a good reason for leaving the room just then, to get rid of stolen goods. But then, perhaps George did, as well. No, not George. He was their ally now. She really did not care so much about the missing items, would have shrugged them off, but it hurt to know that someone would steal from her and she did have quite a liking for that old Spanish pistol.

"I should think you would exercise some restraint over Max's outlandish behavior," Lady Margery accused.

Veronica jumped when she realized she was being held accountable for Max out of habit, and perhaps because Flurry had chosen not to join them. What was she thinking? Flurry had probably helped with the lightning inventory that had occurred at the end of dinner.

"What outlandish behavior?" Veronica said. "It seems quite reasonable, not to say heroic of Max not to want me to be robbed."

"You were always defending him." Lady Margery wrapped her shawl about her in a huff. "Come Mercia. It is easy to see we are not welcome here."

"I think I shall stay awhile, Mother."

Veronica turned to stare at Mercia but did not see open revolt in her face, just a speaking look cast at her mother. Mercia had realized she gained nothing by surrendering the field to Veronica and Etta.

"I cannot tell you how sorry I am this has happened, Veronica," Mercia said, "but you cannot seriously suspect one of the family."

"Who do you suggest?" Veronica asked.

"The way the windows are left open all night long, it could very well be any wandering beggar."

"Quite true," Steeple said. "That is most likely what has happened."

"Thank goodness we will not have that worry any longer," Max said, handing the lists to Veronica as though they now bored him.

There was an awkward pause of deliberate creation

as Max closed his eyes and pretended to meditate. Veronica would have applauded except that it would spoil the effect and she wanted to know what he meant, as well.

"What do you mean?" Steeple finally asked.

"I have had all of the art work moved into the library tonight with a guard stationed at the door."

"That is absurd," Steeple said. "What if one of us should need something?"

"Such as?" Max opened one eye to ask.

"Such as a book," Henry replied.

"Mustafah or Rajeev will get it for you."

"There may be papers I have to consult."

"You have already made off with all the papers in Papa's desk, creating quite an impediment to our finding the treasure he spoke of," Veronica contributed.

"But who knows what he may have stuffed in those old books of his?" Steeple speculated. "There could be banknotes in there, or maps . . ."

"Good point," Max agreed. "Make a note to check the books, Vee."

"You are cutting me out of this and I will not have it." Steeple pounded a small table so hard his glass jumped.

"It would be better if you cooperated with us. We are quite willing, so long as you will agree to leave Vee alone once we find this treasure."

"You know where it is?" An avaricious light came into Steeple's eyes.

"No, we think we know *what* it is," Max corrected.

"How much is it worth?" Steeple's teeth gleamed in the candlelight.

"Hard to say. Will you abide by the terms of the will and leave Byerly once it is found?"

"Of course, of course." Steeple rubbed his hands together.

"Will you sign a document to that effect?"

"I should have to see the document," he replied suspiciously.

"Oh, you will write the document," Max assured him. "After all, you are the lawyer in the family. Come, let us set to work."

Max walked out with Steeple in his wake, leaving Mercia uncertain what to do. Finally Dora beckoned her to sit down and drew her into conversation with her, Etta, and Lady Eustace.

Veronica got up and went slowly out of the room. What was Max thinking, placing a guard on the library? Had he forgotten that she was to come to him tonight? Of course she could get into his room from the small greenhouse, but most likely he had taken care of that entrance, as well. She would rather lose all her art than spend the night alone.

After waiting for two hours in her room while she tried to contrive a way of seeing Max, Veronica did actually gather up a shawl and head back downstairs. A floorboard creaked at the other end of the hall, but she could see nothing in the darkness. From the sound of men's voices behind the oak door of the library, she surmised they were still working over the agreement.

It was upsetting in the extreme to realize one encounter in four days was enough to satisfy Max, but not enough for her. Was there something abnormal about her that she should desire him so much? She would just have to school herself to do without him for a short while.

Gathering her resolve about her she started up the

stairs. The drawing room door opened and Dora came out, looking much surprised to see Veronica.

"I could not sleep," she said.

"Neither could I," Veronica confessed. Veronica went up the stairs wondering why Dora felt she needed to explain her presence in the drawing room. Probably because someone had taken some of the artifacts and she did not want Veronica to think it was her. Besides George, Dora would be the one least likely to do such a thing. Her generosity in the neighborhood was well known, her open-handedness with the servants a legend in the household. And she had also a comfortable jointure from her marriage to Robert. Money would be no motive to Dora. Veronica felt almost as sorry for her as for Etta.

A step creaked under her foot. What would happen to the old house when they made their escape? Max had spoken of leaving George in charge. Perhaps she would speak to him about letting Dora stay on. It was the least they could do for her.

Once again Veronica had a reason to dream of foreign lands. Max had promised her all of them.

19

Max tried to ignore the throbbing in his head as he glanced around the breakfast table at Vee, Flurry, and Etta. It had taken a quantity of brandy for him to get Henry Steeple to write and sign the agreement he had in mind the previous night, and by the time they were finished he was in no condition to go climbing oak trees, let alone try to make love to Vee. He would rather not have her at all than make a mull of it or not satisfy her. Now she was sitting there in a new dress and as close to a pout as she came, and he would have no chance to explain to her what had happened for some hours.

Mustafah had just come in with two steaming china pots and Max could hear footfalls on the stairs. Their peace was over for now, unless it was only George. Max leaped up to pour himself more tea, but immediately choked on it.

"What is the matter?" demanded Flurry.

"Coffee!" Max gasped as though he had been poisoned. He cast the contents of the cup out the window. "Who in the house drinks coffee?"

"Only your mother, Max," Flurry replied. "She grinds the beans herself because she says the servants do not get them fine enough. It is good of your men to see to her wants."

"They should warn one," he complained, getting himself a clean cup and more tea. "Can you be ready to set out for Losely House by nine o'clock, Vee? You seem to be dressed for an occasion."

Veronica smiled involuntarily. "I have only to get my sketchbook."

"I will need to get my shawl," Flurry said, warning Max that he had best not spurn the company of Veronica's chaperon.

"I imagine Etta might need a wrap and a bonnet too," Max said. "We will be outside most of the day and it is likely to be windy."

Etta stared at him. "I am to come too?"

"Unless you would dislike it," Max said generously. "I have ordered a picnic luncheon prepared rather than lunching at an inn." Max turned to observe Veronica frowning at him. "If that meets with your approval," he added.

"Sounds delightful, Max." Veronica said, wondering why he was suddenly deferring to Etta, not her. Then it hit her that the attraction of Etta to George, if obvious enough for her to notice, was probably in Max's mind as well. "I am of the opinion George may be of some use to us today, since he is interested in the artifacts from Nonsuch."

"Just what I was thinking," Max said, smiling at her.

Etta and Flurry preceded her out the door and Max followed them into the hall to shout after Veronica. "I do not suppose you want Henry Steeple included in the expedition as well?"

"Quiet, Max," Veronica said as she set her foot on the bottom stair step. "We are trying to make a getaway. You will spoil it."

George was just trotting down the stairs. "Getaway?"

"Yes," Max confirmed. "If you can breakfast while the ladies get their wraps, we could use your help on this expedition to Losely House today. Veronica says you can take the measurements."

George stared at Max with keen interest in his eyes. "Losely House is where many of the pieces from Nonsuch ended up. Of course, I want to go." He felt his side and pulled a small tablet from his waistcoat pocket.

"I shall have the carriage brought around to the front," Max offered.

Dora rounded the head of the stairs. "Where are you going, Max?"

He arched his right eyebrow at his mother. "Taking my intended on a pleasure jaunt. That should please you."

"If you wait Lady Eustace and I will come," Dora said as she came down the stairs.

"Completely destroying the notion of pleasure," Max said acerbically.

"Well, she cannot go alone with you," Dora replied with a scowl.

"I would have thought you would have wanted . . . at any rate, Miss Flurry is coming."

"Very well then, we will not come if you do not wish it," Dora said as she walked past him toward the breakfast parlor.

"Sorry, Mother," Max said without even turning to face her. "But it would not serve my purpose to have you there."

Dora rounded on him. "What purpose should you

have but to marry Etta as quickly as possible after this interminable delay?"

"There are one or two other things I must accomplish. Now go have breakfast. That abominable coffee of yours is getting cold."

Dora looked alarmed for a moment, but Max thought it was because she did not know how to take his teasing. He was so unused to seeing her anything but assertive that he found himself softening his criticism. "How did you come to be a drinker of such a bitter brew?"

"You sent me some years ago," she said almost like an accusation. "You do not even remember, do you?"

"I . . . no. I do not remember."

"I am past having my feelings hurt. I shall be satisfied if you are a husband to Etta."

His mother did turn and go into the room, then, leaving Max wondering how often he had succeeded in hurting her without knowing it. But then he remembered that she had ruined his whole life.

Flurry took charge of the picnic basket and Veronica got in beside her. Max helped Etta in, but she voluntarily took the seat opposite, generously allowing Max to sit beside Veronica. George got in beside Etta and Max was on the point of giving the order to start when Mercia came running out of the house with her pelisse flying and her curls bouncing.

Veronica gave a sigh of impatience as George slid over to make room for his sister. Vee had wanted to sit next to Max but she was acutely conscious of his thigh pressing against hers and his shoulder, so warm and solid she could have leaned over and fallen asleep against him, if not for that familiar throbbing that her body set up. She knew her lips must be suffused with red. This simply would not do, to be getting excited about him on a day when there was no possibility of stealing away with him. She must distract herself from thoughts of Max and his anatomy with the prospect of discovering something about Nonsuch.

"Well, did you accomplish anything last night, Max, when you were closeted with Henry Steeple for hours?"

Max looked surprised and gave that tempting half smile. "Yes, he signed an agreement that he shall administer the Nonsuch treasure and quit any claims of the estate upon the artifacts in the inventory."

"I am so glad you achieved something," Veronica replied, "even though it took forever."

"I cost only one night and there are many nights," Max promised.

Vee took that as an assignation, however vague. "I have not been idle either. I have made some inroads into Papa's notes."

"Have you found anything of moment?" George asked.

"Yes, Papa must have gone to Losely House himself when Flurry and I were at Janey's. He describes some of the panels so minutely, there is no other possibility."

"It is too bad he could not tell you about the treasure before he died," Mercia said unhelpfully.

Veronica stared at her, knowing such a clumsy remark was not meant to wound, and yet it did. "I should never have left his bedside," Veronica said passionately.

"Perhaps we have laid more emphasis on Losely House than it deserves," George said, drawing the conversation away from death. "It has surviving relics of Nonsuch, but that only tells us what we are not looking for. As you said yourself, Veronica, there were many artisans employed. Even if we found a statue from the palace we would have the devil of a time authenticating it unless someone had described that particular piece."

"I had not thought of that," Veronica said, thinking back over all the descriptions of artwork she had transcribed. "Papa may have said nothing because it was a dry well."

"We shall at least have a pleasant outing and be away from the oppressive ... house for a few hours." Max smiled, quite proud that he had not stumbled and said *family* instead of *house*.

Etta cast him a dubious look, which as good as said she had not fallen for that. Max found he did not like to have a fiancée he could read like a book. She would forever be throwing him speaking looks at dinner or the theater and expecting him to understand and act on her mute requests. A wave of regret seized Max, for he had thought of Etta as his wife, as though the knot were tied, when he still meant it never to be. He had looked into the future with complaisance, and he had not liked what he had seen. His heart thudded in his chest. There was a way to save them all from this fate. It simply was not an honorable one. He would provide for the girl and her mother, certainly, but he would never marry her.

"Veronica was talking to you, Max," Flurry said sharply.

"Sorry, I was woolgathering, Vee."

"Do you think this expedition will help us find the treasure?"

"Well," Max gave one of his momentous hesitations and spoke slowly. "It is not like looking for something from a building that still exists. As George said, most of the accounts we have read, no matter how detailed, would be worthless in identifying a piece. In fact, when you think about it, it seems extraordinary that more was not saved from Nonsuch Palace."

"That is what I was thinking," George agreed.

"Yes," Veronica said, her investigative spirits astir once more. "Does it not seem people have been rather careless to mislay such a piece of history?"

"Oh, I do not think it was a conspiracy," Etta replied. "By what George says, the building survived several of Henry's successors, did it not?"

"Henry who?" Mercia asked.

"Henry the Eighth, my dear," Max said as though he were humoring a child. "Yes, had it been demolished by an invading army, people might have paid more attention and even tried to recover some of the art. As it was legally purchased and demolished it caused no great stir. They were thinking of what to build from the pieces and probably selling the fountains and statues for what they could get."

"It still seems a shame to me," Veronica said.

"Would the statues be made of gold?" Mercia asked, her eyes glittering.

"No, ground up stone," George replied.

"What is the point then?" his sister asked.

Veronica sighed and stared out at the countryside, trying to pretend Mercia was not there.

It was obvious Max had made extensive arrangements for their visit since the retainer who showed them the decorative panels was most obsequious. Max barely glanced at the pieces, having probably looked his fill before, Veronica thought. Instead he took Mercia to walk in the gardens and spout her inanities there where she was not as likely to get on Veronica's nerves. Veronica sent Max off with a grateful smile as she began sketching. Flurry watched her work as George pointed out to Etta the devices of Henry VIII and his last queen, Catherine Parr, a maiden's head rising from a Tudor rose.

"George?" Veronica said when there was a lull in the conversation. "Something has been niggling at my mind since we came, the look of these lions. Do they remind you of anything?"

"Of course!" George smacked his forehead with the palm of his hand. "The lion's head bosses in the stable, the ones we use to hang tack on. My God. That is proof that pieces of Nonsuch made it as far as Byerly."

"That is a good sign then," Etta surmised as Veronica continued to sketch.

Veronica glanced up to see Etta's young face glowing with excitement. Yes, when not repressed by Lady Eustace or stubbornly bearding Max, she was quite pretty.

"You seem to have taken a great interest in our quest," George replied.

"It is very romantic. To think that the king built Nonsuch Palace just for Catherine Parr," Etta said wistfully.

"Henry was rather old then," George replied.

"But he must have been quite enamored of her," Etta insisted.

"He always was in love with his wives . . . at first," Veronica said darkly.

Flurry left off her scrutiny of the panels and came around to look at Veronica's sketch. "At least Catherine Parr kept her wits about her, and her head," Flurry replied.

Veronica stopped drawing to stare at Etta. "Even if Max were to marry you, Etta, that does not mean your life would be easy."

George looked concerned. "Etta, you said once you were afraid of Max."

"I have gotten over that," the girl claimed.

"That does not mean he will treat you well," George said. "He means to go off and leave you here. You may never see him again."

"But will he not expect me to take care of Byerly?"

"No, he has hired me to manage the estate," George replied. "And Max has not made my stewardship of the estate contingent on finding this cursed treasure."

"You have that firmly from him, George?" Veronica asked.

"Not in writing, but I have never known Max to go back on his word," George said, pulling out his notebook to jot down some figures.

"That is an odd thing for you to say." Flurry stared at him.

"Max promised to make us all regret the way we treated him and he has."

Etta looked up at George in a worshipful way. "Max has sworn revenge on me, as well. Mother and Dora keep telling me that our marriage settlement is unbreakable, but Max has vowed to find a way out."

"Why not simply release him?" George asked.

Veronica could see a few tears building in Etta's eyes and was surprised. George supplied his handkerchief so solicitously that it caused Veronica to smile with satisfaction. Her instinct told her that Etta would be happier with anyone other than Max, but George actually seemed to have some sympathy for her.

"Because I am too old now to find someone else. I

suppose that was his plan, to wait until I gave up on him."

"Stop breaking your heart over Max," George advised. "You are beautiful enough to have your pick of men."

Etta laughed in a watery voice. "Oh, I do not really love Max, so there is no broken heart, just a very weary one."

George stared at her intently. "And you would marry him anyway?"

"I have no fortune, so I have no real choice. But I am used to being trapped."

"Max is not," Veronica said. "I just hope you do not provoke him to violence."

"You have nothing to fear from him while I am here," George said staunchly.

Etta looked at him, clear-eyed and frank. "It is not necessary that Max like me, only that he keep his word."

"I see," Flurry said. "I wish you luck, child. Well, Veronica, are you nearly done?"

"With the first one." Veronica filled in some of the area with colored chalk, wondering how much the panels had faded over time.

Flurry wandered toward the door. "I do believe I will go outside. It hardly seems fair for Max to be charged with entertaining Mercia by himself."

"Confess, Flurry," Veronica said. "You are just worried he will throttle her."

The butler returned to the room twice more to check on their progress and offer them all chairs. Veronica thanked him, but said she preferred to stand. She was putting the finishing touches on her drawings when the other three returned. "Now for our luncheon," Veronica said.

"Not yet, we still have to visit the actual site," Max asserted.

Veronica groaned, for she had been anticipating the wonderful fare that must be packed in the basket, but it would be even more delicious if there was a real edge to her hunger. She endured the ride to the site of Nonsuch by closing her eyes and pretending to sleep. Mercia prattled on, but she could be ignored like Aunt Margery and Henry Steeple. There was such a lot of repetition in their conversation one could usually get by with an occasional nod or murmur of assent.

The grounds at the site of Nonsuch were a sad disappointment, for Veronica could discover none of the paths cut through the woods she had read about, no woods in fact, since they had been cut down for timber long since. There were not even any building stones lying about. And the grotto with the statue of Diana and Actaeon, if it still existed, must have been filled in. There was nothing of any interest to her now except the contents of the picnic basket and she commanded Max's man, Karim, to lay the cloth in the sun and let them have at it.

Veronica was not disappointed in the fare and reflected that if she were to continue to feast like this she might eventually grow quite stout. She would have liked to have a real nap now, while the others dawdled over the remains of the meal. Instead she took up her sketchbook and started a study of Max and Etta, sitting nearly back to back, to see if she could capture any expression that she had missed in the portraits. Mercia was on the other side of Max, but that only made it appear Max was distracted by something. Mercia finally got up to shake the wrinkles out of her dress. She came around behind Veronica and gave a snort of disgust.

"You have drawn me out of the picture," she complained.

"You were extraneous to the composition," Veronica said unkindly.

"What does that mean?" Mercia asked.

Veronica opened her mouth, but only said, "Oh, for a shovel."

George choked on a sip of wine and Max guffawed in spite of himself. "Trust me, Vee, if there is anything here, it is buried too deep for you to find it."

Veronica glanced at him. "Max, what made you think—"

"Ladies," Flurry commanded. "If we dawdle any longer we will have no time to examine the site." She extended her hand and Max sprang up and graciously raised her as though he were helping her up from a deep curtsey. George was helping Etta up, so Max gave his other hand to Veronica and pulled her up as though she weighed nothing. She did not think she would ever get used to how strong he was and what fearsome potential he had.

Once again she forced herself to focus on the investigation as she pulled out her papa's hand-drawn map of Nonsuch and oriented herself with the traces of the foundation. She closed her eyes and pictured the dining pavilion on the hill and where the woods would have been. Then she started pacing toward where the grotto had resided. Max followed her and when they reached the spot jumped down over a rotted log and examined the depression in the ground.

"I do not imagine it would be worth digging even if we had a shovel," Max said. "Surely everything of value has been looted from here long since."

"Then what was the point of coming all this way to sit on the cold ground?" Mercia complained.

Max and Flurry stared at her and only Veronica answered. "To make sure we had covered all the ground, that we had omitted nothing in our investigation."

Mercia shrugged. "Max, I am getting chilled."

Twenty minutes later as he was handing Veronica into the carriage he whispered, "Perhaps we should turn Freddy loose here with his pick and shovel."

Of course she could not comment on the advisability of this with Mercia in the carriage. Her presence had come close to ruining Veronica's whole day.

Max was surprised that Vee had not seen the value of throwing George and Etta together before. With any luck, and if he made George's situation attractive enough, his cousin would take Etta off his hands, and that would solve their chief problem. That left only two mysteries and the constant scheming he had to do to get Vee alone.

§ 20 §

They returned to a house in chaos. The doctor's gig was drawn up at the front door, a strange riding horse had been tied to an ivy shrub, and there was terrible wailing coming from the downstairs. Veronica could not make out who it was and ran into the drawing room to find Lady Margery prostrate on one of the sofas with Dora attending her. The others crowded in behind her.

"But what has happened?" Veronica demanded.

"He is dead!" Lady Margery said. "Poor Henry, taken off in the prime of life."

"Dead?" Max and George repeated.

Lady Margery gasped and scrubbed a sodden handkerchief across her eyes. "I . . . I found him. I had let him sleep since he was tired from his trip, but it was getting on toward luncheon and when I went to wake him he was dead." Her voice rose to a wail. "And there was blood."

Max strode from the room and up the stairs with George close on his heels. At the doorway into Henry's room they encountered Dr. Morris. He introduced Mr. Perth, the magistrate from Oakham.

Beyond them could be seen the shrouded body still on the bed.

"Poison?" Max asked, causing the magistrate to stare at him, but bringing a curt negative shake of the head from Dr. Morris.

"No, but not a natural death by any means," Morris replied. "This seems to have been the murder implement. We extracted it to find out what it was." He held up a long thin metal rod, still rusty with blood.

"But that looks like a knitting needle," Max said.

"But Miss Flurry was with us," George replied.

"Why did you mention Miss Flurry?" Perth inquired.

"Because she knits," George answered, staring at the man as he made a note.

"When did this happen?" Max asked.

"Sometime in the night," Morris replied. "He has been dead for twelve hours or so."

"But anyone could have done it," Max said.

"Does anyone besides Miss Flurry knit?" Perth asked.

"I have no idea," George replied numbly.

"I think we need to talk to this Miss Flurry," Perth insisted.

"George, can you introduce him to Flurry, and do not let him browbeat her." After the other men had left, Max asked, "You are certain this was the cause of death?"

"It was driven right through the bedclothes and straight through his heart. He did not even have a chance to struggle."

"But that would have taken strength. An old woman could never have managed it."

"Well, someone did it. Is there any chance that his valet had a grudge against him?"

"He has no valet. They brought no servants with them at all."

"You know what this means?" Morris asked.

"Yes, it has to be one of us," Max replied.

When they went down to the drawing room Flurry was still sitting on the other sofa calmly answering all Perth's questions. Her knitting bag had been emptied onto the worktable and contained only one needle. Dr. Morris laid its mate beside it and Flurry drew in her breath. "It was missing this morning from my knitting bag," Flurry said. "I had left it in the drawing room last night."

"Max," Veronica pleaded. "Make him go away. We know Flurry did not do this thing. Anyone could have got her knitting needle from the drawing room. In fact, I saw Aunt Dora coming out of there late last night."

"What time were you up until, my lady?" Perth asked, flipping to a clean page in his notebook and provoking an exasperated sigh from Veronica.

"Where is Freddy?" Max asked.

"Not my Freddy," Lady Margery wailed. "Freddy liked Henry."

"I simply asked where he was," Max said. "He frequently comes in late. He might have seen someone."

"I shall go look for him," George volunteered and left the room.

"Max, I want to take Flurry to her room," Veronica said.

"I shall have to ask you all not to leave the residence," Perth stated.

"No one is going anywhere," Max said as he helped Flurry to her feet. "I assume we can begin to make funeral arrangements."

"Yes," Dr. Morris said. "We shall be back tomorrow."

* * *

Veronica spent the following two days at Flurry's side. Max was never far from them. He realized now that they were in more danger than he had ever guessed. Had Henry been killed because he was helping Max break his marriage contract or because he had agreed to vacate Byerly if given administration of the treasure? Neither seemed a likely motive for murder. Or had Henry been deep into something that Max did not even suspect yet. Freddy had turned up, unkempt and tired from a day of digging. He had displayed little emotion except surprise when informed of his stepfather's death, but thereafter gave Flurry and the Indian servants a wide berth as though one or all of them had conspired to kill Henry.

With one of Max's men on guard in the library at all times, the other two had been sleeping on the third floor and had heard nothing in the night. Max had slept soundly after what he had imbibed and he imagined Steeple had, as well, never knowing what danger he was in. Now that the killer had struck again, the safest thing would be to take Vee and Flurry with him to London, but it seemed such a cowardly act. He would be abandoning others to their fate and he had never done such a thing.

Subsequent visits by Perth and Dr. Morris revealed no additional information that would lead one to suspect one member of the family above another. A search of Henry's room turned up no ivory elephant, nor any of the other missing items, and Max had the conscience to feel stricken about this. Henry had been a greedy man, but not inherently evil. He was probably dead now because of Max.

The evening after the funeral Max could not stand yet another evening of Lady Margery weeping into her handkerchief. Scarcely had the ladies vacated the dining room than he left George and Freddy with a full brandy decanter and a box of cigars. Steeple had been killed because of something that had happened since Max had returned. In a way this meant that the trail of the killer was hot again. He had only to figure out whether the murder had to do with the will, the inventory, the marriage contract, the agreement he had just made the man sign, or some other action of which he was yet unaware. He knew he needed a place to think as he turned his footsteps toward the stairs.

Veronica excused herself early from the drawing room, before the men had even come in, aiming to have a comfortable chat with Flurry. But her old friend was still below stairs in the servants' hall, where she had been taking her meals since the murder. Veronica felt so lonely she went to her room and got out all of her paintings of Max again, standing them around on the furniture. She had captured his every expression and knew his dear face better than her own. It seemed, indeed, that she understood Max a great deal better than she understood herself. Certainly she was better at managing him than her own wayward inclinations. She wanted him with a hunger that was almost painful.

She walked slowly around the room trying to decide which painting was her favorite. She paused in front of the one she had done the night of his arrival, with the lightning flashing in the background. It was as though the two sides of his face did not belong to the same man. The right side was arrogant, petulant, and forbidding in the stark light from the exploding sky. But the left shadowed side of his face held all the fears and pain, all the uncertainty of Max the boy. She loved both Maxes and was nearly drunk with desire for him. A jolt went through her as she remembered his hands on her hair, stroking her body. If he came to her now she was lost. With trembling fingers she opened the trunk and uncovered the final painting of Max unclothed. His arrogance was softened by a seductive smile.

"I had no idea," Max said softly.

Veronica gasped and dropped the large painting. Max picked it up and placed it on the dressing table. "All of me," he said in awe. "Whenever did you do them?" He spun on his heel to take in all the images, amazed that she had spent so much time on him, for these were not the work of a week or two, but a lifetime.

"I did not hear you knock," Veronica said breathlessly.

"And announce my presence at your door? That would be stupid. I was already here, waiting for you, thinking you might get undressed in front of me again." He saw her sway and was at her side in one stride. Always before she had been aware of his presence, but this time he had shocked her. She fit against his side as though she were a part of him and he enfolded her in his arms as he gazed at the paintings. "You did most of these from memory," he concluded, examining each portrait, from the smallest miniature to the large likeness of him in the nude. "But why, unless . . . unless you have always loved me."

"Of course I have," Veronica said impatiently. "But it was different when I was young. You were my hero, my rescuer, the one I knew I could count on to save me in the end."

Her small arms encircled his waist and she made him feel strong and competent in spite of all that had gone amiss.

"I fear I am a sad disappointment when it comes to

being a hero." He gazed into her eyes, assuring himself that she was all right. "I have brought nothing but confusion and trouble since I returned. Now another murder."

"Max, how can we all go on as before, as though nothing has happened?" She pillowed her face against his chest. "If we ever had any hope that Papa's death was a natural occurrence, that is at an end."

"I know. Now my chief concern is keeping you and Flurry safe." Max stroked her hair and gripped her even tighter.

"What do you mean?" Vee looked up at him. "Who could have any designs on us?"

"If I knew that, I could do something about it. You said something once about how cold Etta is, as though she has no human feelings." He felt her tremble in his arms and wondered if there was yet some horror she was not telling him.

"Yes, but we are talking about a particularly brutal way to kill someone, Max. I have nightmares about what Steeple must have gone through in the instant he knew."

"It was more than a murder. It was also an attempt to blame someone else," Max said. "Etta would have had the strength."

"I cannot believe it of her," Veronica said. "She and I may not be on the best of terms, but we are honest with each other. She would never do something that would hurt me so much."

"She plans to keep you from marrying me."

"I know," Veronica whispered.

"Who then?" Max rested his chin on the top of her head as he rocked her against him.

"Max, if I had a clue, do you not think I would tell you?"

"That is why I am asking you to pretend that we have conceded to her, that Etta's marriage will take place."

Veronica turned in his arms, puzzled at his request. "To what end would you raise her hopes when you know you have no intention of fulfilling the marriage contract?"

"To keep you safe," he said desperately. "That is my only aim. Would it be so hard to pretend for a few days, or a week, until I can resolve this?"

He stroked one long elegant finger along her cheek and felt her shiver again.

"So much for avoiding scandal," she said, closing her eyes. "To pretend Etta is to be your wife means faking indifference to you, and I am not at all sure I can do that."

"I was not thinking," Max said. "And I just asked you to lie for me. I am sorry." His hands slipped down her arms to her waist and rested on her hips. Something fired in his brain that extinguished both worry and reason. He bent to capture her lips and kissed the coldness away with a single-mindedness that caused her to press against him. His arousal began to throb between them and he wondered how he had managed to keep himself in check so long.

"Let us pretend we are already married," whispered Vee, "and that no one can come between us ever again."

"Whatever you say, my dear. Do we make love every night?" he asked as she escaped from his arms to lock the door.

Max chuckled as he removed his coat. "If we are married, why are you locking the door?"

Vee turned to stare at him in mock surprise. "Max, the children. We would not want them to be shocked if they discovered us."

"Somehow I do not think our children will be shocked, no matter what they catch us at." He sat on the bed to pull off his boots and shed the rest of his garments as though this were his room and he did this every night. He liked the feeling of normalcy this lent their relationship.

"Max, I wanted to help you undress," she said as she stared hungrily at his body.

"Sorry, shall I dress again and—"

"Do not be so provoking, but you can help me," she said as she struggled with the clasp of her pearls.

Max came lithely off the bed and undid the pearls only to drop them down her dress. "Let me find them for you, dear."

He could hear Vee's tiny sighs of pleasure as he fumbled inside her bodice. Finally the pearls dropped through to the floor, but not before he had run his fingers over her nipples, bringing her to full arousal.

He then began undoing her dress, wondering if he would survive this, for his pounding heart was making him rock. The dress crumpled about her feet on the floor.

He knelt behind her to run his hands up her thighs, to untie her drawers and slide her stockings down. She stepped out of the pile of clothing and her shoes, then turned to him, pressing herself against him and teasing his manhood with the warmth of her body.

He knelt again and began kissing her ankles and working his way up, provoking the most delicious giggles from her. He carried the shift up with him and tossed it aside before he gave full attention to her breasts again. She arched her back and sighed with pleasure as he held her by the hips and suckled each breast in turn. "I forgot to ask. How many children do we have?"

"Oh, six or seven," she sighed. "We have been too busy to count them lately."

"I must have given up my seafaring ways." He was about to pick her up and carry her when she locked her hands together behind his neck and snaked her legs up around his hips, giving his manhood a dangerous squeeze.

He grunted but carried her across the room this way to balance her hips on the edge of the high bed. "I forgot to ask how old married people do this?"

"I think we are trying something new tonight," Vee prompted.

"Surely we have tried everything by now," he said, releasing her gently onto the bed, then positioning himself to enter her.

"I think I hear the baby crying," Vee said with a teasing smile.

"Enough of this fantasy," he decided as he slid his length inside her.

She gasped and he let her trembling subside before he moved again, guiding his manhood from his standing position in a roughly circular motion that was driving her to distraction, her fingers clenching convulsively as she fisted the covers.

"Max, you are inventive for an old married man," she gasped.

"Not tired of me yet?" he asked as he began his slow retreat, which caused her to grasp his hips and pull herself toward him. "Afraid to let me go? I will always come back to you," he said with a thrust that caused a small gasp. He increased the speed of his thrusts so gradually that she was able to tolerate it for a time, but when the first wave of her release broke over her, she was like a drowning person, grasping him to her as though her life depended on him. He bit his lip and kept his own fulfillment at bay until she was quiet again. He kissed her and invaded her mouth with his tongue, making a double contact that set her to gasping again. Still on his feet but bending over the tall four-poster, he began thrusting again, capping her shoulders with his hands so as not to drive her across the bed. Her gasps came out as sweet whispers of contentment, and he was able to sustain his forbearance so long as she only called his name or made small sounds, but when her next paroxysm of pleasure took her, he had to stop her sounds with a kiss or risk discovery. Then his release rocked him and he groaned with the long, slow thrusts that delivered his seed and, he hoped, created one of those mythical children.

When he was empty he tried to stand but went to his knees beside the bed. He lay back on the floor and laughed as Vee's impish face appeared over the edge.

"Not bad for an old married man," she said, "and I think we have not wakened any of the children. Now come to bed."

"Vee, it will be some moments before I can even move."

"Does this mean we will only be able to do this once a day?"

"If you think you can stand it more than once a day," he gasped as he pulled himself to his knees, "I think I can accommodate you."

She held the covers up invitingly and he slid between the cool sheets. Vee turned her hot back to him and settled into the curve of his exhausted body with a sigh of contentment. He brushed her hair aside to kiss the nape of her neck. Her warm wriggles now spoke of comfort rather than lust, and he knew he would sleep well as he embraced her protectively, cupping one breast in his hand. He had never felt so alive as now, never so whole. Nothing else mattered to him except her. Tomorrow he might remember all those niggling worries that had been occupying him, but for now there was only sleep with her enfolded in his arms. He knew now they had a love that would last beyond hot youth, and that there was so much more to Vee than desire and fulfillment. There would be children and the thousand other joys of living together.

21

$\mathcal{A}$ stone clattered against Veronica's window, snapping her from an unquiet doze to full wakefulness. It had to be Max. He had been gone when she awoke and she had felt bereft. The pebble against the windowpane was always how he had gotten her attention when they were younger. She was picturing him as he had been that last night before he went away, eyes burning intently under disheveled hair, his lip bleeding, a bruise raising a welt on his cheek, and his white shirt torn nearly to his waist, revealing the marks of George's whip.

But when she slipped out of bed and pushed up the window she blinked and looked at him, then rubbed her eyes. For he was grown, of course, not at all injured and impeccably dressed except for that negligently tied cravat. Much had happened in the intervening years, but she did not want to think about that.

"It is barely dawn, Max. What is it?"

"Let us go for a ride," he pleaded. "It is our one chance to talk."

"I would love to, but if I am supposed to pretend to defer to Etta. I should not be alone with you again."

"We will not be alone. The horses will be with us. Besides, no one else will be up for hours."

Veronica was going to reply that Strider and Bonnie would be no use as chaperons, when she noticed the mists being drawn up by the sun's first rays.

"It may be too hot to ride later," Max insisted.

"Ten minutes," Veronica said and ran to her wardrobe.

Max strolled to the stables and saddled the horses himself. He had been thinking Veronica could not be serious about dressing so quickly, but she was indeed running across the lawn in her riding habit ten minutes later. He saw her take note of the two horses and surmised she had been wishing to ride double with him again. She was a wonder, innocent enough for her desire to show and frank enough to own to it.

Max lifted Veronica up on Bonnie and mounted Strider himself. In consideration for the older horse Max held his mount to an easy pace, stopping often to admire the swirls of fog gathered at the foot of some stretch of woods while treetops poked through. It looked very much like an oriental painting. The valleys surrounding Byerly Hill were still gauzed in shrouds of mist.

"Does it really look like this in the Orient?" Veronica asked in that milky voice that told him she could be pushed to tears for no reason except that something was very beautiful.

Max reined in Strider to stare at her, for they had been thinking exactly the same thing without speaking.

"Sometimes. But in many ways Byerly is more beautiful," he said, feeling more one with her than ever.

"Is it possible you might want to live here someday?"

He laughed. "With you? Yes."

"But for now we must finish our work somehow and make our escape," Vee said as she rocked to the familiar rhythm of Bonnie's walk.

"What if we cannot solve these puzzles we have set for ourselves," Max asked. "I have the most overwhelming urge to spirit you and Flurry away and leave the rest of them to their fates."

"We cannot do that." Vee's curls tumbled about the shoulders of her jacket as she shook her head.

"Why not? Do any of them deserve our help?" Max stared toward the house with disgust. "Keeping in mind one of them is a murderer."

"You would never have deserted one of your convoy when the French attacked, even if it were not a particularly valuable cargo." Veronica urged Bonnie toward a small stream for a drink.

"How do you know that?" Max asked as he loosened the reins for Strider to drink as well. "I have never spoken to you of my business or anything that happened during the war."

"I have seen your scars," Veronica said. "I know you were wounded and that you fought bravely. I know you might have died more than once. How like you not to speak of any of that, just so as not to worry me."

"Someone had to carry troops and supplies to the peninsula and bring the wounded back." Max felt he somehow had to defend his negligence with his own life. "I thought you were oblivious to my . . . side activities."

"I knew you were in danger. I could read between the lines of your letters. I could almost tell where you were by what was happening in the papers sometimes. I would read about some dangerous action and wonder if you had a hand in it."

"Yet you never berated me for those risks," Max said as they splashed across the stream and began the long winding ascent to the house through the woods on the south side of the hill.

"I thought perhaps you did not wish to speak of them, and now that there is peace, I hope you will not undertake anything so dangerous again."

"If I did continue my work for the government, would you try to stop me?" Max halted Strider to look at her.

Veronica rode up to him. "No, I would come with you and help you."

Max groaned. "So, you will not run from a fight so long as you can be part of it. You have not changed a bit, Vee."

Veronica raised an eyebrow at him so much in imitation of his own mannerism that she made him laugh.

"We are one now, Max. You must share everything with me and that includes the worst that life has to offer along with the best."

Max stared at her. "Do you trust me, Vee?"

"I have faith in your love, but no, I do not always trust your judgment, not when you have a penchant for falling off cliffs."

Max blew out an impatient breath. "The truth of it is that as aggravating as Steeple was, we did need him to press our suit through the courts. He was planning on getting the contract overturned since I signed it when I was underage. But he had discovered that it is difficult to find a barrister willing to help you sue your parent. Now I must make other arrangements. Plus there are several other matters that require my attention in London."

"You are leaving again?" Veronica asked, feeling an

even stronger tug of apprehension than she normally felt when Max was out of her sight.

"Only for the day, or at most overnight. Do you still have that dagger I gave you?"

"Yes." She lifted her skirt far enough for him to see it strapped over the thigh of her leather breeches.

He gave a shuddering sigh. "God, do not tempt me like that."

"So it is just as hard for you as it is for me," Veronica surmised.

"Yes, but when I think of making love to you I lose all my reason and even the desire to find the killer. You are both good and bad for me. You make me weak."

"You do the same for me," Veronica replied.

"And if I ask you to take me to that secret glade of yours again?" He looked at her with that seductive smile that she had immortalized in the nude painting. He was almost irresistible.

She bit her lip. "At this moment I would have the strength to say no. It is unavoidable that one or the other of us should be weak. So long as we both do not succumb at the same time."

"But why should we not enjoy each other?" Max pleaded. "We do plan to be together forever."

"As you said, we cannot think clearly when we are close to each other, let alone touching. If we are to find the murderer we are going to have to be able to think very clearly."

"Very well. Promise me that if I do not return by nightfall you will sleep in Flurry's room. It is the only way I will feel that you are both safe. I will have one of my men watch the hall."

"I promise." They rode for a few moments with no other sound than the jingle of the bridles and the thud of the horses' hooves on the packed trail. The morning birds flitted about in the undergrowth at this early disruption to their hunting. They had finally reached the plateau and Veronica let Bonnie graze as a reward. Max loosened his reins as well. "Shall we visit the statuary garden on the way back?" he hinted.

"Max, we have just been through that. I think that would be exceedingly dangerous." Veronica urged Bonnie into a reluctant trot.

"Are you afraid you cannot control me or yourself?" he demanded with a wicked grin.

"Both."

Max watched her easy seat on the horse. "Each time you make love to me I become even more drunk with lust for you. You are like strong poison, Vee. Once in the system, one can never recover from you."

"That is not a very flattering simile," Vee said, urging Bonnie to keep up with Strider, "considering what happened to Papa. I find myself quite sober now, and able to resist you with ease."

"Oh really? Perhaps that was my intent," Max said. "A dalliance with you would delay my departure by an hour or two at least. It would be better for me to leave now."

Veronica shot him a challenging look. "You flatter yourself, sir. Do you really think you can keep it up for an hour or two?"

"You little she-devil. Just wait until I come back from London."

Max left for London before breakfast, letting it be known he might be gone until the next day. Veronica enlisted a bored Etta to made more inroads into her papa's notes, garnering several more descriptions of

Nonsuch pieces and one drawing in John Strake's crabbed hand. For authentication it was nearly useless, but they could make out a lion and Catherine Parr's design, the maid rising from the Tudor rose. Veronica had very cleverly asked George to search and dust all the volumes in the library as they worked there. Veronica frequently noticed Etta gazing up at his lithe figure as he hefted a stack of books down the ladder in his shirt sleeves. If you liked fair men, George was a handsome specimen still in his prime, but he could never compare to Max.

Freddy happened to talk his way past Rajeev when another garden map dropped out of a dusty volume and fluttered to the carpet. This one was so old the paper had yellowed and become brittle. But this only convinced him of its authenticity, and he went back to digging in the hot sun. The three of them took afternoon tea in the library from which they could watch and chuckle over Freddy's struggles.

Max had managed to conclude his banking transaction, complex though it was, and stowed the results in the boot of the coach. He had also arranged to meet with his contact at the Foreign Office to make sure he was not immediately needed, and Henricks seemed mildly amused to discover that Max Strake had a family and that it was just as troublesome as most families.

"Sit down, Strake, I need to talk to you." The portly man poured two glasses of brandy and handed Max one as he lounged tiredly in the spartan office, piled with papers and maps.

"What? A mission?" Max felt himself tense but made a secret promise that he would take no assignment that interfered with his rescue of Vee or his work at Byerly.

"A letter has come our way that causes us concern." Henricks perched on the arm of the other chair, a tenuous position for a man of his weight. "Have you made any enemies recently?"

"Besides all of France and half of Spain, you mean?" Max asked flippantly.

"Yes, English enemies. The letter was not signed, but it was written by someone who knows you well and hinted at . . . well, quite frankly, it called into question your loyalties."

"That is absurd," said Max, a flash of anger meeting the brandy in his throat and almost choking him.

"Yes, I would have thought so myself, but the enclosure is a rather damning missive that indicates you may have taken a bribe. No matter how lightly I—"

"Bribe? What are you talking about?"

"I do not have the papers myself. They are being examined at a higher level, but it was your signature. I would know it anywhere."

"That is impossible. I demand to see these documents."

"I am sure you will if charges are filed. Under the circumstances, the government may simply decide to dispense with your services."

"Dispense with me without even giving me a chance to defend myself?" Max was on his feet, feeling ready for a fight and frustrated that the enemy was not available.

"Strake, I assure you I do not feel this way, but I shall have trouble convincing my superiors that you are not a risk."

"This is a nightmare," Max said, wondering why this had to happen just now when he had the least time to deal with it. "I shall be back in London in a week or so."

Max tossed off the rest of the brandy and left the glass on the untidy desk. "And Henricks?"

"Yes, Strake?"

"I do not want this swept under the rug. I demand to see those documents."

"I will convey your concerns."

"Not my concerns, my demands." Max left him, not caring how the man took the warning. He would not have his character tarnished by . . . who would even know about his activities, let alone have an interest in damaging his clandestine career? It was as maddening as the situation at Byerly.

Mustafah had come to London with Max and had been instrumental in tracking down a particularly elusive bishop by late afternoon, but the chase to the man's country place consumed most of the evening. Max sat numbly in the carriage across from his trusted retainer, wondering if the shock of his disgrace showed on his face. How could it be possible that both his worlds would fall apart at once? At least he had Vee and her love to sustain him, but even if they cleared away the entire mess at Byerly, he now had this to face when he got back to London.

He found himself rather amazed that Mustafah accepted each of his orders without the slightest explanation. Either the man had implicit faith in Max's judgment or had already reached the same conclusion himself. How much he knew of Max's affairs was not an issue. He never spoke of any of them.

Once both the special licenses had been obtained, not an easy task when the cleric suspected him to be two parts drunk, Max leaped back into the carriage and ordered Mustafah to instruct the driver to return to Byerly despite the darkness of the moonless night.

The man's hesitation and pursed lips caused Max to rethink the order.

"Tell him to find us an inn," Max said tiredly. "The horses need rest and I suppose we do as well."

It was not until the next morning after they had breakfasted and were rolling along a country lane in the direction of Byerly that Mustafah handed him the *Morning Post* without a word or warning about the notice. When Max's eyes fell on it he felt his blood run hot through his veins. Out of the corner of his eye he saw Mustafah turn a deaf ear to his stream of invective. If he had had his mother in the carriage at that moment he would not have answered for what he might have done to her.

22

Veronica had slept fitfully on Flurry's daybed. After breakfast she busied herself by finding two matching frames for the state portraits of Max and Etta. She had cleaned the frames, salvaged from the old portraits in the attic, and was trying Etta's in the gold-painted wood when Etta came into the library, her cheeks glowing.

"Any last minute changes?" Veronica asked, holding the painting up to show it to her. "Speak now or forever hold your peace." Veronica felt somewhat resentful of Etta's glowing cheeks and was wondering what had prompted her to quote part of a marriage ceremony to the girl.

"I wish . . ."

"What?" Veronica asked, feeling guilty at resenting Etta's happiness.

"Nothing. Look how the cracks in the wall almost make a design."

"Yes, they unite the portraits. You may want to consider hanging them here on this bare wall that I used for the backdrop. But that is quite up to you."

"Is Max's finished?"

"Unless there is something you want changed. Perhaps a kinder light in Max's eye, a more indulgent smile."

"No, we may compel Max to do what he should, but we cannot really change him. He will remain always alone and untouchable." Etta's short fingers played clumsily over the canvas as though this might be the only way she could touch Max.

"You say that as though you like him that way," Veronica said, snapping Max's picture into the frame and sliding the keepers into place.

"I cannot imagine him in any other fashion."

"You do not think he could be warm, loving even?" Veronica asked without facing the girl, for Veronica knew Max was nothing like the face he presented to other people.

Etta was holding her own portrait and regarding it with wonder. "Max? You must be joking. Veronica, do you wish to work on your father's notes again?"

"Yes, we may as well finish up."

"Are you going to stay until we find the treasure?" Etta asked, not letting Veronica know what answer she wanted from her.

"I am not sure. It does not seem so important anymore. If not, George will be able to help you continue the search. I will, at least, translate all Papa's scribblings."

"Your poor papa." Etta stood the painting on the mantel. "It is so unfair that he had to die for me to come here."

"What did you say?" Veronica asked, her lips dry with shock.

"If he had not died, Max would never have come back to England, at least not to Byerly. And we would never have known each other."

Veronica felt a sudden chill freeze the blood in her veins.

"I can almost see him," Etta continued. "With his pince-nez perched on his nose . . ."

Veronica gasped and spun to face Etta.

"I am sorry," Etta said. "I should never have mentioned it."

"How did you know Papa wore pince-nez?" She was feeling a little dizzy as though she were going to faint.

"Why, I met your father. He visited Dora in London one day when we happened to be there." Etta stood Max's portrait on the other side of the mantel.

"Did he . . . did he know about the engagement?" Veronica asked in wonder.

"I do not know. Now that I think of it, Dora did not introduce me as Max's fiancée."

"You assumed he knew." Veronica felt the blood begin to pound in her veins again and pursued her line of questioning. "Why did she surprise us with it? Have you any idea?"

"No, but I could ask her," Etta offered.

Veronica looked away. "No, do not bother. It matters little now."

"I must go change. George is taking me for a walk," Etta said gaily as she whisked out of the room. It was so odd how Etta had put it about Papa having to die. It seemed that just when Veronica was feeling the closest to the girl, she said something shocking.

There was a sound in the entryway like an enraged bull, and she knew Max had returned, but what was he going on about? She rushed out to see Max thumping all over the downstairs in his boots, shouting Etta's name. By the time the girl ran down the stairs, the rest of the household had gathered, including several of Max's men whom he dismissed with a nod.

"Are you responsible for this?" He thrust a formal-looking document at Etta. She had to uncrumple the paper and press it flat on the hall table before she could make any sense of it.

"Ah, I see they've posted the banns," Dora said, taking the paper from Etta, whose shock was so innocent as to convince even the enraged Max that it was his mother's doing.

"How did you manage that, you interfering witch?" he asked Dora.

"I forged your signature," Dora said coolly.

Max opened his mouth to speak, but could think of no rejoinder to such a blatant confession.

"Since you have neglected to post the banns, I arranged for it," Dora continued. "Someone had to get things moving."

"Are you mad?" Max asked, glaring at her. "You cannot compel me to marry Etta, no matter what you do."

"And with Henry newly dead?" Lady Margery started sniffing again. "How crude to be thinking of a wedding at a time like this, in a house of mourning."

"This is the third Sunday the banns have been posted." Dora's voice droned relentlessly on. "If any of you bothered to go to church like me, you would have known that. We can have the wedding any day we wish."

"You arranged this just the way you put that announcement in the *Post* without my knowledge." He tossed a newspaper onto the table.

Veronica looked at Max, with the coils of Dora's trap tightening about him. It was not his fault, but when he cried off now, even if he broke the engagement by legal means, he would be branded a cad.

"I should like to know," Max said, gritting his teeth.

"I should like to know how often you have made use of my signature."

"Only when necessary and in a good cause. In a few days you and Etta will be married, and we will all leave you alone here to get on with your life."

He stared at his mother as though he could not believe what she was saying. "You think that by destroying my career, you can make me a more amenable husband? You are insane. At least I know the answer to one of my problems." Max turned on his heel and strode toward the back door.

"Max, where are you going?" Dora demanded.

Max suddenly noticed Veronica standing in the doorway to the library. She had painted his face intense, playful, thoughtful, even despondent, but she had never seen him in a towering rage before. She did realize it was not directed against her.

"Back to London," he said brusquely, casting Veronica a speaking look as he turned and went out the back door. She raced through the library and the bedroom to escape through the greenhouse and chase him across the lawn to the stable.

"Max, what happened?" she asked breathlessly as she caught up to him.

He halted when he saw her and smiled wearily. "Has Strider been ridden yet today?"

"No, he is fresh. Max, what is it?"

"Good, I need him." Max strode into the stable and pulled a saddle off the rack.

"You are not going to tell me, are you?" Veronica complained.

"There is no time, Vee. I shall come back to you by nightfall, I promise." He saddled Strider himself as she bridled the horse for him. He led the animal out and kissed her once within full view of the house before he mounted and galloped down the drive.

They saw nothing of Max at dinner, and Veronica went straight to her bedroom after assuring herself that Flurry meant to go to bed early as well. Veronica stared out her window into the night, watching for Max. She began to wonder if they had driven him away for good. Perhaps he would be tempted to ride off to London and forget about Byerly. But she knew he would never leave her.

Then she saw the white horse trot up the steep drive, looking like a ghost in the mist. She could not tell for a moment if he was riderless or if Max was on him. She pictured Max lying broken and bleeding on the road to London. Strider stopped under the oak tree and there Max was on his back. She saw his white shirtfront first and breathed a sigh of relief. He was safe; he had not ridden over a cliff or any of the horrible things she had been imagining.

"Veronica, I must speak to you," he whispered urgently from the lawn.

"I do not think it is a good idea for you to climb this tree again," she whispered. "Come in by the door."

"Do you no longer trust me, Vee? I swear it was Dora who did it, not me."

Veronica sighed. "I know that, Max."

He walked the horse closer so he was directly under her sill. "Vee, I must speak to you. We have to make plans."

"I will come down then," she offered.

Max dropped the reins and slid from the horse, which immediately put its head down to graze. "I will take off my boots." Max said. Once barefoot he scaled the tree easily, using the hand and footholds of his youth.

Veronica stilled the protest on her lips for she wanted him to come to her without the slightest delay. She wanted him in her bed no matter how wrong it was. When she rested her hands on the casement he must have thought she was going to close the window.

"Please, Veronica. Do not shut me out."

"Never," she whispered as she reached out her hands to him. He stepped inside the window, his feet as sun-bronzed as the rest of him.

"You knew I would come," he surmised as his gaze roamed over her figure in the thin nightdress. He pulled her to him, his hands probing hungrily at her breasts and buttocks as he kissed her, awakening the banked fires of her passions. She pulled at his coat, trying to get it off him. He interrupted the kiss with a laugh to strip off his coat, shirt, breeches, and small-clothes so fast Veronica looked at him in amazement as she backed toward the bed.

"I believe you issued a challenge to me," Max reminded her, his eyes glittering in the candlelight, "to last for an hour or more?"

His smile was hungry and seductive, setting up her throbbing pulses again. "I also made you angry," Veronica added as Max knelt at her feet. He ran his hands slowly up her sides, lifting the gauzy material just enough to nuzzle her mound.

"But that wasn't you," he said distractedly.

Veronica gasped at what tricks his tongue was playing with her. Her knees started to tremble, but just as she would have fallen, he came to his feet and tossed the gown across the room, grasping her to his naked chest.

She shuddered at the feel of his manhood throbbing

between their bellies. "I refused to interrupt our ride to make love," she prompted, as she sought his mouth.

"Ah yes. I owe you something for that, as well. Perhaps a riding lesson."

"What do you mean?" She looked at the wicked gleam in his eyes and knew she would do whatever he thought of.

"The first time we did this I observed several deficiencies in your style. Granted you are a beginner . . ."

"Beginner?" Veronica complained. "I do not imagine it takes any particular talent to . . ."

"Ah, but that is where you are wrong."

He teased one nipple into an erect bud with his tongue, then closed his mouth over it, suckling it between his teeth and tongue as a foal would. She gasped and let her head drop back, offering no resistance when he nuzzled her other breast in the same teasing manner. She felt weak in the knees, for all her blood was pounding in her stomach.

"A woman of your caliber could manage to make me last if she had a mind to."

She was tempted to argue with him but knew she was on shaky ground. "Show me," she finally demanded.

"Very well." Max left her swaying and walked to the bed, laying down as lithely as a large cat and looking a challenge at her.

Veronica made a move to straddle him and he said, "Not so fast. Would you leap on your horse like an aide-de-camp about to rattle off down the road with an important message?"

"No," she said. "I would speak to him first and pet him." She began working over Max's body with her hands, stroking his muscles and testing them as though she had to memorize and reproduce him three-dimensionally. She examined every part of him, drawing more than one excited gasp from him. She ended her tour of him with his manhood, where she ran a tentative finger from base to tip and received a response. Max had his eyes shut tightly, his lips compressed but smiling at the corners. She experimentally ran her tongue along the engorged member and was rewarded with a slow groan. She could feel a wetness between her legs and knew she was more than ready for him. She threw her leg over his waist and he opened his eyes, grasping her hips.

"Now, slowly Vee. Do not lay the whip to me as though I were a butcher's nag."

She positioned herself above him and teased his shaft into her as slowly as she could, enjoying every gasp that escaped his seductive lips. His hands were on her buttocks guiding her, and when she had impaled herself on him she looked at him with a sense of accomplishment.

"I can feel waves of heat radiating through you," he said slowly. "I can feel your blood racing, but do not clench those tight internal muscles of yours just yet. You will feel so much more of this if you relax inside."

She licked her dry lips and listened to him, consciously unclenching the muscles that had been built from years of riding. She lay her length on him and discovered that he touched her in new places. Her hands gripped his shoulders as she reached for a kiss. He raised his head and their mouths locked. He slipped his tongue alongside hers and began a back and forth motion. She slowly straddled him again and repeated the motion with her body so slowly as to be torture for her. Their double contact completed some circle of need and fulfillment that she never wanted to end.

His large hands with those long fingers kneaded her buttocks, pulling her tender tissues so that each of her advances and retreats set up a washing wave of muscle contractions that made her dizzy with ecstasy.

She broke the kiss to ask breathlessly, "Max, how long have we been at it?"

"Not very long at all. Be patient, Vee."

"That is stupid. For I can have you now and have you again later. I do not want to wait."

"Then you concede it is you who cannot last an hour."

"I concede anything you wish," she said as she picked up the tempo of her back and forth motion, still careful not to bring her internal muscles into play. But she had not realized how total her loss of control would be when the storm surge of her need washed over her. She was incoherent with passion, rearing against him and grappling with him so that he groaned his need aloud. When she was near exhaustion, he grasped her arms and flipped her sideways onto her back. Instinctively she locked her legs around him and he pursued her with thrusts so slow and deliberate that she knew he was still in control of himself and that she had no vestige of reason left. Finally his own vast hunger for her asserted itself and his thrusts became deliberate and rhythmic, his testes smacking against her bottom in the most lascivious manner.

"Now, Vee," he whispered harshly. Grip me."

She clenched her muscles and he moaned aloud, his manhood engorged even more for the final thrust. When he backed out little by little, shuddering and spilling seed inside her, he gasped his relief in her ear as she stroked his neck, back, and shoulders, whispering reassurances to him.

"I am too heavy for you," he said as he rolled sideways and came out of her, still blowing out breaths of relief.

"Do you want a blanket?" Veronica asked solicitously, cuddling against his heaving chest.

"I think we can abandon the riding metaphor now. It has served its purpose." He settled her against him possessively.

"It has taught me one thing," Veronica said, stroking the hair on his chest.

"What is that, my little jockey?" Max kissed the tip of her nose.

"That you have much more restraint than I."

"That is because I need to. I only get one chance at it, and you can experience such a surge of euphoria again and again."

"Women are luckier than men," Veronica said in awe.

"Perhaps in that one way," he conceded.

"The only truly important way."

"I see I have managed to change your expectations about the world a great deal," Max said with a chuckle.

"Yes, I will always paint, of course, but it does not fill my soul's need as it used to. I think you need to sleep now, Max. You are exhausted."

"But I have left Strider on the lawn."

"He remembers Byerly. He will take himself to the stable."

23

$\mathscr{H}$is first sensation was of a cool breath playing over his naked flesh. He was too tired to open his eyes but wondered that he would not at least have thrown some gauze over the bed to keep the insects away. There was some creature in bed with him, breathing as lightly as a cat. He opened one eye and saw Vee, her black hair tumbling gloriously about her shoulders and those dark lashes of hers fanning her cheeks. Her mouth was slightly parted, revealing her pearly teeth. He wanted desperately to kiss her and enter her again, but he was afraid if he woke her she would regain her reason and send him away.

Secretly he hoped that they were discovered together. There would be no question then. He would have to marry the girl he had ruined. The law said so, and this might encourage the court to find in his favor. There would be a scandal of course, but Vee said she did not care about that. His waking mind ran through all the ramifications of a public disgrace. It was not as though the government would stop seeking his services for that reason. Scandal meant nothing to the English so long as a man's loyalties remained intact, and he had not cheated at cards ... or taken a bribe. He rather thought he had convinced Henricks that his insane mother was the instigator of the incriminating documents. He had, at least, made the man promise to study the signatures more carefully. It was an unlikely tale, he had to admit, his mother wanting him home so desperately that she tried to destroy his career.

And even if Henricks did dispense with him, what did he care? That would assure that Vee would never insist on accompanying him on any really dangerous assignments, though the excitement of such a situation had a certain appeal. No, nothing made as much sense to him right now as going back to sleep and letting Flurry walk in on them. Even that dangerous parasol of hers was no deterrent to him anymore, not after what he had been through.

When Vee awoke she was prepared to feel bereft at Max's departure. She was not prepared for the full sun streaming in the window and Max still tucked up beside her with his muscular arm encircling her breasts. She spun to face him, trying to escape his sleepy embrace. "Max, wake up," Veronica whispered desperately, rubbing his cheek. "It is morning. You must get back to your room before anyone is about." Veronica slid out of bed and pulled her dressing gown on, tying it securely as she bent to toss Max's clothes up onto the bed.

"Do not worry," Max said as he sat up, raking his hair with his fingers and discovering the lump where he had ridden into a limb in the dark. "Now that I know you are mine forever, I will make it right. It does not matter if Flurry finds us."

"It matters very much," Veronica argued. "Put these on. I shall help you."

Max sat limply on the bed and began to draw on his smallclothes and breeches, remembering too late his boots on the lawn. Veronica held his shirt open and helped him shrug it on. Then she handed him his coat and went to unlock the door.

"My little Vee, why so desperate?" he asked, lifting her chin gently with one hand. "Flurry will understand. She means to come with us."

"With us?" Vee asked distractedly. "Of course she will, but we cannot leave yet. What of the murders?"

"I do not think we can solve them," Max said sleepily. "I think it would be best if we left now before some other disaster befalls us."

Veronica stopped dead still to gaze at him, to study every line of his face. She realized that he had a bruise on his forehead and wondered if she had done that in the night or he had come to her injured and she had not even noticed. Perhaps that was why he was so close to giving up on the mysteries, his head hurt and he was tired. She kissed him hastily as she pushed him toward the door. "But we agreed to keep our affair a secret, at least until we leave here. Now go."

"But I need you," Max protested.

"Our needs are mutual. Well, perhaps mine are stronger," Veronica said in a desperate voice. "But I enjoy the secrecy of our affair too much to make it public if I can help it." She pulled open the door to the hall and looked left and right. "Go now, there is no one in sight."

Max stumbled out, shaking his head in confusion. "But I love you and you love me," he whispered urgently. "Sooner or later people will realize that. We may as well leave now before we have another ugly scene."

"Of course I love you, Max. But you said it yourself. It is not safe to let anyone else know until we catch the murderer."

"Veronica, you must—" His sentence was cut off as Veronica pushed him into the hall and locked her door. He was about to pound for readmittance when he heard the shuffle of Mustafah's feet on the stairs. He walked past the man with the intention of ignoring him, but Mustafah was carrying his boots, newly polished, and handed them over without meeting Max's eyes. Max merely said thank you and went downstairs to his room on the first floor.

Veronica washed and dressed herself, feeling more alive than she had in days. Max was like strong drink to her. She could do anything when under his spell, but sooner or later her rational mind reasserted itself and she realized they were no closer to finding any answers than when they started their research. When she glanced out the window she saw Max walking numbly toward the statuary garden. He would probably sit there for hours, trying to puzzle out their mysteries, and he was better off thinking about them alone. The Nonsuch mystery was not important, for she did not think it was linked to either death. What she did not perceive was the connection between the two murders. Who would want both her papa and Henry Steeple dead? She raked a brush through her hair, trying to bring it into some kind of order. She kept coming back to the will, but in spite of the solidness of the estate in terms of rents and production, there was not enough capital or cash to kill someone over. She, Max, and Flurry were the only beneficiaries to get much from it. There had to be some connection she was not seeing.

Still mulling over motives, Veronica went downstairs to find Flurry alone in the breakfast parlor. She ate her breakfast hungrily. It suddenly struck her that she was carrying on one of the most erotic affairs she had ever heard of under her own roof with no one the wiser. She was amazed that she could do it, but when she thought of Max she wondered how any woman could resist him.

"Are you feeling feverish?" Flurry asked.

When the question penetrated, Veronica replied. "I did not sleep very well last night, Flurry."

"Because of Max, no doubt. I thought you had decided not to love him."

Veronica closed her gaping mouth, thinking for a moment that Flurry knew. But Flurry must have thought she had only been wakeful. "I begin to realize that logic has no sway over that emotion. What is worse, I am confusing Max."

"Yes, I know," Flurry said. "I saw him leaving for his usual walk, looking like an unmade bed. He has gotten positively careless in his appearance."

Veronica cleared her throat and took a sip of tea, hot with the taste of India.

Etta bounced into the breakfast parlor in a walking dress. "Has George been down yet?"

"Not yet," Flurry said. "Did he promise to take you for a walk?"

Etta merely sighed and got herself something to eat. "No, but it does not hurt to be prepared."

The rest of the family trickled in and there was a rumble of talk overridden by the clatter of plates and scrape of forks.

"Veronica and I have been talking about our trip,"

Flurry said. "It may be necessary for us to leave before the wedding."

Veronica choked on a sip of tea and stared at Flurry, for there was not going to be a wedding and she felt no urgency about them leaving.

"You must do as you see fit," Dora replied, but with such a look of relief that Veronica realized Dora did want to be rid of her quite desperately.

Of course, Flurry would want to get away from this house, where she was suspected—and had even been accused—of being a murderess. Veronica should have thought of that before instead of selfishly staying to make love to Max and pursue her investigations. Perth had come again to question the servants and everyone who had still been up late that night, laying particular emphasis on anyone who had access to the drawing room and Flurry's knitting bag. He had not been pleased by Max's absence, but when Flurry had asked about going to London, Perth had not forbidden it. The man was clearly no closer to an answer than he had been the first day.

To Veronica's surprise Max came in, but by the door this time. He looked around the room mutely, poured himself a cup of tea, and came to sit by Flurry with such a forbidding expression that even George did not address any remark to him.

"Max, where the devil did you come by that bruise?" Flurry asked, pushing his hair back from his forehead as though he were a boy, and making him flinch.

Max caught her hand and returned it to her lap. "I rode into a limb."

"You were walking this morning, not riding," she corrected.

"I mean I walked into a limb." He took a long drink

of tea. Although he was being cold even to Flurry, his eyes took on a warmth when they rested on Veronica, and she could not help feeling a certain pride in being able to manage Max when no one else could.

Dora stared at him. "If I did not know better I would have thought you were fighting with George and Freddy again."

These two turned such outraged stares at Max that he said in a harsh voice, "Those were boys' games. We are beyond that now."

"I should hope so," George replied.

"Vee, I must talk to you," Max said in a businesslike way that might have fooled the rest of them.

"Not now, Max," Flurry said brutally. "We must start our packing." She got up and waited for Veronica to rise as well. There was a silence as they walked toward the door. Max stared mutely after them, but did not move to follow them.

"Are you all right?" Flurry asked as they went up the stairs.

"Yes, but why such a sudden exodus, Flurry? You can go to London if you wish, but I want to know who killed Papa and Henry."

"And I want you safe away from here. You are too much competition for both of those girls, and someone may be insane enough to do something about that."

Veronica wanted to defend Etta, but how much did she know about her, really. She ran all the suspects they had around in her mind again as though they were on a racetrack, but there was never any clear-cut winner. She paused on the stairs as a sudden fear hit her.

"What is it?" Flurry demanded.

"I have been confusing myself by trying to figure out who would have wanted both Papa and Steeple dead."

"It does not make much sense," Flurry agreed.

"But Flurry, the same person may not have committed both murders."

Flurry stared at her, processing this new information with a growing look of horror. "You are telling me there may be two murderers in the house rather than one?"

"I suppose that is what I am thinking," Vee agreed.

"All the more reason to pack quickly and get away from this place."

"But did not Perth tell you not to leave the country?"

"We need not go so very far. But I have the most uneasy feeling that if we do not leave now, Max may be tempted beyond his will to resist you. I saw him kissing you again yesterday."

Flurry went up the stairs and Veronica stared after her, wondering how strong her heart was, but deciding in the end not to tell her whose will was the weakest.

It had been hard to explain why nothing could be packed in her largest trunk except paintings that she must take with her. In frustration Flurry unearthed another trunk from the box room and had it carried upstairs. In a whirlwind of activity she had them packed in the course of the day, except a few things for tomorrow. Veronica felt helpless, as though the tide that was sweeping her away from Byerly was one that would carry her out to sea and lose her forever. She was sitting near the baby gargoyle later that day, tossing bites of biscuit into his mouth.

"Is he good at catching?" Max asked.

Veronica bit her lip and steeled herself. "Better than your average statue." She turned to look at him and wondered how long he had been leaning against the willow tree.

"I just wanted to ask," he said, coming to gather up the bits of bread from the grass. "We never found the Nonsuch treasure. Was there anything else of use in Uncle's notes?"

"One very bad drawing. We could scarcely make it out."

"Well, what good is a treasure once you find it?" Max tossed a bite and it landed in the gargoyle's mouth. "All the fun is in the quest."

Veronica looked at him out of the corner of her eye to see if he intended a double meaning, but there was no subterfuge about him. His eyes were dead calm and sad. "Max, before we . . . got distracted last night, you said something about making plans." Veronica made the mistake of looking at him and the now-familiar desire began to churn in her again.

He snatched up her hand and locked fingers with her. "I will follow you to London. My ship will take us to Madagascar or the Indies."

"I rather think Flurry has her heart set on Paris."

"Very well. I will take you to Paris," Max offered, feeling the tearing of their parting more than he had suspected he would. He wanted them to go, he wanted them to be safe, yet wanted to go with them himself.

"And never catch the murderers?"

"I shall do my very best, but I— What did you say?"

"Only that it is possible we are dealing with two entirely separate motives, and that means—"

Max sat suddenly on the bench and shook his head. "Yes, I see. What a wretched family. I cannot leave until I find out what happened no matter how long it takes, but I have gone over it all again in my mind and I find myself no closer to the truth than I was a week ago." He stared at the gargoyle as though it might speak and give him some useful information.

"Flurry is very distressed, so I think that I had better go with her. You can catch up with us later."

"Yes, that is best. But I wanted to go with you as your husband, Vee. A week from now will do as well, I suppose." He held the back of her hand to his lips, then closed his eyes and laid it against his cheek. Her hand felt cool to him and he wanted nothing more than to find out what the rest of her felt like at this time of day, but he must restrain himself or he would only make the parting more difficult for Vee.

She bent toward him to kiss him but jumped back at the calling of their names from outside the box hedge. "That is Etta. I wonder what has happened."

Max's face showed his disgust at the interruption.

"There you are," Etta said breathlessly. "You must come quickly."

Veronica ran to her, thinking she had never looked so pretty as now with her cheeks pink from running, and her hair curling in tendrils about her neck.

"We have found the thief," Etta gasped. "The elephant and all the other artifacts."

"Who is it?" Max demanded, as he followed the girls, both of whom were hurrying toward the house.

"Lady Margery," Etta said over her shoulder. "I lend her my maid, Joslyn, from time to time, as she did not bring one of her own."

"A spy?" Max asked with a wry smile.

"Yes, the elephant, the pistol, and the dogs are in a trunk she keeps locked and under her bed."

"Etta, that is amazing," Veronica said, beginning to run.

"Amazing?" Max asked, seeming to get some of his old energy back. "That Lady Margery would steal? I personally cannot own to much surprise."

"No, that Joslyn would be clever enough to discover it," Veronica corrected. "Do not dawdle, Max."

They pelted in the back door and pounded up the stairs like a bunch of children. Flurry saw them in the hall and followed to deliver a scolding. They all came upon an argument in Lady Margery's room, with Joslyn crying and Lady Margery demanding the return of her key. Max strode forward and held out his hand. The maid gratefully dropped the key into it.

George and Freddy appeared in the doorway demanding to know what was the matter. Max pulled the trunk from under the bed and unlocked it.

"This is outrageous," Lady Margery said.

"Yes, an ivory elephant, one antique pistol, two Chinese dogs, and the vase." Max laid the gun on the bed and presented Veronica and Etta each a dog to hold. "Well, Aunt Margery, I am sure you have an explanation."

Freddy was gaping and staring at his mother as much as the others were.

Lady Margery ran one hand through her flaxen hair in a distracted way. "My brother John wanted me to have them. I am sure he said it a thousand times."

"See, there," Freddy said, like a man grasping at straws.

"Papa never said anything of the sort." Veronica turned an angry face on her aunt.

"How would you know, you stupid girl," Lady Margery spit at Veronica. "Besides, he was half-mad near the end. He probably forgot to tell you."

"He was not mad," Veronica protested.

"Of course he was. That is the effect of the castor—"

"What?" George said into the stunned silence.

"How did you know it was the castor beans that killed Uncle John?" Max asked.

"So, it *was* you who poisoned him," Veronica said softly, staring at the woman in horror and holding her hand to her mouth. Flurry came to take her by the shoulders.

Was it the castor beans that you used?" Max demanded harshly.

Lady Margery gaped and tried to speak, but no words came.

"George," Freddy demanded. "Are you going to let Max insult Mother like that?"

"But if she did poison Uncle John . . ." George said.

"I did not poison anyone and these are mine!" Lady Margery wrenched one dog out of Etta's grasp and handed it to Freddy. She was making for Veronica when Max intervened and grasped her by the wrist. Freddy lunged belatedly between Max and his mother, dropping the statue onto the bed and carrying Max to the floor under his greater weight. They wrestled fruitlessly, each trying to gain a hold over the other. The washstand with its pitcher and bowl broke apart as they rolled into it, the china pieces shattering on the wood flooring. Veronica had an impulse to throw herself into the fray, but Max seemed to be gaining the upper hand. In fact, he now had Freddy in an arm lock that he could only escape from by lunging wildly enough to carry Max to his feet. But Max held on as though he were wrestling one of the rams.

George stared at the two men in disgust, shaking his head.

"Let him go," Lady Margery commanded so firmly that Veronica turned to her and gasped.

"Max, she has the pistol," George warned.

Max looked surprised for once, but laughed.

"Have a care, Mother," Freddy warned, the sweat beading on his brow.

"Let my son go, Max."

"Fire away, Aunt Margery," Max goaded.

"Max, duck," George shouted as he pushed past Veronica.

Freddy lunged and Max tightened his hold, dragging him down onto the bed. Veronica saw Lady Margery's finger tighten on the trigger and the hammer click down. In the split second between the powder catching and the retort, George leaped at the crazed woman. The room was full of smoke.

Veronica could see that George, prone on the bed, now held the pistol and gave a sigh of relief.

"I think I am hit," George said in surprise, staring rather calmly at the blossom of red spreading on the shoulder of his coat.

"George!" Etta gasped, dropping the china dog to his death on the carpet. She ran to George and knelt by the bed.

Lady Margery shrieked six or seven times, going rigid with each piercing wail. Then she fell to the flooring, thrashing and kicking. Veronica stepped around her to add her small handkerchief to the pad Max was pressing against George's shoulder.

"What is wrong with Mother?" George asked in a strained voice. "She is not the one who got shot."

"You have heard of strong hysterics?" Max asked.

"Flurry, more bandages," Veronica commanded. "How bad is it, Max?"

"A flesh wound, I think, but nothing to trifle with. I trust no piece of wadding or fabric is embedded. Certainly the ball skimmed over the shoulder and lodged itself in—oh, dear, the other Chinese dog is finished, I'm afraid."

"Blast the damned dog, Max! Will George be all right?" Etta demanded.

"Yes, of course," Max said as he raised an eyebrow at this outburst. "Ah, Mustafah, there you are. Send the stable lad for the doctor, please."

"What about Mother?" Freddy asked of the still prone and shrieking woman.

"You deal with her," Veronica commanded. "Or go find Aunt Dora."

Freddy gratefully disappeared as Flurry slipped back into the room with bandages. Between the four of them they slipped off George's coat and wrapped the wound tightly.

Dora appeared, looking harried, but immediately took command of Lady Margery, holding her wrists together and talking to her in a half-threatening, half-cajoling tone that seemed to calm her.

George got to his feet and asserted he would walk to his room under his own power, Veronica suspected the quicker to escape from the noise of his mother.

Etta pushed Veronica aside as she and Max helped George down the hall.

Veronica trailed after them, carrying the ruined coat. "Max, you idiot, why did you tell Aunt Margery to shoot?"

"Because I knew it was an antique pistol. I thought it would not fire even if it were loaded."

"But I cleaned and tested it myself," Veronica protested. "I kept it loaded in the library in case of prowlers."

"Your efficiency cost you the Chinese dogs," George

said sadly as he made his halting progress down the hall.

"No matter, George. At least we know for sure who killed Papa and will not be forever suspecting other people." Veronica ran into the room ahead of them and turned down the bed as Max helped George down upon it. "I just realized. George, you *did* know the pistol would fire, for I told you I had it working. You saved Max's life."

Max stared at George, twisting his head sideways like an inquisitive dog.

"Max is such an amusing fellow," George mumbled. "I could not let anything happen to him. But who would have thought Mother would stoop to murder. And did she kill Henry Steeple as well?"

"Do not try to talk," Etta said gently. "Actually the dogs were very ugly, certainly not worth shooting someone over."

Veronica sighed. "The worst of it is, if she had asked me for them, I probably would have said to take them."

George glanced at her. "That is handsome of you, Veronica."

Flurry came purposefully into the room with a draught of something in a glass. "Are you children going to keep George talking when he should be resting?"

Veronica and Max gave ground, but Etta stayed to dampen a cloth for George's brow.

Veronica stole a glance at Max and he gave a shrug as much as to say, Who knows where this may lead?

They tiptoed past Lady Margery's room, where Mercia entered with the laudanum she had been sent to fetch. Low moans now issued from behind the door.

When they got downstairs Max saw the stable boy just leaving and hailed him from the drawing room window. Max leaped over the sill and mounted Strider himself, remarking that he knew where Dr. Morris would be.

Since Veronica had done everything she could for George, she went to see if Dora needed anything, but was told by Max's mother that she should not be attending the sickrooms and should rest. Veronica said a silent prayer of thanks for reliable Dora. In spite of how she had treated Max, she certainly knew what to do in an emergency. Veronica went to sit in the library and stare blankly out the window. She was glad to know who had killed Papa, even though she did not know why. A woman who would stoop to stealing might have any number of reasons, including revenge. But that was only half the problem. Margery would have had no reason, and indeed was clearly incapable of what had been done to her husband. So who was it?

Max returned with Dr. Morris within an hour and the practitioner seemed glad but puzzled to hear of Margery's confession. Max thought the man should be more relieved; he certainly was. Morris bandaged George with Max's help, talking bracingly to him as though it were just a scratch, though Max knew any wound could be dangerous if not properly cleaned.

Max invited the doctor to stay for dinner, seeing as he had interrupted his lunch. Etta remained by George's side and Dora was sitting with Lady Margery.

"Young George will be fine in a week or two. That is not to say he should be up and tearing about. The wound could easily become infected. As for Lady Margery . . ." The man paused as he selected a brace of lamb chops. "I ought to inform the magistrate, but I have my doubts about her being able to stand trial."

Max was not eating, but he had already emptied two glasses of wine. "Did she say anything else, such as why she did it?"

"I questioned her, certainly." He paused with his knife and fork poised over a portion of turbot as though he were going to dissect it.

Veronica pushed her plate away and Flurry reached for her hand under the table to give it a reassuring squeeze.

"I asked her what she had given Lord Byerly and she kept shaking her head no. I mentioned ricin and she seemed confused, but when I referred to it as castor bean she got hysterical again."

"I do not think we could prove a case against her," Max said, pushing his unused silverware about. "And I am not sure I want to, especially since her second victim was her own husband. Veronica?"

Veronica swallowed hard. "She looks very nearly as tortured as Papa before he died. I know I should hate her, but I only feel sorry for her."

Freddy swallowed a bite of beef. "Best let it rest, Max. Think of the scandal for the family."

"Think of your mother's sanity!" Max snapped. "I do not give a damn about scandal."

Mercia stopped sniffling into her plate. "Are you saying Mother is insane?"

"At the moment," Dr. Morris pronounced, "she is having a breakdown. Whether she recovers or not depends on the care she is given."

"We will not send her to an asylum." Freddy thumped the table.

"Of course not," Max said. "She will remain here, heavily attended until we see if she regains her reason. I would still prefer to know what could have made her do in Steeple. My hiring him could not have affected her mind that badly."

"And what if she never regains her reason?" Mercia asked tremulously.

"Then she will always have a home at Byerly," Etta said decisively, glaring at both Max and Lady Eustace, daring either of them to challenge the statement.

Mercia rose and threw down her napkin. "I will not stay mewed up here for the rest of my life. I want to go home. I want to go back to London. Freddy, help me."

"Not now, Mercia," her brother said dismissively.

Mercia fled the room in tears, causing the doctor to clear his throat.

"Nerves . . . must run in the family," Dr. Morris said. "Is there any of that ham left?"

When Veronica went into the breakfast parlor George and Max were both there, and though they looked like they had been discussing something serious, they both looked pleased with themselves.

"Shall I go away until you are finished?" she asked. "I assume this is some secret."

"Ah, she is a sensitive child and always knows when she is not wanted," Max jibed.

"As it happens, Veronica, we have concluded our business," George said smugly.

"Are you sure you should be up?" Veronica asked as she filled her plate from the sideboard.

"That is exactly what Max asked me. I was getting restless. Besides, I could hear Mother all night long."

Veronica poured herself a strong cup of tea. It was as though someone had just mentioned a ghost. "Dr. Morris promised to stop by daily to check on her."

"I am so sorry, Veronica, and for you, too, Max," George said. "I never would have thought it of Mother."

"Surprising how you do not really know people, even

your own family," Veronica replied, seating herself at the table.

"Or how they may change a great deal in twelve years," George offered.

Mercia came into the room. "Where the devil is Freddy? His room is mud from one end to the other."

"Oh, I ran into him in the hall," Max said. "It seems he has found another treasure map."

Veronica shook her head. "The lawn looks like a battlefield. I keep telling him there is no such thing as buried treasure and he will not listen."

Mercia got herself a plate of food, shook out her napkin and sat down.

Etta dashed into the room, then relaxed when she saw George. "Are you sure you should be up?" She faked unconcern as she made herself a plate of food.

George grinned at Max.

Dora came in looking grave and tired, reminding them all of the woman upstairs.

"Who is with Mother?" Mercia asked.

"Lady Eustace offered to sit with her since she is quiet." Dora gratefully accepted the cup of coffee Veronica poured for her. "I have been thinking, Max, that since Lady Margery knows me and I seem to be able to keep her quiet, perhaps I should stay on here with her . . . indefinitely." She took a drink of coffee and sat down while they all absorbed this.

"You would be willing to do that, Aunt Dora?" Mercia asked hopefully.

"I will be staying on anyway as Max's agent at Byerly," George said. "I am sure I can find someone to nurse her."

"Yes, I know," Dora said. "But I was thinking it

should be someone in the family because of the way she rambles."

"I see," Max said. "That is very generous of you, Mother, but I do not think you should sacrifice yourself—"

"I would be happy to stay," Dora insisted. "Besides, I enjoy living at Byerly, and other than Etta and Lady Eustace I have no friends in town."

"Well, that is all settled then," Max said, trying not to wonder why his mother would be so generous.

A shout from the yard caused Etta to run to the window. "It is Freddy. He is incredibly filthy and dancing around with a shovel. He says—Veronica, he says he found the treasure."

"But there is no treasure," Veronica said. "Can we never have a quiet meal?"

Mercia ran to the window. "He is carrying something," she reported.

Veronica opened her mouth to repeat that there was no treasure when she glanced at Max. The corner of his mouth was twitching in that way of his.

"George," Flurry commanded as she whirled into the room. "What are you doing up? If you do not lay down this instant, you may faint."

"Not a bit of it," George said, hauling himself up. "I must see what Freddy has found."

Freddy rushed into the room carrying a small chest that he flipped open for his sister's inspection. "Gold!" he shouted, running his fingers through the coins. "It is gold."

"So it is," Max said calmly.

"Let me see," Mercia commanded. "It is the Strake treasure! Give it here."

"Not a chance," Freddy said, snapping the lid shut to

the endangerment of his sister's fingers, and tucking the chest under his arm.

"But it is part of the estate," Mercia said. "Max, reason with him."

"I should say it is more a case of finders keepers," Max said helpfully.

"What?" Mercia shrieked.

"Yes," Veronica agreed. "Freddy has worked hard for this treasure. Let him keep it, I say, and good riddance to him."

"He is the only one who believed in it," George reminded his sister. "Freddy does have a right to it."

"Thanks, George," Freddy said. "I will not forget what I owe you. By the way, how is the arm?"

"Mending," George replied.

"Good."

"How dare you?" Mercia demanded. "This is as good as stealing from me, Freddy."

Max stared at the two of them. "You may use my carriage if you feel you need to get to town, Freddy."

"I am on my way."

"I am coming with you," Mercia said. "It was left to me, so I should have a share even if you did find it, Freddy."

"Those two will fight about it all the way to London," George observed with a grin.

"I had once hoped that they might carry your mother with them," Max observed. "Ah, well, we cannot have everything."

With the team harnessed Freddy waited impatiently for Mercia to pack, but he did wait for her. The house seemed a shade quieter. After dinner that night Flurry helped Veronica make up a tray of food to take to Dora while it was still hot. Veronica found the reek of the strong coffee offensive, but to each her own.

"No change in her?" Veronica asked.

"It might be best if she did not regain her reason," Dora said, thrusting a bookmark into the tome she was reading and taking the tray from Veronica.

"Is she able to eat anything?" Veronica asked, noticing the book was one of her papa's plant books. How bored Dora must be.

"I fed her some broth earlier, but she has no appetite," Dora said as she plowed into the feast Veronica had brought.

Veronica stared at the prone woman, so pale, with the usual blond ringlets in straggly disorder on the pillow. "If one were to believe in divine retribution, one might feel she has gotten what she deserves." Veronica clenched her hands together in front of her.

Dora glanced up. "No one would blame you, Veronica, if you did gloat, if you did enjoy seeing justice served."

Veronica blinked away tears. "But what is the point? It will not bring Papa back."

Dora pushed the tray aside and came to her, taking both her arms in a bracing grip. "In this condition she is not likely to do that to anyone else. That is the real reason for stopping someone like her, to protect others." She smiled approvingly as Veronica nodded. "The wedding is set for tomorrow, a private affair in the drawing room. I just wanted to warn you. Will you be able to see it through?"

"I . . . I do not know," Veronica said desperately, wondering if Max knew anything at all about this. Etta had been harping about her wedding dress for weeks now, but Veronica had discounted all that. What would the girl think when Max laughed in her face?

"What? Are you going to lure Max away, then?" Dora accused.

"No, Flurry and I plan to leave as soon as Max's carriage comes back and the horses are rested. I do not think my presence would add anything but uncertainty . . ."

"Good girl. You feel Max will find it easier to say 'I do' without you as a witness."

"No, I fear I should cry."

"Everyone cries at weddings. No one regards that."

"I wonder why." Veronica shook her head and turned to go. "I hate to leave you with Lady Margery to care for."

"That is what family is for. Besides, who else is there? It is not a fit task for you or even Mercia if she could steel herself to it. Do you depart from London for Paris?"

"Yes, Max promised we could go on one of his ships."

"That is best then," Dora agreed.

Veronica was feeling very unsettled and even a little unwell. She went to the library and got out her paints again. She wished she could use them to conjure up enough love between Etta and George for Etta to release Max. It would be better than him leaving her at the altar, so to speak. She began a study of George. His face was not as well known to her as Max's but by closing her eyes she could picture him well enough to achieve a likeness. But she was not transported to a trancelike state by the work; she was pretty sure nothing would come of it except a backache. Nevertheless she stood the portrait on the mantel between Max and Etta, whispering a prayer that George would come between them.

* * *

They took tea in the library that night, all but Dora. Veronica had declared the portraits complete and offered no explanation for the sudden appearance of George's likeness. If there was some symbolism as to how she had arranged them, no one commented on it. Veronica watched Etta looking from Max's likeness to George's, comparing them. Looking at them objectively, even Veronica admitted that George looked the handsomer of the two, but it was all in what one preferred.

"Is it not odd how it all worked out?" Etta asked as Flurry poured the tea.

"Yes," Veronica answered. "The Strake treasure turns out to be negotiable after all, and Freddy and Mercia have been carried away by their greed."

"That is rather severe," Max said, raising an eyebrow at Veronica. "With George sitting here listening to you."

Veronica smiled at Max, knowing that he had not told George his suspicions about Freddy. That was kind of Max.

George snorted. "What did it cost you, Max, filling that chest with gold? As I recall it used to contain your boot blacking."

Etta stared at George, then at Max, who shrugged and smiled. Then Etta turned a speculative gaze back on George, pleased perhaps that he had not been deceived.

"About twenty thousand. Gold coin is not all that easy to come by. And I had to make it convincing. Freddy is no fool. The hardest part was finding a place to bury it that he had not dug up yet."

"You mean that you buried that chest?" Lady Eustace demanded. "But why? Why give that young jackanapes anything?"

"I know why," Veronica said. "If Max had bought

them off it never would have ended. They would have been back for more, again and again."

"Exactly," Flurry agreed. "Max has given them no reason to expect any generosity from him. Moreover, he has divided their loyalties. And he can hold the poisoning of John over Lady Margery's head, should she ever regain her sense— Sorry, George."

"I am the one who is sorry," George replied, his brows furrowed. "I watched over the poor man and I had not a clue Mother was doing him in."

"So did I watch it happen," Flurry said regretfully.

Into the dead silence that followed Etta dropped the emotional clinker of saying yet again, "It is too bad John had to die for me to be able to come here."

After the initial shock Veronica began to wonder if Etta was quoting someone, the way she kept saying it. To be sure Max might have dawdled outside the country for years had her letters to him not been so insistent. He had come back, albeit too late, at her own request. And, Veronica admitted, she never would have written so emotionally if Papa had not been so ill. But how could it have been to Lady Margery's advantage to end her brother-in-law's life at that particular time? Mercia might have inherited something, but surely Lady Margery was enough in Henry's confidence to know there was nothing left over for Mercia. Had they counted that much on the treasure? Harking back to the first evening, Veronica rather thought Aunt Margery had planned on playing on Max's sympathy and family pride. Or since she knew nothing of his engagement, perhaps she had hoped to throw Mercia at his head. Neither would have been likely happenings if one knew Max at all.

But perhaps Lady Margery was deranged then and

hiding it. Certainly she must have been when she applied the poison. Not in an angry start, though. Veronica gave a trembling sigh. It had taken many doses and many days.

"Then Max planned it all," Etta said in wonder.

"Well, not getting George shot," Max said with an arched brow. "That was an accident. Veronica, are you feeling unwell? You look so pale."

"Max seems to have solved everything," Veronica agreed, her lips trembling. "Papa's murder and the treasure hunt. There is nothing left to do."

"Except find the real Nonsuch treasure," Max said regretfully. "Perhaps that will be for another man to do. George, in your new post as steward you should have the leisure to search it out."

Veronica smiled at him. "If you could not find it, Max, no one could."

Max sighed and looked across the salon to where three portraits now stood on the mantel. "They are finished, then," he said. "Including one of George for good measure. Very fitting."

"Yes, it is always hard to decide when something is finished," Veronica replied. "But it has to be admitted eventually."

Max glanced sharply at her, his brows knit in pain. He rose and went to scrutinize the paintings, his teacup still in his hand.

Veronica looked from the paintings to the plaster wall against which she had set them. She supposed it should be repaired again, but every time they tried the same cracks reappeared, the one shaped like the woman's head, the one like the lion's claw— Veronica's sharp indrawn breath caused everyone to look at her.

"George, you were carrying around a drawing of a

lion, the hind leg especially . . ." Veronica said as she set her cup down and walked toward the wall, staring at it.

George pushed himself out of his chair with one arm and walked toward the mantel. When he saw what Veronica was pointing at he gasped, stepped back and looked at the wall, then said, "My God. Etta, run to my bedroom and get my notebook, will you?"

Max came to stand beside them. "What are you looking at?"

"The cracks in the plaster," Veronica said. "I put them into the portraits just as they are."

"Yes . . ." Max said as he examined the tracery of lines. "Oh!"

Veronica enjoyed immensely that startled look of excitement on his normally bored face.

"Right under our noses!" Max chanted, "All these years, right under our noses."

By now Flurry had risen to examine the wall, causing Lady Eustace to stare at her.

Etta returned and handed the notebook to George, her cheeks flushed with excitement.

George unfolded an aged drawing. "We found this in one of Uncle's books. Look at the lion's hind leg. He held the drawing up against his painting. "What do you see, Max?"

Veronica ran to the desk and snatched a lethal-looking letter opener out of the drawer.

"I do not see anything," Etta complained.

"Max," Flurry said happily. "The cracks in the wall match the drawing exactly."

"Yes, this entire inside wall of the library must house a relief from Nonsuch, a work given up as lost centuries ago." Max grabbed Veronica's hand just in time to prevent her from attacking the wall with the letter opener.

"Gently, Veronica," George said. "We would not want to destroy a particle of it."

"But we must be sure," Veronica insisted.

Max pried delicately at a corner of the wall, and a surprisingly large chunk of plaster came away with some sort of canvas backing.

George examined the fragment of plaster. "They put this layer on first to protect the castings. The removal should really start at the top. Otherwise a large chunk coming away may cause a plaster landslide and damage some of the relief."

"Why did I not see it before?" Veronica asked as she dragged a chair over to stand on, the better to examine the pattern of cracks.

"If I mistake not," George said, "it was moved to Durdans, then brought here when that place was pulled down. We may never know."

"But why plaster it over?" Etta asked.

"Yes, why hide it?" Veronica repeated. "And how could a family possibly lose track of such a treasure?"

"Possibly because only one member of the family knew of it, the one who built the library," Max replied.

"The fourteenth viscount," George supplied.

"Still, I do not see what point it was to have it if he was going to hide it," Flurry insisted.

"It is my guess this was the only way to keep it. The family fortunes had dwindled by that time to the point where—"

"Max, he never stole it." Veronica looked conspiratorial.

"No, I think he acquired it legally enough, though he would not have been above failing to pay for it, or perhaps even claiming it did not arrive in one piece."

"That would be a reason to hide it," Lady Eustace agreed.

"I have studied the period," George said. "The palace existed during the Roundhead era. Since it was not in danger then, religious concerns would have been no reason to mask its presence."

"It could have been a simple matter of taxation," Max said, stepping back to look at the size of the wall. "The more a house was worth, right down to its number of windows, the higher it was taxed. I shall send a crew of restorers out from London. You will have charge of them, George."

"I think I had rather take care of this personally. If word of this gets out we may have more treasure hunters than Freddy digging up the yard."

"As you wish, George. But it is a large undertaking for one man."

"I shall help him," Etta said loyally.

"Do not worry," George replied. "By the time Veronica and Flurry return from their travels, the work will be completely restored."

Veronica smiled. It was the first time she had thought of returning to Byerly as a certainty. She might still be unmarried when she and Max came back. Perhaps by then Etta and George would have formed some kind of alliance. Max would follow her and Flurry up to town in a few days and they would sail away, leaving George in charge. She felt a sudden sense of completeness as though she had finally accepted the loss of her papa. The pain of it had dulled with the discovery of his murderess. The puzzles here were at an end and after one very difficult scene tomorrow she would find new scenery to paint.

"This will be the first time it has been looked upon in

hundreds of years," Veronica said. "When I return I shall do a painting of it."

Max smiled at her. "Was it worth the struggle, Vee?"

"Oh, yes, for now the treasure is very much a part of the house," Veronica said. "I like to think that Papa figured it out before he died." She turned to Max.

"I am quite sure he did, but had the same problem we do. If anyone finds out about it . . ."

"Such as Freddy and Mercia," George said. "It would be better if no one ever knew of it, at least until I can get Mercia to sign off on any claim to the estate."

They all nodded their agreement and vowed secrecy.

25

The next morning Max put on the shirt Mustafah had laid out for him, but angrily tossed the formal black suit aside and dressed as carelessly as usual in leather riding breeches and his old hunting jacket. The thought that Dora had given his servant an order and he had obeyed it disturbed Max.

He tucked a piece of parchment under his arm along with his cane and went down the hall toward Etta's bedroom. His hand shoved into one pocket encountered some objects that he discovered to be the ricinus seeds Vee had handed him weeks ago in the garden. He had been drunkenly happy that day, falling in love with her and not yet aware of it. He shoved the mottled seeds back into his pocket and knocked on Etta's bedroom door.

"What is this?" Etta asked as she pulled her robe closed at the throat and stared suspiciously at the paper Max held out to her.

"A list of what I am willing to offer for my freedom. This is what I will sign over to George if you agree to marry him."

Etta shook her head no without even looking at the

list in Max's left hand. He stared at her as though she were mad.

"Surely you do not need me."

"But I do not want mere money," Etta said.

"You cannot pretend you want me," Max said angrily.

"Not you personally," she said, biting her lip.

"I have no real position in society."

"A position in society is Dora's ambition and mother's, not mine. I want security, and marriage to you will give me that. You are noted for sharp but fair dealing, for always winning your gambles, for always paying your debts, and for always keeping your word."

Max cringed at this last. "I may not be able to marry Vee, but I will not marry you either, and you will have nothing."

"I have studied you, Max, under Veronica's guidance. I am sorry for her because she does love you."

"If you cared about her you would release me. Marriage to me will be pure hell for both of us."

"I do not require that it be blissful, only that it has the outward appearance of a solid marriage."

"No matter what your private life is like, no matter that you have a husband who hates you?" Max asked.

"Do you hate me?"

"You stand between me and Veronica," Max said. "I cannot help but hate you."

"But you can marry me and still have Veronica."

Max stared at her as though he had misheard her.

"I only want you as a husband, not as a lover."

"So you will have George, after all," Max concluded.

"I do not even care to have children with you," Etta continued.

"What are you saying? You do not mean to consummate the marriage?"

"It is a matter of indifference to me."

"A matter of indifference!" Max shouted with disgust. "It will not be a matter of indifference if I throw you down on that bed and take what you are selling so blithely."

"You may, of course, execute your rights as my husband once we are married. I will not fight you. But I do not think you will, not out of spite."

"Was there ever such a calculating, scheming . . .?"

"Such qualities would be admired in a man. Ironic, is it not? But I accept your recriminations. You will get over it, Max. Eventually you will accept this marriage to me as the best course for all of us."

"Never!"

"I am trying to tell you that our marriage is no impediment to you and Veronica being together."

"Did you say that to her? Did you suggest she set herself up as my mistress?"

"Are you angry?"

"I am past angry. I am incensed."

"Nevertheless I must hold to my decision. What you and Veronica do is up to you."

"And you expect that George will fall in with this plan and become your lover? My God! No wonder you are ambivalent about children. George would be able to supply those and they would inherit the Strake title."

"There is nothing you can do about it, Max. If you refuse, Dora will make you marry me."

"I know what she has been up to with those forgeries of hers and I have taken care of that," Max said, gripping his walking stick.

Etta licked her lips, looking for the first time uncertain of her position. "How will it reflect on Veronica if it comes out that she was the cause of our breach. That strikes at something you care about."

"The only thing I do care about," Max growled.

"I must marry you. This is what we have planned for all these years. I will not throw all that work away because you are in love with Veronica."

"You could marry George. You still get to live in the house. We would scarcely ever be here."

"But no title," she said.

Max swung on her, the light of battle in his eyes. "If you insist on marrying me I will abdicate the title."

"You would not dare!"

"I will dare anything to escape you." Max tramped down the hallway to his own room and slammed the door.

This brought George out of his room. When he saw Etta still in the hallway he warily approached her. "What is going on now?" George asked.

"Max is being difficult," Etta said breathlessly.

"You are still set on this course? You still mean to marry him after everything that has happened?"

"What other course is there for me?" Etta asked. "I cannot back down now. I have nothing to fall back upon."

"You are worried about your pride," George said with surprise. "I had not thought women even concerned themselves with such things."

"Pride was all I have had to live on for a long time."

"So Max's refusal did hurt you."

"I have always been good at hiding my hurt, which is fortunate, for Max informs me my tortures have only begun."

"You could marry me," George offered. "I have not nearly as much money as Max but we would be well off and . . ."

"And what?"

"And I have a great regard for you. I know that is stupid of me. You are a mercenary little thing, but I cannot help myself."

Etta stared at him. "You have no very high opinion of me, yet you would marry me anyway?"

"I was always an easy mark," George said. "Mother egging me on to compete with Max and bringing me to heel no matter what outrageous project she had in mind, and Freddy involving me with his gambling friends. They were no friends. Max and Veronica are the only ones who ever dealt fairly with me. And now that I have a position and need never fear want again, I lay that at your feet. Why, I do not know." George took a step nearer, gazing into her eyes. "There is something so very compelling about your avarice."

"If I make Max go through with the ceremony he has threatened to abdicate the title."

"Etta, that would be disastrous! Neither of us would get to live at Byerly then."

"But who would be viscount?"

"No one. The male line dies out with Max. If he gives up the title, it is gone. You must not let Max do this. Marry me now. Max does not want to live here; neither does Veronica. All he wants is to be with her. As Max's steward I shall have an income no one can touch and Max will pay for repairs on the house. Perhaps it has escaped your notice, but . . ."

"What?"

George held her chin in his free hand and brought his lips down on hers in a kiss so gentle it should not frighten the shyest of maids. Force would never work with Etta. She had a mind of her own. He felt her hands creep up his lapels and snake around his neck. He felt the kiss deepen and thought perhaps he would win her after all.

"Nothing escapes my notice," she said.

"Marry me, not Max. Forget about your pride for once."

Veronica went to answer a knock on her door and was surprised to see Max on the threshold. She glanced at the open window and he grinned tensely.

"I am so used to your usual entrance, having you come by way of the door seems tame," she said.

"We need to talk before Flurry comes charging in here and stabs me with her umbrella."

"I can talk while I pack." Veronica looked down at her black carriage dress.

"Did you mean to leave without saying good-bye?"

"Yes, very gutless of me, was it not? Your coach is back. As soon as the horses have had a few hours' rest . . ."

"I told you I will not marry her. Have a little faith, Vee."

"Are you going to leave her standing at the altar, then?"

"Altar?" Max asked impatiently. "The ceremony is to take place in the drawing room. And Etta can be married in an hour if that is what she wants. But I have a few cards left to play."

"The game is over, Max," Veronica said, "and George has lost."

"Never mind that now. She hurt you last night."

"Not on purpose."

"She stumbles too often to suit me. I sometimes wonder if it is not all an act, that wronged-maiden stance of hers. If I did not know better . . ."

"What?" Veronica asked. "How can she be anything but what she appears?"

"When you think about it, Etta is the one who benefits from Uncle John's death."

Veronica gasped and stared at him, shaking her head. "She did let slip that she had met Papa, but there is no way, Max. She and her mother were not even at Byerly."

"Sorry," Max said, folding her in his arms. "Now I have hurt you."

"You give me a chill when you talk like that. But when I look at Aunt Margery now I see only a victim." Veronica looked up at him with the tears sparkling on her lashes. "Max, what if Lady Margery did not do it?"

"But she confessed," Max said.

Veronica took his hand and held it. "That is what we thought, because that is what we hoped. But all she revealed was that she knew which poison killed him. What if she only witnessed it. What if she let Henry Steeple into the room."

Max groaned. "Then she is still as guilty as he is. I had not thought of a conspiracy and I must know before I leave. Stay, Vee, and help find out who killed Steeple."

"I cannot," Veronica said, pulling away from him. "It hurts too much. I thought I had started to heal, but I find that the pain of loving you gets worse each time I see you."

"At least stay to see how I manage the day."

"If I leave I shall not know until you come to me and tell me. I think I would prefer that. I am so terribly tired of scenes."

He bent his head toward her lips, but she laid her small hand over his mouth. "No, do not kiss me. Your kisses are much too persuasive. We would end up in that bed as surely as we have every other time we have thought that we could resist each other."

"Do not worry. Trust me. Dora has no way to compel me to this act. I will give you a head start and ride Strider up to London. We shall be together in a few hours."

"Max, I hope and pray it all works out as you say, but I have the most terrible feeling that something may go wrong."

"I love you, Vee. Nothing can alter that. No one can come between us. You shall see." Max peeled himself from her arms and walked slowly toward the door. He turned and looked at her and she saw it fleetingly, the confident man and the uncertain boy in that same look. He closed the door behind him, softly, as though she were sleeping.

She stared at the old wood, wishing he would come back and dreading that he would at the same time.

*A*n hour later Max strode past the flowers that adorned the hallway, unseeing, and pushed his way into the library, where the bride was now waiting, without bothering to knock. Both Lady Eustace and Dora moved toward him, scolding, but Etta merely said, "Mother, leave us."

To Max's surprise, Lady Eustace did leave the room. Dora had not been similarly dismissed and Max could only think that Etta needed her.

"Veronica and Flurry are leaving," Dora answered unbidden. "They thought Veronica might be a distraction to you."

"I think it is best Veronica leaves, if it will pain her to watch," Etta said quietly.

"Watch what?" Max asked, clenching his fists. "Do you really think I will consent to this insanity?"

"Are you meaning to be difficult?" Dora asked as though he were a little boy who could be dragged where she wanted him to go.

"Difficult? I am meaning to make it plain to you

once and for all that I am not marrying Etta. If she wishes to marry George, that is another matter."

"There is no choice now, Max," Dora said. "You know the consequences if you back down."

"That you will sue me for breach of promise?" Max laughed. "If you had any idea how little that would bother men in the business world you would not have fallen back on it as a threat. I can afford any judgment passed against me."

"You can afford the money, but it will cost you time. Can you really afford lengthy court appearances?" Dora challenged.

"I shall settle out of court."

"My demands will be such that you will never meet them," Dora threatened.

"Your demands?" Etta asked, the color high in her cheeks.

"Quiet child, I am doing this for you," Dora said sharply.

"I used to believe that, but now I am not so sure." Etta looked at her, trying to divine the struggle that was going on between Dora and Max. "You are punishing him for something. What is it?"

"I said be quiet!" Dora thundered.

Etta stepped around her and fled the room, leaving the double doors open. Max watched her go with a crease between his brows. Dora rounded on him. "See what you have done? Lady Margery always said you were a bastard and she was right."

"How do you mean that? If it were true it would not reflect well on you at all, Mother." Max folded his arms with satisfaction. "Besides, Vee gave me proof that I am the head of the Strake line."

"What do you mean?" Dora's face had gone pale now

and her eyes glittered like obsidian under their heavy lids.

Max went into his uncle's bedroom and emerged with a package. He tore the paper away and held it out to her. "Allow me to present to you the fourteenth Viscount Byerly. Remarkable resemblance, I think. Veronica saw it right away."

Dora held up her head loftily and scanned the painting.

"That is just one of Veronica's renderings of you," she said boldly.

"I can have it authenticated if I must," Max replied. "I have proof that I am a Strake."

Dora turned away from him, fuming and breathing hard. "I said you were a bastard," she spit at him savagely. "I did not say whose."

Max stared at her for a full minute in confusion. "What on earth are you talking about?"

She turned to him, the glitter of victory in her eyes. "You resemble the fourteenth viscount so much because you are a Strake. You are John's son."

"Great-Uncle John?" Max staggered backward. "But then—but then—"

"But then Veronica is your half-sister," Dora said savagely.

Max felt as though his heart had been frozen, then shattered with a hammer. This could not be. Vee, his sister? He would have known if that were so. He stared at his mother as though her face were some mask from a nightmare. But she opened her mouth and her lips moved to drive the words through him like spikes.

"You can understand my reluctance to tell you this, but I have no choice now. I have done everything in my power to assure you would marry someone else, but your attraction for Veronica is obvious and dangerous."

"Oh my God!" Max dropped the painting with a heavy thud and stumbled across the room, searching for any salvation. He saw the glass cabinet with the liquor in it and pulled at the door. Locked. He smashed the glass carelessly, making Dora jump. He reached in and pulled out the decanter of brandy. With blood streaming down his hand and sopping the lace at his cuffs, he drank from the decanter, trying to burn the memory of his incestuous seduction from his mind.

"A fine spectacle you will make at your own wedding."

"Wedding? Do you truly expect me to marry Etta after this betrayal?"

"I meant it when I said you have no choice. If you go to Veronica unwed she will expect you to marry her. Then you will have to tell her."

"No!"

"Marriage to Etta is your only path, Max," Dora said slowly. "If you do not take it, you will have to explain why to Veronica."

Max felt the walls closing on him as though he were in a paper house that was folding up on him, collapsing like his world. There was no escape now. He looked back and saw everything his mother had done to push him in this direction. She must have thought she was doing the right thing.

"You had better hope I can get drunk enough to go through with it," Max said when he could speak. "Why in God's name did you never tell me this before?"

Dora came to confront him. "Why do you think I have been so adamantly trying to marry you to someone else? I thought never to have to tell you, but there is no choice now that you are both grown and pawing each other at every opportunity. You must marry Etta or I will have to tell Veronica, as well."

"No!" He whirled to face her. "You must never tell her."

He took another long pull at the bottle and coughed.

"Then marry Etta."

He stared down at the blood dripping onto the carpet. If only it had been a mortal wound.

"You witch. You sent me here every summer. Did it not occur to you I might someday fall in love with Veronica?"

"Never," Dora said with a sneer. "She was so much younger."

"Why take the risk? I had always thought I was supposed to be ingratiating myself with my uncle."

"You were and you did. But you had an in." Her voice dripped with accusation. "He was predisposed to like his natural son."

"You have ruined all," Max said in despair. "Why?"

"Revenge on the family for never really accepting me. If Veronica is hurt that is not intentional. I will be accepted now, by the Eustaces and the family, if they ever want to come to Byerly again. Etta will let me stay here where I am known and respected. You can ask any of the servants or the people in the village. They all think well of me."

"What a long plan you have made, Mother." Max's jawed clenched with hatred. "I do not know a general in the world who would have had your patience."

"I shall regard that as a compliment, the first you have ever offered your own mother."

"As for being ruthless . . ." Max closed his eyes and swayed a little. "I admit that I am shocked and it takes much to do that. You would have let nothing stand in your way."

"It has never been my desire to hurt you, Max," Dora said lightly as though she had not just ripped his heart out.

"I think you have miscalculated, you know," he said shakily. "You have figured without Etta."

"Etta will do as she is told. It is the only way Veronica will be safe. You must marry Etta, Max." She snapped her mouth shut after this pronouncement and Max would have liked to throttle her. But that would not change his crime or the fact that he could never be with Vee again.

He nodded slowly, took one more long pull on the decanter, and set it down. With an effort he pulled out his handkerchief to wrap around his hand. Dora awkwardly helped tie the improvised bandage.

"You were never as good at this as Flurry," he said sadly, shaking his head to try to clear it.

Dora glowered at him and opened the door. "Now, Max."

"I need a few minutes," he said remaining where he was.

"Are you going to abscond through a window?" Dora demanded.

"No, but I need some time. Consider it a last request before the firing squad."

Dora tramped impatiently to the drawing room and went inside.

Max thought of Vee and all the times they had made love. The scenes came back to him in flashes of warmth and lust. He had known they were sinning, but he had no idea . . . He took a deep breath and stepped out into the hallway just as Vee was running back in the front door.

"I . . . I thought you had gone," Max said, swaying a little on his feet.

Veronica tore off her bonnet and cast it down on the hall table. "No, I made them turn the carriage around at the bottom of the hill and come back. I am not leaving without you. Oh, no, what have you done to your hand?" She came toward him and he backed up a step.

"I . . ." he tried to say something but the words would not come.

"Let me," Veronica offered, pulling a handkerchief from her reticule. He stared at her as she tied up his hand, thinking, *This is the last time I will see her. This is the last time she will touch me like this. What have I done?*

"Max, what is it? You look so tragic. We will get a surgeon to see to your hand in London."

He cleared his throat. "If I were a coward I would tell you that I would see you in an hour or two."

The silence stretched between them as Vee stared at him, and the tears came by instinct to her eyes. "You are not coming," she said, then pressed her lips together. She reached her arm around his neck to give him a kiss, to persuade him, but he was stiff as though he were already dead. She almost suspected that he had swallowed some strong poison and was only waiting for her to leave before he fell.

He let her kiss him, but his lips were cold. He lifted his good hand and brushed the tears off her cheek, then carried that finger to his lips and kissed it.

"Good-bye, Vee."

The dismissal hit her like a bath of ice water. She should take her tattered pride and leave before she made a fool of herself. But this was her Max and he was in pain. Not just from his wound. Something had hurt him so badly it had shaken the foundations of his character. How could she leave him now?

"I will not leave unless you tell me why," Veronica said, setting her jaw firmly. "I will not leave you like this. What has she done to you?"

He groaned and pulled Veronica into the library. Flurry appeared in the doorway and followed them.

"What is it, Max?" Veronica demanded.

"Lady Margery was right about me being a bastard, Vee." The word tasted bitter on his tongue.

"Impossible," Veronica said. "You look too much a Strake."

"But which Strake? Robert or John?" Max cleared his throat. "I hear they looked much alike."

Veronica staggered a little, staring at him, seeing all their love poisoned in her mind with those few words, with that thought wherever it had come from, but loving him still.

"Who told you such an absurdity?" Flurry demanded.

"Veronica is my sister." He choked on the words and wiped his bloody sleeve across his eyes.

"Sister?" Flurry stared at him as though he were mad. "She is nothing of the kind. Would I have given my permission for you to marry her if she were?"

"Mother told me," Max croaked. "I am John's son, not Robert's. I have been so blind."

Flurry grabbed his arm and shook him to get his attention. "Listen to me, Max. Dora has lied to you again."

"What?" Max staggered and stared at her.

"Do you really think John Strake would have died without letting you know that important fact by some means, if it were true?" Flurry paced back and forth, wringing her hands. "You are Robert's son. You are a bastard on the maternal side."

Max shook his head, trying to make sense of what she said. "I do not know what you are talking about."

"Dora's child died inside her, but your father Robert knew he had begotten another child Dora could raise as her own.

Veronica thrust herself under Max's arm and he leaned against her, staring at Flurry in shock.

"No wonder she made such a rotten job of it. She did not want me because she did not love me. She simply used me like she has used everyone else. Then Veronica is not my sister." Max felt as though he were waking up from some nightmare, that he could actually think again.

"No, she is your second cousin and no more. I knew Dora was cruel, but I had no idea she was capable of something like this," Flurry said.

"Dora is not even my mother," Max said numbly.

Veronica hugged him even tighter. "You should never have listened to her, Max."

"Your own mother—" Flurry began.

"Do you imagine I even care who my own mother is?" Max growled. "It only matters that Vee is not my sister."

"When I tell you, you may care," Flurry said, causing him to fix his attention on her face, which was looking tired and old.

"Who then?" he asked impatiently. "A poor serving maid, an opera dancer, perhaps another actress?"

"A well-educated woman, a vicar's daughter, seduced by her romantic nature into a disastrous alliance." Flurry wrung her hands. "But the brother of the man who ruined her took pity on her. She went on to become a governess."

Max gaped at her. "Flurry? You?" Max came to take Flurry in his arms. There were tears in Max's eyes but he was laughing. "If only I had known."

"When you were born, I promised never to tell anyone if Robert and Dora would raise you as their son. Dora has held that over me all these years. If it were known it would be as bad as some scandal about Veronica."

Veronica came and hugged her too. "We do not care at all."

Max stared at Flurry so hard she protested.

"What is it, Max? Are you angry with me?"

"Who had the most reason to want Uncle John dead and not able to refute anything?"

Flurry stared at him, the tears drying unnoticed in her eyes. "Dora!"

"She poisoned Uncle John to get me home," Max said. He sat abruptly on a chair, breathing hard. "I must have blocked out any possibility of her doing it just because I thought she was my mother."

"Max, I feel so much to blame," Veronica said, bursting into tears. "She used me. By writing you and compelling you to come home I snared you into her trap."

"But why?" Max asked. "Does she love Etta that much?"

"She did it to get this house and the power it represents," Flurry said. "This the only place she has any consequence."

"But I would never have wanted her here, not after what she did to me."

"You would never have stayed," Veronica said. "And Dora must have known that."

"But Max, we can never bring her to justice for it," Flurry added.

"What a lot of dirty linen we Strakes seem to wash. There must be a way to bring the crime home to her. Max paced to the door and motioned for Mustafah. He told him in Hindi to send for Dr. Morris at once. The servant's answer pleased Max. Dr. Morris was with Lady Margery now.

The door opened and Dora poked her head in. "Well, Max, what is the delay now?" Dora started when she saw Flurry and Veronica.

"Surprised to see me here?" Flurry asked.

"I do not care what Flurry has been telling you, Max. It was time you assumed your responsibilities," Dora said.

"After you have been to such pains to get me home," Max said.

Dora stared at him. "It only matters that you are home now, after all my letters."

"It was really Veronica's letter that touched me, not yours. But this is what brought me." Max reached into his waistcoat pocket and pulled out one of the castor beans.

When she saw what was in his hand Dora turned pale and backed away, oblivious to Dr. Morris entering the room behind her.

"Afraid to touch it, Dora?" Max taunted. "I imagine you must have handled many of them, to extract enough ricin to kill Uncle John."

Morris said nothing, just watched the woman.

Max grabbed Dora's hand and squeezed her wrist until she opened her palm. He planted the seed in it and closed her fingers over it, leaving a smear of blood on her wrist from his recent wound. She cast the object from her.

"You are insane!" she shouted. "You can prove nothing."

"Probably not without a witness, someone who saw you give John a medicine not prescribed by Dr. Morris, but who was afraid to say anything, or saw an advantage to John's death."

Veronica sent Max a startled look. "The coffee," she said.

"My God. You used to grind your own coffee beans," Max added. "You could have ground the seeds up in there. I wonder if we might still find traces if we looked."

Dora was looking pale, her dark eyes open so wide the whites looked hideous.

Max saw George enter the room behind the Doctor and stand there stock-still.

"We only suspected Aunt Margery because of her slip about the effect of . . . a certain poison," Max continued. "We thought it was perfectly safe to let Dora nurse her. We applauded Dora's charity, not knowing we almost signed Aunt Margery's death warrant."

George stared at Dora in horror.

"Fortunately," Max continued relentlessly, "It is early spring. The ricinus plants will not be ready to yield another harvest of poison until late summer. Had we not discovered the murderer now she would have done Lady Margery in then for what she saw."

"I had to do something!" Dora spit out with an angry growl. "I had to get you home before Etta lost her looks. I thought of poisoning Flurry. I knew that would bring you, Max."

"My God!" Max shouted over Vee's murmured protest. "You would have murdered Flurry?"

"She was the last one who knew anything about your birth. I would have been safe then."

"She is right, Max," Flurry said. "John, his wife

Olivia, and Robert were the only ones who knew you were my son. Did you wait your chance and get them one by one?" Flurry accused.

"You can prove nothing," Dora repeated. "No one will believe such an absurd tale from a lovesick girl, a wanton woman, and a half-mad rake."

"And why did Henry Steeple have to die," Max asked in the ensuing silence as Etta and the clergyman appeared in the doorway as well.

"He was going to find a way to break the contract. He came back from London bragging about it," Dora said it as though it seemed perfectly reasonable to shove a knitting needle through someone's heart for such a reason.

"But to blame Flurry . . ." Veronica said.

Dora's face turned hateful. "She had too much hold on Max and she knew too much."

A shocked gasp from Etta finally got through to Dora that she was not alone with the three of them.

Veronica pulled the bell rope, and when Mustafah came to do her bidding she said, "Please help Doctor Morris lock Aunt Dora in her room and then send for the magistrate. She is the one who killed Lord Strake and Henry Steeple and . . . I suppose we will have to make a list."

Mustafah opened his eyes wide, then bowed before taking Dora by the arm. She looked from one to the other of the family and clamped her mouth shut, turning so purple in the face Veronica thought she was going to burst a blood vessel.

"If only we could have figured it out sooner we could have saved Henry Steeple," Veronica said.

"I should have guessed," Flurry said, wringing her hands. "And all those other deaths."

"How could you know, Flurry?" Veronica asked. "The problem is we all forgot that Dora used to be an actress."

"Yes, she told many lies over the years and all she wanted was Byerly," Max said. "She did not care who she had to hurt to get it."

The vicar sat down and closed his eyes in prayer. "I can see there will be no wedding today, so I should take my leave, but I feel . . ."

"Oh yes there will," Etta corrected. "George Comish has declared himself. Please be so good as to marry us now before the magistrate arrives."

"But . . . but, you were to be married to Lord Byerly," the vicar protested. "The banns were posted."

"That was Dora's doing and, as you can see, she is quite mad. It is George I wish to marry."

"But . . . you need to post the banns or get a license."

"You mean this license?" George asked, handing the cleric a folded document.

The carriage wound its way slowly down from Byerly Hill, crossing the riding trail and the stone bridge over the stream. Veronica, secure in Max's arms, looked out the window the whole way.

"Will you miss it, Vee?" Max asked.

"After a while, perhaps. But George and Etta will take good care of it."

"We can come back to Byerly whenever you wish," he said gently.

"Just think," Flurry said. "Had you not insisted on going back for Max, he would have married Etta and we would be going to London alone."

"Max taught me what is important," Veronica said. "And pride is not even on the list."

Flurry stared at her and smiled sadly. "Had you chosen the coward's way, letting Max take the blame and escaping to London to wait for him, he would never have come."

"Max, would you really have married Etta just to spare me the pain of Dora's lie?"

"At the time it seemed like the only way to put you

beyond my reach without telling you. You saved me again, Vee."

"Veronica insisted on the truth, and that is what saved you, Max," Flurry said with satisfaction.

Veronica leaned her head against Max's shoulder. "It was a good thing I did not listen to you for once, Flurry. You wanted me to escape and be safe."

"So I was wrong once in twenty-three years," Flurry chided. "That is nothing compared to the mull Max has made of things."

Max smiled tiredly at Flurry's easy dismissal of an illegitimate child kept secret for thirty years. "Just do not make a habit of it, Flurry," Max said.

He could afford to be generous now that he had Vee in his arms and no one could ever part them again. It amazed him that he had found the true purpose in his life and achieved it in a few short weeks. But with a woman like Vee, anything was possible.

"And that wedding." Flurry shook her head. "Was there ever anything so ramshackle? At least Etta had a dress, a ring, and flowers. I do not see why you and Veronica could not wait until we got to London."

"Once Etta married George, I was free, and I did not want to take a chance on anything else going wrong." Max brushed his bandaged hand across his forehead.

"I cannot believe you forgot to buy a ring," Flurry continued.

"Max had a lot on his mind, Flurry. Besides, I like this ring," Vee said of the large emerald, that she only held on her small finger by clutching the stone on the inside of her hand. "It is deep and mysterious like Max."

"Max is a sham. He is no powerful, awe-inspiring

hero. He is just as desperately passionate and reckless as when he was a boy."

"I know. He is wonderful," Veronica said.

Max laughed and kissed Veronica longingly. He locked his arms around her as though he would never let go.

"Enough of that, you two," Flurry demanded, poking her umbrella between them. "This is disgusting to watch. Save it for your wedding night."

"But Flurry, we have already—" Veronica's confession was interrupted by Max's renewed kiss and when he paused for breath she had forgotten what she was going to say.

"You will do as you please, both of you. You always have." Flurry tsked, gave them a disgusted look and pretended to stare out the window.

Veronica looked into Flurry's clear gray eyes. Those eyes that Flurry had only once let Veronica capture on canvas, and with good reason, of course. Flurry was Max's mother. Why had she not seen it before?

"It will be just we three again, like old times," Veronica said. She rested her head on Max's shoulder and took his wounded hand to hold between her own as though she could cure everything that was wrong with him by holding him long enough. She felt his lips brush the top of her hair. She did not want Max to be a hero. She wanted him unconditionally, with all his dear imperfections, sure now that she had just as many. She wanted to argue with him and laugh with him as they made up their children's names.

Most of all she wanted to make up for all those years, when they might have been falling in love safely and sanely rather than in a mad rush of discovery and desire. Their eventual union she regarded as inevitable, if they would have had to cross oceans, break laws, or ruin themselves to achieve it. She was joyful that they had come together without harming anyone and that she had had the courage to go after Max and demand the truth when it mattered the most.

**Visit the
Simon & Schuster Web site:**

www.SimonSays.com

**and sign up for our
mystery e-mail updates!**

Keep up on the latest new releases,
author appearances, news, chats,
special offers, and more!
We'll deliver the information
right to your inbox—
if it's new, you'll know about it.

SIMON & SCHUSTER
A VIACOM COMPANY
www.SimonSays.com

2345

POCKET BOOKS
PROUDLY PRESENTS

My Phillipe
Barbara Miller

**Coming in October
from Pocket Books**

**The following is a preview of
*MY PHILLIPE***

turned her attention back to the Appalasian, hoping that

*A*rabella looked up at the horse dangling helplessly in the sling as the boom swung the gray mare over the side of the ship toward the London dock. Sebastian, her father's great white warhorse, nickered reassuringly from the quay where Carlos held him. Maria had taken Jamie, Bella's young son, to sit safely on their baggage wagon with his mongrel dog. Bella's grooms, Rourke and Greenley, held the other two mares. She smiled at Greenley, her late husband's only servant. The others had, one by one, returned to England, unable to stand the privation of the war in Spain. Greenley grinned back at her. He had been a boy when the war started seven years ago. Now he was a man and she was . . . a widow. She thought of Edwin, her dead husband, so short a time a duke. She thought of him with his blond hair tousled by the wind and that apologetic smile of his, not how she had last seen him when she had helped to bury him after Waterloo. Already Edwin's features were beginning to blur in her mind—or was it tears come to betray her regrets?

Bella ran the back of her hand across her eyes and turned her attention back to the Andalusian, hoping that it would not panic the first time it was being unloaded in this manner. The ropes squeaked through the chocks as the mare was lowered. The graceful horse started writhing in the sling and Bella spoke soothing words of comfort to it. Above the noise of the docks and creaking of the ship's gear Bella heard a carriage arrive, with a tramp of hoofs and a squeak of harness, but could spare no attention for the passengers except to hope that they did not further frighten the animal.

"Phillipe! Phillipe!" Jamie called.

In her concentration on the horse, Bella did not stop to wonder why Jamie would be calling for his dead father's cousin, whom they had not seen in nearly a year.

As she stared upward, a rope parted, the frayed ends singing through the pulleys as the mare and sling slithered down toward her. With no purchase, the animal instinctively tried to jump. A strong arm closed around Bella's waist and scooped her out of the way as the mare landed with a grunt on the wooden quay. Its shod feet sent splinters flying, and in its struggle to get to Sebastian, the creature knocked both Bella and her savior onto a pile of baggage.

"What were you going to do?" Captain Phillipe Armitage demanded gruffly. "Catch her?"

"Phillipe! What are you doing here?" Bella flashed him her most brilliant smile as she leaped to her feet and watched him struggle up, the stiff leg still giving him some trouble. In spite of his being in England this past year, his blond hair still bore the burnish of the Spanish sun and his bronzed countenance was more handsome than ever. He looked so much like Edwin it was uncanny. But his voice was not silken and pleading. Phillipe's voice always held the hard edge of anger even when it need not have.

"And you are your usual careless self," he said coldly as he examined her dark looks with his brooding brown eyes and brushed the dust off his black coat. "What if that horse had fallen on you? What would have become of your son?"

Her smile melted away as it always did when he criticized her. "But nothing did happen."

"But you might have been killed," he insisted gloomily. "You always take too many chances."

"That has been true any time these past seven years." She wanted him to remember what they had been through together during the war and have that count for something, rather than have him be angry with her.

"I know," Phillipe said bitterly, looking her up and down, his brown eyes, so unusual for a blond man, skipping critically over her person. "Your father was a fool to take you with him into that war."

Bella became conscious of the dust on her serviceable black riding habit and gave the skirt an ineffectual swipe. "Many other officers took their wives and their families as well. At least I was of some use."

"Tending the wounded," he said bitterly while glancing at his stiff leg. "That was no fit work for you."

"I could say haring all over Spain by yourself and drawing maps for Wellington was not fit work for you." Bella rested her hands on her hips, ignoring Rourke's throat-clearing and Greenley's stifled laugh.

Phillipe gritted his teeth. "That is different . . . I am a man."

"Are we going to argue immediately?" she asked, trying to joke him out of his foul mood.

Phillipe shook his blond hair out of his eyes, turned, and walked slowly to the mare, displaying only a slight limp. As Bella followed him she thought that, considering how badly his leg had been torn up by the bullet, it was surprising Phillipe moved as well as he did. She had fought the surgeon to get Phillipe under her care, and she had managed to convince the doctor that she could save Phillipe's leg without endangering his life. She did not expect Phillipe to be grateful for that, but she wished he would not scowl at her so.

He talked soothingly to the mare and the creature stopped trembling and sweating. Bella could remember how soothing Phillipe could be when he chose, and she felt a pang of envy. The mare nuzzled his ear and hair. Bella remembered the feel of his fingers running through her hair, pressed against her cheek, moving across her skin. She blinked and brought herself back to attention.

"You always did have a way with women," she said, giving flattery a try.

"Some women." Phillipe's lips curled at the corners. He was not in a good mood, but the encounter might yet be salvaged.

"But how did you know we were coming?" she asked, watching his hands stroking the mare.

"Rourke wrote to me. Thank God one of your household has some sense."

"Would you like to ride that mare to our hotel?" Bella asked. She had half a mind to give the horse to him since it liked him so well.

"You are not going to a hotel," Phillipe stated flatly. "Which horse were you planning to ride?"

"Sebastian." She nodded toward the pawing warhorse. "You know what havoc he can cause in a city. Just like a conquering army, he can never behave himself."

"I shall ride Sebastian. The mare will be quiet by the time they are saddled."

Bella bit her lip rather than argue the point with him. His leg might be healed well enough to cope with a restive stallion. She did not think false pride was one of Phillipe's besetting sins, so she passed over the matter of the horses to light on his other statement. "We can hardly ride straight to father's farm in what's left of today." To demonstrate, she drew a map out of the pocket of her short jacket. "It must be seventy miles, and I have no idea what the roads are like."

"This is England, not the outback of Portugal," he said, grabbing the much-creased map and flipping it around to look at the line she had drawn. "I merely meant that there is no need for you to stay in a hotel when the Duke of Dorney"—Phillipe nodded toward her young son—"has a perfectly comfortable town house at his disposal in London."

"Has he?" Bella teased. "I keep forgetting my son is a duke."

"I do not forget it," said the young man who had driven up with Phillipe. "That small scapegrace has done me out of a fortune. I am your brother-in-law, Hallowell Armitage. Call me Hal."

Bella looked skeptically at the slight, brown-haired youth, but the mocking tone seemed in good humor. "I am Bella," she said bluntly, reaching out her hand and meaning to shake his. "Edwin spoke of his brother, but I had thought you much younger."

"Your Grace," the youth said, taking her hand and kissing it as he bowed. "I am nearly twenty."

"You do that very well," she returned. "You put me in mind of Edwin."

"I always put people in mind of my brother. I wondered if they would keep saying it now that he is dead."

Bella dipped her head to shadow her face with her flat black Spanish hat. When she had schooled herself not to react to this heartless statement, she looked Hal in the eye. "I am sorry for your brother's death."

"It can scarcely be considered your fault, Your Grace," he returned with a shrug.

Bella winced. Did that mean he really did not blame her, or that he did not care about Edwin's death? And how would he regard Jamie? At a motion from Carlos,

Bella remembered her manners. "Allow me to introduce Edwin's aide, Lieutenant Carlos Quesada."

"Rather young to be a lieutenant," Hal remarked as he shook hands with Carlos.

"Carlos is Maria's son," Phillipe added with a nod to the gaunt woman who held Jamie, "and the son of Captain Quesada, who was attached to Bella's father's brigade in Portugal."

"It pleases me to meet you, Hal," Carlos said with his charming smile and the slightest of accents. When he bowed, his black hair, parted in the middle, licked his forehead.

"If I may inquire," Hal said, regarding the buttons on Carlos's red coat, "since you are Portuguese, how did you come by that British uniform?"

"His Grace, the duke, arranged it," Carlos said formally.

"I take it mighty hard that he granted your wish and refused mine," Hal said with mock affront. "I do not think my brother cared for me at all."

"Perhaps he cared enough *not* to buy you a commission," Carlos suggested, raising one black eyebrow.

Hal shrugged and turned to Phillipe. "I perceive you are going to ride, Phillipe. That means I shall have to drive your team."

"You mean the young duke's team, so mind you do not gallop them and overturn the curricle. In fact, I think you should take Jamie and Maria up with you so they do not have to go in the baggage wagon."

A petulant look passed over Hal's face but was replaced almost immediately by a smirk. He wandered off to make the duke's acquaintance, cozening Maria, Bella's companion and Jamie's nurse, while carefully making friends with Jamie's dog before shaking Jamie's hand. After all this he spared a moment to wink at Bella.

"Playful boy," Bella said as Phillipe helped her to

mount the gray mare. His hands on her waist were strong and possessive—or was that just her imagination? Since it was his left leg that was stiff, Bella wondered how Phillipe would get on Sebastian, but he merely mounted from the right. The horse turned to stare over its shoulder at Phillipe, standing patiently except to throw its head up and sniff the air, curling its upper lip in an effort to catch the scent of any mare in heat.

Since Greenley now had charge of the mares, Rourke looked determined to ride the baggage wagon. Carlos seemed inclined to ride along beside the curricle and talk to Hal, so it looked as though she could have a private word with Phillipe. But when their strange train started through the London streets, she found she did not know what to say to him after all these months. "What are you doing here anyway? No one could have known what ship we would be on."

"No thanks to you. Rourke wrote me. And why would I not be here? I am responsible for your household now that Edwin is dead. At least until your child comes of age."

"What do you mean?" Bella asked. "Why am I not Jamie's guardian?"

"If he were an ordinary little boy, perhaps you would be. But Edwin was a duke when he died, and this is how he left things."

"He trusted you," Bella said, glancing at him under the low brim of her hat. "He said I could trust you as well."

"Too bad that does not work both ways."

"What do you mean?" she asked, feeling they may as well get this out in the open. Her proud stare lit a fire in his dark eyes and he looked almost angry.

"You could have waited for me," he growled desperately, then looked away as though he had not meant to voice the thought.

Bella was silent for a moment as the horses' shod hooves

rang smartly on the cobblestones. "The men said you were dead. Every one of the soldiers who saw those French lancers drag you away swore you were dead. And I did talk to every one of them, looking for some thread of hope."

"And Edwin, whom I trusted. I should have known he would be as eager to marry you as any of the others. A beautiful young English girl was a rare commodity in the Peninsula."

Bella ignored his reference to commodity. "I waited three weeks, but I was so worn down, losing both you and Father in the space of days, I did not particularly care what happened to me." She turned toward him. "Phillipe, after my father died I had to marry someone. You know that."

"Three weeks is such a long time for a woman to mourn," he almost whispered. "I should feel honored."

"You sound so bitter."

"I used to care about my cousin until you came between us."

"Meaning I did not care about him?" Bella demanded, rising slightly in her saddle.

"You said it."

It was only then that she realized how neatly he had trapped her. How could she say she had not loved Edwin when he had done everything in his power to make her happy and provide for Jamie. But if she did claim Edwin's love, that meant she forever denied her yearning for Phillipe. She expelled an impatient breath. "If the truth be known, I did not love him, but I did care."

"I do not think you are capable of love, Your Grace, only agility. I had Edwin's promise to look after you while I was away. I imagine it took little of your skill to turn that into a betrothal."

The arrow went home. So nothing was changed at all, not even by Edwin's death, Bella thought. Phillipe still hated her for what he perceived to be her betrayal. The love she had always felt for Phillipe had still to be tamped down and kept secret, just as she had hidden her feelings during the war, during her four years of marriage to Edwin.

Phillipe thought there was no more infuriating woman in the world than Bella. He bit his lip and glanced sideways at her and was surprised to observe a momentary look of hurt before Bella turned her face away to stare straight ahead. She said nothing, which was her way of ending conversations that were beneath her. Damn her. He had never won an argument with her in the six years he had known her. If he said something truly devastating, her generous mouth pulled down at the corners and she stopped talking. Those blue eyes iced over, that aristocratic chin came up, and he saw only her profile revealed by the nearly black hair pulled back into a braid.

She had cut her hair short at Vitoria because of the heat, and the men had competed for locks of it. Now it was long again like he remembered. If it were undone, it would ripple over her shoulders far enough to cover her breasts. He looked away, trying to dismiss the image of Bella from his memories, but if he had not been able to do so in all these months away from her, what chance had he with the woman herself only an arm's length away?

He had wounded her—that much he knew—but it was not what he had set out to do. There was so much he wanted to tell her, how he had loved her, loved her still. But she brought out the worst in him and he could never understand why. He had seen other men making protestations of love to her, Edwin included, and she had laughed off their gallantries. The words "I love you" would have no more left his lips than she would have laughed them back at him. He had lost much to the war, but he would not shed his self-respect. He could never let her know how much he wanted her.

She watched his hands after that, perhaps worried, he thought, that he would mistreat her dead father's prize horse. Sebastian picked that moment to scent a mare and neigh a greeting. The creature answered him and the great horse turned to look at Phillipe. "Walk on!" he heard himself say so harshly that even the warhorse snapped back to the matter at hand and forgot the mare.

Was that how he sounded to Bella? Always harsh and commanding? Suddenly it occurred to him that she watched his hands to see which way he meant to turn. She had no idea where he was taking her. This gave him a slight feeling of control, but he knew it was an illusion. No one could control Bella or make her do anything she did not wish. He would have to remember that. No matter how much the law was on his side, he could not control her except by force, and he did not want to use that.

When they reached the house in Portland Place, he had the satisfaction of seeing her gape at the four-story town house of rose-colored brick.

"This is Edwin's house?"

"Yours now, Your Grace. Or, rather, your son's."

"Stop calling me that," she ordered, giving him a sharp glance.

"It is one of the penalties for marrying a duke. Get used to it."

"Edwin was not a duke when I married him. He was a major."

"His father had been in ill health for years," Phillipe reminded her. "Waiting at his deathbed kept me in England when I should have rejoined the army in Brussels. It was only a matter of time until the old duke died. You must have known that."

She did not wait for him to dismount, throwing her leg over the pommels of her sidesaddle and sliding off the mare herself, reluctantly turning the reins over to a liveried groom. Phillipe dismounted stiffly and watched Bella stand uncertainly on the steps. She had pulled off her black leather riding gloves and was drawing them through one hand over and over, an old habit that spoke of her nervousness.

"Surely Edwin told you what to expect," Phillipe said with satisfaction as she scanned the facade of the large house in agitation.

"We never spoke of England at all. He did not want to come back."

"He might have sent you home after he knew you were with child."

"Never!" Bella picked up the tail of her riding dress.

"Why not?"

"He . . . he had his reasons. Besides, I could not bear to leave him, just as I could never leave Papa. And I was right. Had I come back to England . . ."

"Edwin might have sold out of the army," Phillipe said bleakly.

"Never," she said as she watched Carlos carry the sleeping child out of the carriage. "Edwin meant never to return but to always reside abroad."

"Leaving me to look after his affairs. How like Edwin," Phillipe said as he watched the tousled blond head, wondering if the boy really was Edwin's or if Jamie was his son. Moreover, could he ever trust Bella to tell him the truth of it?

The great doors were flung open and a small army of liveried footmen issued forth.

"The servants will take care of your baggage," Phillipe said more gently. "Come inside and meet the Dowager Lady Edith."

"I had rather wait until I have bathed," Bella said as she followed Carlos and Maria, who were being directed upstairs by the housekeeper.

"She does not like to be kept waiting," Phillipe remarked, halting Bella in the foyer.

Bella stared at him, making him writhe uncomfortably in his tight riding coat.

"Jamie is covered with ship dirt. You do want him to make a good first impression?"

"I was not considering. By all means, take as long as you like. Hoskins, where is Her Grace?"

"Her Grace has not descended yet," the butler said stiffly.

"You make her sound like a hot air balloon," Bella remarked, startling a smirk from Hoskins. "When does she usually descend for the day?"

Hoskins turned a wary eye on Phillipe before answering Bella. "Not before noon, Your Grace."

"See, Phillipe? There is plenty of time for me to bathe. I rather think I shall like being called "Your Grace" the way Hoskins says it, so genteelly. Thank you, Hoskins."

"My very great pleasure, Your Grace. I shall have hot water carried to your chamber immediately." So saying, he clapped his gloved hands and sent three footmen scurrying to do his bidding. "Allow me to escort you."

"Thank you, but first I wish to see where they have taken my son."

"I shall show you the nursery first, Your Grace. By then, your trunks will be unpacked and your bath ready."

"You run an efficient household, Mr. Hoskins," Bella said as she marched up the stairs beside a servant who almost instantly had become her devoted slave.

Phillipe stared after them with a smile. The faint smile faded when he recalled all those empty nights of coveting Bella. He had thought he was over her, that he had cured himself of that painful infatuation. But she no more walked back into his life than he began fantasizing about her undressing, bathing, and going to bed under the same roof again. No, he would never get over Bella, he thought.

"Phillipe? Phillipe?" Hal demanded.

Phillipe started. "I need a drink," he rasped.

"Now you are talking. Let us go wait in the red salon. There is always brandy in there." So saying, Hal led the way into the large room, poured the amber liquid, and handed one glass to Phillipe, who leaned against the mantel as a more comfortable alternative than sitting on one of the stiff Adam chairs. Hal lounged on the matching sofa.

"That Carlos seems like a nice enough chap. Bit irregular, though, him being her nursemaid's son and still accompanying Bella."

Phillipe glanced at his cousin, who had never worried about propriety in his life before now. "Maria and Carlos are of a noble family. They have been with Bella for years. Edwin took them into his household after Bella's father was killed."

"That's all very well, but to be traveling together . . . I tell you, Phillipe. It does not look right. If Mama asks about him, say he came on another ship or something. Say he is going back to the army."

"He is, once he sees Bella safely settled. And he will not shrug his duty there. Edwin made him promise to take care of Bella and Jamie."

"Well, they are now safely settled. I tell you, Phillipe, if Quesada hangs about, half the women in London will fall in love with those black eyes and that white smile. A mortal man has no right to be so handsome."

Phillipe smiled. So Hal was not interested in Bella; he was simply jealous of Carlos. "After what he has been through, do not grudge Carlos a few months of pleasure."

"Gadding about in a cavalry uniform and, moreover, one that should have been mine."

"You have some strange ideas about army life. The first

time I encountered Carlos and Bella, they were helping to tend the wounded sent back after the Battle of Talavera."

"What?" Hal sloshed his brandy on his riding breeches and swore as he searched for a handkerchief.

"They faced some horrendous wounds and knew that most of those they helped would die anyway. I asked her why they bothered. She said simply so that the soldiers would know someone cared."

Hal left off his blotting and turned a shocked face toward Phillipe. "I . . . I had no idea."

Phillipe tried to close the door on that look into the past. When had that idealistic child turned into a hardened fortune hunter? Had the war done that to her, taught her to look out for herself? Or had it been the result of having a child to provide for? But the child came after her betrayal, after her marriage to Edwin. At least that was what everyone thought.

Look for
MY PHILLIPE
Wherever Books Are Sold
October 2000